The
MX Book
of
New
Sherlock
Holmes
Stories

Part II: 1890-1895

The MX Book of New Sherlock Holmes Stories

Part II - 1890-1895

SOUTHAMPTON STREET

359

EDITED
By
David
Marcum

OFFICES

TRADITIONAL HOLMES
ADVENTURES
COMPILED FOR THE
BENEFIT OF THE
RESTORATION OF
UNDERSHAW

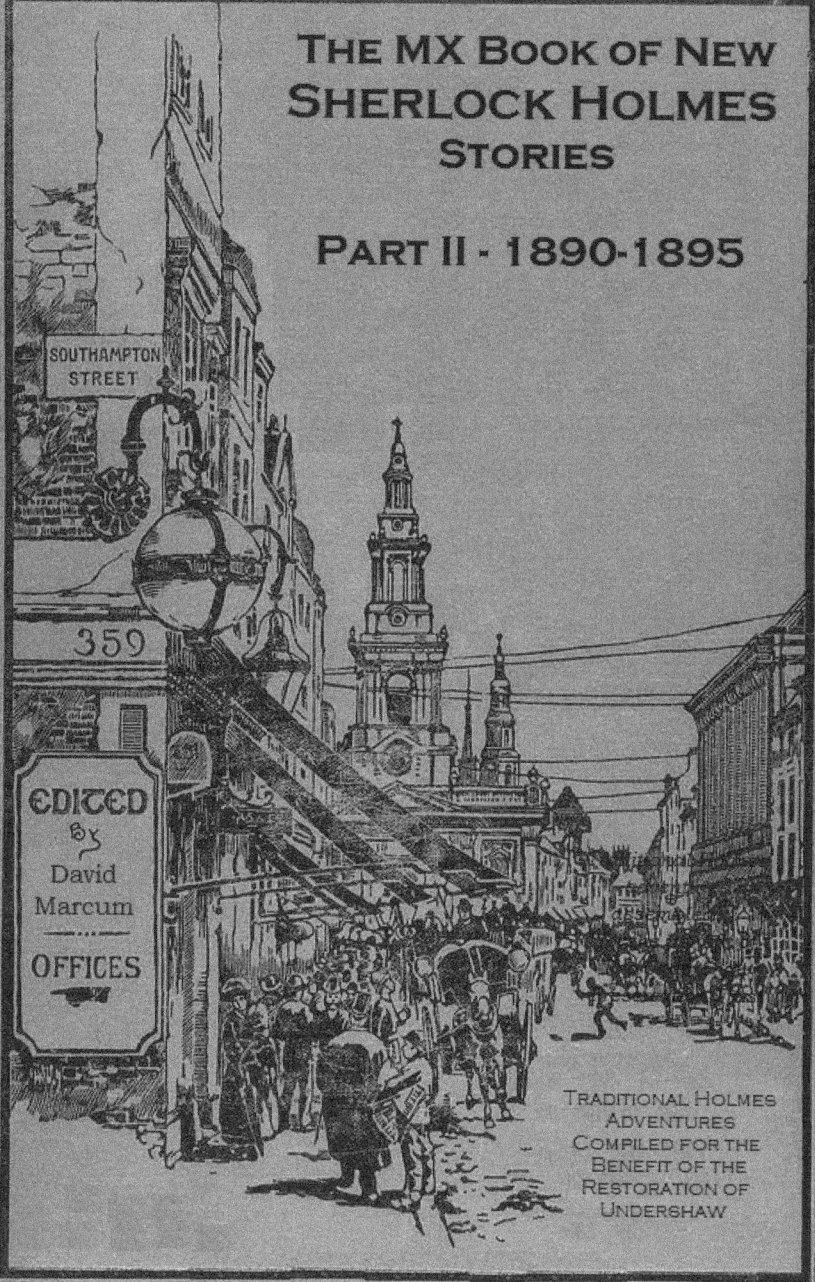

ISBN 9781780928289 Hardback
ISBN 9781780928296 Paperback
ePub ISBN 9781780928302
PDF ISBN 9781780928319

Published in the UK by MX Publishing
335 Princess Park Manor, Royal Drive,
London, N11 3GX
www.mxpublishing.co.uk
Cover design by www.staunch.com

CONTENTS

PART II: 1890-1895

(Continued on the next page . . . .)

**These additional adventures are contained in
The MX Book of New Sherlock Holmes Stories**

(Continued on the next page . . . .)

COPYRIGHT INFORMATION

Editor's Introduction:
The Whole Art of Detection
by David Marcum

Part I: *The Great Watsonian Oversoul*

According to Merriam-Webster, a *pastiche* is defined as a literary or artistic work that imitates the style of a previous work. Almost from the time that the first Sherlock Holmes stories began to appear in print, there were Holmes pastiches as well, side by side with the official sixty tales that are known as *The Canon*. Some from that period are more properly defined as parodies, but a few were written to sincerely portray additional adventures featuring Our Heroes, Holmes and Dr. John H. Watson,

I personally discovered pastiches at around the same time that I found the original Holmes stories, and began reading them just as eagerly as I did the material found in The Canon. In my mind, a well-written pastiche, set in the same correct time period as the originals, was as legitimate as anything written by the first – but definitely *not* the only! – of Watson's literary agents, Sir Arthur Conan Doyle. In the past, I've described the whole vast combination of Canon and pastiche as *The Great Holmes Tapestry*, with each providing an important thread to the whole, some brighter or thicker than others perhaps, but all contributing to the big picture. Perhaps another comparison would be to say that the union of Canon and pastiche forms a *rope*, with the Canonical adventures serving as the solid wire core, while all the threads and fibers of the additional pastiches bound around it provide greater substance and strength, with the two being indivisible.

I believe that pastiches have contributed immensely to the ever-increasing popularity of Holmes and Watson throughout the years. Additional cases and adventures only serve to feed the Sherlockian Fire, and ideally refocus interest back to the original narratives. There are some Sherlockian scholars who want nothing at all to do pastiches, and there are others who don't even want to classify all of the original sixty stories as being authentic, stating in various essays and books that this or that Canonical tale is spurious. I cannot agree with them.

In my essay, "In Praise of the Pastiche" (*The Baker Street Journal,* Vol. 62, No. 3, Autumn 2012), I argue that just sixty original stories relating incidents from Holmes's career are simply not enough. There must be more *about* the world's greatest consulting detective to justify that he *is* the world's greatest consulting detective, rather than just a few dozen "official" stories that leave too much unanswered. Pastiches fill in the gaps and cracks.

In "The Adventure of the Abbey Grange", Holmes tells Watson that ". . . I propose to devote my declining years to the composition of a textbook, which shall focus the whole art of detection into one volume." The vast amount of stories that make up the combination of both Canon and pastiche may not be – in fact, it certainly isn't! – what Holmes had in mind, but it is the closest we'll get to seeing and observing that overall tapestry of his life and work, the *Whole Art of Detection.*

Over the years, an incredible number of people have added to the body of work initially introduced by Watson's first literary agent. Sometimes, people discover lost manuscripts, usually written by Watson, but occasionally narrated by someone else – a Baker Street Irregular perhaps, or a client, or Mycroft Holmes, or a passing acquaintance, or maybe even by Sherlock Holmes himself. On a regular basis, an adventure is discovered in one of Watson's Tin Dispatch Boxes – and there must have been several of those to hold so many tales! These stories may be narrated in first person, or they may have a third-person omniscient viewpoint. No matter how they are found or transcribed, I believe that each of the "editors" of these later discovered adventures has tapped into what I like to call *The Great Watsonian Oversoul.*

When I was in high school, my award-winning English teacher, (who sadly never ever taught anything at all about the literary efforts of one Dr. John H. Watson, leaving that joyful task for me to capably take care of for myself,) introduced us to the concept of an "oversoul" – she was using it in relation to how it influenced some poet. Essentially – and I am no doubt remembering this somewhat incorrectly – the idea is that we are all tiny pieces of a greater entity, split off for a time from it, out here in the darkness and trapped in our own heads, before returning at some later point to the protection, warmth, goodness, and omnipotence of the greater whole. I, however, appropriated the idea to describe the overall source of the Holmesian narratives.

To my way of thinking, all of the traditional Canonically-based Sherlock Holmes stories are linked back eventually to this same basis of inspiration, no matter how the later "author" accesses it. Since the mid-1970's, I've read and collected literally thousands of adventures concerning the activities of Mr. Sherlock Holmes, and since the mid-

1990's, I've been organizing all of them – both Canon and pastiche – into an extremely detailed day-by-day chronology, now covering hundreds of pages and literally thousands of narratives. Among the things that have become apparent to me over the years are: 1) There can *never* be enough good Holmes stories, relating the activities of the *true*, *correct*, and *traditional* Holmes of the Victorian and Edwardian eras; and, 2) The people who bring these stories to the public, no matter how they go about it, or whether they even realize it, are all somehow channeling Watson.

So one way or another, the spark of imagination that sets these narratives in motion originates in the *Great Watsonian Oversoul*. That's not to say that a lot of authorial/editorial blood, sweat, and tears doesn't go into all of these "discovered" stories, and these efforts should not be negated at all. These works don't simply appear as finished products – even the ones that are found essentially complete in Tin Dispatch Boxes. It takes a lot of work to first make contact with the Watsonian Oversoul, and then to transcribe what is being relayed in such a way that the public can understand and enjoy it. Sometimes the person relaying the story might misunderstand a fact or two along the way, leading to an odd discrepancy, or the "editor" channeling the tale may weave some little thing from his or her own agenda onto Watson's original intentions that isn't quite consistent with the big tapestry. But if the writer listening for that still small Watson voice within is sincere, the overall sense of the Sherlockian events that are being revealed within the story remains true.

Part II: *The MX Book of New Sherlock Holmes Stories*

This collection of new Sherlock Holmes adventures came about by listening to that still small voice. One Saturday morning in late January 2015, I popped awake, several hours earlier than I had intended, having just had a full-fledged and vivid dream about a new Holmes anthology. Now, I've tapped into the Oversoul and "edited" a few of Watson's works myself, but I hadn't tried anything like this before. If I'd rolled over and gone back to sleep, the idea would probably have disappeared. But it had grabbed me by then, so I quietly got up and started making a wish list of "editors" of Watson's works that I already knew and admired, in order to see if they would be willing to go through the effort to come up with some more new adventures

I emailed Steve Emecz of MX Publishing, and he enthusiastically liked the idea. Early on, we agreed that the author royalties for the

3

project would be used to support Undershaw, the home where Sir Arthur Conan Doyle was living when both *The Hound of the Baskervilles*, as well as some of the later Holmes adventures, were written. MX Publishing has supported this effort in the past, so this decision was an easy one.

The same morning that I had the idea, I began to email authors, and I immediately started receiving positive responses. I was then emboldened to start asking still more people, and quickly the whole thing escalated. I reached out to friends to help me track down some authors in England that could only be reached by the old-fashioned mail. People already participating suggested still more folks who might also want to tap into the Oversoul and contribute a story to the anthology. It quickly grew to the point where it obviously needed to be two volumes, and sometime after that, it became three. (If it hadn't been split into multiple books, the whole thing would have become so fat that the book spines would have cracked apart.) It was always important to me that this collection, although finally presented under three covers, be considered as *one unified anthology*. As such, it is the largest collection of new Sherlock Holmes stories assembled in the same place.

These volumes have contributors from around the world: the U.S. and Canada, all over Great Britain, India, New Zealand, and Sweden. There are a couple of British expatriates who were living in Asia at the time they made their contributions, and two American ex-pats in London and Kuwait as well. Early on, I let all of the participants know that, since we had contributors from all around the globe, the format and punctuation of the books would be uniformly consistent, but they could use either British or American spellings in their finished works. Therefore, if you see some stories with *color* and others with *colour*, for example, that's why.

The contributors to these anthologies come from a wide variety of backgrounds. Some are professional best-selling authors. Others, like me, write for fun, but have day jobs elsewhere. A few are noted fan-fiction authors, taking this opportunity to write for a wider and different kind of audience. (I've always felt that some of the best Holmes writing has appeared as fan-fiction, and that a great Holmes story doesn't have to be found in a published book.)

There are several here who are writing a Holmes story for the first time. In the case of a few of these, I specifically invited noted Sherlockians who have worked long and hard to promote the World of Holmes but haven't written a pastiche before, with the idea that someone

– and I can't think of who – once said that every Sherlockian should write at least one pastiche in their lives. This was their chance, and they did a great job with it.

A number of our authors have not been previously associated with MX. Welcome to the MX family! I'm aware that a few of these authors have already caught the Holmes-adventure-writing bug and are working on additional stories for future MX books of their own. I can't wait to read them!

Early on, I decided to arrange the stories chronologically, extending from 1881, when Holmes and Watson first met, to 1929, the year of Watson's death. This allowed for a logical arrangement of the stories, covering the entire period of Holmes and Watson's friendship and professional partnership. I was greatly influenced by that wonderful volume edited by Mike Ashley, *The Mammoth Book of New Sherlock Holmes Adventures* (1997). He also arranged the stories within by date, and as a hard-core chronologist, I have a great appreciation for that method.

My conditions for participation in the project were very basic. First and most important, as the editor of this collection I was very firm that Holmes and Watson had to be treated with respect and sincerity, and as if all involved were playing that fine old Sherlockian tradition, *The Game.* For those unfamiliar with this idea, Holmes and Watson are treated as if they were living, breathing, historical figures, and as such they *cannot* be transplanted to other eras, or forced to do something that is completely ridiculous for the time period in which they existed, such as battling space aliens. The stories had to be set in the correct time periods, ideally from 1881 to 1929. There could be no parody, nothing where Holmes was being used as a vampire-fighting Van Helsing, and nothing where he was incorrectly modernized, as if he is some version of Doctor Who to be reincarnated as whatever version of hero the current generation needs him to be.

Additionally, the stories had to be approximately the same length as the original short stories, with no novellas, and no fragments, such as something along the lines of "The Return of the Field Bazaar" or "How Watson Learned Another Trick". Also, I initially stated that the submitted tales all had to be narrated by Watson. However, there were a few that showed up in my email (t)in-box that stepped away from the Watsonian viewpoint – specifically, a case narrated by Wiggins, a couple by Professor Moriarty, one by a passing acquaintance of Holmes during The Great Hiatus, and two about the Professor told in third person. These provided valuable insight, they were set within the correct Holmesian world, and they were simply too good to miss.

Another goal that I set was to make use of completely new stories for the collection, in one format or another. With this in mind, I was *almost* completely successful . . . but not quite, if you wish to be technical about it. I must admit that, by way of a tiny bit of Watsonian Obfuscation, a few of the items herein have appeared in other locations or in other mediums, although they have never been published in this format before. One story was previously in a rather obscure local publication, and I believe that it is almost completely unknown to the larger audience, and might not be read by a lot of people otherwise. (In fact, with all my pastiche collecting, this was one that I didn't know about until it was submitted for this anthology.) A couple of the submissions have previously been on the internet for a short time, and two of the submissions are in the form of scripts that were previously used for radio broadcasts in the U.S. and the U.K. This their first appearance as text in book form.

As a side note, mentioning the scripts reminds me to acknowledge this volume's unintended but happy association with Imagination Theatre, which broadcasts traditional radio dramas weekly throughout the U.S., and has recently passed 1,000 broadcasts. As part of their rotating line-up, they feature a series of original tales, *The Further Adventures of Sherlock Holmes* – as of this writing numbering 117 episodes – and they are also in the process of broadcasting adaptations of the original Holmes Canon as *The Classic Adventures of Sherlock Holmes.* Currently, they are close to completing radio dramatizations of all sixty original Holmes stories featuring the same actors as Holmes and Watson throughout, John Patrick Lowrie and Lawrence Albert respectively, and with all adaptations by the same scriptwriter, Matthew J. Elliott. One of the scripts in this collection, never before in print, is by Imagination Theatre founder Jim French. A number of other Imagination Theatre writers besides Mr. French have contributed to this collection, including Matthew Elliott, Matthew Booth, John Hall, Daniel McGachey, Iain McLaughlin and Claire Bartlett, Jeremy Holstein, J.R. Campbell, and me (David Marcum) – that's a sizeable chunk our authors!

Part III: *With many sincere thanks . . . .*

Throughout the process, everyone that I've contacted about writing a story has been more than gracious, either by immediately stepping up and offering to provide one, or – when he or she couldn't join the party due to other obligations – continuing to offer support in numerous other ways. As the editor, being able to read these new adventures straight out of the Tin Dispatch Box is an experience not to be missed. Having never before tried to put together such a diverse Sherlock Holmes anthology, I must say that the whole thing has quickly become addictive, and I cannot promise not to do another one, although one of this size and scope, which was truly jumping into the deep water and *then* learning to swim, is unlikely.

Of all the people I'd like to thank, I must first express my gratitude as a whole to the authors – or "editors", if you will – of these new adventures from the Great Watsonian Oversoul. You stepped up and provided some really great stories that didn't previously exist. You also put up with my reminders, nudges, and story suggestions when I had to don my Editing Deerstalker. Along the way, as I was able to read these fine stories, I also met some really nice new people.

More specifically, I'd like to thank the following:

- My wife Rebecca and my son Dan, who mean everything – and I mean *everything*! – to me. They constantly put up with my Sherlockian interest, my ever-increasing pastiche collection, and my tendency to wear a deerstalker as my only hat for three-quarters of the year.
- Steve Emecz, publisher extraordinaire and the hardest working man in show-biz. Thanks for the constant support and for always listening!
- Bob Gibson of *staunch.com* – an amazing graphic artist, who let me keep tinkering with the cover, which became two covers, and then three . . . .
- Joel and Carolyn Senter. Years ago, my family knew to start my birthday and Christmas shopping with Joel and Carolyn's "Classic Specialties" catalogs. Later, when the original version of my first Holmes book was published, they enthusiastically got behind it and were responsible for selling almost every copy that was sold. They've encouraged me at every step, and I'm so glad that they could be a part of this anthology.

7

- Roger Johnson, who is so gracious when my random emails arrive with Holmesian ideas and questions. Visiting with him and his wife, Jean, during my Holmes Pilgrimage to England in 2013 was a high point of my trip. More recently, he located some wonderful pictures of Holmes and Watson for use in these books. In so many ways, I thank you!
- Bob Byrne, whom I first "met" by emailing him a question about Solar Pons – if you don't know who Solar Pons is, go find out! – and then we ended up becoming friends.
- Derrick Belanger, who hadn't specifically channeled Watson before, and is now on his way to becoming one of the best. Thanks for the friendship, the back-and-forth discussions upon occasion, and the support.
- Marcia Wilson, an incredible author and friend who received my first fan letter, long before I ever started thinking about writing anything myself. I've always said that, with her complex tales of Lestrade and his associates, she's found *Scotland Yard's* Tin Dispatch Box.
- Denis O. Smith, who was at the top of my pastiche wish list. I'm so glad that I was able to track him down, and I've really enjoyed the ongoing e-discussions we've had along the way since then;
- Lyndsay Faye, who said yes the very first day that I invited her to submit a story, and who also educated me about contracts.
- Bert Coules, for his advice and contributions, and for helping put together the Holmes and Watson that I hear in my head, Clive Merrison and Michael Williams.
- Carole Nelson Douglas, who – among many things – gave me some invaluable advice about foreign editions.
- Les Klinger, who spent part of a Sunday afternoon in a cross-country phone call, giving me some really valuable advice.
- Otto Penzler, who helped me several times when I pestered him for advice, and who wisely told me that "editing anthologies isn't quite as easy as drawing up a wish list and signing up stories".
- Chris Redmond, who jumped in early, and for all that he does, and just for having that incredible website, *sherlockian.net*.
- Kim Krisco, whom I met (by email) along the way, and was a never-ending source of encouragement.

- Tim Symonds, also an email friend with a lot of great ideas and support. I look forward to catching up with you at Birling Gap someday.
- John Hall, whose books – both pastiches and scholarship – I've enjoyed for years.
- Andy Lane – Thanks for the clever back-and-forth emails. I'm sorry I couldn't make it to New York when you were over here. I'll catch you next time!
- James Lovegrove, who corresponded with me way-back-when about the *true* location of Holmes's retirement villa on the Sussex Downs. (You know where I mean.) I'm very jealous of where you live.
- Steven Rothman, editor of *The Baker Street Journal*, for always responding so nicely whenever one of my emails drops in from out of the blue.
- Matthew Elliott, for all that he's done, and also for helping with the description of what he's accomplishing at Imagination Theatre.
- Maxim Jakubowski, who introduced me to a great new set of people.
- Mark Gagen, who gave me permission to use that absolutely perfect picture of Holmes on the back cover.
- And last but certainly *not* least, Sir Arthur Conan Doyle: Author, doctor, adventurer, and the Founder of the Feast. Present in spirit, and honored by all of us here.

This collection has been a labor of love by both the participants and myself. Everyone did their sincerest best to produce an anthology that truly represents why Holmes and Watson have been so popular for so long. This is just another tiny piece of the Great Holmes Tapestry, which will continue to grow and grow, for there can never be enough stories about the man whom Watson described as "the best and wisest . . . whom I have ever known."

David Marcum
August 7th, 2015
163rd Birthday of Dr. John H. Watson

Questions or comments may be addressed to David Marcum at
thepapersofsherlockholmes@gmail.com

Study and Natural Talent
by Roger Johnson

Greenhough Smith, editor of *The Strand Magazine*, hailed Arthur Conan Doyle as "the greatest natural storyteller of his age". Over a century on, Conan Doyle's genius keeps us reading, and, because many of us feel that sixty adventures of Sherlock Holmes just aren't enough, we write as well. The original tales are exciting and often ingenious; they're intelligent without being patronising, and they're never pretentious. The characters of Holmes and Watson – the apparently contrary forces that actually complement each other like Yin and Yang – stimulate our imaginations. Surely every devotee believes that the world needs more stories of Sherlock Holmes, and as, barring a true miracle, there'll be no more from his creator's fondly wielded Parker Duofold pen, we should provide at least one or two ourselves. We know the originals inside-out, or we think we do; we have a grand idea for a plot, and the style seems to be – well – elementary. How hard can it be?

In fact it's a sight harder than most of us think. Believe me: I know! To set a story convincingly in late Victorian or Edwardian London can require a fair deal of research just to avoid simple anachronisms and similar errors of fact. There are aspects of personality that may need careful attention – not just Holmes and Watson, but other established characters such as Messrs Lestrade and Gregson, and Mrs. Hudson (who really *was* the landlady at 221B, and *not* the housekeeper). Vocabulary and speech-patterns are important . . . .

Some will say, of course, that it's impossible to replicate the Doyle-Watson style. Nevertheless, there are writers who have come acceptably close to the real thing. Edgar W. Smith declared that *The Exploits of Sherlock Holmes* by Adrian Conan Doyle and John Dickson Carr should be re-titled *Sherlock Holmes Exploited*, but it is actually a remarkably good collection. Nicholas Meyer, L. B. Greenwood, Barrie Roberts, and Michael Hardwick are other names that come to mind, of authors who have, as Holmes himself said in a different context, applied both study and natural talent to the writing of new Sherlock Holmes adventures. For the current monumental collection, conceived and published for the benefit of the house that saw the rebirth of the great detective, David Marcum has coaxed stories from the best of today's generation of

Holmesian chroniclers. Some of the contributors are famous, and some perhaps are destined for fame, but all of them bring intelligence, knowledge, understanding and deep affection to the task – and we are the gainers.

Roger Johnson, BSI, ASH
Editor: *The Sherlock Holmes Journal*
August 2015

Foreword
by Catherine Cooke

It all depends on your point of view. Fifty-six short stories and four long stories. Sixty cases of Sherlock Holmes spanning forty years. Sir Arthur Conan Doyle thought that was quite enough – probably too many even. While some commentators have opined that not all reach the same high standards, it cannot be denied that for the legions of Holmes's students, 60 is not nearly enough. They beg, *desire*, DEMAND more.

Sir Arthur was a man of action. His wife Touie was diagnosed with tuberculosis. He took her abroad to climes more suited – to Switzerland and Egypt. Hearing from a friend about "Little Switzerland", an area of Hampshire considered to have a climate as beneficial, he rushed down to Hindhead, bought a plot of land, and had a house built, specially designed for himself and for his ailing wife: shallow stairs, easy to open doors, and a couple of splendid heraldic windows. It is a tragedy of recent years that this house, Undershaw, and its beautiful grounds have been allow to fall into rack and ruin while legal disputes rumbled on.

But now there is cause for rejoicing on both fronts. A collection in three volumes (count 'em, *three*) of new Sherlock Holmes stories from well-practiced, well-known pens, as well as from newer writers – surely here there is something for all tastes. Furthermore, all royalties are to go to projects in the redevelopment of Undershaw by Stepping Stones. Conan Doyle's house will rise again offering specialist educational facilities to enable its students to achieve their full potential.

Congratulations are due to the editor, David Marcum, to MX Publishing, and to all those writers and supporters who have given their time, talents, and money to make these volumes possible. Now settle back and enjoy new accounts from the classic years of Holmes and Watson's partnership, which may shed new light on the mysterious years of the Great Hiatus.

Catherine Cooke, BSI, ASH
August 2015

Undershaw
Circa 1900 *(Source: Wikipedia)*

Undershaw:
An Ongoing Legacy
for Sherlock Holmes
by Steve Emecz

The authors involved in this anthology are donating their royalties toward the restoration of Sir Arthur Conan Doyle's former home, Undershaw. This building was initially in terrible disrepair, and was saved from destruction by the *Undershaw Preservation Trust* (Patron: Mark Gatiss). Today, the building has been bought by Stepping Stones (a school for children with learning difficulties), and is being restored to its former glory.

Undershaw is where Sir Arthur Conan Doyle wrote many of the Sherlock Holmes stories, including *The Hound of The Baskervilles*. It's where Conan Doyle brought Sherlock Holmes back to life. This project will contribute to specific projects at the house, such as the restoration of Doyle's study, and will be opened up to fans outside term time.

You can find out more information about the new Stepping Stones school at *www.steppingstones.org.uk*

Sherlock Holmes (1854-1957) was born in Yorkshire, England, on 6 January, 1854. In the mid-1870's, he moved to 24 Montague Street, London, where he established himself as the world's first Consulting Detective. After meeting Dr. John H. Watson in early 1881, he and Watson moved to rooms at 221b Baker Street, where his reputation as the world's greatest detective grew for several decades. He was presumed to have died battling noted criminal Professor James Moriarty on 4 May, 1891, but he returned to London on 5 April, 1894, resuming his consulting practice in Baker Street. Retiring to the Sussex coast near Beachy Head in October 1903, he continued to be involved in various private and government investigations while giving the impression of being a reclusive apiarist. He was very involved in the events encompassing World War I, and to a lesser degree those of World War II. He passed away peacefully upon the cliffs above his Sussex home on his 103rd birthday, 6 January, 1957.

Dr. John Hamish Watson (1852-1929) was born in Stranraer, Scotland on 7 August, 1852. In 1878, he took his Doctor of Medicine Degree from the University of London, and later joined the army as a surgeon. Wounded at the Battle of Maiwand in Afghanistan (27 July, 1880), he returned to London late that same year. On New Year's Day, 1881, he was introduced to Sherlock Holmes in the chemical laboratory at Barts. Agreeing to share rooms with Holmes in Baker Street, Watson became invaluable to Holmes's consulting detective practice. Watson was married and widowed three times, and from the late 1880's onward, in addition to his participation in Holmes's investigations and his medical practice, he chronicled Holmes's adventures, with the assistance of a literary agent, Sir Arthur Conan Doyle, in a series of popular narratives, most of which were first published in *The Strand* magazine. Watson's later years were spent preparing a vast number of his notes of Holmes's cases for future publication. Following a final important investigation with Holmes, Watson contracted pneumonia and passed away on 24 July, 1929.

Photos of Sherlock Holmes and Dr. John H. Watson courtesy of Roger Johnson

PART II: 1890-1895

The years between 1890 and 1895 were times of upheaval for both Holmes and Watson. While Watson continued to enjoy married life with his wife, Mary, Holmes faced an ever escalating battle with the Napoleon of Crime, Professor James Moriarty. The contest between the two culminated on 4 May, 1891, atop the Reichenbach Falls. While Watson was decoyed away, Holmes and Moriarty met and fought on the slippery ledge. Moriarty fell, and Holmes did not. However, seeing the opportunity to continue his work in secret if he was thought to have died, and also as a way to protect Watson and his wife from the last remains of the Professor's organization, Holmes allowed Watson to believe that he, too, had fallen. Watson returned home heartbroken, while Holmes journeyed all over the world, carrying out missions for the British Government and his brother, Mycroft. From May 1891 until April 1894, Holmes traveled to various locations, including Lhasa in Tibet, Mecca, Khartoum, and Montpellier, France (as recorded in "The Empty House".) In addition, he also visited many other locations that are not recorded in the Canon.

While Holmes was away from England, Watson faced both the grief of losing his best friend, as well as the death of his wife Mary in 1893. When Holmes returned to London in April 1894, Watson was amazed to learn that his friend was alive after all, and he soon returned to sharing rooms at 221b Baker Street. The years that followed, particularly 1894-

1895, were extremely busy, and the cases literally tumbled upon them, one after the other . . . .

The Bachelor of Baker Street Muses on Irene Adler
by Carole Nelson Douglas

Kings *do not impress him, especially from Bohemia.*
Women do not obsess him, with their vapors and anemia.
Watson is wrong. His brain thrives on opium dreams and smoke.
Yet sometimes they unite against him, and, uninvited, invoke
A vision of The Woman.

He brushed off a monarch's hand, but when it comes to her now,
He remembers a kindly touch to an aged clergyman's brow.
His injured cleric now seems a shabby trick, thought nothing of,
When she was fighting for her freedom and the cause of true love
Always paramount to The Woman.

Yet such cheek! Feminine features under muffler and bowler hat,
His own name appropriated at his very doorstep, audacious that!
His name, with the honorific "Mister" muttered in a youthful male tone.
He should have known. Not a former Baker Street Irregular grown,
But a woman in wolf's clothing.

All is fair in crime and punishment, and disguise a commonplace.
So she mastered it herself, but she was fair in more than face,
Accepting only her own honor from the prideful and possessive King,
Leaving her true adversary an eternal portrait of her leave-taking.
He too refused the Royal ring.

He smiles as he fingers the gold "sovereign" dangling on his watch
chain.
Him she tipped. The King she slipped. What an ironical refrain.
To sum up the same old story, that last letter left for him lingers near.
She called him hers, she called him dear, terms he had never longed to
hear
From any woman.

And then Baker Street reclaims its own. He will no longer be alone.
Knocking at the lower door, footsteps pounding up a floor to his own.
His blood is up, his pulses race, he wonders what new enigma he will
    find.
He banishes past and pipe dream, leaps up from his chair. And leaves
    behind
The Woman on his mind.

Kings do not impress him, especially from Bohemia.
Women do not obsess him, with their vapors and anemia.
He still finds his muse in opium dreams and smoke,
And the not unwelcome recollections they provoke
Of The Woman.

The Affair of Miss Finney
by Ann Margaret Lewis

It was in the third week of June, in 1890, that Sherlock Holmes encountered a case the likes of which he'd never before had the misfortune to solve. Women had always been a puzzling topic for Holmes. After my marriage to Mary, he exhibited no overt ill will toward my bride, and yet he made it clear that he was not happy about our nuptials. It is with the Miss Finney affair that I believe he came to see my wife with new eyes.

That day, I'd stayed late into the evening with one of my patients. In fact, I returned home at such an hour that I was certain Mary had gone to bed. The house was dark, save for a solitary gas lamp in the front hall that she left up for me so I could find my key in the dark. I did my best not to wake her, but instead turned the corner and surprised her in the hall, candle in hand. She wore her lavender dressing gown trimmed in white lace, and her hair fell to one shoulder in a single, blonde braid.

She gasped. "James!"

I smiled and kissed her cheek. It was a personal affection of ours that she'd address me in a form of my middle name. "I'm sorry, dear; I didn't mean to startle you."

She placed her hand on her breast and sighed with relief. "That's all right. I wasn't expecting you to be there. My, but you were quiet."

"I thought you were asleep."

"Did you have anything to eat?"

"Yes. The housekeeper insisted on feeding me after the baby was born. Child gave us a bit of a fright, but ultimately it all went well."

"Boy or girl?"

"Girl." I smiled. "Charming little thing."

Suddenly, the bell rang downstairs.

"Who might that be?" Mary asked.

"There's only one person who would ring at this hour." I charged with a stiff gait down the stairs and swung open the front door.

Sherlock Holmes stood on the step. "I'm glad you are here, Watson. I see your wife is still awake. Excellent. May I come in?"

"Of course."

Mary looked askance at me as I led my friend up the stairs. I gestured for her to precede us into our parlour. "Is something wrong?" she asked as I closed the door behind us.

"Mrs. Watson," Holmes said. "I came here to find you, especially, in the hope that you might assist me."

"I'm always happy to be of help, Mr. Holmes."

He began to pace the carpet, his nervous energy evident in his stride. He removed his hat, and I realized his hair was mussed as if he'd been asleep. Whatever it was, it had apparently awakened him.

"In my entire career," he said, "I have been fortunate that I have never dealt with a case such as this. I have always known it was possible that something of its ilk might walk through my door, but I'd hoped I'd never see it." He stopped at my fireplace and continued in a hoarse voice. "It is heinous, monstrous, depraved, and vile. It is pure evil."

"Whatever is it, Mr. Holmes?" Mary asked.

"There is a young lady, who waits for me now at Baker Street. I came here, leaving her in the care of the maid. I fear she has been ill-used."

"Ill-used?"

"In a most unspeakable way."

Mary's fingers went to her mouth. "Oh . . . ."

"Good Lord," I whispered.

"She does not know the man who attacked her. He abducted her, rendering her unconscious with chloroform. The man gagged her, put a burlap sack over her head so she'd not know where she was, and later held a knife to her throat as he did . . . what he did. After, that he beat her and left her alone in this fashion for three days in some sort of prison, giving her only marginal food and drink, if any at all. Around ten-thirty this evening, she managed to twist herself free of her bounds and crawl through a coal chute to escape.

"A cabby named Preston, whom I know from other cases, brought her to me tonight believing I might help her. Even so, I have sent word to Stanley Hopkins at the Yard. He is a compassionate sort, someone a woman in this state might find consoling." He shook his head. "Meanwhile, I have tried, in vain, to interview the lady at length, to glean more definitive details about her ordeal, but her upset renders her unable to speak of it coherently. Much of what I've told you I was able to deduce by observation, but when I attempted to examine the blood under her nails, she recoiled from me as if my hands were laced with acid."

"The poor girl." Mary shook her head.

24

"Mrs. Watson, I have the faculties to help this young lady, but she cannot reveal what she must to me because . . . ." He paused, his lips turning downward in a troubled frown.

"You are a man," she finished for him.

He nodded. "Despite her desire for my assistance, she is not entirely . . . comfortable . . . in my presence, which I understand completely given the circumstances." He continued in a subdued voice. "Mrs. Watson, you've read your husband's narratives and you know that I have not always spoken of the fair sex in the most sympathetic terms. Nonetheless, I would never wish to see such grievous harm done to a woman."

"I know that, Mr. Holmes," Mary said in a gentle voice.

My friend averted his gaze from her and turned to pace the rug again. "The loathsome vermin who did this must be found, but without more data I am in the dark. There is grain powder and saw dust on her dress, along with mechanical oil, indicating she was kept at a mill or some similar place. Where, that is the question. I need her to reveal more. She fears me, though, which, while irrational, is, as I said, understandable."

Mary nodded. "What would you have me do?"

"I would like you to interview her while the doctor and I listen from the adjoining room. Mrs. Hudson may have helped, but she is with her son this evening. Besides, I think someone close to her own age may comfort her. The housemaid would be of little use in this regard, for I need someone with a quicker intellect."

"But, Mr. Holmes, I am not a detective. I am hardly qualified – "

"On the contrary, you are uniquely qualified for what I am asking. You are reserved, but not shy. You are also personable, and what she needs now is a friend. I believe she will respond to you better than I because, in addition to being female, you have a genuine, sympathetic character. And yet . . . ." He leaned on the fireplace mantel and pressed his knuckle to his lips.

"What is it?" Mary asked.

"You have never done this before. Perhaps I am asking too much of you. It is just that I can conceive of no other way."

"If there is no other way that you can think to manage this situation," Mary replied, "then I must do it, must I not? At the very least I should do the very best I can."

Holmes looked from my wife to me, and back again.

"All right, then. If you feel confident enough to try."

"I confess, I am not entirely confident, but I will find my way. What sort of questions must I ask?"

"It is best to concentrate on her senses, what she smelled, heard, etcetera. Anything that she can remember to describe this man, for she could not see him. Also, the location is important. He took her someplace she'd never been before, to her knowledge."

"Did she not come to your rooms from there?" I asked.

"She hid under a tarpaulin in barrel cart that was next to the building and allowed it to take her away, so she was not aware of the path she took. When that stopped, she apparently came upon Preston, who immediately thought to bring her to me. He wondered if he should to take her to a hospital, and in truth, that may not have been a bad idea considering her condition."

"I should examine her, then, Holmes," I said. "She will no doubt have some serious injuries with the treatment she's received."

"I agree, but given her reaction to my touching her hand, doing that may be difficult at first. You should wait until your wife has won her trust."

"Should I write down her answers for you?" Mary asked.

Holmes pursed his lips thoughtfully. "That would be a fine pretence. As I said, I plan to eavesdrop with your husband from my bedroom. I'll make an excuse and pretend to leave the house, perhaps that I am going to find the doctor. She need not know he is even there – you'll wait in my room, Watson – then I'll enter my bedroom from the hall. When I've heard enough, I'll return as if I'd returned from the outside. You may then show me what notes you have, so she does not suspect that I was listening through the wall."

Mary sighed. Her clear blue eyes glistened once more with uncertainty.

"This will certainly be a challenge, Mrs. Watson," said my friend.

"Yct you say you cannot convince her to speak to you."

"No," he said. "I am afraid this case is doomed to failure at my hands alone."

"Very well, then." Mary nodded. "Let me dress and we shall go."

After a few moments, Mary emerged from our bedroom dressed in a simple, emerald green gown accented with ivory, with her hair neatly wrapped in a bun. She carried over her arm two other gowns and personal linens.

"I thought perhaps she might like some clean clothes. These dresses are different sizes."

"Very good, Mrs. Watson," said my friend. "Let's be off."

We summoned a hansom cab. As we made the short drive to Holmes rooms down the street and around the corner, Holmes gave my wife some additional guidance on the sort of questions to ask. He then added, "You should be aware that she is in the condition she was in when she arrived. The maid wanted to clean her up, but I asked her to wait until you have seen her."

Holmes led us up the stairs, gesturing us to be quiet. He directed me to enter his bedroom door, and when I did, I went immediately to the small peep hole Holmes had created in the wall to see into the sitting room. In the room it was hidden by a moulded glass wall decoration that expanded the field of vision so one could see the entire room laid out. As I peered through the hole, I froze for a moment, mortified at the site that met my eyes.

A young woman around the age of three and twenty sat in the chair at Holmes's hearth. Her pale red hair was ratted and dirty, and her fair skin layered in grime. Her dress, a soft pink calico, was ripped in several places and soiled with oil, muck, and dust. She was missing a shoe and her stocking was rent, leaving her foot nearly bare. A crocheted afghan blanket of red and blue had been laid about her shoulders, and yet she still shivered as she lifted a cup of tea to her swollen lips with fingers cut and covered with dirt and blood. Black and blue bruises coloured her right eye and cheeks, the sides of her mouth, her arms, and red, raw burn wounds circled her wrists.

I looked at my Mary, who had preceded Holmes into the room, and I could see alarm in her opened lips and widened eyes.

"Miss Finney," Holmes said in a quiet voice.

The young woman twisted in her chair as if stung. "Mr. Holmes?" Her voice had the lilt of Irish.

"This is Mrs. Watson. She is the wife of my dear friend, Doctor Watson."

"The gentleman who writes of you?"

"Yes. I thought she might keep you company while I find the doctor. I am hoping he will assist me with your case."

"Oh." She blinked at Mary with pale blue eyes that seemed lifeless. "Thank you, Mrs. Watson."

"You are so very welcome." Mary walked across the room and tugged the bell rope. "Why don't I have the maid bring up a wash basin with warm soap and water, and we can clean your wounds a bit? Won't that make you feel a little better?"

"I think that's an excellent plan, Mrs. Watson," said Holmes. "Meanwhile, I shall be on my way. Good-bye, Mrs. Watson, Miss Finney." He nodded his head and stepped into the hall, closing the door solidly behind him. He then entered his room silently from the hall and came to stand beside me near the wall, to listen.

The maid answered the summons and brought Mary's requests. Mary then sat before the young woman on the ottoman to ring out a towel with warm water and soap.

"Thank you, Mrs. Watson," Miss Finney whispered. "You are very kind."

"Why don't you simply call me 'Mary'," my wife said. "We are about the same age, are we not?"

"I am twenty-five," Miss Finney said. "My name is Melinda."

"Melinda is a beautiful name." Mary smiled warmly. "Let me start with your face, dear." She began to clean the young woman's cheeks with gentle touches.

"Mr. Holmes is a good man," my own lady continued as she worked. "On our ride here he told me he wants to help you, but you'll need to tell him more of what happened to you."

"I know," Miss Finney said with a quivering voice. "But . . . it's so difficult to . . . talk about it . . . there's so much . . . ."

"I cannot imagine," Mary agreed. She patted the young woman's face with a dry towel. "But perhaps if you and I break the whole ghastly thing up into tiny, little pieces, discussing it won't be so trying. In fact . . . ." Standing, she went to Holmes's desk and took up a piece of foolscap, pen, and ink. "I shall write some notes, and we can tell him these little pieces when he comes back."

"Little pieces? What do you mean?" Miss Finney's pale eyes were wide.

Mary set the paper next to her on the side table. "Thinking about everything at once is just overwhelming, so we focus on one little thing at a time. For example, when you were in the room alone, I understand your eyes were covered so all you could do is listen. Did you hear anything?"

"Yes."

"What?"

Miss Finney swallowed hard. "The rats."

My eyes shot over to my friend standing across from me. He winced.

"Good God," I whispered.

28

Holmes again held his finger to his lips and I went silent once more to listen.

"Shall I roll up your sleeves, dear, so I can wash your hands?"

Miss Finney tenuously put forward her arms, and allowed Mary to wash the dirt, blood, and ichor from her arms and fingers.

"Did you remember hearing anything from outside?" Mary asked as she worked.

"Church bells."

"Church bells? You are certain it wasn't a clock tower?"

"Yes. The bells didn't ring every quarter hour, but every few hours. I am sure it was the Angelus. I prayed it . . . ."

Suddenly, the clock on the mantelpiece chimed midnight. Miss Finney started, but Mary soothed her by placing a firm hand on her shoulder. Dropping her face into her wet hands, Miss Finney sobbed.

Mary pulled the young woman to her shoulder and let her cry there. She rocked her gently, stroking her tangled hair. I turned my gaze to my friend, who stood by the door wearing a thoughtful expression.

"It's all right, dear," Mary said finally. "It's another little piece that'll help him find where you were imprisoned. It could help lead him to . . . to the one who did this."

"Y-yes. I see." Miss Finney sniffed.

Mary brushed loose hair from the woman's face. "Did you hear anything else that you recall?" Mary asked, she dabbed Miss Finney's tears away with the towel, and returned to bathing the young woman's wrists and fingers.

"A gurgling and swishing, like water in pipes . . . only louder."

"Excellent. That's another thing that Mr. Holmes might find useful. I'll write that down." Mary set aside the rag a moment to write on the paper.

I looked over at Holmes and saw a gleam in his eyes. This had apparently indeed triggered a thought in his mind.

"Now, in this room . . . did you smell anything that stands out in your mind?"

"Oh." Miss Finney rolled her eyes. "That I shall never forget. It smelled so foul there. There was waste . . . some of it my own, I fear. But mostly it smelled like . . . bread yeast . . . only the strongest I have ever smelled. It was mixed with the scent of beer. It was overwhelming. I don't know that I shall make bread or smell beer for an entire year after this."

I saw a slight smile curl at the edge of my friend's lips.

29

"Did the . . . man who attacked you smell this way, too?"

"Yes, he smelled strongly of it. That, and tobacco. A very acrid tobacco, much like what I smell here. I'm afraid when I entered Mr. Holmes's sitting room, I wanted to retch."

Holmes sighed. He closed his eyes and rested his head against the wall.

"He put a gag on you, I understand," Mary prompted.

"Yes, it was . . . so horrible."

"I don't doubt it," Mary said gently. "Did the cloth he use taste of anything?"

"Oh, it tasted rank. Like stale beer."

Holmes nodded, as if he expected to hear this. "Now the man," he murmured. "Ask about the man."

"Now here's one more thing, and I think this may be the most difficult of all, dear." Mary shifted her seat closer to the young woman and taking the younger woman's hands in her own, held them tightly. "Was the man who did this . . . could you tell if he was large or small in size?"

"He . . . was . . . broad shouldered, average build, I think. But not so tall."

"Were his hands rough, or smooth?"

"S-smooth. If I'd not known him otherw-wise, I'd say he was a gentleman. And the way he spoke was educated. He had a rasping voice, not very deep."

"So he spoke to you. Did he say anything that stands out in your mind? Something specific?"

"Not much I'd repeat. He said such foul things."

"But you'd recognize his voice if you heard it again."

"Yes. I don't think I can ever forget it."

"Melinda, you are doing brilliantly. See how much easier it is to take it piece by piece?" Mary wrote these down on the paper she had beside her.

"I feel badly that I could not tell Mr. Holmes this. He asked some similar questions, but I just c-couldn't . . ."

"It's all right, dear. I'm sure he understood. But you see? We have all these notes here that will help him."

"There's one more thing you might write down."

"What's that?"

"He had a beard. A short one. It was very strange . . . coarse, like horsehair. He had a moustache, too, but it was not as rough."

30

"Very good. I know that will be helpful."

Holmes patted me on the shoulder and gestured with his head for me to follow him. He went out into the hall, walked quietly downstairs and led me out the front door.

Once downstairs, he reopened the front door noisily and walked up to the landing, taking care to walk heavy on the stairs. I did the same. Holmes knocked lightly on the door, and heard my wife say, "Come in."

"Hello again, Miss Finney, Mrs. Watson," Holmes said, entering the sitting room. "I have located the doctor."

"I think Miss Finney is doing better, Mr. Holmes," my wife said. "She shared some things about her ordeal that I recorded for you."

Holmes took up the paper my wife held out to him and glanced over it. "Ladies, this is marvellous. It will help tremendously." He folded the paper and put it in his pocket. "Miss Finney, I assume you live with relatives?"

"Yes. My father."

"Do you wish me to contact him to let him know where you are?"

"Yes, please. He is the proprietor of the Celtic Knot Public House, on Surrey Row in Southwark."

"If I may," I interjected. "I'd like to examine her injuries."

"Of course, Watson. Miss Finney?"

I sat before the young woman, and when I reached out to touch her chin to inspect her bruises, she shied away, pressing against my wife who sat beside her. Mary placed her arm around her shoulders reassuringly. "It's all right, Melinda," Mary said. "My husband is very gentle."

With Mary's reassurance, she allowed me to give a superficial inspection of her injuries. She needed a more thorough exam, but I determined that she would be all right for the time being.

Mary then said to me, "Do you think I could have the maid draw a bath for Miss Finney? Then I can finish caring for her?"

"That is an excellent idea, dear. I can give you some ointment and bandages for her wounds."

"Meanwhile, the doctor and I have some other work to do," said Holmes. "Thank you for your help, Mrs. Watson."

"You are very welcome, Mr. Holmes."

After Mary led Miss Finney from the room, Holmes went to the mantel to fill his long clay pipe from the tobacco slipper. Halfway through this process he paused, set aside the pipe, and took a cigar from the coal scuttle.

"Holmes, this is simply monstrous."

31

Holmes lit his cigar and paced the floor, puffing and thinking.

"Southwark." He stopped in his tracks.

"Southwark?"

"Anchor Brewery, Watson. It is right next to St. Saviour's Church in Southwark. That is where she was imprisoned. I'm certain of it. The smell of yeast and stale beer. The gurgling pipes, rather loud from her description. A good deal of water, malt, and hops. Clearly a brewery. The Celtic Knot Pub is also in Southwark, and her father would likely order from a local brewer. I believe this monster works for her father's beer supplier. He probably kept her in the brewery's cellar. The closest supplier is Barclay's Anchor Brewery."

"It cannot be that simple, Holmes. Can it?"

"Usually it is. Most victims of this crime know their attackers in some way. Human nature, really. We covet what is most familiar to us. The difficulty lies in finding the man within a brewery establishment that fits her description, but I believe I know where to start."

There was a knock at the door.

"Come in, Hopkins."

The youthful, primly-dressed Scotland Yarder stepped through the door. "How the devil did you know who it was through the door?"

"I was expecting you, and you have thick knuckles."

"Of course." He gave my friend an amused grin. "What's this about then, Mr. Holmes?"

As Holmes explained in delicate terms the situation at hand, Hopkin's expression clouded.

"Dark business," he said. "There was a report this morning of a missing young lady from Southwark. It wasn't my case, so I don't know the details, but I wager it's the same one. I can send word to the Yard." He pulled out a notebook. "So you want to look in at the brewery? No one will be there at this hour."

Holmes went to the closet and took out a dark lantern. "Which is precisely when I wish to go, my dear fellow."

"Now, wait just a moment. There are laws to follow."

"And you should follow them, of course. I place all the legal formalities of entering the building in your capable hands. You shall meet us there when you have papers."

"Meet you there? You mean – ?"

"The rest shall remain unsaid, Hopkins, lest you find yourself in a position of having to lie to your superiors. Here is the address. Join us as

32

soon as you can. Watson, I trust you have your revolver? Right then, let us be off."

As we made our way to Southwark in a hansom, Holmes asked, "What do you make of it, Watson?"

"As I said before – monstrous."

"What of her description of the man?"

"Medium build, I think. With a beard."

"Yes. She said the beard was like horsehair. What does that suggest to you?"

"It was fake?"

"I believe so."

"Then the man would be clean-shaven."

"Most likely. Ah, here we are." Holmes tapped the roof of the cab with his cane.

The brewery loomed dark and large in front of us as we approached it. Holmes lit the lantern in his hand, and began to walk around the building.

"Wouldn't it be better to see what's here in the daylight, Holmes? Why did we have to come at night?"

"Seeing evidence would be better during the day, I admit. Now, however, our quarry will not be here. He took her in the evening, left her alone late at night, and abused her, I would surmise, earlier the next day. She was gagged so she could not be heard as he left her here. That's why she took the late night opportunity to escape, for she knew he'd leave her to herself. I wanted to find this prison now and inspect it before he can return."

"Will you have enough light?"

"I've found clues in less light than this, my friend. Hello, here is a coal chute." He held his lantern over the rusted entryway and crouched. From the edge of the rusted metal chute door, he removed a tiny piece of fabric and thread.

"Hold the lamp won't you, Watson?" I did as he asked, and he examined the fragment closer to his eyes.

"Pink calico. This is where she crawled out of her prison. The room is beyond this wall."

I walked a few steps along the building. "There's a window here, Holmes, but it seems to have been blacked over on the inside."

He looked over my shoulder. "Close the lantern."

"Why?"

33

"A precaution. Let me see if we can open this window." He bent down in the dark, and I could see his shadow moving in a pushing motion. "Ah, for shame. It is a crank window, locked from the inside. Very well, then, I must break it or find another way in."

"Someone will hear you if you do that."

"Yes, I'd rather find another way." We walked together down the length of the wall, and around the back of the building. There we found a simple wooden door, which was locked with a padlock. I opened the lantern slightly so he might inspect it.

"This Aquire model is not much of a challenge." From his the pocket inside his coat, Holmes pulled out what I recognized as his lock picking tool kit, selected and instrument and went to work. It wasn't long before we were inside and making our way down a set of creaky wooden stairs into an unused portion of the giant brewery cellar. I say "unused" in that it didn't seem to be currently employed for the brewing and ageing of beer. It was, however, filled with old barrels, equipment, bottles, sawdust, and tools which were layered in dust.

Holmes took the lantern from my hand and stood gazing at the slate floor. Footprints were clear in the dust, leading to the end of the room and another singular, wooden door, which was bolted shut.

Holmes slid open the bolt and stepped into the chamber beyond. A foul odour struck me first as we passed into what had been the young woman's prison. I took my handkerchief from my sleeve and pressed it to my nose and mouth to block out the stench. Holmes held up lantern to illuminate the entirety of the grim space.

"Here are her bonds," he said, touching bits of thick rope with his cane. "Being a tiny woman, she wriggled free of them. What have we here?" He handed me the lantern, and bent down. He then lifted up a small glass bottle in his gloved fingers. Opening the top, he sniffed.

"Spirit gum. That confirms the fake beard, Watson."

"He put it on here?"

"I think not. Most likely he carried this small bottle in his pocket to re-affix the hair piece as necessary. They fall off with oil from the skin and perspiration when worn too long. This bottle is not empty, so he probably did not drop it on purpose."

"He then left the premises wearing the beard."

"I think so."

"There doesn't seem to be much else here," I said, walking the length of the room to the coal chute. "Other than that burlap sack, which you say covered her head, and this cloth." I picked it up off the floor. "Her blindfold, I'd assume."

"Yes, and this is the gag." Holmes said, pointing with his cane to another crumpled, stained rag. "No, nothing much else, Watson. He brought her here three days ago, used her, and left her here for his next convenience. Ultimately he would have killed her, I believe."

A slight movement near my boot caused me to jump. "Good heavens. The rats. I'd forgotten. It seems we've startled them." I looked up at Holmes, and saw he was gazing at me with a peculiar glint in his eye. And yet it was as if he was not seeing me. His jaw and fists were clenched tight and his lips were pressed into a firm line.

"Holmes – " I began.

"Let's go, Watson. I have had enough of this atmosphere."

I followed him outside, and, as we returned the way we had come, we encountered Inspector Hopkins with two constables.

"There you are, Holmes. You've been inside?"

My friend described the inner chamber we found, and handed Hopkins the bottle. "You might want to leave a constable here in case he returns."

"Are you off then already?"

"Yes, to the Celtic Knot Pub. The owner is Miss Finney's father, and I suspect he knows who this villain is, though he might not realize it. The villain works for this brewery, and knew Miss Finney already. He knew when she'd be vulnerable, and he followed her. He also knows where that room is, knew it was abandoned, and that he could use it with impunity."

"You don't mind if I come along, do you?"

Holmes smiled. Hopkins was a student of his methods, if an imperfect one.

"Of course, Inspector. Let's hail a cab, shall we? The pub is in Southwark but too far too walk."

When we reached the pub, we encountered the owner turning down the gas lamp outside the shop. He was a small man, whose pale face and shock of white hair betrayed his own Celt heritage.

"Ach, fellows, I cannot help you tonight. As you see I'm closing the doors a bit early. We've had some family trouble."

"We are aware," said Holmes. "That's why we are here. My name is Sherlock Holmes, and these gentlemen with me are Inspector Hopkins of Scotland Yard, and my associate Doctor Watson."

"Sherlock Holmes – Scotland Yard." He nodded. "You are quick, gentlemen. I only submitted a missing person's report today, as they'd not let me do it sooner."

"Shall we go inside?"

"Surely, surely." He led us into the pub, and locked the door behind us once we were inside. It was a clean, bright establishment inside, not as grim or dark as others I've visited. In fact, I'd say that while the establishment was one a man would frequent, it had the prim, orderly touch of a woman's influence, with shining glassware, well-swept floor, and dust-free artwork and lamps.

"Would you like a pint, gentlemen, or anything else to drink?" Mr. Finney ushered us to a large table at the centre of the floor and we sat together. *"Gratis*, of course. You're here to help, and I'll not take a farthing."

"I'm on duty, so nothing for me," said Hopkins. "Though Holmes and the doctor can indulge."

"If I had something now, it may put me to sleep," I said. "Holmes?"

Holmes shook his head. "I think you might want something for yourself, Mr. Finney. What we have to tell you might be a shock."

The barkeep paled visibly and sank into the open chair beside Holmes. "It doesn't serve to drink the profits," he said in a subdued tone. "You might as well tell me what you must."

"First, let me begin by assuring you that your daughter is alive."

"Oh, thank God." Finney rested his face in his hands.

"But there is more," my friend continued. In a gentle tone, he revealed the facts of his daughter's misery, and as he spoke the barkeep's eyes welled with tears.

"Dear Lord in heaven," he muttered, when my friend finished. He wiped his eyes with his fingers. "My sweet Melinda. Where is she now?"

"The doctor's wife is caring for her at my residence. She's sleeping in the guest room now, I hope. We shall bring her home tomorrow, late in the morning."

"Why late?"

"She must identify the culprit, and you also may help with that goal. The man who did this worked for Anchor Brewery and would have been here regularly. Do you know anyone that fits that description?"

The elderly man dabbed his eyes once more with a handkerchief. "There are three that I know. Charles Hamming is the nephew of the owner and the salesman who takes my orders. The delivery driver is Paul Somersfield, and then there is Joshua Gable. He's an odd fellow, a

36

bookkeeper for the brewery, and he comes here frequently after he leaves work. He doesn't say much, but he has a queer look in his eyes."

"Are any of these fellows clean-shaven?" I asked.

"Clean-shaven? Yes, Gable is clean shaven. The other two have moustaches, and Hamming has a beard after a fashion."

"After a fashion?" I asked.

"He's been trying to grow one, it seems. It's not filled in."

"This has been a helpful interview, Mr. Finney," said my friend, rising from his chair. "Let's leave you to your rest, confident that your daughter will be returned to you tomorrow."

"Thank you, gentlemen," Mr. Finney said, shaking our hands. "Thank you so very much."

As Holmes and Hopkins stepped outside, I paused a moment with Mr. Finney. "Sir," I said, "Your daughter will have great difficulty returning to your pub, I think. It is where she was taken, and the memories of her experience will be quite raw. Does she have anywhere she can go to stay for a time to calm her nerves? Somewhere in the country perhaps?"

Mr. Finney nodded. "I have a sister in Yorkshire. I'm sure she'd be happy to have Melinda to stay with her for a while."

"Excellent," I shook his hand once more. "And if there's anything I can do to help in anyway afterward, pray, let me know."

When we arrived at Baker Street, Holmes, Hopkins, and I found Mary in Holmes's sitting room, sleeping in the chair by the fire. I touched her shoulder and she woke with a start. "Oh! You've returned. I am sorry. I tried to stay awake."

"Do not apologize, dear," I said. "Is Miss Finney in bed?"

"Yes. She's clean and her wounds are bandaged. The maid gave her one of her nightgowns and put her in your old room. I stayed with her until she fell asleep."

"I think sleep is a fine idea for all of us," I said. "I don't believe we can do much more until morning. Or, rather, later this morning."

"I'd rather not leave her, though. The maid said there was a room downstairs where I might sleep, but I wanted to wait until you came back before I went to lie down."

"I hope you would both stay if you can," said Holmes. "Tomorrow morning may be a trial for her, and your presence would be a great help to me."

"That room will accommodate both of us, as I recall," I said. "I'll send a boy over to our flat gather some clean collars for me and some things for you as well, Mary."

"Hopkins," Holmes turned to the inspector. "Those three men can be collected when they report for work in the morning. Do you think you could bring them here?"

Hopkins shrugged. "We've done it before, so I cannot see why not. With some good constables with me, I believe we can have them here around ten o'clock."

"Then you should all go get some much needed sleep. I will stay up a bit longer and smoke – " He paused. "A cigarette or two."

I smiled. "Very well, then. Good night, Holmes."

The next morning, I awoke at eight o'clock. Mary had already risen, dressed, and gone to look after Miss Finney. I washed and dressed quickly, and, upon entering Holmes's sitting room, discovered a breakfast laid out for us. Holmes, Miss Finney and Mary were already seated at the table. One of the windows, I noticed, was opened slightly, allowing a fresh morning breeze to billow the curtains.

"The maid has anticipated our needs, Watson," Holmes said. "Come join us."

I did as he suggested, and we ate together in silence for a few moments, until Holmes said, "Miss Finney, there is something I must tell you."

She looked up at him, her right eye more a vivid blue in contrast to the grey-blue bruise that surrounded it. "What is it, Mr. Holmes?"

He placed his napkin and looked around at all of us. "This morning, Inspector Hopkins will be bringing three men here, one of whom is most likely your assailant."

Miss Finney set her fork down on her plate with a *clink*. "Oh."

"Do not fret, dear lady. I will not ask you to face him. However, if you desire justice, you must identify him for the police."

She shook her head. "But I did not see him."

"You heard his voice. Therefore, I will interview the men in this room. You will listen to the conversation from my bedroom, which is adjacent to this one." Her eyes widened at the suggestion of being in his bedroom, but he held up his hand. "Mrs. Watson will stay with you, will you not, Mrs. Watson?"

"Of course," Mary said.

"There, on my chemistry table, you will see that I have an Edison light bulb in a lamp stand. I have attached it to a switch that I'll give to you. When you hear a voice you recognize, you will flip the switch to signal to me."

"Will they not see the light go on?" Miss Finney asked.

"They may, but that need not concern you."

Miss Finney looked to Mary, who, in turn, placed her hand gently on her arm. Miss Finney straightened her shoulders and turned back to my friend.

"I can do it," said Miss Finney. "I *will* do it."

"Capital. There is only one thing more." Holmes leaned forward with his elbows on the table and asked in a voice that was most gentle. "Are you certain that there is no particular word or phrase that the man used, nothing he said that stands out in your mind? Anything he said may be of help to us."

Her delicate lips turned down in a frown. "Patience."

"Patience?"

"The first morning, just before he left me, he said that. He mocked me by saying 'patience is a virtue.' It was horrible . . . he made it sound as if I wanted . . . ." She covered her mouth and wept once more.

Mary rested her hand on her shoulder. "Mr. Holmes – "

"No more, Miss Finney. I have precisely what I need. Watson, would you escort the ladies next door? I have set some chairs in there so they may be comfortable. I'll ask the maid to clear these dishes, then I'll prepare the light switch."

I did as he asked, and when I opened the door to his room, I was surprised at the site that met my eyes.

It was tidy to the point of being pristine. Holmes had, no doubt, spent a better part of the night cleaning it. The window was also cracked open like that of the sitting room, allowing in the fresh air. He'd set two padded chairs near the wall where he and I had stood the night before to listen to Mary's conversation with the young lady. There was also a small side table with a pitcher of cool water and drinking glasses.

"Well, then," I said. "Here you are, ladies. Is there anything else you think you might like?"

"I may close the window later if there's a chill, but I think we're fine for now."

"I'd recommend a book," I said. "But reading the detailed lives of criminals might be a bit much."

39

"I think we'll be all right," Mary said with a smile. "What time do you expect Inspector Hopkins to arrive?"

I glanced at my pocket watch. "Any time now. He said he would be here around ten o'clock."

"Then we haven't long to wait."

Suddenly the door to the closet opened, and Holmes stepped into the room.

"Good Lord, Holmes," I said. "What . . . how did you . . . ?"

"I'm sorry, ladies. Watson." He held up a bit of rubber-coated wire linked to a small black box with a switch. "This is for Miss Finney. I had to pull the connection through."

"But your closet . . . what did you do?"

He glanced over his shoulder. "Oh, that. After you married and moved, I knocked a hole in the back of my closet, and another in the sitting room which is covered by those additional drapes. Having a hidden way into my room is useful, especially when one must string wire." He smiled and placed the box in Miss Finney's hand. "Simply flip this switch. Watson, let's you and I go in the other room and test it. We have little time."

I followed him back to the sitting room. There he stood in the centre of the room and called out, "Miss Finney, flip the switch please." The lightbulb on Holmes desk lit. "Excellent, you may turn it off now."

"Will you interview all the suspects at once, Holmes?"

"Of course, Watson. If a man is interviewed alone, his voice isn't natural. Put him in a conversation with three or more people, and he'll speak normally. That is what we want. Ah, I believe that is Hopkins' ring downstairs. Watson, sit over at my table near the lamp, won't you?"

Holmes then paced back and forth as we heard several men tramping up the stairs. "Come in, Hopkins," Holmes called out, before the officer's knuckles had struck the door.

Hopkins entered followed by three men and two constables.

"Sit, gentlemen, please," Holmes said, gesturing to the chairs at the dining table. "I fear I haven't much time. I have more pressing matters to attend to today, but I promised the inspector I'd assist him with his case, so let's get on with it."

Hopkins raised an eyebrow at Holmes, then turned his gaze to me. I shrugged my shoulders, wondering what this meant.

"Now, gentlemen, you have been asked here by the inspector because a crime has been committed, and we wish to know if you were involved." Holmes paced around the table, not looking at the suspects. It appeared to me as if he were not interested in them at all. "You sir, are a bookkeeper are you not?"

This question was posed to the man who sat at the end of the table. He was not overly tall, but his eyes were squinting and his mouth turned in an awkward scowl. Clean-shaven and of middle years, he did not meet my friend's gaze.

"I am. How would you know?"

"I was told one of you was a bookkeeper. You seemed most likely, with the mark of a pen on your thumb and forefinger, ink stain on your cuff, and the wear on your sleeve. You also have indentions from a pair of spectacles which are currently in your breast pocket. Your attitude is also lacks the confidence of a salesman. Therefore you are Joshua Gable. This man here," he pointed to the bearded young man who sat beside Gable, "has that confidence. You are Charles Hamming, are you not? Nephew of the owner of the Anchor Brewery?"

"I am. But I fail to see – "

"Of course you do. And that means you," he said to the third, moustached, muscular fellow, "are Paul Somersfield, the delivery driver. Your build belies that line of work."

"Aye, that'll be what I do, but I have no idea why I am – "

"You are here because a young woman was abused and assaulted in the brewery basement."

"Good God," said the bookkeeper. His scowl softened. "Who would do that?"

"One of you three. All of you have association with the Celtic Knot Pub, and all three of you work at the brewery. It can only be one of you. To be frank, I'd rather one of you simply confess and spare me the agonizing tedium of working it out of you. I swear, Hopkins," he turned to the inspector suddenly. "Could you have brought me a less interesting case?"

"I . . . bring it to . . . you?" Hopkins repeated. He crossed his arms. "What do you – ?"

"I grow tired of having to solve the simplest little problems for Scotland Yard," Holmes interrupted. "Is there not one that you could puzzle for yourselves? Why must I be the one to labour for you when the answers are always so obvious?"

"Well if the answer is so obvious," said Hopkins, his voice dropping to a growl, "why don't you just give it to us now?"

"I think you should be patient," Holmes snapped in return.

The salesman snickered.

41

"Why are you laughing?" Holmes said.

"You're asking him to be patient. You are the one who needs patience."

"I need *what*?"

"Patience. You do most of the talking, you cut others off, and do not let them finish. Who do you think you are?"

I felt heat on my left hand. Glancing next to me, I saw that the bulb was lit.

Holmes did not appear to notice. He leaned over Hamming as if examining a bug under a microscope. "Tell me, Hamming. What happened to your cheeks?"

"My cheeks? What do you mean?"

"There are small abrasions on your skin, just above the line of your beard. It looks to me like the skin has been ripped away."

"I'm not used to shaving above the beard line and I scraped it by accident."

"No, no, that is not from shaving. That injury happens when one pulls off a fake beard affixed with spirit gum. If you remove it after a short time without solvent, it hurts like the devil. I know what that injury looks like, as I've done it to myself a few times. When did you do it? Two, three days ago? It's not quite healed. Do you see it, Hopkins? I must admit, hiding a real beard under a fake one shows some cleverness, but if you're going to use a disguise, you might at least learn how to remove it properly."

As Holmes spoke, the light went on and off several times next to me, then finally remained lit.

"Here now," said the delivery driver. "What the deuce is wrong with that bulb there?"

Suddenly the door burst open and Miss Finney entered, followed by a rather anxious looking Mary.

"Mr. Holmes, did you not see the light?" Miss Finney cried with some exasperation.

"I did," Holmes replied. "I was merely confirming your identification."

Jumping to his feet, Hamming spat a word toward the young lady that I shall not record in this memoir. It was so vulgar that everyone froze with shock.

Everyone save Holmes, however. He sprang forward with a solid right cross that sent teeth and blood shooting from the man's lips. There was also a loud *crack* when he connected, and I surmised he'd broken the man's jaw. Spinning from the force of the blow, Hamming crashed to the floor in an unconscious heap.

Releasing a contented sigh, Holmes straightened his jacket, then turned to the women in the doorway.

"I apologize for that, dear ladies. Though I must admit it did give me tremendous satisfaction. I hope it did for you as well, Miss Finney?"

She gave him a slight smile. "It did, indeed."

"Well, there you are, Hopkins." He waved at the unmoving lump on the floor as if it were a fly. "Pray, have your men drag this vile refuse from my sitting room."

"With pleasure," said Hopkins. "I admit I thought you'd lost your mind for a moment there. All that about bringing you boring cases . . . ."

"It's often true," said Holmes said with a smile. "But not in this instance."

Hopkins gave Holmes a wry grin as he followed his constables and the others out the door.

"Holmes, Mary and I would be happy to take Miss Finney to her father," I said. "If there's nothing else you'll need from us . . . ."

"No, Watson. We are finished here."

Miss Finney went to my friend and, with a slight hesitation, laid her hand on his forearm. Holmes's eyes widened slightly at the gesture. He did not shrink away, but remained still at her touch.

"Mr. Holmes, I know that I wasn't the easiest client for you – "

Holmes shook his head. "It is all right."

"Yes, but, I want you to know. You've helped to restore my faith in men and you have given me hope. Thank you."

"You are welcome, of course. Be well."

As we helped Miss Finney into a carriage outside, I heard Holmes's violin playing a sweet, melancholy melody. From that day, I noticed he seldom made negative references to women or marriage in my presence. I wonder now if seeing Mary's effectiveness in this case amended his point of view, not only of her but of all women, or if seeing Miss Finney's strength in her suffering made him less apt to deride them. If it is either, I can only say that he's has become, and always will be, a better man for it.

The Adventure of the
Bookshop Owner
by Vincent W. Wright

As I look over the files concerning the cases in which Sherlock Holmes and I became involved, I find a particular one from the summer of 1890 that had initially presented itself as fairly conclusive on all points, but like many others turned out to be less so.

I had not seen Holmes for some weeks, and found myself in a recurring state of longing for a telegram or visit that would spark an adventure once again. My practice kept me busy, and while I was perfectly content with my work, it could turn dull quite quickly and become routine. My loving wife had lately spent a good deal of time visiting an ill friend in Birmingham, and I felt as if I were a bachelor once more. The recent sun-bathed mornings encouraged me to amble through the streets and listen to the bustle of life, while nights were when I ignored the hubbub and enjoyed Tennyson. Still, I pined for the days when my pulse quickened from the ceaseless, yet unpredictable, cases London would deliver to our door.

On the morning of July 1st I received a short message from Holmes requesting my attendance that evening. No other hints or clues were to be found in the terse missive, but I was certain a visit would be worth my while. My appointments for the next few days were trivial and light, and I arranged for a capable colleague to attend to the cases while I made plans to be gone until at least the weekend.

It was a perfect, cloudless late afternoon when I set out. An occasional breeze carried with it the smell of wet soil from last night's rain. The hansom came to a stop in front of 221, and I stepped down onto the damp street. Mrs. Hudson greeted me with her usual cordiality, and I hurried up the familiar steps. As I entered our old sitting room, I found Holmes already engaged with a visitor.

"Watson, so very nice to see you. Six o'clock! Perfect. Please join Inspector Chamberlain and me for what promises to be a most intriguing conversation," Holmes declared, gesturing toward a strapping young man.

"Hello, Holmes. It's always good to see you. Inspector Chamberlain," I said, turning to him. "I've followed your exploits in the papers. Allow me to offer my congratulations on attaining your position at only thirty. Putting away that sadistic animal Parker and his assistant was indeed a feather in your cap."

Chamberlain rose to greet me. He stood as tall as Holmes but cut a much stouter figure, and bore the large, roughened hands of a man who preferred to use them. His patent leather shoes and dark brown Scottish tweed suit indicated a man of business and professionalism, as did his neatly groomed beard and moustache.

"Thank you, Dr. Watson," Chamberlain said while shaking my hand. "It's a pleasure to meet you and Mr. Holmes. I trust between the three of us we can come to some conclusion about a most curious affair."

As I took my usual chair, I could see a fire in Holmes's gray eyes. It was a familiar sight, but given the unkempt state of the room, it had been some time since he had experienced it.

Newspapers were strewn about, some sliced to ribbons, and no doubt articles had been clipped out for his files. Books teetered in uneven piles on chairs, spilling onto the floor like some miniature mountain range. The humidity that had muffled London for the past few days had left the room stale and musty. A haze clouded the front windows, doubtless due to the acrid smoke from Holmes's preferred mixture of shag. He had not had a case in weeks, but to my relief I saw no evidence of the damaging syringe. In the middle of the room sat the dining table, surprisingly clean, upon which rested a small wooden box partially wrapped in torn paper.

"This will be a welcome change from summer colds and dog bites." I sat, rubbing my hands together in anticipation.

"Chamberlain was providing the details about a murder that happened in Harrow. If you would be so kind, Inspector, could you start over for my friend?" Holmes sat opposite me in his faded dressing gown, crossing his legs. He lit a cigarette and slowly blew a column of smoke toward the ceiling.

"My pleasure, Mr. Holmes," Chamberlain said, sitting down and re-opening his notebook. "Yesterday at 8:45 a.m., I was called upon to investigate the murder of one Jacob Collier. A neighbor found him face down in the mud behind his house. He was killed by a single stab from behind, angled upward to the heart. Hunting knife, seems to me. Other than those of the neighbor that found the body, there was a single set of footprints that led straight to Collier from the road and back. The rains

45

made some of the prints visible in the muck. Sharp new edges on them. Had an imprint on the sole. I could make out the name F. Pine. That and a lion, I believe."

"F. Pinet. It's a French brand," Holmes said.

"Right. Pinet. Well, the tracks went back to the road, then disappeared. Got in a carriage, no doubt. I don't think we can gather anything from them, though."

"Pray continue," Holmes said quietly.

"I searched the home and found a business card. Collier owned a bookshop on Uxbridge Road in Southall – a place called Falstaff Books. Near as I can make out from some papers I found in his desk, he left Manchester three years ago. After I finished having a look around the home, I headed for the bookshop." He sat forward and shook his head. "What I found there was quite odd. The door was unlocked, and the shop appeared open for business. There weren't any signs of a robbery, though, as the register still had a few pounds in it. But there was no one tending the shop. While we were giving the place a look over, a young boy came in. He said he worked for Collier from time to time, pushing a barrow of books. He confirmed that the place had been opened by Collier that morning, and that he had spoken to him before heading out to push his cart."

"What time did you go to the shop?" Holmes asked.

"I arrived at half past ten."

"And when was the last time someone saw Collier there?"

"A gentleman across the street runs a little haberdashery – a Mr. Arnold George," Chamberlain said, looking at his notes. "He recalled seeing a postman enter the place around ten. I confirmed this with that postman once I found him."

"So this postman saw Collier?"

"Well, according to the postman, he didn't notice who signed for the package. Seems he was busying himself with a volume about photography. A little hobby of his, he claimed. Now I figure it must have been the murderer who was behind the counter. He obviously went to the store to rob the place with the owner out of the way."

"What of the delivery signature?" Holmes asked.

"Unreadable. Shaky. Seems as though the murderer made a poor attempt at Collier's signature, for it appeared to read Jack, not Jacob. The two names look enough alike, I guess. Nerves, perhaps."

"Perhaps. Were there any receipts in the register?"

"None. The gent across the street said business was slow that morning. Not much foot traffic to speak of."

"Thank you. Please go on," Holmes said, closing his eyes and rubbing his temples.

"Well, I found nothing at the shop that would indicate what happened to Collier except for this package. It was on the main counter."

Holmes handed it to me, and I turned it over in my hands. How many times had I watched Holmes take a mundane object such as this and deduce its history? Sheer repetition should have left an impression, but I was unable to discern anything useful. It was a simply built wooden box wrapped in plain off-white butcher's paper, tied with twine. The paper had been ripped open, one end of the box was pried off, and any contents had been removed.

"There was blood on the box," Chamberlain continued, "as you can see. The blood was far from fresh when I arrived there. Some had dripped down to the papers under it. Inventory papers that were dated from the same day. Someone opened the box and then left it sitting there. I thought it might be important, so I brought it with me. One thing I noticed was that the handwriting on the package matched perfectly with that on the papers under it, and to other papers about the place. The high loops and slant made it easy to identify."

"You have a good eye, Inspector. What do you make of the box, Watson?" Holmes leaned forward.

"I can see nothing about it that would lead to any conclusions," I said. "It's of simple construction, about the size of a small cigar box, and the address of the shop is in a man's hand. The paper has been torn away rather savagely, and the twine is still knotted. Strange that the box wasn't fitted with a hinge or panel, so the only way to open it is to destroy it."

"There isn't much to be gathered from the box, that is true, and unfortunately the postmark has been smudged. I can make nothing of it," Holmes said as he took the box back. "However, there are a couple of minor points. The person who made it has little experience with carpentry, is right-handed, enjoys black sausages, and may have spent time in the Navy. The last point is purely speculative, I'm afraid."

I frowned at the box. "Once more I am at a loss about how you come to these conclusions," I said.

"Allow me to enlighten you. The box is made from scrap wood, unevenly cut, with nails much too large for this size box. They have caused the wood to split in one or two places." Holmes pointed to cracks in the side panels. "Add to that the marks of a hammer from a right-handed man who missed his target several times, and you can conclude this was not made by an experienced woodworker. The paper and twine are types regularly used by butchers, and you can just smell the hint of sausage – a rather unique recipe, I might add. There were no contents in the box, so we must conclude that someone took them."

"And the Navy?" I asked.

"Again, this is pure speculation, but the type of knot used to tie the twine is called a figure-eight knot. It is used primarily by sailors, but can be found anywhere there are boats. I cannot see a sailor making the box, however, for that well-known nautical neatness of hand is contradicted by the shoddiness of construction."

"I'll be, Mr. Holmes," Chamberlain said, shaking his head. "I've heard of your abilities when it comes to reading things, but I'm glad to finally see it for myself."

Holmes eased back in his armchair.

"Can you describe the dead man?" I asked. Holmes shot a quick glance and smile at me.

"Mid-forties, fifteen stone or so, about five and a half feet, with graying hair. Had a scar on his left cheek just below the eye. He was wearing working clothes, and his muddy boots were old. Certainly not the ones that made the footmarks. Blood had pooled on his back and ran down both of his sides. Mud caked his pant cuffs."

"What can you tell us about the home?" Holmes inquired.

"Quiet place. Small. Country furniture. Local items. Nothing of any terrible cost." Chamberlain again opened his notebook. "A kitchen table and chairs, a writing desk, a small fireplace, one large bed, wardrobe, and a couple of parlor chairs. One big room for everything. Sits on about an acre or so with a small barn in back. A few pigs and chickens. No signs of a wife or children. Simple, really. Rather fond of his own face, though. Had a painting of himself hanging on the wall. Scar and all. Nice frame, too."

"Did you look in the barn?" Holmes asked.

"Of course, sir. Found some work clothes like the dead man was wearing hanging on a line in the loft, and a small unmade bed in there, as well. Curious as the one in the house was perfectly made. Looks like Collier preferred to sleep near his animals. Outside of that it was a standard barn. I should also add that there were no witnesses to the crime."

"What of the bookshop? Any footprints?" I asked.

"Several in the store, but only one person's behind the counter, Doctor. The light rain last night left enough mud to leave tracks, but I could find only the one set past the counter and down into the cellar," Chamberlain said.

"No signs of a struggle? No forced entry?"

"Nothing."

Holmes clutched his hands together, closed his eyes, and leaned his head back against the worn fabric of the chair.

"What do you make of the blood on the counter, Inspector?" I asked.

"It must have come from the man who opened the box."

"Yes. The blood," Holmes interrupted, "was from the man cutting himself when he opened the box. He was desperate to get at what was inside, and in his haste caught his skin on the splintered wood. There is nothing more to be learned from it.

"This case certainly has some curious points about it, Inspector. I should like to contemplate it further. Thank you for stopping in," Holmes said as he stood and walked to the door.

"Very good, Mr. Holmes." Chamberlain's brows rose. "I do have a murderer to catch. I'll inform you if we find anything more, but, to be honest, I was hoping for better tonight."

"I'm afraid there is nothing more I can tell you. Goodnight, Inspector."

Chamberlain shook our hands and made his way to the door. "Good evening, gentlemen," he said with a tip of his bowler.

The door closed behind him, and Holmes smiled at me.

"An excellent case to end my dreary days. What do you make of the whole business, Watson?" Holmes asked as he retook his chair.

"Perplexing. It seems to me that the murderer certainly could be the one who signed for the package at the bookshop. He must have gone there looking for something. Who else would have known the place would be vacated?"

"It is a possibility," Holmes said softly. "He could easily have assumed the role of an employee. And if he were searching for something, it could very well be whatever was in that box." Holmes sat forward, put his elbows on his knees, and pressed his fingertips together. "Curious that it has the murdered man's handwriting on it. He must have sent it to himself to avoid having it found. But why? Why not just take it along with him when he went to work? It is paramount that we find out what was inside."

"I must confess at being absolutely befuddled. What do you think we should do next?"

"Dinner and a walk. What do you say, Watson – are you up for a little night air? I find it most restorative to the senses."

"I should be delighted."

We dined and passed the time in splendid conversation. Many and varied were the subjects we spoke of. I talked about the newest advances in medicine, and how I was enjoying my married life, after which Holmes thrilled me by recounting the recent championship boxing bout between Dixon and Wallace in Soho. The evening was brought to a close with both of us lounging at Baker Street with pipes in hand, and enjoying the occasional recollection or memory. Not a word was spoken about the case. We retired early, both ready for the resumption of the case the next day.

The next morning dawned fair. I made my way down to breakfast to find Holmes already dressed and drinking his coffee.

"Good morning, Holmes."

"Ah, Doctor. I trust you slept well."

"Very. Thank you," I said as I picked up the newspaper. A small article had been emphatically circled.

"The piece you see there is about the murder. Nothing new to be reported. It reflects everything we already know. However, I have a few items I would like to look into concerning the matter. Would you care to join me?"

"Certainly. Where are we going?"

"The paper that wrapped the box is nothing special in itself, but the smell of the sausage it had once covered was a particular type that is only made in one or two places in the city. I have some questions I would like to ask the proprietor."

"Sounds like the perfect way to spend a morning," I smiled.

"Excellent. Let us finish Mrs. Hudson's fine eggs and toast and we'll be on our way."

Within the hour we were in a cab headed for Southall. Our ride, like many before in our partnership, was spent in silence.

We stopped on High Street in front of a butchery. The windows displayed the rather grotesque and elongated carcasses of numerous hogs and fowl. A breeze carried the smell of cooking animal flesh. The bakers, confectioners, and brewers that lined the street added their own unique smells, resulting in an aroma that confused the senses but roused the appetite.

We stepped inside and found ourselves between two long glass counters which contained all matter of headcheeses, rumps, and shoulders on mounds of ice. Sausages and hams hung from hooks above, and bones for soup and stock were in buckets on the floor in front of the display cases.

"Fancy a taste of somethin', gents?" From behind a curtain stepped a small, thin man with large sideburns and liver spots beneath the remaining strands of hair on his head. He took off his bloodied gloves, tossed them behind the curtain, and wiped his hands on a clean corner of his spattered apron.

"My name is Sherlock Holmes. This is my friend, Dr. Watson. I was hoping I might take a moment of your time and ask about a customer of yours."

"Mr. Sherlock 'Olmes. Pleasure to meet you, it is. Stevens is my name. C.L. Stevens." The man gave a nod to Holmes. "Fine work on that nasty murder of the Prime Minister's cousin. Read about it in the paper, I did."

"Thank you. Now, to the matter at hand, my good man. It is my understanding that you have done business with Jacob Collier."

"'Ow come you be needin' to know that?" the man said, cocking his head to the side.

"Forgive me, Mr. Stevens. Collier is an old acquaintance of mine. Back to our college days, actually. Rugby players. I'm responsible for the scar under his eye."

"Scar, Mr. 'Olmes?" Stevens asked in some confusion.

"Well, that was many, many years ago. Perhaps it has healed up completely." Holmes pointed at the links around the ceiling. "Mr. Collier said your black sausage was the best in the city."

"Best anywhere. Recipe passed down for several generations," he said smiling.

"Excellent," Holmes said. "I was hoping you could tell me the last time you saw Mr. Collier. His shop is closed, and I can't seem to locate him."

Stevens rubbed his chin. "Always odd for someone to up and leave without tellin' no one. Can't say, though, if that's the case for Jacob. Been a customer of mine since 'e bought 'is shop. Nervous little man. Likes to live the peaceful life. Tends a small farm. Supplies the 'ogs for

51

the sausage, 'e does. Just did some dealin' with 'im a couple days ago. Monday, it was."

"Can you tell me what time you saw him that day?" Holmes asked.

"Oh, 'e sent a runner with a note. Does that sometimes. I'll 'ave the time in me ledger." He stepped into a side door and back out a moment later. "Well, 'ere it is. Just as I told you," he proclaimed, pointing to his ledger. "I wrote it in me book at a quarter to ten. 'Ere's the note 'e 'ad brought in," he said as he thrust the paper toward us.

Holmes took the paper and studied it carefully. "Does he ever send one of his workers?"

"'E only 'as the one, Mr. 'Olmes. Young boy. Pushes a cart for 'im."

"When was the last time you actually saw Mr. Collier?"

"Oh, it's been since the week prior. Often comes in 'imself. Once a week. Really loves me sausages. Must eat them and nothin' else. Orders enough for two people."

Holmes placed a half-crown in the butcher's hand. "I would like to thank you for your time and bid you a good day."

"Well, sure, if that's all you be needin'."

Holmes tipped his hat and started out the door. We stepped out into the sunlight of the day and stood silent for a moment at the edge of the street.

"Holmes, Collier was dead an hour before that. How can this be?"

"There is something most foul here, Watson. Nothing is at it seems. That note had Collier's handwriting on it. He must have sent it."

"A forgery, perhaps."

"But about sausage? To what end? No, there is something deeper here. Something we haven't seen." Holmes tapped his cane impatiently on the ground.

"Perhaps we should take a look at his home in Harrow," I said.

"I do not believe there is anything more to be learned there. Chamberlain's notes were extensive enough. Also, there is no doubt that the place has been carelessly searched and the grounds tromped over.

"There are a number of things about this case that make it quite unique, my friend. I suspect that we will find out more about Jacob Collier than he ever wanted known."

"So what now?"

"Back to Baker Street. I am expecting a telegram – a response to one I sent this morning before you rose. It will confirm an idea I had this morning concerning a case in Greater Manchester."

Upon our arrival Mrs. Hudson met us in the hall.

"Mr. Holmes? There's a gentleman waiting to see you. Been here about twenty minutes."

"Thank you. Could you send up some tea, please?"

We entered our sitting room and found a gentleman standing before our fireplace. He was dressed in a worsted suit with high black boots, and on the table lay his top hat and yellow leather gloves. He turned to look at us, clutching his lapels. One of his hands was bandaged, and the wrapping had loosened.

Holmes hesitated for a barely perceptible moment and then walked over to the man. "My name is Sherlock Holmes. This is Dr. Watson. Who do we have the pleasure of meeting?"

"My name is not important," the man said curtly. "I am not one to mince words so I shall get to the point. I understand you have some interest in the murder of a bookshop owner named Jacob Collier."

"I'm afraid I'm not at liberty to discuss the matter. Perhaps you should approach Scotland Yard with your concerns," Holmes said.

"Then you *are* looking at it."

"Without making an admittance of any kind, I will ask how it is that you believe I am familiar with this murder at all?"

"Everyone has a price, Mr. Holmes, including a constable ordered to guard the door of his bookshop."

"Sir, whatever I may or may not know about the situation, I will not be discussing anything with you or anyone else save the Inspector who has been assigned to the case."

The man's jaw tightened and his fists balled.

"Your bandage is tattered," Holmes said. "Watson, would you be so good as to change the dressing for him?"

"Leave it be," the man barked, hiding his hand behind his back. "Jacob Collier was a friend of mine," he continued. "He disappeared, and I've only recently found him. I hear, however, that he has been murdered. As I am still acquainted with his family, I am interested in conveying any news I can. I can make it worth your while to tell me what I want to know."

"I am terribly sorry, sir, but I cannot help you. I am certain that Mr. Collier's family appreciates your concern, and I ask you to give them my condolences. Thank you for stopping in," Holmes said with an insincere smile.

The gentleman scowled and breathed deeply through flared nostrils. Without another word he grabbed his hat and gloves and hurried through the door. His steps checked, and he slowly descended the stairs. The front door slammed closed.

"Well, that was unsettling. What do you make of him?" I asked.

"What I make of him is that whomever we were just addressing is not who he says he is. Also, he was wearing lifts in his shoes to make himself appear taller. His high-heeled boots added to that deception. Did you notice how slowly he descended the stairs? He is not comfortable wearing the lifts."

"Incredible."

"His moustache was real enough, but it and his hair were dyed darker."

"So, who were we talking to?"

Holmes peered out the window. "I have a suspicion, but I cannot commit at the moment."

"Should we follow him?"

"No. I saw the unmistakable shape of a revolver in his right-hand pocket, and any man who is brazen enough to pay off a policeman and then bribe others for data regarding a murder is not a man to be taken lightly.

"Watson, I need to step out for a few moments. I shall return shortly." Holmes grabbed his hat and was downstairs in seconds.

Mrs. Hudson appeared with a tray. "I apologize for the delay, Doctor. Where is Mr. Holmes going?"

"Thank you, Mrs. Hudson. He'll be back soon. I'll keep the pot warm for him until he gets back."

No more than fifteen minutes passed before Holmes reappeared. "I think we should have this little problem unknotted by tonight, at least if my sources don't fail me."

"Where did you go?"

"When one wishes to know what happens on the streets of London, one has to go to those streets."

"Ah. You've been to see the Irregulars, haven't you?"

"They are the most valuable institution for information, next to the press. As you know, they have been helpful on a number of occasions. I have Wiggins and his friends gathering some data for me, and if my suspicions are correct, we should have an answer to my query in no more than a couple hours."

54

"And until then?"

"I have sent for Inspector Chamberlain. I would prefer having an official member of the Force with us. Unless I am very much mistaken, he will have learned nothing about the murder of Jacob Collier. Ah! I see you've kept the tea warm. Excellent."

As the clock on the mantel sounded four, we heard heavy footsteps climbing our stairs. The Inspector appeared at the door.

"What's this all about, Mr. Holmes?"

"I was hoping you might bring us up to date on what you know concerning the murder of Mr. Collier," Holmes said.

"I'm afraid there isn't much to tell." Chamberlain sat. "Since we have no witnesses to give us a description of the killer, no usable evidence left at the crime scene, and no way to know what happened at the bookshop, my men have come up with nothing."

"Any theories?" Holmes asked as he rose and stood at the window.

"I still believe the man in the shop who signed for the package was the murderer. It all went so. Collier left for work that morning and arrived at his usual time – probably about seven, as I understand it. Sometime around eight he realized he had forgotten something important at home and returned to retrieve it. In doing so he unintentionally left the shop door unlocked. When he arrived home he must have interrupted a robbery and was stabbed while running away. The killer then went to his shop to rob the place, and was nearly unmasked when the postman arrived. After that he disappeared. I've yet to find him, but I will."

"Excellent, Inspector. However, I believe there is more to this story than you may have realized," Holmes said as he gazed down at the busy street. Suddenly a slight smile crossed his lips and he started across the room. "And unless I am mistaken part of the answer should be coming through our door in seconds."

Holmes opened the door just in time for a young page to enter.

"I have a message for you, Mr. Holmes," the boy said, holding out a folded sheet of paper, and trying to catch his breath.

Holmes took the paper and opened it. His smile grew and he dug into his pocket. He handed the lad a coin. "Thank you. Your expedience is very much appreciated."

"Thank you, sir. Good day," the runner said. He turned on his heel and left.

55

"Well, gentlemen, one half of the mystery has been cleared up. Now we only have to wait for the answer to the second half. I suspect it will be here very soon."

"Out with it, Mr. Holmes," Chamberlain scowled. "We *are* talking about a murder here, you know."

Holmes handed the paper to Chamberlain. As he read it his brow furrowed. "What's the meaning of this? We already know this," he exclaimed.

"Read it aloud for the good Doctor, if you please."

"'JACOB COLLIER IS DEAD.' If this is some kind of joke, Mr. Holmes, I'll have you spend a night looking through bars."

"I assure you it is nothing of the kind. What the note *doesn't* say is confirmation of a clue you didn't even know you had, Inspector."

"You little rascal, you!" Mrs. Hudson's voice was shrill. "I'll take my broom to your breeches to teach you some manners!"

Seconds later a scruffy ragamuffin burst through the door.

"We found him, Mr. Holmes. We found him," the boy said with excitement. "Here's the address."

Holmes glanced at the message.

"Good work, my boy." Holmes scribbled on a new sheet of paper and handed it to the boy. "Please take this to the man."

"Yes, sir."

"Here is your promised sixpence. Make sure to have each of your associates who aided you stop by for theirs tomorrow, will you?"

The boy smiled, gave a quick salute, and left.

Holmes turned to Chamberlain. "Inspector, if you would care to accompany Dr. Watson and me to Southall, your name should appear in the papers once again by tomorrow."

"This best work out, Holmes," grumbled Chamberlain as we descended the stair. "Valuable time has already been wasted."

In Southall, our brougham pulled up to the curb. We climbed down. Before us rose a fashionable, narrow-windowed building of five stories.

Chamberlain frowned at Holmes. "All right, Mr. Holmes. What are we doing here?"

"Isn't that Collier's bookshop across the street?" I asked.

"It is," Holmes said, "and it's under observation."

"By the murderer?" Chamberlain asked.

"Patience, my good man. Note that we are standing just down from The Grand Garden Hotel? Inside is a man with whom you will need to

56

speak. If my calculations are correct, he should be in the lobby very soon. I would ask that you have your revolver ready, as he may not go easily."

We entered the doors of the hotel and found a quiet spot in the corner on a pair of Chesterfields. After several minutes Holmes quietly pointed to the stairs at the far end of the room. We stood and followed closely behind him along the wall and columns, getting to within about ten feet of the man.

"Jack," Holmes said in a low tone.

The man – the same one we had spoken to a short time ago at Baker Street – spun around with a look of sheer horror on his face, his hand already slipping into his waistcoat pocket.

"That'll do you no good, sir," said Chamberlain, pulling his pistol and pointing it at the man.

Holmes walked over and stared hard at the man. "Gentlemen, I would like for you both to meet Mr. Jack Collier – brother to Jacob Collier."

"What?" cried Chamberlain. I shared his confusion.

"Let us find someplace more private, shall we?" Holmes asked. "We need not put this man in any more danger."

Chamberlain took Collier by the arm. "Don't do anything stupid, Mr. Collier. I'm a quick shot, I can assure you of that. In fact, I'll have the piece in your pocket," he said as he gently pulled the gun out. Once we were ensconced in a private room, courtesy of the hotel proprietor, the Inspector shoved Collier into a seat and turned to Holmes. "Now, Mr. Holmes, what is the meaning of all of this?"

"Gentlemen, let me start by saying that Jacob is the poor soul who was murdered in Harrow," Holmes began. "He was mistaken for his brother Jack here and lost his life as a result. This killer had discovered the whereabouts of Jack and went to his home to exact revenge for a past crime. He mistakenly killed the brother. Jack was at work and was not aware of the situation until the mysterious package arrived at his shop. That package was a signal that something was amiss."

Collier shifted in his seat and glared up at Holmes. Chamberlain's grip tightened on the man's shoulder.

"Jack is the identical twin of Jacob," Holmes continued. "Thus the mistaken identity. The only true way to tell them apart quickly was the scar on Jacob's cheek. The painting in the house in Harrow was of your brother. Is that correct, Jack?" Holmes looked down at the man. Collier stared straight ahead and said nothing.

"I first began to suspect the existence of a twin when I spoke to your butcher, Mr. Stevens. I made a passing mention of the scar, but he had no knowledge of one. It was also impossible for someone to send a runner with an order an hour after he was dead. The thought of a twin had not occurred to me before then, but it seemed a plausible theory after that. By using this possibility, I was able to construct a timeline of events. At ten a.m. the postman entered your shop with the package. You recognized it immediately, cut your hand forcing it open, removed the contents, and were so shaken that you left the shop without even locking the door. From there you put into motion a plan already conceived."

"What was in the box, Mr. Holmes?" asked Chamberlain.

"Money, Inspector. Enough to disappear again if necessary. It had been stolen from Jack's old boss, Mr. Benjamin Tower."

Collier looked at Holmes, his mouth hanging slightly open.

"Jack here found it necessary to use Jacob's name in place of his own because he had declared, just before they disappeared into London, that Jacob had died. There was even a funeral. All this was necessary to fool the Tower family into believing they no longer needed to hunt Jacob. If they saw that name they wouldn't think twice about it. Jack was the name they would be looking for."

"My gracious, Holmes. Why?" I asked in astonishment.

"Mr. Tower is a well-known criminal. His power and money have maddeningly allowed him to slip the bonds of justice. Politicians and judges may be swayed, you see, and as a result of some of his more monstrous crimes. I have kept a file on him. A number of things associated with this case seemed familiar, so I sent a message to a colleague in Manchester, asking him to look into the facts of a three-year-old case."

Collier's shoulders sagged.

"Your brother killed one of Tower's sons in a heated exchange – an exchange about missing money that *you* were suspected of taking. It got out of control and Jacob stepped in and beat the man to death. For his protection, you faked his death, and then you both disappeared into London. When you arrived, you changed your name to your brother's. Shortly thereafter, you bought a bookshop. Meanwhile, Jacob led a hidden life in Harrow. No one knew he existed anymore."

"I'll ask you not to think ill of my brother, Mr. Holmes. He did what he did out of loyalty. He was merely protecting me. The only sin he ever committed was being born a little slow in the mind, and without the ability to stop when he was angered. He was all I had in this world. Our

58

mother died when we were very young. I took care of him, and vowed to always do so. Jacob was the reason for the money being taken. I had emptied our reserves. Our father died from consumption, leaving us nothing. It drove him mad that neither of his sons would follow in his footsteps as a Navy man."

I looked at Holmes and saw a slight grin on his face.

"I used Jacob's name out of my love for him," Collier continued. "Tower's people thought he was dead, and we had moved over two hundred miles away. I even went so far as to purchase passage on three different ships to three different countries under my actual name to throw them off my trail. For three years I never suspected a problem. I was certain we were safe and would never be found."

"How did you come to be discovered then?" Chamberlain asked.

"A simple slip of the tongue, sir. Nothing more. A customer in town on business was looking at a book about Manchester, talking about being from there, and I made a few careless references to my past. He must have put things together once he knew that I was from the area and saw the name on the business cards on the counter. I have talked to so many people, but never once made a mistake in talking about myself. Overconfidence or stupidity, I suppose. That devil, damn the fortunes, must have been one of a thousand men in Tower's network. He alerted them, and by that night they had probably found out all they needed to know. They came to the house early thinking I wouldn't have left for the shop yet. Found poor Jacob out back feeding his hens. Mistook him from behind for me. Had they seen the scar, which the Tower boy created with his knife during their struggle, they would have known. But, they didn't." Collier let out a deep sigh and lowered his head. "Jacob made that box for me, and I filled it with all the money I could afford. I had to wrap and tie it, though. I saw it at your flat, Mr. Holmes, and even though I wanted it back, I thought it best to leave, as I didn't want to give you any clues as to my true identity.

"I would put the box out every morning for the postman, and Jacob would bring it back inside before the man was scheduled to arrive. That was the arrangement. If the package shipped it meant that something was wrong, and that I needed to flee. If I didn't see it by lunch I could rest a little easier that the morning had passed uneventful. When I saw the package I left immediately. I jumped in a hansom. There is a room I keep in Brentford should I need it. Near the docks."

Holmes nodded. "Of course. But as you were leaving, you saw Thomas Cady lurking about."

59

Collier straightened and once again stared at Holmes in disbelief. He sat for a moment in silence and then cleared his throat.

"Tower's money has long arms," he said, nodding. "Cady would stop at nothing for him. I knew it was Cady, though I only caught a glimpse of him. He prefers to do his work in the mornings. That's the reason a signal between Jacob and me wasn't necessary later in the day. After I saw Cady, I hurried back to the shop. I quickly made my way into this hotel here and got a room that gave me a view of the shop. I watched it constantly. Every moment I was awake. I was going to wait until I saw no one I might even slightly recognize, but with my nerves being on edge it seemed everyone looked suspicious. My mind was torn between staying long enough to see my beloved brother buried, and leaving the city for my own self-preservation. I could not even claim Jacob's body for fear of being seen. It has torn my heart apart. I have, however, paid to make sure he gets a proper burial. Anonymously, of course."

"How could you be certain that the package arriving meant his death?" I asked.

"It would almost have to be," Collier said. "Jacob was very healthy, and as strong as Samson. He lived a clean life. Never had a vice. Didn't know of them. He had put on a few pounds recently because of those awful smelling black sausages. Still, it wasn't a concern."

"And when you came to Baker Street earlier, you thought perhaps I wouldn't realize I was talking to someone in disguise?" Holmes asked. "The lifts in your boots were a clever touch, but merely made you look clumsy. I will compliment your attempt, however, as you managed to add four inches to your height."

"I needed this disguise. I'm thinner now than my brother, but we still resemble each other. I couldn't risk being seen. I would have been a dead man for sure. So, I dyed my hair and moustache this morning and then went out to buy the shoes. I did it just so I could come to see you and find out what you knew. I had no idea what was happening with my brother's murder case. I went out bundled up late last night and spoke with the constable across the street at the shop. That's how I came to know about your involvement." Collier removed his hat and used a jacket sleeve to dab his brow. "I must say, I was shocked to get your message. Figured I must have given myself away again. However, I was on my way."

"It was necessary to draw you out," Holmes said. "The closeness of your room here would have been dangerous for everyone involved."

"How did you ever find me? I gave you no idea of who I was," Collier said.

"I took note of the cab you used as you left. The mare pulling it was brown and white, the rear legs themselves being completely white. The cab itself had damage to the right side window. It was easy enough to have found. I could only hope you didn't stop and change carriages, but I suspected you wished to get back to wherever you were staying and take off those uncomfortable boots. It took my informants only a couple of hours to determine where you had been taken. After that, they only had to wait to see someone matching your description."

"That seems to be everything, but who is this Cady fellow you talked about, Mr. Holmes?" asked Chamberlain.

"He is one of Tower's henchmen, and the murderer of Jacob. I know of his crimes, even though his name is always kept out of the paper. However, he does have a fondness for a particular brand of French boot."

"I'll track him to Hell's doorstep if needed," Chamberlain said. He lifted Collier up by the arm. "I'm afraid I'm going to have to take you in, sir. I believe there's a charge of embezzlement you'll have to answer for."

It was some weeks later I read in the Times that Chamberlain had shot and killed Thomas Cady on a foggy morning in Derby. The murderer of Jacob Collier, as well as countless others, was dead. Chamberlain was unable to connect him to Benjamin Tower, and so Tower was never brought to trial for any of the crimes of which he was suspected. Upon speaking with Holmes afterwards, I had the impression that he was unlikely to stop trying to make sure he paid for his offenses.

Jack Collier had pleaded his case before a Manchester judge. He was not allowed to go free, but instead was given a sentence of two years at Wandsworth and ordered to pay back any money he had left that had belonged to Tower. Upon his release he promptly disappeared again.

The Singular Case of the Unrepentant Husband
by William Patrick Maynard

Of the many adventures that I shared with Sherlock Holmes, the case I record here may well stand as the most troubling. It began, unremarkably, with a telephone conversation. My wife had come to rely upon that infernal device which so often disturbs a man's thoughts at the most inconvenient hour for the most mundane reasons. It was not unimportant in this instance, as it happened, and my wife insisted that I pay a visit to my old friend as a consequence.

It was half past twelve in the afternoon of the following day when I arrived at the great house on Baker Street. Mrs. Turner answered the doorbell and I saw a glimmer of relief flash across her features.

"Good afternoon, Mrs. Turner. Is he home?"

The matronly Scotswoman rolled her eyes theatrically as she stepped aside to allow me to enter.

"Where else might he be, Doctor Watson? Where else could he conduct his odious scientific experiments or pace the floor at all hours of the night? How my sister tolerates that man is beyond my ken. I'll be the one needing the holiday once she returns."

"Right you are. Silly of me to have asked in the first place, I suppose. Well, never mind. I'll soon have him out of your hair."

"You have a case for him, I hope?"

I detected the hint of anticipation in her voice and knew that Holmes must have driven the poor woman to her limit.

"If all goes well I do, Mrs. Turner."

The last I saw of her was the smile creasing her lined face as I made my way upstairs to Holmes's rooms.

My old friend lay sprawled upon the davenport. Street maps were unfolded and lay strewn over the table and on the floor. An empty tea cup was overturned on top of the map nearest the front legs of the table.

"What is it this time, Mrs. Turner?"

Holmes did not even glance up as I entered the room. His toneless voice betrayed his boredom with his enforced solitude. I was relieved he

62

had long since broken his addiction to that awful drug that so often claimed him at times such as this. I cleared my throat pointedly.

"Watson! What an unexpected surprise!"

His face registered what appeared to be genuine delight at seeing me.

"It shouldn't be unexpected, Holmes, I have rung you three times since yesterday morning. You told Mrs. Turner on every occasion that you had no wish to speak with me."

"Did she tell you that?" Holmes asked as he sat up, stiffly. "The woman's incorrigible. It's high time I had her put down for distemper. Perhaps I'll have her stuffed. I could keep her in the hallway next to the hat stand. She'd make a lovely conversation piece."

"One must entertain visitors if one is to have conversations, Holmes."

"That is a fair point, Watson, and a welcome reminder that you have business to attend to unless I'm very much mistaken."

"Did I say anything of the sort?"

"Well, I certainly didn't extend an invitation."

"That's perfectly beastly of you, Holmes, but also oddly appropriate."

"Is it? Pray tell me more."

"I have a case for you to consider taking and, coincidentally, it involves an acquaintance of mine who will not stay dead."

"You interest me, Watson. Go on; go on . . . while I search for my socks."

"Try looking at the end of your feet."

"Not these socks, Watson!" he shot me a reproachful glance as he wriggled his toes. "I mean the socks I removed when I retired last night – or this morning."

"Alfred Habersham is the gentleman who refuses to rest in peace."

"Habersham . . . Habersham . . ." Holmes muttered as he leaned over to peer underneath the davenport.

"Yes, the late Alfred Habersham was a patient of mine. Not a particularly lucrative one, but respectable nonetheless. He was an author as well, although I daresay he couldn't have made a go of it had he not been fortunate enough to come into a princely sum of money at an early age which allowed him to indulge his passion without fear of wondering where his next meal was coming from."

I had started to wander about the room as I spoke. It was the only way to keep my concentration while Holmes continued to be preoccupied

63

with his missing socks. I spied the stray animals resting on the small writing desk by the window. Lifting them gingerly, I brought them back to Holmes, who was on his hands and knees like a hound upon a scent, peering intently under the davenport. I dropped them on his back as I continued.

"Very conservative fellow our Habersham was. He spent precious little of his wealth except when absolutely necessary. He married well. A nice sensible girl, although I fear she left her girlhood behind quite some time ago. No children, but he did have a ward. A distant relative he sent to a boarding school in Switzerland."

Holmes sat upright suddenly and the socks fell from his back and onto the floor in front of him.

"Ah! There they are! Darn socks!"

"Really, Holmes, such humor is beneath you."

"Humor is beneath everyone. That's what makes it humorous."

"Are you paying attention? I daresay you haven't heard a word I've said."

Holmes's brow furrowed in irritation at my rebuke. "Of course I have! Alfred Habersham died leaving a widow and a ward well off since he was a miserly old sod, and you have yet to get to the interesting bit about how he is refusing to stay dead. Not very respectable behavior for a chap you seem to consider so respectable."

I smiled with unhidden amusement.

"Well said, Holmes. Although I should make it clear that it is the claim of Mrs. Habersham that her husband is not resting peacefully in his grave. She claims he has appeared to her twice during the past week. The first time she thought she was dreaming. The second time she says she was wide awake and had only just retired for the night."

"Sounds like her nerves are frayed."

"There is little question of that, yet somehow . . . I believe her."

Holmes raised an eyebrow quizzically.

"You see, there's more to it than just seeing her late husband. He speaks to her."

"He speaks to her?"

"Yes, he speaks to her. Confesses might be the more appropriate word. He apparently cannot rest with a guilty conscience and has told her some rather terrible things."

"What sort of terrible things?"

"Crimes he claims he committed when he was younger . . . indiscretions that she knew nothing of during their long marriage."

"Are these claims credible?"

"Well, his wife certainly thinks so."

"What do you propose I do about it, set a trap to catch a ghost?"

"What I expect you to do, Holmes is to restore peace to a poor widow. Prove that these ghostly visitations are the result of nervous excitement or grief. She is beside herself with the thought that the man she loved was a blackguard. Imagine her pain to hear that he wronged others when he was a young man and, worse still, was unfaithful to her for decades. She could scarcely keep from crying when she told Mary about it."

"Ah, your scheming wife put you up to this. I might have known."

"That is uncalled for and you know it, Holmes. Mary merely relayed the story to me and I sought your aid on my own."

Holmes sighed and sunk back in the davenport, arms folded across his chest.

"You're being disingenuous on that last point at the very least."

"Oh for heaven's sake, Holmes, I've known Alfred and Olivia Habersham for ages, and Mary and Olivia have become quite close since we've been married. You have only to speak with her and make her see reason."

"Watson, the woman sees and converses with her husband's ghost. She is not likely to be receptive to anything approaching reason."

Silence hung over the room. I stood still and stared at the well-worn carpet beneath my feet.

"Oh, all right. I'll come along, but not more than twenty minutes, do you understand? If she has not come round to the idea by that time, I want to hear no more about the matter."

I shook his hand effusively.

"Thank you, Holmes. Mary will be thrilled."

He grumbled in response, but I caught the flicker of a smile cross his sullen face.

"You know . . . you're not nearly the curmudgeon you pretend to be some of the time."

My old friend snorted derisively.

"I fear that I never mastered the art of disguising my feelings."

"That is hardly true and we both know it, Holmes."

He sat there silent for a moment before breaking into a hearty laugh.

We arrived at the modest Praed Street residence of the late Alfred Habersham a short while later. Olivia Habersham answered the door to

65

their apartment. She was an attractive woman whose beauty remained undimmed by the passing years. I noted that her eyes betrayed both exhaustion and emotional fragility. Her eyebrows arched in irritation, a tell-tale sign of her Irish heritage, at being disturbed by unwelcome visitors, but her features quickly softened when she recognized my face.

"John! My word, what brings you here? Do come in. You should have telephoned first. Oh dear, I must look a fright. Is Mary with you?"

Olivia's mouth quivered as she caught sight of Holmes standing to my left, just out of sight of the door.

"Good afternoon, Olivia. Allow me to present my dear friend, Mr. Sherlock Holmes of Baker Street."

Olivia stared at him a moment, her mouth curling into a look of mild repulsion.

"Oh dear," Olivia repeated, listlessly. "You're that consulting detective everyone talks about, aren't you?"

Holmes responded with a slight inclination of his head.

"If it isn't too much trouble," I asked, "might we come in, Olivia?"

She stepped aside for us to enter, but never took her eyes off Holmes.

"I can't understand the need for it myself, what with Scotland Yard and all."

"Yes, well that's why we've dropped by you see. Mary mentioned to me this morning that you have been troubled of late, and while Scotland Yard would not be of much use, I do believe Holmes, who has considerable experience handling some fairly peculiar cases such as yours, might be of some assistance."

Olivia blinked a few times, her mouth hanging agape.

"I don't know what to say, John, other than you really should have telephoned first. I don't wish to be rude, Mr. Holmes, but this is a difficult time right now, and I don't see what you could possibly do that would . . . ."

"Mrs. Habersham, I beg you . . ." Holmes's tone was calm and conciliatory, "please at least share with me in your own words what you have experienced and then let me judge whether or not I can prove to be useful to you."

The Irish eyebrows arched once more as her cheeks flushed with emotion.

"I'm sure you both mean well, gentlemen, but this is hardly a matter for Scotland Yard, much less consulting detectives. However, should I find myself in need of such services as you render, I would not hesitate to call. Good day to you both, gentlemen."

Without a further word, we were ushered back out into the hallway as the door promptly closed in our faces and was bolted shut.

"I'll be damned!"

"Oh, I shouldn't go so far as to damn you for this wasted trip, Watson," Holmes sighed, "so long as you listen to me and not your well-meaning wife the next time round."

The incident left me in a foul mood the rest of the day. I was sullen and ill-tempered with Mary and retired for bed early, instead of staying up late reading as was my fashion. I awoke dreadfully early the next morning to an unexpected phone call.

"John?" the voice on the other end trembled.

"Yes. Who is this, please?" I asked, bitterly rubbing my bleary eyes.

"It's Olivia."

"Olivia . . . ." I repeated the name, momentarily puzzled, ". . . of course, Olivia! Good morning! What can I do for you?"

"Your detective friend . . . ."

"Holmes?" I asked, genuinely puzzled.

"Yes. I need him. I don't think I can stand another night in this house. I don't know whether I'm going mad or whether Alfred really is speaking to me."

I scratched my uncombed hair, absently.

"Olivia, please try to relax . . . ."

"John, do me the favor . . . the tremendous favor of bringing your friend round right after lunch or sooner still. I must know what is happening. I must know the truth. I cannot bear the thought of another night of Alfred coming to me and telling me those ghastly things he's done."

Her voice trailed away in uncontrolled sobs.

"Keep your spirits up, Olivia. We will get to the bottom of this, I promise you."

I returned the receiver to its cradle and sank back in the bed.

"What was that all about?" Mary rolled over and asked, groggily.

"Poor old Alfred is still appearing to Olivia and confessing his misdeeds. She wants me to retain Holmes's services to set things to right."

"Well isn't that a good thing?" Mary asked.

"I don't relish the thought of convincing Holmes to make the trip a second time. You know how he is about having his time wasted. Add to the fact that Olivia treated him as if he were a leper and you can imagine why I am dreading speaking to him."

Mary clicked her tongue at me as she rolled back over in bed, "I don't know why you insist on sticking your nose in other people's affairs, darling."

I sat there a moment, dumbstruck, before replying, "It is what a doctor is paid to do, dearest."

"I am not paid to be insulted, Watson."

To say that Holmes was obstinate this morning was a considerable understatement.

"If you have nothing further to say to me," he said burying his eyes in the newspaper, "then I suggest you return home and leave me to my own work."

I sat there a moment, considering the best course of action before settling on righteous indignation.

"What work, Holmes? You haven't taken a case in weeks. You told me so yourself!"

Holmes slapped the newspaper down on his table in irritation.

"You bring up an excellent point, Watson."

"Thank you," I nodded my head, hopefully. "Olivia Habersham personally requested that I ask for your help. I'm sure that you won't be insulted in any way now that . . ."

". . . now that she knows she needs me," Holmes finished my sentence, ruefully.

"We could still make lunch if we hurry," I said quietly.

Holmes stared at the newspaper again before sweeping it off the table with a hurried gesture, "Oh, botheration! I'll never enjoy a moment's peace until I agree."

He wiped his mouth clean of the crumbs from his morning toast as I clapped my hands together jubilantly.

The Olivia Habersham who quickly ushered us into her apartment that afternoon was a very different woman from the one we had last seen. Her hair was in complete disarray, and the dark circles under her eyes betrayed the fact that she had slept very little. She had a haunted look about her, and her lower jaw trembled a bit as she spoke.

"Thank you so much for coming, Doctor Watson . . . Mr. Holmes. I feel as if I'm coming apart at the seams."

"Why don't you start at the beginning, Olivia?" I asked as we sat down at her kitchen table.

"Well . . . the beginning of it all or . . . ."

"The beginning of when your husband's ghost first appeared to you, Mrs. Habersham," Holmes said, bluntly.

I blanched as I watched Olivia visibly wince at his words.

"I am not a hysterical woman, Mr. Holmes nor am I given to flights of fancy involving ghosts. If I appear rattled today it is because I have good reason to be."

"Quite. Now kindly explain what occurred the first night."

Olivia gave vent to a deep sigh and shut her eyes, composing herself before speaking.

"It isn't so simple, Mr. Holmes. It started with voices . . . or maybe they were just thoughts . . . or dreams while I was still awake. I would hear Alfred speaking to me as if he were in the room chatting as we are now. He would speak of a specific incident, a memory we both shared only . . . it would go all wrong."

"All wrong . . . in what way?"

She placed her hands before her on the table and played with her wedding ring in nervous agitation.

"He would say to me, 'Remember the time we did such-and-such?' A picnic or a holiday or something . . . and then he would tell me how he went off with the maid or . . . or with some other woman he met in passing. It was . . . it was awful."

She was fighting tears, but Holmes stayed focused.

"These were dreams you say where you were not quite asleep?"

"Yes, it was as if he were whispering in my ear. No, that's wrong. Not as intimate as that. It was more as if he were in the room with me . . . speaking softly."

"Did he apologize to you for what he had done?"

She paused for a moment and appeared lost in thought before answering.

"No, no, he didn't. He was rather matter-of-fact and detached about it all. It was as if it were some horrible joke he was choosing to share with me now that he is . . . gone."

"Was your husband given to such ill humor?"

"No, Mr. Holmes. Most assuredly he was not."

69

"Have you considered the possibility, Olivia, that this is simply your grief manifesting itself in this queer fashion?"

She looked at me sharply and I felt compelled to explain myself better.

"You and Alfred had a good life together. It would not be uncommon in your sadness to experience . . . doubts . . . about his integrity. Fears perhaps that you have harbored over the years and kept silent and unspoken that may now be coming to the fore."

"You should give up medicine to follow Doctor Freud, Watson," Holmes chuckled.

"There were no doubts, John," was Olivia's stern response. "I understand why you might suggest that and I would be half-inclined to agree with you, if only to offer some form of rational explanation, but I assure you it is a theory without basis in fact. These . . . experiences continued on this way for some time . . . not every night, but most of them. Then . . . I started seeing him."

Her voice trailed off. I couldn't tell if she was fearful of the memory or doubting her own sanity. Perhaps it was a bit of both.

"I heard him calling my name. I lay there for a few moments, hoping it would stop, but it didn't, so I got out of bed and went out into the corridor. He was at the opposite end, by the stairwell. He stood there looking at me and said, 'Olivia, I have been a sinful man. I have ruined others for my financial gain'. And then he would proceed to tell me the most . . . heartless stories imaginable."

"What did you do?"

"What could I do, Mr. Holmes? I cried. I told him to stop. I asked him why."

"Did he approach you? Did he take you in his arms and reassure you?"

Her jaw quivered terribly and I marveled at her endurance.

"No, Mr. Holmes. He simply backed up a step and vanished into thin air."

"How many times has this happened?"

"I don't know. I lost count. Seven, maybe eight times if we count the dreams where he only spoke to me . . . four times now that I have seen him . . . last night was the worst by far."

"What was different about last night?"

"He stood over my bed, leaning near me. He was young again. Younger than I had seen him in years . . . and he said, 'Olivia, I killed a man. He threatened to ruin me so I bludgeoned him to death in his stable

70

and doused him with kerosene and threw a lit match upon his body and let him burn. I am not sorry, Olivia. I am glad I did it.' Oh, God, Alfred, how could you do such an unconscionable thing?"

She put her head down on the table and sobbed. It was clear she had been fighting for too long to keep her emotions bottled up, and now she gave vent to tremendous pain. Her sobbing was so great that she took in great gulps of air in order to breathe and appeared to rock back and forth as she did so, like a child in its cradle. For half a minute, I worried she might require medical attention, but presently she regained her composure and sat upright in her chair.

"There you have it, gentlemen," she laughed humorlessly. "Now tell me, what am I supposed to do?"

"Wait until nightfall and let us see your ghost for ourselves."

"You mean to stay here all day?"

"I suggest no impropriety, Mrs. Habersham, nor have I any intent of causing a scandal. Watson and I will depart for now and we shall return later . . . discreetly, I might add. Certainly there is a servants' entrance in the rear."

Olivia's face flushed with relief.

"Thank you, Mr. Holmes, most sincerely."

"Oh, one more thing before we go, ma'am."

"Yes?"

Holmes smiled for a moment as he considered his words carefully.

"Have you any photographs of your husband that I might see."

Olivia paused, clearly disturbed by the request.

"Yes, of course. I'll get them. I won't be a moment."

When she returned, she set a large dust-covered picture book before us. Holmes turned the heavy pages and studied the photographs closely. Seated across the table from him, I glanced at the faded sepia prints wrong side up. I always found picture books rather unsettling. It is a bit like looking through other people's stolen memories. Holmes was engrossed in the images and appeared to be studying them with great care.

"You certainly enjoyed quite a few holidays together."

"Yes, we were very fortunate in that respect. Alfred was very frugal, but we shared a passion for travel."

"Yes," I added, "Mary was always quite envious."

"And now it is I who envies her," Olivia added forlornly.

I exchanged a glance with Holmes. He nodded almost imperceptibly.

71

"Well, I think we will be going now, Olivia. Brave heart . . . we will return soon."

As we stepped outside, Holmes took me by the arm and steered me in the direction of the nearest cab. Climbing into the back seat, he barked an unfamiliar London address to the driver.

"Do you have business in the City, Holmes?" I asked.

"I have business with a solicitor, one Basil Carruthers. I need to see his files on the late Mr. Habersham, specifically his last will and testament."

"That is a most irregular request, Holmes."

"Isn't it? It is also crucial that Mr. Carruthers comply with the request immediately. We haven't the time to spare."

It was extremely rare for Holmes to use his brother's name and position within the government for influence, but in this instance he felt justified in doing so. His request was quickly granted, and a private office afforded us in which to pour through Alfred's files. Several hours later, he closed the last of the large stack of folders and rose from the table with a sigh.

"It is ten minutes to five o'clock, Watson. We must make haste."

"Is there an appointment I have forgotten?"

"The Habersham residence, of course!"

"So soon?"

"We should have left already!"

"But what about the files?"

"I have finished with them."

"You haven't told me what you were looking for."

"Correct, Watson, I haven't. Now come along or I shall be forced to leave you behind."

Holmes would not be drawn into conversation for the duration of our cab ride back to Praed Street. The rain fell in a light drizzle that left smearing wet circles on the windows of our cab. I stared through these blurred portals to the world outside while the horses' hooves clattered against the crumbling road beneath their feet. When we arrived at our destination, Holmes had the driver pull round to the back so that we could enter through the rear entrance, as he had promised Olivia we would do just a few hours earlier.

I felt a sense of disquiet, as if the old house were staring at us in resentment as we made our way inside through the servants' entrance. Holmes's eyes darted furtively round the darkened corridor as we entered by the backstairs. Not a sound disturbed the silence to give any indication that our entrance had been noted. Holmes placed a finger to his lips to indicate we should do our utmost to maintain our silence.

Presently, he stepped with great caution to the rear of the staircase. A small cubbyhole was visible beneath the stairs. He indicated that I should crouch and enter the cramped space. As I stepped inside, cobwebs pulled against my face. A sense of revulsion washed over me as I watched a thick brown spider with crimson stripes on its back scurry up its web to escape through the opening between the steps above my head.

Holmes ducked into the cubbyhole to join me and smiled sympathetically in recognition that our lodging for the night was to be an unpleasant one. Soon my eyes adjusted to the gloom. We stood there crouched down and silent for what seemed like several hours until we heard it. The door to the servants' entrance had opened.

My heart raced, but I quickly regained my composure. There was no reason to fear this unknown arrival. Admittedly, it was likely far too late to be a cleaning woman. I reached for my pocket watch to check the hour when Holmes's hand shot out and touched my wrist. He shook his head slowly to insure that I did nothing to give away our position.

Presently, the new arrival began to quietly climb the stairs unsteadily, one step at a time. At first I feared my movement had been overheard, but I resolved it was likely only an elderly person struggling to ascend the staircase. I looked up as each step creaked beneath the weight of their shuffling step. I could make out shoes and dark pant legs in the dim light that shone between the cracks in the stairs, but nothing else. Holmes's face strained as he listened intently, but what he was expecting to hear I could not imagine.

The footfalls quietly moved down the second floor hallway above us. A door creaked open somewhere in the distance. I had no sense where Olivia's flat was located from the back of the building, but Holmes suddenly appeared electrified as if he'd received an unexpected jolt. He pushed his way out of the cubby hole and, before I could react, he was bounding up the stairs two steps at a time.

Excitement gripped me and I hurried to race after him. When at last I reached the top of the stairs, I found myself frozen to the spot. The disturbing sound of someone snoring unnaturally loud filled the air. I had heard it before, but I could not recall where at the moment. It frightened me for some reason. My subconscious seemed to associate the sound with terror, though I was unable to recollect the particulars of the memory.

All thought flooded from my mind as a mighty crash sounded and a man came hurtling through a doorway on the right hand side of the corridor. He smashed into the wall and slid to the floor. Holmes was upon him before he could pick himself up. My friend was not, by nature, a violent man, which made the scene before my eyes difficult to reconcile. Holmes grasped the man by the lapels with both hands and threw him forward several feet where he landed hard upon his back. Along the corridor, several doors were opening and faces of tenants were peeking out at us in concern.

"In the name of God, Holmes, what are you doing?"

"She's dead, Watson."

His chest was rising and falling from the exertion.

"Who is dead? Make sense, man!"

"Olivia Habersham is dead. He killed her."

He gestured toward the cowering figure on the floor before him.

"Olivia is dead? How did this happen?"

"He frightened her to death. Meet the unrepentant Alfred Habersham."

My mind reeled from this revelation. It could not be, but as I stared down at the face in the dark of the hallway, I recognized my old friend's features.

"Good Lord, Alfred, how could you?"

It was only then that I had moved close enough to my old friend to be startled by what I saw. The man before me was indeed Alfred Habersham, but as he must have looked thirty years ago!

Holmes and I found ourselves ensconced a short time later at the Metropolitan Police Department. Inspector Jones was somewhat less than welcoming to find that we were already involved in a matter that had just been called to his attention.

"So let me see if I understand this correctly, Doctor Watson. The deceased was a friend of your wife whose late husband was also your patient. The deceased confided in your missus that her late husband's ghost was paying her nightly visits. You took it upon yourself to contact Mr. Consulting Detective here to sort the matter out and, in short order, your friend ends up dead while our Consulting Detective assaults the man he claims scared her to death. A man you believe, incidentally, to be

74

the deceased's late husband as he appeared thirty years ago. Is there anything I have missed?"

I sighed with frustration. There was no way this was going to be a simple task.

"Yes, Inspector, that is correct."

"I'm finished. I'm finished with the lot of you," the Inspector said, slamming his fist down upon the top of his desk.

"Wonderful. Then perhaps you might let Mr. Consulting Detective speak for himself for a change."

"Do you have anything to add, Mr. Holmes?" the Inspector sneered with mock politeness.

"As it happens, Inspector Jones, I have some considerable information to impart. The man you are holding is not Olivia Habersham's late husband."

"But, Holmes," I cried, "you said so yourself!"

"I did no such thing, Watson. I said the gentleman in question was Alfred Habersham. That is an entirely different matter in this instance."

"Is Alfred Habersham not the name of the deceased's late husband?" the Inspector hissed through gritted teeth.

"It is," Holmes replied.

"Then what, by God, are you talking about?"

"Alfred Habersham is also the name of his son."

My head was reeling.

"Holmes, you're mistaken. Alfred and Olivia had no children."

"That is true, Watson. Alfred and Olivia Habersham had no children."

Inspector Jones slapped his forehead and muttered an oath beneath his breath.

"The young man being held for Olivia's murder," Holmes continued, "is the son of Alfred Habersham and a woman whose surname I presume is Clovis."

I sputtered for a moment as I followed his meaning.

"Alfred . . . Clovis . . . you mean you believe that man is Alfred Habersham's ward?"

"I certainly am not entertaining any doubt about the matter."

"No, no, no. A thousand times, no. Alfred Clovis was a distant relation that Alfred took as his ward because the boy had no father and would otherwise have suffered a life of destitution. We reviewed the paperwork in Basil Carruthers' office only yesterday."

"Yes, we did. Tell me, did Master Clovis ever live with the Habershams?"

I paused a moment.

"No, he did not. As I've said, Olivia was unable to have children and, if you must know, she told Mary she objected to the idea of taking the boy in. I suppose because they were an older couple at the time. I never questioned her on the matter, but I knew it was a sensitive one, of course. When the boy was made Alfred's ward, it was agreed that Alfred would pay for his education. His school holidays were spent with his mother, I presume. To the best of my knowledge, he never once visited his benefactor."

"Yes, quite. And one more question, Watson. Did Master Clovis benefit financially from Alfred's will?"

"Well you read the will yourself, Holmes, you must certainly be aware of the answer. He did not. Alfred left everything, that is to say, the apartment building he owned, as well as his considerable savings, to Olivia."

"And what arrangements did he make were something to happen to Olivia?"

"Well in that event . . . ."

I paused as a terrible recollection of what I had read only yesterday in the will returned to me.

"By Jove, Holmes, you're right."

"Thank you, Watson."

"Don't tell me," the Inspector covered his eyes and winced.

"In the event of Olivia's death, his entire estate passes to his ward, Alfred Clovis. Alfred Clovis is the spitting image of his father. Alfred Clovis is Alfred Habersham's illegitimate son!"

I would like to say that ended the matter conclusively, but sadly it did not turn out quite so well. Whilst it was true that Alfred Clovis was indeed my old friend's son, he denied any wrongdoing in Olivia's death. He claimed he had recently made an effort to establish a relationship with his father's widow for the purpose of better understanding the man who had sired him. He had no idea that Olivia was suffering from nightmares of being visited by his late father's ghost and claimed that he had only just let himself into the apartment with a key Olivia had personally given him when he discovered his stepmother dead. When Holmes set upon him, he erroneously believed my friend to have been Olivia's murderer.

76

There was little we could say to counter his claims. He did indeed possess a key to Olivia's apartment. Propriety alone would have precluded her from telling Mary about the boy. It was all entirely plausible, except for the fact that I did not believe his innocence. I was convinced he had indeed posed as his father to frighten his stepmother to death in order to get at the inheritance. The question was how to prove his guilt.

"Oh, for heaven's sake, Watson," Holmes complained bitterly one evening in his study when I paid him an unexpected visit to run through the facts with him yet again. "This is real life, not some penny dreadful. What do you expect me to do, dress up as a ghost myself to trick the murderer into confessing his wrongdoing? We accomplished our task. We solved the case, but we cannot prove his guilt. He was the cleverer of us and he's gotten away with the crime. End of story. There is nothing more to be done with it."

"Holmes, I cannot believe you are willing to accept defeat so easily."

"I am a rational man, Watson. That's why I knew there were no ghosts involved, no matter how convinced Olivia was to the contrary. I was certain that the only rational explanation for Alfred Habersham to appear from the grave seemingly decades younger was for a close relative, such as an unknown son, to be masquerading as him. That made sense, and the mysterious unseen ward fit the puzzle perfectly. There ends the matter. There is no logical way to prove our suspicions are correct. One must accept that he has earned his earthly reward by foul means and, if one believes in a Christian heaven, perhaps justice will be done there. For the present, there is nothing more to do."

"Won't you even speak with him?"

"For what purpose, Watson, to give him further cause to bring charges of harassment against us? We were very fortunate he chose to be understanding, considering the circumstances of his arrest. His level-headedness would only sway the court in his favor. I certainly would command no respect. Inspector Jones is certainly not inclined to look with favor upon our theory that Alfred Clovis killed his stepmother. Again, I beseech you to see reason. There is nothing more to be done."

"Very well, Holmes, you leave me no choice but to follow your example with Basil Carruthers. First thing tomorrow morning I shall refer the matter to your brother."

"You can't be serious," he scoffed. "Do you honestly believe my brother will lift a finger to help in this matter? I gave you credit for greater intelligence than that, Watson."

"I'm happy to hear it, Holmes. I do not intend to enlist your brother's aid. I merely wish to inform him of how badly you bungled the matter and how quick you were to admit you have been bested by a common swindler."

Holmes's features froze as he stared at me aghast.

"You wouldn't dare!"

"I trust you know better than to doubt me."

"That isn't cricket, Watson."

"No, it isn't, but then nothing about this case has been. Now . . . how do you propose to proceed from here?"

Holmes stared at me in something resembling admiration for the first time.

"Do you know, Watson, you have a distinct touch of the blackmailer about you?"

"Don't be vulgar, Holmes. When one heals the ill for a living, one must learn to be persuasive. Blackmail is for the uncouth layman. In any event, there is still the vexing issue of under what pretense we are to approach Mr. Habersham. His story is a reasonable one. His stepmother gave him the key with which he entered the apartment to speak to her when he found her dead . . . ."

"Found her dead," I repeated my own words, startled by a sudden thought. "He couldn't have."

"Why is that? The inquest revealed nothing to suggest otherwise."

"We don't need the coroner's report, Holmes; we need only to use our own senses."

"I'm afraid I don't follow you, Watson."

"Do you recall the specific details when you entered Olivia's apartment?"

My old friend paused a moment. His face appeared conflicted.

"No, I cannot recall precisely the sequence of events. Normally I'm very observant about any such matters, as you well know, but I was so preoccupied with what was happening that I rushed blindly forward in the dark."

"That explains your confusion, Holmes, but I know for a fact that Olivia was not yet dead when Alfred entered the apartment. I should have realized it sooner."

"Explain yourself."

"I know because my first recollection was of hearing a terrible sound emanating from the apartment . . . a sound I now recognize as Olivia swallowing her tongue during the throes of a seizure. I mistook it for an unnatural snoring at the time. I have heard that same awful sound many times before a patient died. I first heard it as a boy the night my mother died. It . . . it has haunted me ever since. Recurrence has done nothing to accustom me to its terror. Do you recall hearing it now?"

Holmes paused a moment and shook his head.

"I cannot be certain. You may be right, but I could not swear to it. I will trust your recollection better than my own in this instance. The trouble again remains there is no proof, of course. It is simply your word against his. This is no basis for confronting him with his actions."

"Surely, you will think of something?"

"I can but try, Watson. Leave me to my thoughts."

The next morning, I eagerly rang Holmes shortly after breakfast, but there was no answer. I tried several more times to no avail. Frustrated, I took a cab to Baker Street, but was surprised to find Mrs. Turner did not answer the door.

"He's not in."

I spun and saw the bundled form of an old woman walking an ugly little dog.

"He's in hospital."

"Who is in hospital?"

"The detective . . . who else would it be? You're standing on his doorstep."

"What happened to him? When was this?"

She shrugged her shoulders and pulled on the lead to move her little beast along. Without wasting another moment, I hurried to the corner and hailed a cab. My heart was racing when we reached St. John's Wood and I rushed inside the hospital. I found Mrs. Turner in the corridor outside Holmes's room.

"Oh, Doctor Watson . . . I should have rung you, sir, I am sorry."

"What happened, Mrs. Turner? What is wrong with him?"

"Brain fever, sir, like his mother before him, I fear."

I felt my legs start to give way beneath me.

"What . . . what has the doctor said?"

Mrs. Turner shrugged.

"There is nothing to be done except to watch over him. It is the terrible sleep he may never wake from."

79

I saw the toll this ordeal had taken on the poor woman. Mrs. Turner cared for Holmes in spite of the frustration he caused her. She was exhausted. I kept vigil with her for several hours, but eventually insisted she go home and get some rest. I had already rung Mary to tell her I would be staying the night. After several hours, I leaned my head forward and rested my chin on my chest and fell into a fitful sleep.

I dreamed the queerest thing as I slept slumped outside of Holmes's hospital room. I saw my old friend appear out of nothingness on a street outside a grand estate. I did not recognize the location, but I knew it could not be England. Tropical trees filled with ripe fruit of a kind I did not recognize grew tall in the forecourt. Dust blew up from the street and mingled in the air around Holmes as he approached the large iron gates. Rather than stopping at them, he simply passed through them as if his body were immaterial. My mind's eye followed him as he approached the grand estate and passed through its walls as easily as he had the gate.

Inside those walls, it became clear the estate was actually a castle. Alfred Habersham, or rather Alfred Clovis, for I now knew it was not my late friend, sat upon a throne at the back of the cold, expansive, stone-tiled room. His face rested in his right hand as he sat in decadent boredom before us.

"What business do you have here, detective?"

Holmes continued to walk, or rather float, toward the throne. He came to a stop, hovering just before that great chair. Young Master Clovis appeared unmoved by this extraordinary visitation.

"My business, as you say, is justice," my friend answered. "You shall find you are still answerable to a Higher Authority than your own cunning."

Alfred Clovis snorted in amusement, but his posture remained unchanged.

"Oh, am I now? And what authority would that be, pray tell?"

"That which none can deny when facing their Judgement. I speak of the Truth, of course. It is not a game from which the clever trickster can hide forever."

"You have no proof," Clovis sneered at Holmes. "These meaningless accusations are mere trifles without proof to substantiate them, and you have none to offer. Go home, detective. You are as unwanted here. Tend to your own business and leave your betters to themselves."

"You speak of proof," Holmes replied. "Will this suffice?"

My friend held up his right arm and a mirror seemed to appear beneath it framed by some ethereal tapestry. Upon the mirror played a series of images that I saw as if I were now staring through the eyes of Alfred Clovis. As I watched these images coalesce and recede, I obtained an understanding of what they signified.

I saw Alfred Habersham, my old friend, in his younger years looking uncannily like Alfred Clovis. I saw a young woman graced with a terrible beauty. I saw Alfred succumb to her charms. I saw my old friend, hardened with the bitterness of his falling, faced with the child that resulted from this adulterous union. I saw Olivia covered in a stony silence to mask the pain of Alfred's betrayal. I saw Alfred Clovis grow up a privileged young man with no parents to love him, no family to nurture him, no identity to anchor him from the wayward path he chose. I saw Clovis and Olivia, but my comprehension now began to fade. I read torture upon Olivia's face, but I could perceive nothing to indicate the nature of her interaction with Clovis. Did she know him? Was she being blackmailed or was he deceiving her into believing she was being haunted by his father's ghost as she maintained?

The mirror went dark, and Holmes pointed a bony finger at Clovis upon his throne, "You know that for which you are condemned. Face your sins, Alfred Clovis. Accept the Judgement your actions warrant."

Clovis' face contorted in pain. His only response was to scream in vain like a guilty man going to the gallows.

I awoke with a start, realizing someone was shaking me.

"What is it, Sister?"

"The doctor says you may go in now," the matron replied. "Your friend's fever broke overnight. He is on the road to recovery."

I was elated at the news. Holmes was extremely weak and his face was covered in sweat, but he expressed some relief at seeing me at his side. I was not allowed long to stay in the room with him, but those precious few minutes meant more than the many hours of boredom I endured as their price.

It was with the greatest pleasure that I found myself present to witness Mrs. Turner's joy when she returned and discovered her sister's famous tenant on the mend. Exhausted, I managed to find a cab to take me home just a few minutes before noon. Mary greeted me with enthusiasm and listened patiently to the good news about Holmes's miraculous recovery.

"Before you go off to bed, John," she said, patting my arm with affection, "I should let you know that Inspector Jones rang you up this morning."

"Oh no, what did he want?"

"Now, now, don't be ill-tempered. He only rang to tell you of the tragedy that had befallen that awful Alfred Clovis boy."

"What tragedy? What are you talking about, Mary?"

"It seems his heart burst from shock in the middle of the night. He was asleep in his bed at the time. When the cleaning woman found him this morning, she said he looked as if he'd seen a ghost. The Inspector said to tell you that word for word. It is the queerest thing. I half-wondered whether he only wanted to make sure that Mr. Holmes and you had played no part in the matter. You know how he is about him."

"Of course I do," I replied, as if dreaming. "The Inspector needn't worry. Holmes couldn't possibly have been involved while he was in hospital suffering from brain fever . . . could he?"

I climbed the stairs, pulled the blinds, undressed, and retired into my soft, warm bed. Sleep soon claimed me, and I lay slumbering through the afternoon, undisturbed by dreams and feeling numb to the tragic end of a child born of sin who would not break the fateful chains that bound him to this world.

The Verse of Death
by Matthew Booth

Those members of the public who have taken such an interest in this series of accounts of my association with Sherlock Holmes will recall that the dark affair of the Agra treasure and the revenge of Jonathan Small resulted in my own marriage to the lady who brought the case to Holmes's notice. The natural result of my union with Mary Morstan was an inevitable yet unwelcome disassociation with Holmes. My own happiness and the domestic responsibilities with which I became endowed were sufficient to absorb all my attention but, as often as was practicable, I endeavoured to make every effort to remain in contact with him. My correspondence was seldom reciprocated, unless it was in that austere and terse manner which was peculiar to him, but when it was possible for me to visit him in his rooms in Baker Street, I think that my presence was welcome. It was on one such visit that the story of Edmund Wyke, and the sinister mystery of the verse of death, came to our attention.

It was late one afternoon towards the end of September of 1890, I have reason to recall. As we had done so often before, Holmes and I were sitting beside the fire in the familiar rooms, the smell of tobacco and close friendship hovering in the air between us. Holmes was regaling me with the details of some of his most recent exploits, the circumstances of which made me long to have been by his side. He had only that moment completed his explanation of how he had solved the riddle of the Seventh Serpent when Mrs. Hudson showed in our old comrade Inspector Lestrade, of Scotland Yard.

I had not seen the sallow official for some time and I confess it was a pleasure to shake his hand and see him sitting once again on the settee before us. Whilst my domestic happiness was not to be questioned, there was something about this familiar triumvirate in these particular circumstances and surroundings which both thrilled and comforted me.

"Well, Lestrade," said Holmes, "what brings you to our door? I trust you have been busy since we saw you last during that little affair of the McCarthy murder at the Boscombe Pool?"

Lestrade shook his head. "A bad business that was, Mr. Holmes, I can't deny it, but it was nothing compared to the investigation upon which I am currently engaged."

Holmes's eyes glistened in anticipation. "Having a little difficulty, eh?"

"It is a queer business, sir, and no mistake. You may perhaps have heard of the retired financier, Edmund Wyke?"

"The name recalls nothing to my mind."

"He is a man of considerable wealth, known both for his ruthless sense of business and also his philanthropic endeavours. He is patron of a number of charitable foundations but, conversely, he is responsible for the ruin of many a competitor. He resides in an isolated house called Cawthorne Towers, down in Kent. When I say isolated, you may take it I am not exaggerating. It stands in its own extensive grounds, protected by any outside influence by a high stone wall. Any guest to the house is, I gather, permitted only by express invitation and after careful consideration. I hesitate to say that you could find any property or household so self-contained or cut off from outside influences."

"This man, Wyke, is a man who craves his privacy, it seems," remarked Holmes.

"You may say so."

"And what has befallen him?"

"He is dead, Mr. Holmes. He was found last night, in his bed chamber, stabbed through the heart."

Holmes considered his fingernails. "There does not seem to be very much in the way of interest for me, Lestrade. Despite our friendly rivalry, you are an able and efficient officer. Is a case of simple murder not within your own province?"

"In normal circumstances, I should not dream of disturbing you, Mr. Holmes. But, you see, the man was dead in the room and there was no trace of any disturbance, nor any means by which any human agency could have entered the room."

"No forced entry?"

"None."

"The doors and windows?"

"All locked. A rat could not have entered the place."

Holmes yawned. "I have yet to investigate any crime committed by a flying creature. A locked room mystery always has an explanation. You recall the Speckled Band case, Watson? That, too, was presented as an impossible mystery, but the solution was only too evident once the facts were considered."

Lestrade shifted in his seat and, from his pocket, produced some folded papers. "I did not think to entice you with the sealed room alone, Mr. Holmes, although that in itself is enough to beat me. But, I thought you might be intrigued by these."

Holmes took the papers from the inspector. "What are they?"

"Mr. Wyke received them over the course of the week prior to his death. They are little poems, Mr. Holmes. But, if I am not much mistaken, they warn the man of his own impending death."

I confess that at these words a shudder passed through me, but Holmes remained as impassive and controlled as ever. His eyes betrayed that glimmer which told me that, despite his austere exterior, he was inwardly excited by Lestrade's news. I moved behind Holmes and leaned over his shoulder to examine with him these strange portents of death. They were written in printed capitals and there was nothing distinctive about either the ink or the paper.

The first ran as follows:

> In hatred and shame you die.
> Of guilt must be made your coffin.
> Lay down your head and perish.
> For it comes for you as it came for me,
> A death which none can deny,
> Not least those souls who are innocent.

The second ran thus:

> The maiden of vengeance must serve
> As my cruel replevin.
> Centuries of wrong will she avenge;
> And to our deaths will she lead us.
> Her lips will touch us both and carry on them
> The kiss of the guilty.

For some moments, Sherlock Holmes read the curious verses over and over again, his brows furrowed and his eyes squinting against the tobacco fumes of his pipe. For our part, Lestrade and I remained silent, both of us more than aware that in such moments of concentration, Holmes's greatest ally was silence.

85

"What do you make of them?" Holmes asked suddenly.

Lestrade shrugged. "I can make nothing of them."

Holmes gave a quick smile. "I fancy that the author of these fascinating verses gives Shelley and his comrades no reason to fear for their reputations. But there is something very serious behind this, if I am not mistaken. Who alerted you to these messages?"

"It was Mrs. Agatha Wyke, the dead man's wife. A stern and proud woman."

"She knew of their existence?"

"Mrs. Wyke says she and her husband had no secrets."

Holmes lowered his gaze momentarily. "Every man has his secrets. Who else knew of these curious threats?"

"Mrs. Wyke insists that she was the only one aware of them."

Holmes gave a curt nod. "Now, tell me, Lestrade, who are the other members of the Wyke household?"

Lestrade aided his memory with the use of his official notebook. "There is the dead man's wife, as I have told you, and there is their son, Sebastian, a somewhat wayward young man if I am any judge, Mr. Holmes. There is a small staff, led by the butler, Jacobs."

"Is that all?"

"No, there is a friend of the family who is staying with them for the weekend. His name is Dr. James Lomax."

"I have heard of him," said I. "He wrote a splendid article in the *Lancet* not so long ago on the hereditary nature of disease."

"He is a level headed man, fiercely practical from what I have seen of him," advised the inspector. "He it was who took charge of the situation when the body was discovered."

Holmes leaned forward in his chair. "Pray, give us the precise sequence of events."

"I had better start with the previous night, that is to say two nights ago. The household, including Dr. Lomax, had assembled for dinner and the evening had been pleasant enough. Over the post prandial brandy, however, Wyke and Sebastian exchanged heated words which resulted in a somewhat fraught quarrel. It culminated with Sebastian asking Dr. Lomax for the hour, as he wished to retire and he could stand the company of his father no more. He wished Wyke would go to the Devil, and that if he would it would cleanse the very air they breathed."

"Violent words which he must surely regret now," I observed.

"Just so, Doctor, and words which you might expect me to interpret with some suspicion in light of subsequent events. But, Mr. Holmes, if I have learned one thing only from my association with you, it is to keep an open mind."

"Very wise," murmured Holmes with a sardonic twist to his voice.

"Well, after Sebastian had stormed out of the room, Lomax strove to convince Wyke to make it up with his son at once. He said it did no one any good to go to sleep without resolving an argument, but Wyke was defiant. 'If the lad wishes to make up before sleep, he may do so,' said he, 'but I see no reason to do so. Let him calm down before I make any attempt to speak to him.' This approach is, I believe, typical of the man."

"What was this quarrel about?" asked Holmes.

Lestrade shrugged. "What are quarrels between father and son ever about? Love or money, in my experience. In this case, it was money. Sebastian is an errant youth, as I have said, Mr. Holmes, and he is in deep with the wrong crowd."

"The gaming tables?"

"Precisely so. His father has been too generous with him before over money matters, and he now refuses to come to his aid. Sebastian has viewed the refusal as some form of betrayal." Lestrade looked back to Sherlock Holmes. "Now, Mr. Holmes, we get to the core of the matter. The following morning, Mr. Wyke did not appear for breakfast. It was his custom to rise early and take a stroll in the grounds, so he was usually the first to rise. The fact he was not up and about when the rest of the house rose was sufficient to cause concern. Lomax, Sebastian, and Mrs. Wyke all went to Wyke's bedroom, accompanied by the faithful Jacobs, and they found that his door was locked. Sebastian knocked but could get no response. Lomax made his own attempt but got the same reply. He kneeled to the lock and found that he could not see into the room, which showed that the key was in the lock. Thus, together, the three men threw themselves against the door and broke into the room.

"Once inside, they found Wyke lying on the floor. He was on his back and, in his heart, there was one of his own ceremonial daggers which was known to be one of a pair which hung on the wall of his study. The alarm was raised and the local police called in. I was summoned almost at once, and I have spent the morning making my enquiries. As soon as I heard about the threatening poems, I thought of you, Mr. Holmes, and I came straight round to see you."

Holmes had been sitting with his fingertips together and his eyes closed, but now he rose from his chair and stood before the fire. "You did wisely, Lestrade. Now, tell me. Has anything in that bedroom been touched?"

"Nothing. I have a constable on guard by the door."

"Excellent. Now, I have one or two other matters to attend to today. Would it be convenient if I came down to this house early tomorrow morning, Lestrade?"

"Certainly," replied the little professional.

"Capital. Watson, you are not averse to accompanying me? I trust the redoubtable Mrs. Watson and your long suffering patients can spare you for one day?"

Having heard the prelude to this strange story, I felt unable to deny myself the opportunity of witnessing its conclusion. "I would not miss it for the world, Holmes, and my practice is never very absorbing."

"Splendid, my faithful Watson. Be back here for seven o'clock and we shall breakfast together before catching the train. Farewell, Lestrade, and we shall be with you tomorrow morning to continue our investigation into what promises to be a most fascinating case."

I have stated elsewhere that Sherlock Holmes had the remarkable power of detaching his mind at will. When I met him on that following morning, it was as though the whole story surrounding the inexplicable murder of Edmund Wyke had never come to his attention. For myself, I confess that the previous evening had found me distracted by the whole business, and I fear I had been poor company for my wife. She had retired early, but I had stayed up beyond a reasonable hour, trying to discover some clue in the sequence of events which Lestrade had set out. My researches, I confess, were in vain. However, when I met with Sherlock Holmes for breakfast, he was full of energy, and I had that familiar sensation that already he had seized upon some clue which remained far beyond my grasp. Not one word would he utter of the whole business, though, until we had arrived at the railway station and been greeted by Lestrade.

"Well, Mr. Holmes, have you had chance to consider the matter?" asked the detective.

"Certainly. There are particular features of interest to the student of crime which make the matter of specific interest."

Lestrade glowed with a triumphant arrogance. "I have not been idle myself, although I confess I ought to have spared your time. With the exception of a few loose threads, the matter is at an end."

"You do not mean that you have solved it?"

"I have my man, although he has yet to confess."

A glance at my companion's face showed that his anxiety had risen. To me, who knew his manner so well, his composure seemed shaken and

88

the pale tone of his gaunt features seemed to intensify. His eyes remained as keen as ever but it was evident that he was disturbed by the inspector's confidence.

"You have made an arrest?"

"Just so." Lestrade reached into his pocket and produced a small envelope. From it, he dropped a ruby encrusted watch charm into his hand. "A further examination of the body has revealed that this was found in the dead man's hand. He must have wrenched it from the culprit's watch as he slumped to the floor."

Holmes had clutched at the charm between his thin fingers and he had begun to examine it with his lens. "There is no sign of damage."

"What of it?"

"Perhaps nothing," said Holmes, with a shrug. "To whom does this belong?"

Lestrade was unable to keep the chime of victory out of his voice. "I have identified it as belonging to Sebastian Wyke."

"The son with the gambling debts?" I recalled.

"The same, Dr. Watson, and a man whose need for money has now brought him into more troubled waters than he could have foreseen."

Holmes handed the watch charm back to Lestrade. "You consider the murder to be the natural sequel to the quarrel of which you told us."

"Do you not agree?"

Holmes shrugged. "Possibly, but I prefer to reserve my position until such time as I have had the opportunity of seeing for myself all that there is to see."

Lestrade chuckled. "You will have your little ways, Mr. Holmes, and no mistake. If you will come this way, I have a dog cart waiting, for it is a fair drive along this country track to the house."

Despite the invigorating briskness of the breeze which assaulted our faces, the weather was not inclement and there was a shadow of the summer sun still in the sky. The surrounding countryside and its rolling green hills was a treat for the eye, and were it not for the memory of the dark crusade upon which we were engaged, I would have admired it with the fond eye of a man who is proud of his country. And yet, the track along which we rattled was sombre and uninteresting. Lestrade was not guilty of exaggeration, for the narrow lane leading to Cawthorne Towers seemed to me to make the journey seem interminable.

Lestrade had spoken of its isolation but I had not been prepared for the extent of it. The high wall of which we had heard was sufficient to discourage visitors, so forbidding was it, and the huge iron gates which formed the entrance to the fortress itself were no less relentless in their obstruction. Beyond these imposing fortifications, the Jacobean manor house glared at us from its incongruously beautiful lawns. The windows were like malevolent eyes peering at us maliciously, as though daring us to approach. It was as though the house had shunned any form of social activity, and as though no external influences were desired or to be permitted, save the passing of time which had left its mark in the lichen and faded colours of the bricks.

We drove up the winding path to the house, and we were ushered inside by a lean, cadaverous old man whom it was impossible not to identify with Jacobs the butler, of whom we had heard. Holmes exchanged a few words with him, but nothing of any further importance could be added to the account which Lestrade had given us in Baker Street, and we made our way upstairs to the bedroom which had been the scene of the tragedy. We were halfway up the stairs when a man's voice called out to Lestrade and halted us in our tracks. Looking to the foot of the stairs, I saw a man of rather more than forty racing up towards us. He was a handsome man, with hair as black as the most fearful twilight, and eyes which betrayed a keen intelligence.

"Is this Mr. Sherlock Holmes, of whom you spoke?" he asked of our official companion.

It was Holmes who spoke. "That is my name, Dr. Lomax."

The man stared. "How do you know my name, sir?"

"The inspector here advised me that there was a man by the name of Dr. James Lomax in the house, and your watch chain bears the initials "J.L". If any doubt remained, it is not difficult to discern a doctor from the trace of iodine on his left forefinger."

The doctor let out a wry chuckle. "For a moment, I thought you had done something extraordinary, Mr. Holmes, but I see that it is nothing more than a conjuring trick."

"Just so. Now, gentlemen, perhaps we can continue to the bed chamber."

The room in question was along a dark, oak panelled corridor on the second floor of the house. It was furnished opulently, if in a somewhat old fashioned style. A large four poster bed with delicate veils tied to each post was the central, imposing figure of the room, and the dark crimson stain next to it, which was so familiar a sight to us in our dark investigations, showed where the man Wyke had fallen down dead. The body had been removed, but the mark on the carpet at our feet gave the unmistakable impression that it still lay before us, its horror displayed for us all to see.

"May I examine the weapon?" asked Holmes.

"Yes, I have it here," replied Lestrade, handing over the blade. "It is of a rather ornate design, as you can see."

It was a beautiful object, although its present purpose had diminished its splendour. The handle was carved ivory, decorated with a number of emeralds of the most vivid green. The guard was carved into two claws of advancing menace, and the blade itself curved slightly to its deadly point. There was still the trace of the dead man's blood smeared across the blade.

"A fascinating object," said Holmes. "And it is one of a pair, I believe."

"That is correct."

"It was no secret that they were kept in the study, as I understand it?"

"No, they were displayed on the wall."

"It is certainly a dramatic choice of weapon," remarked Holmes. "It is of course a ceremonial dagger, used by a certain ancient cult of assassins for specific forms of executions."

Lomax nodded his appreciation. "It is a dagger of the El-Khalikan Cult of ancient Egyptian assassins. They used it to execute those members who had transcended the code of conduct."

"In particular, those assassins who knowingly murdered innocent people who were not political targets, if my memory serves me well."

"It serves you perfectly well. You are well read, Mr. Holmes."

"I have been told that I am an omnivorous reader with an immense knowledge of sensational literature. You, sir, are not so far behind, it seems."

Lomax blushed at the compliment. "I have listened to Edmund talk about the ancient history of Egypt many times. It was one of his passions."

Holmes handed the knife back to Lestrade and walked over to the door of the room. He bent to his knees and, with his lens, examined the lock and the hinges. Finally, with his lens close to his eye, he picked up the key from the carpet and examined it in minute detail.

"This key fell to the floor when the door was forced, no doubt," said he.

"I suppose it must have done," said the doctor.

Holmes rose to his feet. "I believe, Doctor, that you attempted to look through the key hole but were unable to see into the room."

"The key was in the lock. We had tried the door several times."

"Quite so. Did anybody else look through the hole?"

"No, I decided it was best to get the door down as soon as possible."

"You acted wisely," said Holmes. "When you rushed into the room, did you ascertain at once that Mr. Wyke was dead?"

"It was perfectly obvious in any event," said Lomax. "Sebastian said, 'My God, he is dead,' and I went over to confirm it."

"You had remained by the door until that moment?"

"Yes."

"Thank you, that is very clear."

"It is a terrible thing, a son murdering his father in this fashion," said Lomax with some sadness.

"You are sure of the young man's guilt?"

Lomax looked at my companion with the expression of a confused man. "Do I take it you are not?"

"I form no biased judgment, Dr. Lomax. I walk where the facts lead me and draw only those conclusions which the facts allow. Now, Lestrade, perhaps I might be permitted to speak to the widow."

In spite of her obvious grief, Agatha Wyke was a stoic and proud woman of perhaps sixty years of age. At Holmes's request, he and I interviewed her alone. Lestrade offered no objection, for he had already spoken with the lady and he had other matters to which he had to attend. When we entered the drawing room, Mrs. Wyke greeted us with dignity and a demure elegance which only seemed to increase my empathy for her. Her features were blanched with sadness, but they retained a delicacy of expression which must once have been captivating, but which the passing of time had slowly sought to eradicate. She took my friend's hand in hers and spoke to him in a voice which was soured by tragedy.

"Can any woman say she has suffered more than me, Mr. Holmes," said she, "to discover that my husband is dead and my son thought to be responsible for it?"

"Might I ask whether you believe that he is truly guilty?"

A flash of colour rose to her sallow cheeks. "Bless you for giving me hope! Do I take it from that question that you believe in his innocence?"

"I have reason to believe so."

"Might I enquire what those reasons are?"

Holmes shook his head. "If I am to be of service to you, you must possess your soul in patience and allow me to act as I see fit, including permitting me to disclose my thoughts when I consider it appropriate."

"I am at your service, Mr. Holmes. I wish only to have justice for my husband and vindication for my son."

"I hope I shall be able to bring you both, madam. You have told Inspector Lestrade of these strange verses which you husband received. I believe they mean nothing to you?"

"I cannot explain them."

"Were they delivered by hand?"

"No; they came through the post."

"Did your husband keep the envelopes?"

"I am sorry, he did not."

"That is unfortunate. An envelope can tell many secrets to the trained observer." Holmes paused for a moment. "I believe no one else knew about these verses."

"No one."

"Not your son?"

"Certainly not. Edmund was at pains to keep them secret from Sebastian."

"How long has your husband known Dr. Lomax?"

The lady thought for a moment. "Perhaps five years."

"How did they meet?"

"A mutual friend introduced them. I am not aware of the details, alas."

Holmes nodded and sat for a moment in serious thought. "I have one final question, Mrs. Wyke, and then I may leave you in peace. Did your husband ever mention a woman by the name of Violet Usher to you?"

The question took the lady by surprise and for a moment she could find no words of response. Finally, with her hand to her cheek in surprise, she gave her answer. "Do you suggest that there was another woman in my husband's life, Mr. Holmes? How did you come by this information?"

Holmes held out a hand of calming gentleness. "Have no fear, madam, I am suggesting no infidelity of that nature."

"Then who is this woman of whom you speak?"

"A woman of great sadness, like you, madam."

"I have never heard the name."

"The fact that you have not may well have kept you alive, Mrs. Wyke," said Sherlock Holmes. With those cryptic words, he ushered me out of the room and we left the lady to her sorrow.

"Come, my dear Watson," said he in hushed tones when we were in the hallway once more. "Let us find a quiet corner and consider the position."

We spent half an hour in each other's company, strolling around the beautiful stretches of lawn which surrounded the house in which these dark deeds had occurred. Holmes walked in silence, and I did not dare to break it for I knew that his mind was turning over all the facts of this strange business into which we had walked. Instead, I allowed the soothing song of the birds and the gentle balm of the breeze to seep into my soul. So peaceful did those gardens seem when contrasted with the dark mystery inside the house that I was startled when Holmes's voice invaded my reverie.

"Your gift of silence is invaluable to me, Watson," said he, "and your presence by my side is always a comfort as well as an aid."

"I did not like to interrupt your thoughts."

"It is well you did not. My mind is now quite made up on the matter."

"You have solved it?"

"The identity of the murderer was never in question. It was the verses which piqued my interest, for in their solution we hold the key to this crime and a serious error of justice."

"I am afraid I do not follow you."

"That is understandable, my dear fellow, and no cause for shame. Come, we must find Lestrade at once. It is time to bring this matter to a close."

We made our way back to the house. Holmes sent at once for Jacobs and requested that the butler find Dr. Lomax and bring him to the study. The request made, Holmes made his way to that very room, where we found Lestrade, collating his reports of his investigation. Holmes sat on the corner of the desk and peered at his professional colleague. "I wonder, Lestrade, whether you may wish to amend those reports in due course. I must advise you that Sebastian Wyke is innocent."

"Why do you say so, Mr. Holmes?"

"The watch charm is a clear indication of his innocence."

Lestrade scoffed. "It is the clearest indication of his guilt!"

Holmes shook his head. "And yet, you gave me the proof that the charm cleared the son yourself."

"How so?"

"In your statement to us in Baker Street, you said that Sebastian Wyke asked Dr. Lomax for the hour as he wished to go to bed. Now, why should he need to ask the time if he was wearing his own watch with the very same ruby watch charm attached to it? Furthermore, is it not inconceivable that he would put his watch on before he stepped out to murder his father? Why on earth should he do such a thing?"

"But the charm was found in the dead man's grasp," protested Lestrade.

Holmes waved aside the objection with an impatient gesture. "Then it was placed there. That much is also evident by the lack of damage to it. If it had been wrenched off, as you claim, the link attaching it to the watch chain would surely be bent out of shape. No, Lestrade, the charm was removed from the chain and purposefully put in the dead man's hand. "

"But who could have placed it there?"

"Someone who wished to implicate Sebastian Wyke, naturally. Someone who saw in the argument between father and son a possible motive for murder and a means of diverting suspicion."

"But the only other person present during that argument was . . . ."

There was a knock at the door at that instant and Holmes leapt to his feet to answer it. He threw open the door with a flourish and ushered in the visitor. "Come in, Dr. Lomax. We should very much value your assistance."

"If I can be of service, Mr. Holmes, I am eager to help."

"Pray, sit in this chair before the inspector, then." Holmes indicated one of the chairs at the desk and guided Lomax into it. "Now, the best way for you to assist us, Dr. Lomax, is to explain to us why it was that you murdered Edmund Wyke."

The doctor made a move to rise from the chair in protest but Holmes had his grip on the man's shoulder and any attempt to move from the chair was futile. "Do not be noisy, Dr. Lomax. You have no chance at all."

For a moment or two, Lomax considered his options, but he must have seen that the three of us were not about to allow him to escape. The snared rat glowered at my companion. "What right do you have to accuse me?"

"I suspected you from the first, my dear doctor," declared Sherlock Holmes. "I stated at the outset of this case that any apparently impossible crime has a solution somewhere. It is my experience that the solutions to such mysteries are invariably very simple. The answer to this particular problem lay in your own statement of your conduct, Doctor. You told us that when the door was broken down, Sebastian ran to his father and stated that he had been murdered."

"Yes, I recall saying that."

"Very good. Then you will also remember saying that it was at that moment that you walked over to the body."

"I see no importance in either remark."

"Very likely not. But the significance of those comments struck me at once. I was forced to ask myself why you remained at the bedroom door when you had previously appointed yourself commander of the situation outside. What was the reason behind your sudden passivity? It was surely natural that you would approach the body with Sebastian, especially in your capacity as a medical man."

The sneer on the man's face intensified. "And what conclusion did you draw, Mr. Holmes?"

My friend smiled but there was no humour in it. "All in good time. My next consideration was the key in the door. You had stated that you, and only you, looked through the key hole before the door was forced."

"So I did."

"And do you maintain that position?"

Lomax nodded. "I do."

"And there is the point. The fact that only you looked through the keyhole means that we only have your word for it that the key was in the lock at all. In fact, it was not, because it was in your pocket. You were admitted to the bedroom by Wyke, where you murdered him, took the key from the door, and locked it behind you. The following morning, when the alarm was raised, you made sure that you were the man who was in control of the situation. It was imperative that it be you who checked the lock and no one else. You declared that the key was in the lock and no one had any reason to doubt your word. When the door was forced, everybody but you rushed into the room and attention was focused on Wyke's body. Thus, no one noticed you drop the key on the inner side of the door at the approximate place it would have fallen, had it been in the lock when the door was broken down. You had to remain close by the door in order to drop the key, of course, which is why you held back whilst everyone else entered the chamber and why you did not approach the corpse immediately."

Lestrade had listened to this exchange with increasing interest. Now, he leaned forward and clasped his hands on the desk. "Is this true,

Dr. Lomax? I should warn you that what you say may be used against you."

"I see no reason to deny it," replied the prisoner. "Perhaps Mr. Holmes can explain why I did what I did."

Sherlock Holmes reached into his pocket and drew out the two threatening verses which had been the commencement of this dark investigation. "I would not have known your motive were it not for these. You wanted Wyke to know that vengeance had come upon him. Whether he knew from where or whether he interpreted these messages as you intended, we shall never know."

"I will always know. The look on his face showed he had glimpsed the truth behind those poems," said Lomax.

"What is the truth?" asked Lestrade.

Holmes pointed to the verses. "There is a hidden message in those two poems of death. In the first, you will note that the end of the second line and the beginning of the third line form a name. So too do the end of the fourth line and the beginning of the fifth line. The same pattern in the second verse also spells a name. The message is completed by the final word of each poem. Read concurrently, you will see amid these verses the messages 'Finlay Meade innocent' and 'Vincent Usher guilty'."

Lomax raved in the air. "And guilty he was, the villain!"

Holmes turned to me. "You will recall, Watson, that I asked Mrs. Wyke whether she had ever heard the name of Violet Usher. Mrs. Usher was the wife of Vincent Usher, a cruel and violent blackguard. When he discovered that his wife was seeing a man by the name of Finlay Meade behind his back, Usher went berserk. In a violent rage fuelled by jealousy, he beat the woman to death. He escaped justice by placing the blame on her lover, Meade. After the trial, Usher disappeared and was never heard of again. No doubt fearful that his crime would overtake him, he changed his name to Wyke, as we now know, and began a new life as a different person. "

Lestrade nodded his comprehension. "I remember the case, Mr. Holmes. The evidence against Meade was conclusive. There was never any suspicion that it was fabricated and the verdict was obvious."

Holmes's cold eyes were on Lomax. "It was a cruel miscarriage of justice. It must have struck you as a poetic justice when Sebastian and his father argued, Lomax. What more fitting revenge than to kill the villain and put the blame on his son, just as Wyke had done to Meade."

Lomax nodded sombrely. "It was a temptation I could not resist. My mother's maiden name was Meade. Finlay was her brother. I never knew my parents, Mr. Holmes, but my uncle was a great influence in my life. His death was a crushing blow to me and I could never believe the charges against him. For years, I dreamed of seeking out the truth about what really happened. My researches led me nowhere, however, and my frustrations began to pollute my mind.

"I had not known Usher, but his name was with me every day of my life. When I met Edmund Wyke in Egypt, I could have no way of knowing that the man who had taken my dear uncle from me was gradually becoming one of my best friends. The irony punishes me even now. Naturally, Wyke was unaware of my identity, and there was no reason for either of us to think what a cruel twist of fate our friendship was.

"One day, I met an old family acquaintance quite by chance. I had not seen him for many years and I barely recognized him at first, but as he spoke I began to remember him as a friend of both Usher and my uncle. His name was Harry Coombes, and what he told me shook me to my core. He said that he had witnessed the attack on Violet Usher and he knew that Finlay was innocent. Naturally, I asked him why he had not gone to the police at the time, but he had set sail for the new world soon after the murder and was not in the country for the trial. Besides, he said, he knew what Vincent Usher was capable of and he dared not cross him, even to save another's life.

"This was shattering news to me, as you can imagine, but Coombes had still more to tell me. He had seen me in Wyke's company on a number of occasions, and he had assumed I was unaware of who my friend was. He could not understand why I would be in close company with a man who had so wronged me otherwise. You can appreciate what a devastating blow it was to me to learn that my dear friend was my sworn enemy. It was only when he showed me a likeness of Usher that I was forced to accept it. My soul cried out for justice and my mind raged at the cruelty of truth.

"I urged Coombes to come with me to the police but he refused. At last, I convinced him but, again, fate was against me for the old man died that very night. It is easy to suspect foul play in those circumstances, but it was not. His life had been long and his heart gave out, unburdened at last from the weight it had borne all those years.

"Of course, now I had no proof of Usher's guilt and Finlay's innocence, but my thirst for justice had not been quenched either. I cannot say what made me do it. Perhaps it was the years of frustration and anger poisoning my mind, or perhaps it was that my faith in justice had long ago evaporated. Whatever the cause, I would have vengeance for Finlay Meade, but the law would only fail him again whereas my own breed of revenge surely would not. I wanted him to know that death was upon him. I did not want to be a dagger in the shadows. I wanted to be cruel justice revealed, shining brightly in the sun. Those messages were my advertisement of death. If Wyke, or Usher as he was, saw through them, then he would know why his end was close. If he did not, I cared little, for I would know what those portents of death represented, but I know that he did see through them."

Holmes had listened to this statement with a keen interest. Now, he paced around the room with a troubled expression on his gaunt face.

"I have been known to empathize with criminals before now," said he. "There are times when I have battled with my conscience at the conclusion of a case. I fear I cannot do so now. Your vision is blurred so much by this private retribution of yours that you fail to see that your plan to murder the guilty and incriminate the innocent makes you no better and no different to Usher himself. That is why I cannot show you any mercy."

Lomax looked up at his with eyes of granite. "I ask for none of your mercy, Mr. Sherlock Holmes. I neither want nor need it. I go to my death with my own conscience salved. I am ready, inspector, for whatever punishment your frail system of justice sees fit to bestow upon me."

It is not necessary to prolong my narrative by telling how we explained the true facts of her husband's death to Mrs. Wyke. Nor do I need to dwell on the details of the release of Sebastian Wyke and his reconciliation with his mother. How we told them of Edmund Wyke's dark past is a matter which I feel must remain private, for I cannot help but think that mother and son have suffered enough for the old man's sins. Justice did not fail them, however, and Dr. James Lomax was sent to his death in accordance with his crime. When I read the announcement in the newspaper to Sherlock Holmes, he turned his face towards the fire and shook his head.

"Our system of justice is a fair and honourable one, my dear Watson," said he. "But it is not infallible. If it were, it would not be the law of mere men such as us. Instead, it would be the unfailing Court of a far greater power than ours."

Lord Garnett's Skulls
by J.R. Campbell

At the urgent command of the cab's occupant, the horse skidded to a stop in the busy London street. A familiar voice called my name in an impatient tone I had learned to endure. My morning walk interrupted, I turned to see my good friend, Sherlock Holmes, holding the cab door open and beckoning me to join him. It was, as Holmes correctly anticipated, an invitation my somewhat latent sense of adventure compelled me to accept. My well-intentioned schedule for the day forgotten, I leapt aboard the cab and fell into my seat as the driver urged his horse onwards.

"Holmes?"

Recognising the intent of my barely uttered question, Holmes explained the urgency of our trip. "We are bound for Lord Garnett's."

"Young Cambers' case?" I asked, remembering the youthful, thin-faced Detective Constable who had visited Baker Street last evening. Cambers had struck me as rather slight for the rough and tumble of police work, and every thought, every emotion, experienced by the earnest young detective seemed to parade across the thin, handsome features of his open face. Perhaps it was simply the contrast to Holmes's aquiline but often stoic face which misinformed my first impression of the Detective Constable, for it soon emerged that young Cambers had already made quite a name for himself. He'd solved a difficult and gruesome matter in Bedford and, as a result, Scotland Yard offered him an opportunity to practise his trade in London. Having caught the attention of his superiors, the young man was anxious to advance his career – however, a difficult theft blocked his upward path. Having heard his new colleagues at the Yard speaking of the Baker Street consulting detective, Cambers ventured forth to request Holmes's insight into a rather macabre theft from Lord Garnett's London stately home.

"Apparently there has been a new and disturbing development," Holmes informed me. "How much of Cambers' investigation do you recall?"

"To be honest Holmes, I did not consider the matter important," I admitted. "Certainly the nature of the theft was unusual but, really, it seemed of no great consequence. I understand Cambers' desire to impress his Lordship – he is an ambitious young man – but I'm surprised to see you in such a hurry over so trifling a matter."

Holmes, amused by some private thought, looked out the window. Turning to me, he said, "Indulge me."

"Very well." I proceeded to recite the facts of the case. Lord Garnett had recently returned from an inspection of his North Borneo holdings and, fancying himself a man of science, hosted a dinner party to which several prominent patrons and scientists had been invited. The highlight of the evening was the unveiling of artifacts Lord Garnett had brought back from the steamy, far-off jungle. Specifically, a net containing four smoke-blackened skulls collected from a Borneo long-house, trophies of that distant land's savage headhunters. Apparently, Lord Garnett intended to author a paper concerning the display and could not resist the opportunity to announce his upcoming publication to those who would envy such an achievement. The following day, Lord Garnett locked the drawing room containing the bones, assuring the grisly artifacts were safe from those who might covet his gruesome souvenirs. When Lord Garnett returned four days later and unlocked the drawing room, he discovered his net of skulls missing.

"According to Cambers, the room had not been tampered with," I completed my recitation. "The doors had been locked and the windows securely fastened from the inside."

"Quite true," Holmes agreed. "It was, after all, for that very reason Cambers sought my assistance."

"Yes," I admitted. "So why are we rushing to Lord Garnett's? You provided Cambers a written list of questions to ask, and you seemed quite confident it was all the detective would need to solve the matter."

"This morning I received a message from Cambers," Holmes explained. "It seems another of the skulls in Lord Garnett's possession was taken."

"Another one? Good heavens! How many skulls did Lord Garnett bring back from the jungle?"

"It's worse than you know, Watson," Holmes assured me. "This particular skull was still in use by Lord Garnett's son."

"What?" I exclaimed. "You mean the boy was kidnapped?"

"It is too early to make that assessment," Holmes insisted. "All we know for certain is that the boy disappeared sometime last night. Cambers returned to Lord Garnett's residence early this morning with the intention of putting answers to my list of questions. He was present when the child's absence was discovered."

"Well, Cambers seems a talented detective," I offered my opinion.

"You think so?" Holmes asked.

"You said he'd done well with that matter back in – where was it? – Bedford?" I reminded Holmes. "He seems quite an ambitious fellow."

"In my experience, the mere presence of ambition is not indicative of talent," Holmes argued. "I should also point out that crimes occurring in Bedford are markedly different than the crimes of London."

"Surely crime is crime, wherever it happens," I suggested, earning a long-suffering look from my friend.

"Not so, Watson," Holmes argued. "Regrettably, we do not have time to debate the point. There is Lord Garnett's. Ah, and here comes your rising star." Holmes leaned forward and, in a conspiratorial whisper, added, "I will admit this detective shows some promise."

"Oh?" I said, somewhat surprised.

"He knows enough to call for me," Holmes explained.

Cambers waited anxiously as the cabbie brought his horse to a stop. Detective Cambers' open face was twisted into an expression of calamity. His eyes darted to and fro, reminding me of a frightened rabbit. Holmes dismissed the cabbie and turned to the Scotland Yard man.

"You've completed a search of the grounds?"

"I have Mr. Holmes," Cambers answered. "We've found nothing, nothing at all. I was just on my way in to inform Lord Garnett."

"How many constables are with you?" Holmes asked.

"Four," Cambers reported. "They're good men."

"And my list?" Holmes asked pointedly. "Have you managed to gain the answers I instructed you to seek?"

Cambers looked surprised by the question, but, seeing Holmes's unfaltering expression, the young man grimaced and confessed, "I'd just begun, Mr. Holmes, when the kidnapping – "

"Kidnapping?" Holmes interrupted the Scotland Yard detective. "Has that been determined?"

"Well," Cambers prevaricated. "The boy is only seven years of age. It seems unlikely he'd just wander off alone in the night."

"Seems unlikely?" Holmes shook his head. "I trust we're able to do better than that, Mr. Cambers."

The young detective's expression rearranged itself into a guarded look. "Of course, Mr. Holmes, any help you can provide will be appreciated."

Holmes nodded, indifferent to whether his assistance would be appreciated or not. "How many of my questions were you able to answer before abandoning them?"

"I'd been speaking to the chief cook, Mr. Holmes," Cambers explained. "She'd just completed the questions on your list when the alarm went up. As you might imagine, Lady Garnett is hysterical. Her physician has visited, and I believe her Ladyship has been sedated."

"Have you the cook's answers?" Holmes asked.

Cambers dug in his pocket and removed the sheet of questions Holmes had written out for him the previous evening, and another sheet of paper, presumably from the chief cook.

"Very well." Holmes examined the cook's list. "And the other question you were to ask her?"

"She says she had no idea as to the nature of his Lordship's stolen foreign treasure," Cambers said.

"Was that the phrase she used?" Holmes asked. "Foreign treasure?"

"I think it was, yes," Cambers answered. Shuffling his feet impatiently, he added, "I should really report to Lord Garnett. He's most insistent that he be kept informed."

"You must proceed as you think best," Holmes declared. "Watson and I shall make some inquiries of our own. I assume the head butler waits inside?"

"I believe so," Cambers said without conviction.

"Then we shall gather answers for your neglected list." Holmes gestured for the Detective Constable to lead the way into the house.

"If you discover anything – "

"I will keep you informed," Holmes assured the detective. We hurried up the stairs and into Lord Garnett's grand house. Detective Cambers, anxious to make his report, waved us towards the kitchens where the household staff might be found before hurrying away in search of Lord Garnett. In short order, Holmes was questioning the head butler, a white-haired elderly gentleman with a timid but impeccable appearance.

"I wish you to write a list naming everyone who visited this house during the two days before Lord Garnett's dinner party," Holmes requested.

"Of course, sir," the butler replied. "Anything to assist the young master's return."

"You are aware of the other matter?" Holmes asked the butler.

103

"The theft?" The butler shook his head. "I'm afraid his Lordship has not seen fit to inform me of it."

"Even so, you know of it. Surely the police spoke to you? Asked you if you'd seen anything suspicious?"

"No, sir, they did not." The butler's formal demeanour and neutral expression still managed to quietly express his disapproval.

Holmes scowled in a manner that, to my eyes, seemed somewhat theatrical. The detective complained, "I was hoping you could tell me what was stolen."

"Well, sir." The butler looked left and right before leaning forward and conspiratorially lowering his voice. "I believe it was some object he brought back from his Borneo holdings. Although I don't know the item's exact nature, I did see the trunk in which it arrived. If you care to examine the trunk, I believe it is still in the drawing room."

"Indeed," Holmes said. "The drawing room is down this hallway?"

"By the stairs, sir," the butler agreed.

"Once you've completed your list, please bring it to us there."

The drawing room fitted Cambers' description perfectly. A large, elegant space filled with an assortment of seats scattered around a small fireplace. Two doors opened to the interior of the room and four large windows looked outside. Holmes inspected the lock on the door through which we entered.

"Well, Watson," Holmes mused as he examined the door. "Does it seem strange to you that neither the chief cook nor the butler are aware of the nature of Lord Garnett's stolen items?"

"It is a large home," I reasoned. "Likely the kitchen staff does not normally have access to the drawing room."

"And the butler?" Holmes asked, shifting his attention to the first of the windows.

Frowning, I considered the problem. "No doubt a busy man – "

"No doubt," Holmes agreed, moving to the next window. "However, that explains nothing. If the head of staff was not aware of the skulls' presence, it follows that none of the staff knew of them."

"Can you be certain of that?" I asked.

"Gossip, Watson, is as much a force of nature as sunlight or sea tides," Holmes explained. "If any of the staff had seen the skulls, they would have spoken of it and, once uttered, word surely would have reached the ears of one of the household chiefs. Imagine if I placed a skull on my mantle in Baker Street. How long do you think it would be before Mrs. Hudson informed you of the addition?"

Chuckling, I conceded the point. "But what does it mean, Holmes?"

"Only that Detective Cambers has been shockingly misled as to the nature of the thefts. He believes a net of skulls has been taken, when in fact a mysterious foreign treasure has gone missing." Holmes finished his examination of the last window and turned his attention to the remaining door. I moved to follow when something outside the window caught my eye. A branch of one of the rose bushes had been recently broken, a few dark threads were tangled in its thorns, and at the edge of the garden a partial footprint was visible in the soft soil.

"Well-spotted, Watson," Holmes commented as he examined the door. I continued to look out the window.

"You saw it too." It wasn't a question, I knew Holmes's methods too well to believe he had missed such evidence. "Why didn't you tell me?"

"Because it is meaningless," Holmes declared. "It has nothing to do with the theft of the skulls or the missing child. As I'm sure you'll agree, the matter of the missing boy is too urgent to allow us to loiter over such trivia. However else he was misled, Cambers was correct when he stated the doors and windows had not been tampered with. Meaning the thief had a key or found another way in and out this room."

Turning his attention upward, Holmes surveyed the high ceilings. "Now Watson, never having visited a Borneo long-house, I must confess to a degree of uncertainty regarding how best to display a net full of skulls. However I suspect that hook in the ceiling would serve, don't you agree?"

"It seems secure enough," I answered.

"And it is a recent addition. You can see a hand print where the workman braced himself as he put it in. And yet – " Holmes turned around, his eager eyes searching for something by the fireplace. "Ah! There it is!" Striding over to the small fireplace, Holmes recovered a long, slender pole with a metal catch on the end. Holding the pole aloft, he retraced his steps to the ceiling hook. The pole easily reached the hook, leaving no doubt it had been constructed for just that purpose.

"And here is the trunk the butler mentioned," Holmes observed, resting the pole between the mantle and a green trunk lying open on the floor. Holmes bent to examine the trunk with his lens. For a moment Holmes was silent. Then he stood suddenly upright with an alarmed expression on his normally reserved features.

Holmes turned to me, putting away his lens, and began to speak. "Watson, I fear – "

Fate deemed I would have to wait to discover what had wrought so sudden a change in my friend's demeanour, as the butler chose that moment to enter the room. He announced his presence with a deferential, "Sir?"

"Quickly man, quickly!" Holmes exclaimed, rushing towards the servant. "You have the list?"

"Yes, sir," the butler replied, holding a folded sheet of paper in his gloved hand. "I only just completed it. I thought, perhaps, you – "

But Holmes snatched the list from the servant's hand and unfolded it quickly. As he did so, I saw Detective Cambers approaching, no doubt reacting to the urgency in Holmes's loud voice.

Behind Cambers came another figure. From the stout man's harried expression, I knew it must be Lord Garnett. The strain of his situation showed clearly on the strong features of his face. Beneath dark brows, his Lordship's brown eyes seemed wary, as if cringing in anticipation of the morning's next blow. Yet even in the midst of these troubles, a ghost of the old adventurer remained. Thick, dark hair and a moustache he had not yet attended to, a tan darkening his face and the back of his strong hands. There was doggedness to his movements, as if his every step was an act of determination, and anyone who dared hamper his way had best be prepared to pay a steep cost for their insolence. Yet, even as he approached, my reaction towards his Lordship was not one of intimidation or respect, but was, rather, one of sympathy. It was plain to my senses Lord Garnett was very close to being overwhelmed by the unexplained disappearance of his son.

Such were my impressions of Lord Garnett. Holmes seemed to take no notice of his Lordship's approach. Holmes's formidable powers of concentration were focussed on the butler's list and, in his other hand, the chief cook's list he'd pulled from his pocket.

Detective Cambers and Lord Garnett entered the room together. His Lordship, seeing his butler waiting, raised his hand and started to give instructions to his servant. "Ah, I wonder if you might see to – "

"I have not yet finished with this man." Holmes interrupted firmly, though he did not look up from the lists he was examining.

"I beg your pardon?" Lord Garnett asked, blinking in surprise. Apparently his Lordship was not accustomed to being interrupted while addressing his servants.

"I have further need of this man," Holmes insisted.

Turning to acknowledge his employer, the butler seemed intent on ignoring Holmes and letting the matter drop. Whatever else he had

106

endured, it seemed Lord Garnett was not willing to suffer impertinence such as Holmes was displaying.

"And who, sir, are you?" Lord Garnett asked, his voice a threatening rumble.

"My name is Sherlock Holmes." Pulling the butler's coat until the man was forced to turn and acknowledge him, Holmes pointed to a name on the list. "I require an address for this man."

"I regret, sir, that I do not know the address offhand."

"Then find someone who does!" Holmes demanded forcefully. "And hurry!"

Shocked by Holmes's insistence, the butler turned pleadingly to Lord Garnett. His Lordship seemed quite taken aback by Holmes's manner and was about to voice his displeasure when Holmes spoke first.

"Lord Garnett, your son's life may depend on the speedy resolution of your butler's errand. If you value your child's life, I suggest you give him leave to go."

"Of course," Lord Garnett nodded to his servant, who promptly left the room at a pace seeming, for one so dignified, a run. "Now then, Mr. Holmes, is it? I fail to – "

But Holmes had turned his attention to Detective Constable Cambers. "I will require two of your uniformed officers, those you judge to be most capable, and I require them now."

Cambers, his face clouded with displeasure at being addressed so in front of his Lordship, frowned. "Now see here, Mr. Holmes – "

"Now!" Holmes repeated. "We must act quickly if we are to capture this villain."

Cambers opened his mouth to argue, but snapped it shut when he noticed Lord Garnett's formidable attention on him. With an uncertain shrug, Cambers hurried from the room, much as the butler had before him.

"Now then, Mr. Holmes," Lord Garnett started, but, to the surprise of both his Lordship and myself, Holmes set off down the hallway at a quick run. For a moment Lord Garnett seemed at a complete loss. I had the impression it had been quite a long time since his Lordship had met anyone as insolent as Holmes. His Lordship watched Holmes's slender figure disappear beyond the doorway, and then he turned to me in a manner reminiscent of heavy artillery.

"And you are?" Lord Garnett asked me.

"Doctor John Watson," I said, offering my hand. Lord Garnett shook it firmly, apparently relieved to be dealing with someone familiar with the concept of courtesy.

"Are you with the police?"

"No," I answered, somewhat embarrassed. "I'm here with Sherlock Holmes."

"Ah," Lord Garnett nodded. "Then perhaps you can tell me: Who is this Sherlock Holmes? Is he a policeman?"

"No," I admitted. "He is a detective, a consulting detective. Cambers came to seek his advice last evening and sent word this morning of your misfortune. Naturally, we came to offer what assistance we could."

"Assistance?" Lord Garnett repeated in surprise. "Is that what he was doing?"

"I assure you, Lord Garnett, my friend's methods may seem odd but he is a remarkable detective." Yet I had barely finished uttering these words of confidence when Holmes rushed back into the room bearing a large basin of water. Ignoring both Lord Garnett and myself, Holmes hurried to the fireplace and, upturning the heavy basin, doused the burning coals. An enormous plume of smoke and steam spilled from the fireplace and when it cleared Holmes was standing surprisingly close to Lord Garnett.

"Lord Garnett," Holmes addressed the missing child's father directly for the first time. "Can you tell me when this room was last cleaned?"

"Have you lost your mind?" Lord Garnett sputtered, waving away the last of the steam.

"It was cleaned before you locked the room, was it not?" Holmes asked, refusing to be distracted by Lord Garnett's outrage.

"Of course," Lord Garnett answered.

"Naturally." Holmes turned to me and explained. "It would make little sense to lock the servants out of the drawing room if it had not already been tidied. And as the staff was unaware of the nature of his Lordship's souvenirs, it follows the skulls were closed up in that trunk. Correct?"

Lord Garnett's complexion changed to an unhealthy ruddy colour as he replied to Holmes. "Who the devil do you think you are, coming into my house and – "

108

"Oh, I am sorry," Holmes apologised, much to Lord Garnett's surprise. "I thought I had introduced myself. My name is Sherlock Holmes, and your son's life depends on me."

Holmes's reply had a profound effect on Lord Garnett. The man's bluster seemed to disappear, his ruddy complexion paled in horror, and he reached for a nearby chair to steady himself.

"The skulls were closed up in that trunk, correct?" Holmes repeated his question.

"Yes," Lord Garnett answered meekly.

"I see no evidence of the trunk having been locked," Holmes mused. "Yet it seems likely the skulls were not simply laid inside. There must have been something more."

"There was," Lord Garnett agreed. "A bag, I purchased it from a sailor. It was – "

"Forgive me, your Lordship," Holmes interrupted Lord Garnett dismissively. "I hear your man approaching."

Just as Holmes predicted, the butler appeared in the room, a slip of paper in his hand.

"You have the address I requested?" Holmes asked.

"I do, sir."

Detective Cambers, with two of his constables in tow, followed on the butler's heels. The expression on Cambers' open face made it clear he intended to regain control of the situation. Holmes, however, completely ignored the detective.

"Give the address to the constables here," Holmes instructed the butler. "Gentlemen, you are to go to this address and search the premises for Lord Garnett's missing skulls. Take note of all you see there, with a special eye towards any children you might observe. Find the man and ask to see his certificate. I doubt he has one, despite the law concerning his trade. Regardless of what excuse he provides, take him to Scotland Yard for questioning. If he has the temerity to ask what he is to be charged with, inform him the charge is murder."

"Murder?" Lord Garnett whispered, his face paling even more. His Lordship staggered against a seat and fell into it.

"Courage, Lord Garnett," Holmes instructed the missing child's father. "There is still hope. You were about to describe the bag you purchased from the sailor, the one you used to store your net of skulls. If you would be so kind as to share your description with the constables?"

"What?" For a moment Lord Garnett looked confused, and I feared the events of the dreadful day had overtaken his reason. After a moment however, sensing the rapt attention of the constables, Lord Garnett managed to speak in a curiously disconnected, uncharacteristically soft voice.

"The bag? Oh yes, I purchased it from a sailor. It fit quite neatly into the trunk and was made of sealskin. Waterproof, you see, very handy. It opened at one end and I threaded a chain through the grommets so I could lock it with a padlock. I didn't want anyone to look inside. It could give someone quite a fright and I was planning to write a paper. I didn't want to give any of my rivals a chance to examine them. Of course, I lined the inside of the bag with wool. You cannot allow the skulls to get cold, you know, or else the souls of their owners will come back and haunt you."

Lord Garnett's eyes had grown quite wide as he uttered the last part of this speech, weaving a macabre spell which held the constables, Cambers, the butler, and myself captivated.

Breaking the spell, Holmes proved himself immune to the fascination gripping us. "How charming. Constables, you know your duty. See to it!"

The constables started off, completely oblivious to the hand Detective Constable Cambers' raised to stop them. Or perhaps the constables merely reacted to the more forceful nature of Holmes's authority.

Cambers was, by this time, glaring at Holmes, and I feared a confrontation between the two men was imminent. Holmes must have sensed the Detective Constable's hostility as he suddenly spoke. "Watson, why don't you show the Detective Constable what you discovered at the window?"

Suddenly I found myself the focus of Cambers and Lord Garnett. "Of course, Holmes," I replied, remembering how Holmes had dismissed the apparent clues as trivial. "I was over here when I noticed – "

"A footprint!" Cambers exclaimed.

"Yes," I agreed. "And you see there, some dark threads tangled among the rose bushes.

"They certainly weren't there yesterday," Cambers proclaimed. "Obviously, the footprint was made by the kidnappers."

"Whoever made the footprint didn't gain entrance into the drawing room," I observed. "The windows were still secure, and there's no trace of mud in here."

"Likely they tried the windows and found some other way in," Cambers judged. "We'll need a closer look."

Cambers left the room, presumably to go out to the garden and examine the footprint. I turned and was surprised to discover I was once again alone in the room with Lord Garnett. Holmes and the butler had disappeared while I was distracted by Cambers.

"They've gone upstairs," Lord Garnett informed me. "Your friend said he urgently needed to examine the roof."

"Whatever for?" I asked.

Lord Garnett simply shrugged. He seemed utterly drained by the experiences of the day. I suspected Holmes's use of the word murder had deeply frightened the man. Wishing I had some comfort to offer, I stood and said simply, "I think I'll join them."

"Yes," Lord Garnett agreed. "Perhaps I'll come as well."

"It might be best if you were to rest." It was, I reflected, not a very helpful suggestion, but the urge to prescribe rest is deeply ingrained in all physicians.

Lord Garnett shook his head. "I know you mean well," he said, "but I couldn't rest. What if they found something and I was asleep? No, it would be best if I went somewhere in case I was needed."

"Then perhaps, before we go, you'll join me for a brandy?" It was all I could think to offer.

"Yes," Lord Garnett agreed. He stood and went to fetch the drinks from one of the cabinets along the wall. Returning, he passed me a glass with a generous measure of amber liquid in it.

"And to think yesterday my most pressing concern was the missing skulls." Lord Garnett shook his head and grimaced. "And now your friend seems to think he has found them."

"Likely he has," I said. "As I said, he is an extraordinary detective."

"Do you believe he can find my son?" Lord Garnett asked, unable to look me in the eye as he voiced his deepest wish.

"He will find him," I assured the man. "Of that I have no doubt."

Lord Garnett nodded sadly, hearing the unspoken fear in my voice. In truth I had no doubt at all regarding Holmes's ability to locate the child but there was no way of knowing what condition in which we would find the boy.

"Henry is often a difficult child," Lord Garnett confessed. "Headstrong and quite independent, despite his young age. We've often quarrelled, but I am extremely proud of him. Do you think I will have the chance to tell him so?"

"Honestly, I don't know," I admitted. "But if anyone can find the boy, it's Sherlock Holmes."

Nodding, Lord Garnett drained his brandy and set the empty glass on a nearby table. Though I had barely tasted mine, I set my glass next to his. The brandy had done Lord Garnett a world of good, returning some colour to his complexion and easing some of the strain in his determined features.

"Let's find Holmes, shall we?" I suggested.

"Yes," Lord Garnett agreed, leading the way out of the room. I caught a glimpse of Cambers and his remaining constables through the windows as we passed.

Apparently Lord Garnett saw them as well. "Your friend tricked them. He saw Cambers was spoiling for a fight so he had you point out the footprint in the garden. He only did it to keep them out of his way, didn't he?"

"I believe so," I admitted, following Lord Garnett up the stairs. "When I first noticed the footprint in the garden, Holmes told me it meant nothing. He seems to be in a dreadful hurry, but I don't understand why."

"Well," Lord Garnett said, "I suppose that's a hopeful sign."

We found the butler on the uppermost floor of the house, standing on a small balcony and clutching a precariously perched ladder which Holmes climbed down with a fearlessness that bordered on the reckless.

"Watson! I trust Cambers is occupied in the garden?"

"He is," I agreed. "But Holmes, why – "

"Sorry Watson, time is short," Holmes forestalled my question. "Lord Garnett, could you show me to your son's room?"

"Of course," Lord Garnett nodded. "This way."

"Lord Garnett," Holmes asked as he followed his Lordship out to the stairs. "Your son came to see you late last night."

"How on Earth did you know that?" Lord Garnett asked.

"He must have had some complaint," Holmes observed. "What did he say?"

Lord Garnett led the way down the flight of stairs. "It sounded so childish at the time, but it chills me to think of it now. He claimed he'd heard a ghost Mr. Holmes, a ghost moaning in agony."

"You did not believe him?" Holmes asked with perfect sincerity.

"No, I didn't," Lord Garnett admitted.

"That is your son's room there?" Holmes asked, not waiting for Lord Garnett's direction.

"It is," Lord Garnett confirmed, again startled by Holmes seemingly supernatural abilities.

Holmes turned and addressed Lord Garnett and the butler, who had followed us downstairs.

"Go to the garden shed." Holmes instructed them. "Bring me a pick, a pry bar, a lantern, some rope, whatever you can lay hands on. Quickly! Bring them to me here!"

To my surprise, both the butler and Lord Garnett hurried away to fulfil Holmes's command. Holmes turned and looked at me with weary eyes. "I will say this for the headhunters of Borneo, they are honest enough to display their sins in plain view. It is an example we could learn from."

"Holmes, whatever do you mean?" I asked.

"Bones, Watson," Holmes admitted, walking into the missing child's room and pulling out a pocketknife. "My knowledge of the subject is not as extensive as Lord Garnett's, but it is enough to confirm my observation. Headhunters display the fruits of their savagery proudly, rather than hiding them inside walls. You didn't, by any chance, bring your stethoscope with you?"

"No." Holmes had stopped me on the street, between home and my Paddington practice, before I'd reached the tools of my profession.

"Pity," Holmes observed as he unfolded his pocketknife and inserted the blade into the wall.

"Holmes?" I asked, watching in mute horror as Holmes dragged the blade through the wall. He was making a dreadful mess but, after carving a gouge more than two feet long in the wall, he seemed to find what he was searching for. He withdrew the blade, folded it and put it back in his pocket.

From outside came the sounds of men running up the stairs. Lord Garnett rushed into the room, a large pick in his hand. The butler had found a pry-bar, a hammer and a lantern, which he dropped onto the child's unmade bed with obvious relief.

"Some water would not go amiss," Holmes observed as he took hold of the pick Lord Garnett had brought. The butler, his refinement stretched somewhat thin, observed Holmes with a cool look but left to fulfil the detective's request.

"This must be done with some care," Holmes told me as I picked up the pry bar. "The trick is to pull the bricks outward, not to let them fall inside."

"Bricks?" I asked.

In answer, Holmes swung his pick into the wall and, in a shower of lath and plaster, uncovered a section of chimney. Such destruction

113

caused me a measure of surprise, but Lord Garnett, sitting on the edge of his son's bed, simply watched without expression.

"Hurry, Watson," Holmes swung the axe again, knocking one of the chimney bricks inward at an angle. Hurrying to help, though not at all certain the purpose behind this extravagant destruction, I reached in with my pry bar and attempted to pull the brick outwards.

"Back in the hallway, you were going to ask about Cambers and the footprint in the garden," Holmes explained as I worked. When the brick fell out, he swung the pick once more, loosening more bricks. "No doubt by now you've reached the obvious conclusion. The footprint and remnant of cloth were left by one of the police constables as they searched the grounds this morning."

Hearing this, Lord Garnett was unable to contain a bleak chuckle.

"Can you be certain of that?" I asked.

"Of course," Holmes said as he swung the pick again. "You saw the footprint, the distinctive pattern of a hobnail boot. And the colour of the threads match the police constable's uniform precisely. While I do not wish to mention the constable's name, I have matched the evidence to the subject. If his name was mentioned, I fear the poor man would suffer Cambers' displeasure. It is a peculiar conceit of Scotland Yard investigators, they seem convinced all the footprints in the world belong to someone else."

"And the skulls?" I asked. "What makes you believe you know where they are?"

"Believe?" Holmes swung the pick again. "Watson, your lack of confidence is astounding. The man whose address the butler found is the chimneysweep who finished tending to Lord Garnett's chimneys the morning of the party."

"A chimneysweep?" I shook my head. "Holmes, there's no possible way a grown man could fit down that chimney."

"No?" Holmes asked. "It would, of course, depend upon the man, but you are most likely correct. Unfortunately, and to our nation's great shame, chimneysweeps discovered a method of overcoming such obstacles centuries ago. There are laws against the practise now, a system of certification designed specifically to bring an end to the dreadful practise. Surely you see it now, Watson? Lord Garnett?"

At that moment I was prying out bricks, enlarging the hole Holmes had knocked in the chimney.

"Lord Garnett, if you would be so kind as to light that lamp," Holmes asked. "The boy's complaint of spirits moaning in the night, that

114

must clarify matters? This is, after all, the same chimney we saw in the drawing room, one floor beneath us."

"Are you suggesting something is trapped in the chimney?" I asked.

"Something?" Holmes shook his head. "No, Watson, someone. The evidence is clear, although the crime itself is obviously based on a series of misunderstandings and random chance. Start with the assumption the chimneysweep is a villain. He comes to Lord Garnett's to practise his trade and hears the servants talking about their Master's return, and the strange trunk he has taken such care to bring back with him. Surely, the servants gossip, it must contain a great treasure! The chimneysweep, being a villain, listens carefully and constructs a plan. He apologises for not being able to complete his work that day, but promises to return early the next morning to finish."

The hole in the chimney was now large enough I could insert my head through it but Holmes urged me to continue widening it. "Early next morning, the sweep returns, carrying the brushes of his trade with him. Hidden in among his tools is the means by which he hopes to accomplish his theft. A climbing boy."

"A climbing boy?" I stopped my task.

"Not so long ago the city was teeming with them," Holmes explained as he gestured for me to continue my efforts. "It is entirely likely this sweep was once a wretched boy earning his living as a sweep's apprentice. The legislation forbidding the use of climbing boys is quite recent, but the sweep, having survived his apprenticeship, feels the law unjust. After all, what is his crime? Teaching children a trade? And if nine of his ten young apprentices perish, well, London is filled with orphans, after all. A child trapped within a chimney brings no harm to anyone, even saving his master the cost of a burial. And those that fall to the fumes or the diseases arising from breathing smoke and eating soot can easily and inexpensively be disposed of."

"Holmes?" I asked.

"Slightly wider, Watson," Holmes said, taking the lit lantern from Lord Garnett. "My fears were first stirred in the drawing room when I discovered a smudge of soot on the lid of the empty chest. They were confirmed when I saw the sweep's name and occupation on the list of visitors the butler prepared. You recall my next action?"

"You fetched water to put out the fire in the grate," Lord Garnett recalled.

"Then proceeded to the roof, hoping to find the boys up near the opening of the chimney," Holmes explained. "Unfortunately, all I found there was a trail of blood."

"Boys?" Lord Garnett asked. "How does my son's disappearance figure into this?"

"The role of the climbing boy was quite straightforward," Holmes explained. "He was to wait in the chimney, enduring the smoke and fumes of the fire below, until nightfall. Then, putting out the fire with water brought for that purpose, he was to climb down, remove the exotic treasure from its case, and bring it to the roof where the sweep waited. Unfortunately for the boy, the sweep betrayed him. Rather than take the child and the treasure, the sweep opted to take only the treasure. He struck the boy, leaving a trail of blood inside of the chimney. The climbing boy fell, becoming entangled in the flue. Whatever his injuries, he still had the water he'd brought to douse the fire. Somehow he clung to life until your return."

"The ghost Lord Garnett's son complained of?" I asked.

"The climbing boy," Holmes agreed. "Finding no one willing to believe his night-time tale, your son acted on his own. Quite bravely too, if I may be permitted to observe. He crawled up the chimney himself. Unfortunately, it appears he also became entangled in the dark. There, Watson, that should be large enough."

Holmes hurried in, sticking his arm with the lantern and his head into the opening we had made. He quickly pulled his head out again. I couldn't help but notice the soot staining his cheek.

"They are there!" Holmes announced. Holmes took off his coat and tied a large loop in the thin rope from the garden shed. Lord Garnett was up and running to the stairs, yelling in commanding tones for assistance.

"Are they – " I couldn't bring myself to finish the sentence.

"They're not moving," Holmes observed. "And they are black as night. Beyond that, I cannot say."

Lord Garnett returned with Cambers and the constables in tow. The butler reappeared, bearing a full glass of water in each hand. It was a tight fit, but Holmes was able to reach into the darkness and loop the rope around the trapped boys. He pulled out the first blackened form, then the other. The two small children were indistinguishable under the soot they wore.

One of the boys coughed and gratefully accepted water from the butler. As the child's face was cleaned I witnessed the joyful reunion of

116

Lord Garnett and his son. The climbing boy was, I am saddened to say, already dead when we pulled his small, broken form from the darkness.

"He'll hang for this," Detective Constable Cambers vowed as Holmes explained the nature of the crime. When the two constables returned from their errand, they reported finding everything as Holmes predicted. A sealskin bag containing the darkened skulls, its lock broken, was found in the sweeps' home, as was evidence of several orphans. The sweep had no certificate and had been practising his trade with no license.

As we took a cab from Lord Garnett's, his Lordship's profuse thanks still ringing in our ears, Holmes expounded on the point he'd been trying to make when we arrived at the manor. "As a rule, the crimes of the countryside are crimes of honest malice, acts of base motive, and Cambers is well-suited to such offences. London, on the other hand, offers its denizens crimes of opportunity. Misdeeds requiring little or no planning, acts of indifference, and Cambers is ill-prepared for such random villainy. I would also point out that it is not enough for a detective to simply ask the correct question. After all, Cambers did ask Lord Garnett for a list of everyone who visited the manor the day of the theft. Yet how was his Lordship to know which trades-people had visited? No, a detective must match the right question to the right person, a lesson young Cambers has yet to learn."

Larceny in the Sky
with Diamonds
by Robert V. Stapleton

I collected a glass of champagne from the waiter's tray, and looked around the room. A string-quartet was playing, elegant young couples were dancing, and I was in search of a victim.

It was the early spring of 1891, and I'd been invited to this society gathering a few miles outside London. For some reason, the hostess regarded me as a philanthropist, and I didn't like to disillusion her on that matter. Organised crime was flourishing, and my greatest adversary was on the run, but I was bored. I needed something to lift the gloom. Sherlock Holmes might resort to cocaine, but I needed a fresh hands-on criminal project to engage my attention. I knew the sort of person I was looking for. He or she would be alone, vulnerable, and brooding. I've discovered that there's always at least one such person to be found at every social event.

I spotted her at the far side of the room. The young woman was standing on her own, not touching her drink, and with her eyes fixed on the unfocused distance. Her mind was clearly on matters far away from this place.

"Her name is Lady Jacinta Pulmorton," the waiter told me. He was one of our men, and he'd noticed my interest in the woman.

"Of Oakenby Hall?"

"The same."

We retreated to an alcove where we could talk freely without being overheard.

"Ah, yes," I told him. "I remember we blackmailed her last year over some personal matter."

"We had some letters she wanted kept hidden from her husband."

"Indeed, a most unfortunate business, but we gave most of those letters back to her in the end."

"That's how I remember it, Professor."

"And my name never came into the affair."

"I believe not."

"Good. That's just as it should be. So, out of a sense of guilt, this lady will now be even more devoted to her husband than ever before. She can't still be worried about those letters. I wonder what's troubling her now."

Through the crowd of guests, I noticed Grimdale's mop of chestnut hair. He was lurking quietly beside the fireplace. He's a good man to have around: a first-rate dodger. He had also seen the young woman, and was watching her like a predacious cat eyeing a doomed mouse. Grimdale turned his hooded eyes towards me. I nodded, and we converged on her from our different directions.

"Good evening," I began. "It's Lady Pulmorton, isn't it?"

She looked up, startled by my interruption to her thoughts. "That's right." Her periwinkle blue eyes were enchanting, but they were clouded by sadness.

"We haven't been introduced," I told her, "but my name is Moriarty. Most people just know me as The Professor."

"Good evening, Professor," she replied. She'd obviously never heard of me before.

"And this is my colleague, Harold Grimdale," I said, indicating my companion.

She gave us each a melancholy smile.

"The evening's going well," I said, trying to break the ice with small-talk.

"Is it?" she said, looking down at her still-full glass of wine. "I hadn't noticed."

I decided to jump straight in. "Forgive me for approaching you like this, your ladyship," I said, "but I was concerned. You appear to be rather unhappy."

She looked up at me. "Is it that obvious?"

"I'm afraid so." I gave her a smile that I hoped would convey deep sympathy. It didn't matter if it was sincere or not, just so long as she thought it was. There was a mystery here that needed to be investigated.

Lady Pulmorton looked as if she was holding back from saying something important. I needed to gain her confidence.

"I can assure you, your ladyship," I told her, "we are both completely trustworthy." I can lie most convincingly when I want to. I gave her another warm smile.

She began to thaw. "It's about my husband," she began.

Grimdale and I exchanged glances. The signs of a profit here were already looking good.

"Is he making you unhappy?"

"Oh, we've had our ups and downs," she admitted, "but we have been extremely happy together. Until recently."

"Recently?"

"You see, Professor, over the last three years, my husband has developed an absurd interest in flying."

"Indeed? Flying?"

"It's become an obsession. He began by building a glider, and then testing it himself."

"That sounds a dangerous pastime."

"So it turned out. He crashed the thing on its very first flight. He was lucky to escape with nothing worse than a broken leg and a dislocated shoulder."

"All part and parcel of the adventure, I believe."

"Then he became obsessed with building a powered flying machine."

"People all over the world are experimenting with powered flight," I told her. "But to build a machine capable of taking a man into the air and then keeping him aloft, now that really is the aeronautical Holy Grail."

"Well, my husband has done just that," she said. There was a hint of pride in her voice. "He's built one."

"Really? You mean to say he's actually got the thing to fly?" I began to imagine the enormous income we might gain from this business.

"Oh, yes. It took off all right. Then it crashed, just like last time. He's been injured yet again."

"I'm sorry to hear that."

"That was nearly two months ago now."

"And has it put your husband off flying?"

"Not a bit of it. He can't wait to have another go."

"And how's his recovery going?"

"He's up and about again, but he still walks with a limp."

Tears welled up in Lady Pulmorton's eyes that would have melted any other man's heart. Pah! I almost felt sorry for the woman.

"I can see how that would upset you," I told her.

"That's not the only problem, Professor," she continued.

Out of the corner of my eye, I noticed our hostess bearing down on us. I was afraid she might make Lady Pulmorton clam up altogether. I needed to hear what more she had to tell me, so I sent Grimdale to

120

occupy our hostess in some engrossing conversation. As a cockney born and bred, that's where his real talents lie.

Meanwhile, I put down my glass and took Lady Pulmorton out onto the terrace. We stood together, looking out over the greening fields of the Thames valley. The cool air was still, loaded with the sweet aroma of new life and fresh growth. The evening was delightful: if you like that sort of thing.

"You see, Professor," she continued, "the engineer who was working with my husband has gone missing. What's even worse is that he seems to have taken my husband's design blueprints with him."

I hesitated for a moment. Then I asked, "Have you informed the police?"

"No. My husband believes it's much more serious than that. He thinks the man might try to sell those papers to some foreign power, possibly to be used against this country. He is extremely upset."

"Naturally. So, it's becoming a matter of national security?"

She nodded. "With my husband confined to the house and grounds, I decided to consult Mr. Sherlock Holmes myself. But they tell me he's away from London at the moment."

"Yes, I believe he's somewhere on the Continent." I tried to keep the bitterness I felt for the man out of my voice. Holmes had been making life very difficult for me recently, and I was glad he was making himself scarce.

"I don't know who else to turn to." Her face clouded over again.

"As it happens," I told her, "I, too, am interested in crime and the criminal classes. Perhaps I could find this scoundrel for you." A criminal operating outside my sphere of influence was a personal matter for me. The man had to be dealt with.

A look of hope filled her ladyship's charming eyes. "That would be wonderful," she said. "Thank you, Professor."

"As time is clearly of the essence," I told her, "we'll come down to Oakenby Hall by the first train tomorrow."

"Moriarty?" said Sir Henry Pulmorton when we arrived at Oakenby Hall on the following morning. "I don't think I know the name."

"I am well known for my academic and charitable work," I told him. Well, at least that was half true.

"In that case, welcome to my home, Professor."

Sir Henry was in the Morning Room, sitting beside a window that looked out over the parkland in front of the house. He was a man of medium height, with dark hair, a pointed nose, and piercing brown eyes.

"Your wife has told me something of your problem," I began. "You think your engineer might have stolen the blueprints to your flying machine."

"Oh, there's no doubt about it," he replied. "I discovered yesterday morning that my safe had been opened and that those papers were missing. He's the only person with anything to gain from taking them. Now the rascal himself has disappeared."

An enterprising fellow, I thought to myself. "What's the man's name?"

"Jeremiah Silt," he replied, in a tone that implied utter contempt.

"Physical description?"

"He's a short, mousy sort of fellow, with grey hair framing a balding head. His most distinctive feature has to be his long sideburns."

"Your wife thinks he might try to sell those plans to some foreign power."

"That is highly likely," said Pulmorton. "He often talked about how useful flying machines might be in times of war. If he can steal from me, then he might well be capable of betraying his country."

"Will you allow us to investigate the matter for you, Sir Henry?" I asked.

"I can't do it myself," he replied, pointing to his ash walking stick, "So yes, please do whatever you can, Professor. Get those documents back for me, and I'll pay you well for your time and effort."

I bowed graciously. I'd willingly have done the job for nothing.

"But first," I told him, "I'd like to see your machine."

"Certainly. Come with me."

Obviously still in considerable pain, Sir Henry picked up his stick, hobbled out through the front door and led us round to the far side of the house. There we approached a vast wooden tithe-barn. From the front of this building, a pathway of hard-packed earth led off across the garden.

When I stepped inside the barn, I was utterly amazed. The flying machine almost filled the place. It was a monoplane, shaped like some gigantic bat, with a wingspan of over forty feet. The bone-like structure of the wings was covered with a black silk-like fabric. The fuselage consisted of an open carriage on wheels, with a wooden seat at the back.

"The carriage would normally be enclosed," Sir Henry explained, "but we've been concentrating on repairing the wing mechanisms first."

122

"Even so," I told him, "it's a magnificent machine."

"It's based on a French design."

"By Clément Ader?"

"You've heard of him, Professor?"

"Indeed."

"Silt got the plans for me. The machinery is complicated and expensive to make, so I was glad of his engineering skills and know-how. He even made a few improvements of his own. Flight is controlled by adjusting the wings. You can alter the flow of air over the front edge of the wings, change their total area, or flex the end-sections."

"And the engine?"

"We're using a steam-powered engine," said Sir Henry. "It's situated just in front of the aviator, and powers a single propeller at the front. The engine is cooled by a radiator directly above. It's a light-weight apparatus, fuelled by alcohol-spirits. We store the alcohol in barrels at the back of the barn."

"Amazing!"

"Again, it's based on Ader's own revolutionary design."

"Did Silt get that for you as well?"

"Yes, but he refused to tell me how."

"In test-flights last year, Ader's machine proved to be underpowered."

"Perhaps, but this one isn't."

"You mean to say it really flies?"

"Oh, yes. It crashes spectacularly as well. While I've been recovering from my injuries, I've been busy putting the machine back together again. As I said, the damage was mostly to the wings. That's now been fixed, so I'm hoping to fly it again very soon."

"Tell me, Sir Henry," I said, "how do you operate the engine?"

"Put simply, you open the tap on the fuel-reservoir, light the boiler jets and wait for the water to boil. Then you allow high-pressure steam into the engine. This drives the cylinders, which turn the propeller."

"Just like boiling a kettle."

"Pretty much. Then hang on for the ride of your life."

Before Grimdale and I left for London, Lady Pulmorton stopped us. "We have yet another problem, Professor."

"Can I help?"

She looked flustered. "In two days' time, an important visitor will be coming to stay with us. A lady from Russia. The Countess of Felixburg."

My eyes lit up. "Isn't she one of the richest women in Europe?"

"I believe she is," said Lady Pulmorton. "It means that we're going to need some extra security here." She turned her heart-melting eyes onto me. "Could I possibly impose on you to take this extra duty on for us, Professor?"

I felt like an alcoholic who's just been asked to take charge of a brewery. "I would be delighted," I told her. "I have some business to attend to first, but I shall return the day after tomorrow."

In the train back to Waterloo, I sat alone with Grimdale in a First Class compartment. We had bribed the guard, locked the door, and drawn down the blinds, so there was little danger of anyone interrupting us.

"Are you really going to help this man?" Grimdale asked me.

"I don't see why not," I told him. "Especially now that the Countess is coming to stay at Oakenby Hall."

"As you say, she is reputed to be extremely rich."

"Indeed, but I'm going to need more details," I told him. "Contact our colleagues in the European criminal underworld and ask them for a description of her jewellery. Somebody will know."

"I'll get onto it the moment we reach the Smoke," said Grimdale.

I tore a sheet of paper from my pocket notebook, wrote a few brief words on it and handed it to my companion. "But first, I want you to deliver this message."

His eyes opened wide when he saw the address. "Are you sure, Professor?"

"Completely."

The message was simple: "Meet me in the Calcutta Room of the Century Hotel, Mayfair, at seven tonight. Come alone. Moriarty."

Sherlock Holmes and I have much in common. We are both chameleons: cold and calculating, whilst at the same time being masters of deception and disguise. He is a worthy but deadly opponent. But it was not Sherlock I'd asked to meet me that evening, it was his brother, Mycroft.

For this meeting, I adopted my persona as a cold fish. I stood at the far end of the room, placed my gloves and top-hat on the table beside me, and leaned on my silver-topped cane.

When he arrived, Mycroft remained near the door. It amused me to think that he didn't want to come any closer.

"I take great exception to being summoned like this," he told me.

"Regrettable, but necessary," I replied.

"I have important state business to attend to."

"No doubt, but I need to consult you on a matter of national security."

Mycroft raised one eyebrow in surprise. He can sometimes appear as unemotional as his brother.

"You may have heard about Sir Henry Pulmorton's obsession with flying-machines."

"He has made no secret of it."

"But what you might not know is that he has now succeeded in building one."

"Have you seen it?"

"Indeed."

"Have you seen it fly?"

"Not yet."

"Then it's a purely academic matter."

"But his assistant believes it can fly. So much so that he has stolen the blueprints. He may try to sell those documents to some foreign power."

In the fading light, I saw Mycroft's eyes sparkle. Now he was interested.

"The man's name is Jeremiah Silt," I told him.

"Someone of that name did make an initial approach to our government," Mycroft admitted, "but we didn't think it was a matter worth pursuing."

"So he may wish to try his luck elsewhere."

"He might."

"You know the diplomatic scene better than anyone," I continued. "Who is there in London who might be willing to pay good money for those papers?"

"What's your interest in this?"

"You may be under the impression that I have criminal tendencies, Mr. Holmes," I told him. "The truth is that I am an intensely patriotic man. I wish, as much as any other true-blooded Englishman, to see to all enemies of our Queen and country vanquished." I was putting on a very convincing show. I could easily persuade myself that all this claptrap really was true.

Mycroft looked pensively out of the window at the darkening sky. "The German Ambassador is expecting a visitor from Berlin," he said. "A man with direct access to the Kaiser himself. I believe he has a particular interest in flying machines."

"That has to be more than a coincidence."

"But whether the Kaiser is also interested is another matter entirely. However, if this fellow Silt is hoping to sell those plans to some foreign power, he might begin by taking them to the German Embassy."

"When?"

"Their visitor arrives tomorrow morning."

"Another foreign visitor!" I exclaimed. "It must be a sign of spring. But the cuckoos are a little early this year. In that case, I shall have my men keep a constant watch on the place until our man shows up."

"He might not."

"But there's a good chance that he will."

From first light, my men kept a discreet vigil outside the Embassy of the Imperial German Government. I'm pretty sure that Mycroft had his own people watching the street as well. I'd have been disappointed if he hadn't.

Later that morning, a young lad, who works for us as a runner, reported to me that the German official had now arrived.

"A posh toff, with a beard as long as Methuselah's," he said. "Came from the station in a carriage as if 'e was the King of Prussia 'isself.'"

I took a hansom to Belgravia and stopped across the road from the Embassy. Grimdale gave me his succinct report. "He's definitely in there, Professor."

"Then all we have to do is wait for Silt to arrive," I told him. "Are your men in position?"

"We've got a newspaper-seller, a road sweeper and some men pretending to work on repairing the road," he replied.

"He mustn't be allowed to reach the front door."

"Don't worry, Professor. The moment Silt turns up, we'll have him."

"Very well," I told him. "I'll wait here."

I made no secret of the fact that I was watching the place. Leaning on my swordstick cane, I stood with my eyes fixed on the front door of the Embassy. All afternoon, diplomats came and went, but I never for one moment took my eyes off that door.

The lamplighter was already doing his rounds by the time Silt arrived. The engineer's sideburns were almost undetectable in the fading light, but I can recognise a guilty man when I see one. There was no mistaking the furtive way he shuffled along the street towards the Embassy building.

The front door of the Embassy opened, and a tall man with an impressive white beard stood in the entrance. But it was too late. Before he could come within twenty feet of the place, my men took Silt in hand.

I crossed the road towards him. "Jeremiah Silt, I believe."

"How dare you treat me like this!" he snapped.

"Because I know all about you."

A look of concern crossed his face. "What do you mean?"

"We both know that you stole those blueprints to Sir Henry Pulmorton's flying machine."

"Stole? I was the one who got them for him in the first place," said Silt. "If I stole anything from anyone, then it was from the Frenchman. I adapted his designs. I added more power to the engine. I was the one who made the thing fly. I am a genius!"

"No doubt," I replied coldly, "but we also know that you came here hoping to sell those blueprints to the German government. You're a traitor to your country, Silt."

"I tried to interest our government in my machine," Silt sneered, "but they didn't want to know. I wanted to develop the design further, but for that I needed money, more than Sir Henry could give me. This country ought to celebrate me as a hero, not condemn me as a traitor."

"Sir Henry wants his documents back," I told him. "Hand them over to me immediately."

He thrust his hand beneath his coat, drew out a bundle of papers and handed them to me, muttering darkly to himself.

Mycroft Holmes now arrived in his own cab. He was looking very pleased with himself.

"At least now those plans won't be used against this country," he said.

"You regard the Germans as potential enemies?" I asked him.

"They are a growing threat in Europe," he replied. "One day, Professor, they will become a direct threat to us."

That was very interesting.

127

"Give me those plans," said Mycroft. "I'll make sure they get safely back to Sir Henry Pulmorton."

"Do you still not trust me?" I asked, trying to sound offended.

"Not in the slightest," he replied.

I handed over the plans.

"I'll keep Silt," I told him.

"This isn't a police matter," Mycroft told me, "so I'm sure I can safely leave him in your hands."

Oakenby Hall was in turmoil when we arrived there on the following afternoon.

"The Countess has arrived from Russia," said the butler. He sounded exasperated. "Together with her entire household."

"I was hoping to speak with Sir Henry," I told him.

"He's extremely busy, sir," the butler replied. "But he is expecting you. He hopes you will both join him at dinner this evening."

"As members of the security staff," I replied, "we shall certainly both be there."

"There are two bedrooms prepared for you and your companion in the south wing of the house," the butler added. "I hope you will find the arrangements to your satisfaction."

"I'm sure we will," I replied. "But where will the countess be staying?"

"In the Blue Room, sir. On the first floor at the front of the house."

After we'd settled into our rooms, Grimdale joined me to discuss our next step.

"What have you learnt about the Countess?" I asked him.

"Following the death of her husband last year, she now owns a great deal of land in her native country," said Grimdale. "Her income is more than enough to keep herself and her entire household very comfortable indeed."

"And her jewellery?"

"She never goes anywhere without it."

"That's what I like to hear," I replied. "It gives us a realistic chance of taking it from her. Do you have any details?"

"There are several pieces large enough to attract attention if sold on the open market."

"Then we must concentrate on the smaller ones."

128

Grimdale laid the complete list of jewellery on the table in front of me. "There's one piece that looks particularly interesting," he told me. "It's described as a necklace made up of three strands of diamonds."

"I have no doubt she'll be wearing it tonight," I said. "So we must find out what happens to it after the meal."

"Sir Henry might lock it away in his safe."

"Perhaps."

Our luggage was light, suitable only for a flying visit, but we both managed to turn up to dinner that evening looking suitably turned out.

"Ah, Professor," said Sir Henry, when we met just before the meal, "it's good to see you again."

"And you, Sir Henry," I replied. "I trust you received your papers."

"Indeed. They came by special delivery from Whitehall this morning."

"That's just as it should be," I told him. I added modestly, "I have my contacts there."

Grimdale raised an eyebrow in surprise at such a pretentious statement.

I ignored him.

"I hope those blueprints are back where they belong."

"They are now once again locked away in the safe in my study."

"That's good to hear." It was indeed very good to hear. If some grubby little engineer could open that safe, then a criminal mastermind like myself should have no difficulty with it.

At dinner, I was seated opposite the Guest of Honour, the Countess herself. At first, we talked of unimportant things, but my attention was fastened on her necklace. It was just as my informants had described it. There were three strands of diamonds, no single stone remarkable on its own, but together undoubtedly worth a fortune.

"That's a magnificent necklace, madam," I told her.

"My late husband gave it to me," she explained. "The stones came from the private treasury of the Tsar himself."

"Indeed? They must be worth a great deal."

"Several millions of roubles, I believe."

"Then, as the man in charge of security here, I must caution you to be on your guard, Countess." I shook my head sadly. "There are thieves active in this country. Are you sure the necklace will be safe during your stay here?"

"I am quite sure it will be," she replied.

129

"Of course," I continued. "Sir Henry has a heavy-duty safe in his study."

She laughed, then fixed me with her steel-grey eyes. "It will not be in his safe, Professor," she said. "I insist on keeping this particular necklace close to me at all times."

"That is a very wise decision, madam," I assured her, "very wise indeed."

I had to get my hands on those jewels. But how? As I watched the wine waiter serving out the hock, the germ of a plan began to form in my mind.

I noticed that the lower button on the man's jacket was hanging loose. As he leaned over me, with the bottle in his hand, I grasped hold of the button and gave it a sharp jerk. It came away so easily that the man failed to notice that anything was wrong.

By the time the meal was over, my plan was complete in every detail. The below-stairs staff would be key to its success.

When nobody was watching, I left the dining room and descended to the servants' hall. There my eyes fell on a charming young chamber maid.

"Excuse me, my dear," I began.

"Yes, sir?"

"Would you like to earn a sovereign?"

She gave me a suspicious look. "What do I have to do?"

"Oh, nothing much." I took out a glass vial and held it in front of her. It's amazing the things a master criminal keeps concealed in his pockets. "All you have to do is to pour the contents of this vial into the Countess's last drink of the day."

"But why?"

"The Countess has had a long journey," I explained. "She needs a good night's sleep."

"Don't we all?"

"You must also make sure that her bedroom door is left unlocked tonight."

"It's the job of her lady's maid to secure the door."

"But not this time," I told the girl. "Tonight, her maid will have her mind on other things."

"What if someone sees me? Are you sure I won't get into trouble over this?"

130

"Quite sure," I replied. "If anyone does question you, just tell them that you saw the wine waiter loitering in the corridor outside her room. That should leave you completely in the clear."

I gave Grimdale the job of keeping the Countess's lady's maid occupied that night. He seemed pleased with the assignment.

"But first," I told him, "I want you to have a word with our coachman."

"Are we leaving tomorrow?"

"Most certainly. At first light."

"What do you want him to do, Professor?"

"Just make sure that our bags are on the brougham and that he's waiting for us at first light down by the old packhorse bridge."

"The stone bridge across the river?"

"That's the one. Then I want you to go to the barn and make sure the flying machine is fuelled-up and ready to go."

"Are we going to fly out?"

"If necessary. As you know, every good burglar prepares an alternative way of escape."

Grimdale nodded.

"Then, first thing in the morning, go back to the barn and light the boiler. Until then, the night and the girl are yours."

Shortly after midnight, I tried the door of the Countess's bedroom. The handle turned easily and without a sound. Inside, the air was infused with the smell of expensive cologne. The Countess was alone, lying on her back; a well-upholstered woman in a well-upholstered bed. She was snoring like a pig. The sleeping potion had obviously worked. It ought to have done. There was enough in that vial to put an elephant out for the count.

Now I had to find the necklace. But where would she have put it? The Countess had boasted about keeping it close to herself at all times. The idea of searching her person didn't appeal to me in the slightest, so I began with the bedside cabinet. I had a lantern with hinged shutters on all four sides. This was the only light I had to work with. In addition, I would have to rely on the well-honed sensitivity of my fingertips.

The top drawer contained only personal documents. I slipped these into my coat pocket. Then I tried the middle drawer. Nothing. Then a stroke of luck. I found the jewels in the bottom drawer. They were in an ordinary jewellery-case, hidden beneath a large fur hat. I took the jewels, returned the case and closed the drawer.

131

On my way out, I dropped the wine waiter's button onto the floor beside the bed. That would see his goose nicely cooked.

It was still dark when I reached Sir Henry's study early the next morning. The safe stood in its usual place, against the wall directly opposite the door. I lit my lantern and knelt down to examine the lock. It was a simple combination affair. I tried the number we'd extracted from Jeremiah Silt just before he died. It was no use. Pulmorton had obviously changed the combination number. I'd certainly have done the same in his shoes.

It didn't really matter. I had it open within five minutes anyway.

I was now glad that I was wearing my voluminous coat with the cavernous pockets. It might look an ungainly garment, but it is extremely practical for a burglar. Faced with a pile of jewellery-cases, and with no time to examine their contents, I transferred them all to the pockets of my coat.

At the back of the safe, I found what I was looking for. The bundle of papers we'd taken from Silt outside the German Embassy. I took them out of the safe and locked it again. Then I stood up and turned towards the study door.

There, in the gloom, I saw Sir Henry Pulmorton. He was standing in the doorway, holding a double-barrelled shotgun, and pointing it directly at me.

"Moriarty!" he exclaimed. "I've had a message from Whitehall warning me not to trust you. Now I see the truth of it. I've sent a telegram to Scotland Yard, asking what they know about you. I expect a reply imminently."

I'd anticipated something like this. That's the trouble with honest people; you just can't trust them. But it was too late now to protest my innocence.

"Damn you, Mycroft!" I hissed. "And damn you too, Pulmorton!"

"No, you're the one who'll be damned, Moriarty," he growled. "Put those things back in my safe, or I'll shoot you as an intruder."

Was he bluffing? Did he have the nerve to pull the trigger? In this world, I consider myself the measure of all things. If the hereafter brings judgement, then I shall have to face it in due time. But I had no wish to be sent to my doom by Sir Henry Pulmorton. Nor, on the other hand, did I wish to return my ill-gotten gains to his safe. The result was a tense stand-off.

It was now that Grimdale appeared. And just in time, as well. He opened the front door and called out, "Everything's ready, Professor."

Instinctively, Sir Henry turned his attention away from me and looked out into the entrance hall.

I am no gymnast, but today I had to act quickly. In the blink of an eyelid, I kicked out at the shotgun in Sir Henry's hands.

The gun went off, peppering the ceiling above us with the contents of both barrels, and bringing down a shower of plaster. The noise was loud enough to waken the dead. The fact that it would rouse the rest of the household was bad enough. Time was now extremely short.

When Sir Henry turned to face me again, I pressed the point of my swordstick blade tightly against his throat.

"Drop the gun, Sir Henry," I told him.

He dropped it onto the floor beside him.

"Now step away from it."

He shuffled to one side.

Without repeating Sir Henry's mistake of taking my eyes off my opponent, I spoke to Grimdale. "We have to get away from here quickly," I told him. "Go back to the barn and open the doors."

When my companion had left, Sir Henry turned his blazing eyes fully onto me. "You'll never be able to fly that machine, Moriarty," he growled. "It took me twelve months to learn, and then I crashed the thing."

"I'm a fast learner," I replied.

"Very well. Take the thing, and break your neck."

I could hear footsteps hurrying along the corridor. It was time to leave. I sheathed the blade, picked up the shotgun and rushed outside. There I dropped the weapon into the herbaceous border. I hoped that might give me enough time to get clear of the grounds.

When I reached the barn, I found that Grimdale had the flying machine ready for me. It was an impressive sight. The boiler was bubbling nicely, steam was bursting out through gaps in the machine's boiler-jacket, and the sweet smell of industrial alcohol was hanging in the morning air.

I climbed onto the seat and jammed the blueprints safely behind a couple of struts. Then I pushed my cane into a space beside the seat and pulled my hat firmly down on my head.

Pulmorton had been right about the controls. They were fiendishly complicated. I was now faced with a confusing array of valves, cranks, dials and foot-pedals.

I tried to remember what Sir Henry had told me on my previous visit. I cautiously opened a valve. High-pressure steam hissed into the engine cylinders. One of the dials indicated an increase in steam-pressure. The four-bladed propeller started to turn. The flying machine emerged under its own power and began to move slowly along the pathway. The wheels rattled noisily on the hard-packed earth.

Then I heard angry shouts coming from somewhere nearby. I needed to make a quick exit. I opened the steam valve still further. The pressure in the engine now increased rapidly, the propeller began to turn more quickly, and the machine shot forward, giving me a violent kick in the rear.

A gunshot rang out. Trust Sir Henry to have another twelve-bore. I was spared a direct hit as shotgun pellets peppered the structures around me. One of them hit the fuel cylinder, and alcohol-spirits began to spray out through the hole. I was lucky the entire thing hadn't exploded there and then.

As the flying machine picked up speed, a gust of wind caught the wings and made it swerve off the pathway. Fortunately, the wheelbase was wide enough to keep it upright when it landed on the lawn. On the other hand, it was now out of control, and careered across the front lawn like a demented chicken. Its wheels gouged unsightly ruts in the carefully manicured turf. I didn't know how to control the thing, let alone how to make it take off. All I could do was to hang on tightly.

The machine soon reached the end of the lawn, where it bounced against the raised edge of the gravel footpath and hopped across the ha-ha. No longer having any solid ground beneath it, the machine began to fall. Desperate to avoid a crash, I opened the steam-valve as far as it would go. The contraption immediately picked up speed, and just about managed to keep clear of the ground. I was flying!

I had no idea how to control the direction of travel. I was having to learn the basics of flying as I went along. At the same time, my mathematical brain was devising possible improvements to the design.

Using a mixture of cold logic and blind panic, I fiddled with the controls until the wings opened to their fullest extent. Then I managed to alter the camber of the leading edge of the wings. These, together with the early morning breeze and increased airspeed, made the flying machine slowly gain height.

But something was wrong. I sensed that the machine was overbalanced at the front. I looked down and saw Grimdale hanging onto the wheel struts for dear life.

"What are you doing there?" I shouted.

"I wasn't going to stay and have that maniac shoot at me," he hollered back.

At that moment, the morning sun rose from behind a nearby hill and bathed the countryside in its bright warming glow.

In its light, the harsh shadow of the bat-shaped flying machine swept rapidly and menacingly across the landscape beneath us. Seen from below, the spectacle must have been utterly bizarre. Black against the clear blue sky, a tall man in a top-hat and flapping coat-tails was riding a gigantic bat, whilst another man was desperately clinging on underneath. The effect it had on the estate workers, who were coming out to begin their daily work in the fields, was startling. When they saw us coming, many of them ran away screaming. Others simply stood still, gazing into the sky, with eyes and mouths wide open in terror.

Superstitious minds might have thought that we were a vampire fleeing the light of the new day, and coming to suck their blood. Scaring people witless always gives me a great thrill.

The land was now sloping downhill. As I'd intended, we were flying towards the river in the bottom of the valley. More alarmingly, we were heading directly towards a line of trees on the far bank of the river. With the additional weight on board, we were flying so low that we risked going straight into them.

I knew I had to jettison something. I now had a choice. Either I choose to throw away the boxes in my pockets, together with the treasures they undoubtedly contained, or else I elect to drop Grimdale off as soon as possible.

It was no contest.

I noticed a willow tree on the nearside bank of the river and decided to direct the machine towards it. I flexed the ends of the wings and leaned over to my left. The machine began to turn. My colleague's extra weight helped, and we were soon making our way directly towards the willow. We flew so close to the treetop that Grimdale became entangled in the upper branches. He released his grip on the undercarriage and fell ten feet into the water below.

Now free from its destabilising load, the machine quickly gained height. Indeed, it rose so steeply that it rapidly lost airspeed. With the fuel also running low, the propeller lost power, and the flying machine plummeted towards the ground.

I struggled frantically with the wings, trying to direct the falling machine towards the far bank of the river. I had no intension of getting wet like Grimdale, but I didn't want to kill myself either, so I looked desperately for somewhere soft to land.

Then I spotted it. Along one edge of the riverside meadow, just in front of the trees, stood a large haystack. My only hope now was to I reach this without hitting the trees. I flexed the wings, held tightly onto my hat, and prepared to hit the ground.

The flying machine landed in the haystack with a tremendous crash. It immediately broke up. The impact threw me out of my seat and into a pile of soft grass. Some might think I didn't deserve such an easy landing, but they can keep their opinions to themselves. I admit I was shaken, but I was also relieved that I was able to walk away from the wreckage.

Which was just as well. A few seconds later, the remains of the flying machine burst into flames. The pall of black smoke drifted across the fields, turning the sweet morning air acrid with the smell of burning hay and scorched textile fabric. The heat was so intense that it forced me to back away. At least I still had my hat and cane with me.

The estate workers, having overcome their initial shock, now came running. They used anything they could lay their hands on to try to beat out the flames and save what was left of the haystack.

As arranged beforehand, our carriage was standing beside the old stone bridge. The coachman now opened the door and helped me climb aboard. Once inside, I sat down and heaved a sigh of relief.

A moment later, Grimdale joined me there. He was soaked to the skin. I had no time for sympathy; my mind was already on other things.

"To the German Embassy," I announced. "Let's hope their government official still wants to buy the plans to Sir Henry's flying machine."

It was only as I looked around for the blueprints that I realised where they were. For safety, I'd pushed them behind some struts on the machine. They were still there, already burnt to ashes.

I roundly cursed my bad luck.

"All that work for nothing," said Grimdale.

I felt like throwing the man back into the river.

"Drive on," I told the coachman.

As we rumbled out of the estate, I took off my hat and pulled something out from beneath the lining. It was the diamond necklace belonging to the Countess.

The sight of the jewels cheered us both up as nothing else could have done at that moment.

Grimdale gave a low whistle. "It must be worth a king's ransom," he gasped.

Then I took out the jewellery boxes I'd removed from Sir Henry's safe. We opened them one by one and took out their contents.

"You must have got every piece of jewellery the Countess owns," said Grimdale.

"She is indeed a very rich lady," I replied.

"Or at least, she used to be," added my companion.

"Scotland Yard are already making plans to arrest me," I said. "This is going to stir them up like a nest of hornets."

"They'll scour the entire country looking for us," Grimdale told me.

"In that case," I replied, "we're going to need a vacation. Somewhere abroad, I think. Possibly Switzerland."

The Glennon Falls
by Sam Wiebe

May 3, 1891
Meiringen, Switzerland

> *The Colonel has found the ideal spot. Far enough up the trail to prevent witnesses, yet scenic enough for a plunge to seem like the wayward footfall of an overeager tourist. One crooked step and my most recent antagonist bows out of my affairs permanently, joining a long line of others.*
>
> *I am well-practiced in removing such nuisances. Since sleep has forsaken me, I have taken pen in hand to document my earliest foray into the world of crime. Yet I must admit to a certain hesitation. While the run-of-the-mill criminal values nothing save his own neck, and cares only about his "get-away," we professionals strive for anonymity. To perpetrate fraud or robbery is a confluence of luck and skill; to convince others no crime has been committed demands a rather Napoleonic genius.*
>
> *There is no vanity as that of an anonymous man, and I find myself desiring a record of this, my first and by some measure, most perfect crime.*

I was from childhood something of a scapegrace, a blight on the Moriarty coat of arms. Mrs. Glennon, my former governess, informed me of my inherent wickedness before I reached my eleventh year.

"James," she scolded on more than one occasion, "you were born ready for the gallows."

Whether Mrs. Glennon was prescient remains to be discovered, but there was no misleading her. Stout and eagle-beaked, she bestrode my childhood, handing down sanctimony and punishment like a wrathful deity. While later in life I would find other antagonists, at that age she was my chief foil and mortal enemy. I loathed her.

I know little of her childhood or upbringing, only that her parents had been liberal-minded and had seen fit to grant her an education. She had some Greek and High German, was familiar with Virgil and the Caesars, and grasped enough of mathematics to make sense of Newton.

138

To hear her speak of this patchwork education was to hear a beggar flaunt her rags.

The Glennon woman had married a dull-witted dogs-body who'd ended up in my father's employ. The wife's services were far from optimal, but my father, a skinflint at heart, granted her employment as well. Their shared living expenses more than made up for the deficiencies in her pedagogy.

I confess that in my early years I displayed no interest or aptitude in studies, and was accounted a dilettante. An accelerated intellect such as mine might find purchase in following its own curriculum, yet not show itself to advantage when corralled with lesser lights. While my father could have provided me with tutors, the miserly soul employed only the Glennon woman, believing her adequate. What impertinence and lack of foresight on both their parts!

Early on in this arrangement, Mrs. Glennon challenged me in one or two trivial details – a Latin declension or two, the difference between Thucydides and Heraclitus. Emboldened by these minor victories, the oat-fed knave saw fit to intrude on larger matters. She became an expert on everything, from Locke's philosophy to the arrangement of coprimes in Euclid's orchard. Even diction – and her unable to conquer her scullery maid's burr. Utter absurdity, and untenable, to say the least.

I resolved to be done with her, and sued my father to end her employment. With an asinine judgment matched only by his miserly nature, he sided with the Glennon woman against his own son.

For those readers whose senses are dull and slovenly – I assume this to be the majority of you, frankly – it may seem childish petulance for an adolescent to resent such a hovering, harping figure to such extent that he would consider transgressing the law to be rid of her. You may never understand what a great intellect feels when stifled by overbearing idiocy. Imagine a child caged at birth, straining to grow, yet bound by the narrow confines of dull iron bars. Now magnify this discomfort considerably, and you may begin to grasp my yearning for a more self-determined existence.

My plan was a perfect engine of such intricate craftsmanship that its memory still causes its author to smile nostalgically. My father possessed nothing so valuable as his collection of rare manuscripts. Religious tomes inscribed on vellum, first editions of Johnson and De Foe – even several Shakespearean quartos, a rough draft of *Lear* lacking Nahum Tate's civilizing amendments. My father fancied himself educated by virtue of possessing such works. I would make better use of them later.

Of particular value was an illuminated Celtic version of the Gospels, something akin to the *Book of Kells* which one can visit nowadays in the Irish colony. The artifice and detail of this work raised it to the forefront of his collection. I doubt the fool read the words of the apostles in the vulgate, let alone parsed through this Latinate version. Yet its ownership caused him great pleasure, and I had little hardship in including this volume in my plan, as a double punishment.

My father had encased the volume beneath a thick pane of glass and the sturdiest hinges and lock available. Heaven forbid he read the book. It was sufficient to gaze at two of its pages through glass, and to acknowledge it was in his possession.

Among my father's acquaintances was the painter Yarborough, a celebrated landscapist of the pastoral school. My father had commissioned him to paint my portrait, with my young self-dressed as a shepherd boy. While degrading to stand amidst our yard in such peasant garb, clutching a crook while a tenant farmer's ewe nudged my ankles, I struck up a friendship with Yarborough, and presented myself as enamored with his skill and desirous of instruction. In this, I will admit to severe exaggeration – his paintings are held in high esteem by those who ought not to be.

In any case, won over by my interest, or perhaps anticipating further commissions, Yarborough and I began correspondence. While his advice on painting went ignored, it wasn't long before Yarborough furnished me with intelligence I could use.

Some months prior, Yarborough had taken on an apprentice, who had since fallen into disrepute. This young man had shown considerable promise, which went unfulfilled due to a fondness for drink and extravagant living. Yarborough soon terminated their arrangement. This young man, whose name was Cutler, appealed several times to re-establish his tutelage. Yarborough demurred.

Cutler, then, had applied his skills to forgery, a trade he found more suited to his talents. Yarborough became aware of his pupil's new trade when a critic congratulated him on a recent canvas of the Lake District – a picture he had not painted. (The critic had pronounced it a necessary and not unwelcome progression from his previous works – if he but knew!)

Yarborough wrote to me of this, only after much prodding on my part. He seemed to wish to unburden himself of the guilt. If he'd only accepted Cutler back; if he'd only been more tractable. I reassured him there was little fault to be found in his decision, and in fact Cutler's actions bore out Yarborough's judgment. At the same time, though, I made note of Mr. Cutler's address and particulars.

My own tribulations under the Scotch witch continued. Mrs. Glennon criticized, prodded, corrected. Her intent was to remedy my weakest skills, namely history and Latin. Every criticism was a lash from a whip held by the most dim-witted of slave masters. Was I not excelling in mathematics, far beyond others my age? Was that not enough? Was mastery of a select few fields truly less praiseworthy than well-rounded mediocrity?

I vowed not to spend my twelfth birthday under the same servitude as my eleventh. I vowed my terrorizer would be removed.

Some months later, upon my father's return from a week's sojourn in Manchester, he found his case empty, his precious Gospels nowhere to be found. The case was locked, the dust atop it undisturbed.

Flabbergasted, he mustered the entire household. A search was conducted of the house and grounds, led by the Glennons, with my father studying them as much as appraising himself on the progress of the search. Finally the volume was located beneath the bed of the Glennons themselves, found by Mr. Glennon, presented to my father, to the astonishment and bewilderment of all three.

Unleashing a monolog of self-serving rhetoric befitting her countrywoman Lady MacBeth, Mrs. Glennon explained to my father how I had taken umbrage at her corrections, and had attempted petty vengeance by somehow unlocking the case and salting the book beneath her bed, to pin the blame upon her. She entreated him to see through my ploy and deal fairly with her, and with myself. She reminded him that kindness to the wicked is cruelty to the righteous.

My father found it easier to accept that fate had cursed him with a disloyal son, than that his own bad judgment had led him to hire shoddy menials. I protested my innocence, which of course went ignored. I was punished, cloistered in my room, my jail now also made physical.

I refused to admit to the crime, or explain how I had unlocked the display case. My father was of a choleric nature but weak-willed, happy to hand down a sentence but happier still to allow someone else its administration. The churlish Mrs. Glennon was allowed to whip me for my bad behavior. I accepted it; I pleaded only that I was not responsible.

For a month I was confined, receiving no visitors, sending nor accepting no letters. The month passed gradually. I returned to the bosom of my loving family a meek exemplar of the benefits of the corporal punishment of children.

141

"We'll speak no more of this matter," my father said. "I've no idea how you unlocked the case, but the book is restored and the locks have been changed and doubled. Let us resume as we have been, with mercy and forgiveness all around. A new start."

And it *was* a new start, for a scant few days after my re-admittance to the household, the book again disappeared. While the case had been picked the first time, the second found the glass smashed. No one had heard the sound; a bundle of thick linen was found near the remnants, indicating that it had been used to muffle the shattering glass.

I was naturally accused and thrashed again, twice as severely, and unceremoniously marched back to my small room. Again a search was undertaken; again Mrs. Glennon was at hand to pour wormwood into my father's ear, and twist father against son.

The book was not found in the house. It was not in my chambers, nor Mrs. Glennon's. Neither was it hidden among the other volumes in my father's overstuffed library. I was questioned, and hit, and hit, and questioned. Then the blows ceased, and a rare burst of logic overtook my father. The book was not on the grounds; I hadn't left the grounds; no packages had been mailed, nothing unusual found in the ashes of the furnace. I was, at least, not the sole instigator.

After much hesitation the constabulary was called for. I've always had a certain disdain for the police, especially the supercilious clew-sniffers and alibi-rattlers whose education seems to be the over-reading of Vidocq's memoirs and certain salacious stories of the American author Poe. This inspector, Collins, was such a martinet. Obviously fancying himself a "great detective," he began his investigation by repeating the same searches and interrogations began by my imbecilic father. Collins reached the same conclusions.

When the search had finished, this Collins turned to me, reigned in his puffed-up demeanor, and attempted a kindly disposition. "Young master James," he said, "I am not accusing you. But since you've filched the book on a previous occasion, I have reason to think you know more than you're telling."

At this I glanced at Mrs. Glennon, then lowered my head and made no reply. Observing my body language, Collins said, "Perhaps a private chat, the two of us, if that is all right with Mr. Moriarty."

"Whatever restores to me what's mine," came my father's reply.

Returning to my chambers, Collins and I resumed our conversation. "Was there something you felt unable to tell me in their company?" Collins asked, going so far as to take a knee and grasp my shoulders.

142

"Someone I should look at more closely? Don't fear them; be forthright, young master."

"Mrs. Glennon is a good woman," I said. "A very good woman. She'd never do anything."

The lummox's line of questioning turned to my governess. Was she violent? Well, I admitted, she had struck me several times. Prone to peculiar behavior? Covetous of objects in the household? I admitted she had been taught to read, and regarded herself an expert and somewhat of a scholarrette.

"She's a good woman," was the invariable conclusion of my every reply.

I've no idea what Collins inferred from this, my answers being whole cloth truth. He soon nodded and we returned to the hallway and the company of my father and the Glennons. All three were questioned, though the Scotswoman received more scrutiny than the other two did, and was invited to a private *tête-à-tête*.

I noticed a softening to Mr. Glennon's features, the longer his wife was absent from the room. He began glancing frequently at the clock and busying herself with needless stoking of the fire.

When they returned, Mrs. Glennon's face was wan. Inspector Collins found pretense to repeat the search, asking permission to include the Glennons' private chambers. Since he had already acceded to such a request, several times, Glennon agreed.

Mrs. Glennon pawed at the grubby coat sleeve of her husband, leaning on his slight frame. She would not meet my eyes. When Collins had started for the domestics' quarters, I whispered to her in a tone I tried to make as reassuring as possible, "Don't worry, I didn't tell him anything."

Collins's heavy bootsteps stopped. He called out to ask if perhaps the Glennons would join him for this leg of the search.

His inspection did not turn up the missing tome, but it evidently turned up something, for I was yet again sent to my chambers, and the four adults remained in conference for the better part of the afternoon. Then suddenly a coach was sent for, and the cook informed me that I'd be dining in my room, alone, while my father and the Glennons accompanied Collins to the East End.

"Something about a note found in the missus's cabinet," the cook told me in his guttural drawl. "Something about a rented room, and a Mr. Cutter or Cutler or some-such, and a great deal of money."

143

Apparently the Inspector had found a scrap of paper in Mrs. Glennon's vanity, a rough note in a hand unlike that of her or her husband. The note supplied an address, an assurance that "the job" would be done "beyond the most expert scrutiny", and reiterated an agreed-upon sum. What the transaction entailed lay beyond the Inspector's knowledge, but his interest was piqued. Mrs. Glennon swore that she'd never seen the note before.

Collins, accompanied by the Glennons and my father, were conveyed to the address mentioned in the note. There was no answer at the door, and the landlady was sent for. She confessed she'd let a suite to a Mr. Cutler, who had insisted on having a separate entrance. She had only met this man twice, and was unaware of his goings or companions. Collins mentioned his police credentials, and the landlady permitted them entrance into Cutler's quarters.

Collins, no doubt believing himself a keen bloodhound, took in the contents and state of the room and deduced the story in full. My father identified various trinkets as belonging to my departed mother – ivory handbrushes, minor bits of jewelry, along with a pawnbrokers' ticket for several other familiar items. Collins inferred them as payment; unobtrusive items which could easily be stored, say in one's skirt or bags.

Among the various paintings and supplies were a series of preliminary sketches of a scandalous nature, featuring the rough outline of a woman of advancing years. Glennon looked at these, then removed himself from the room. His wife stood mute, her face drawn and bloodless, no doubt assembling some cunning justification.

Near the window Collins identified my father's prized book, and next to it, a painstakingly accurate facsimile of several of the pages, one only half-complete. Inks, leathers, dyes, magnifying glass – materials were on hand, enough to produce several ersatz tomes. Collins also turned up a wax copy of a skeleton key, which my father identified as a match to the display case's original lock.

Mrs. Glennon began to enumerate her own beliefs regarding the scene, but she was hushed quite violently by the good inspector. Collins had them open the door to the adjoining room. Himself being speechless, he wished this state imposed on the others until he processed what he saw.

It was a bedroom, in filthy state, with men's and women's hygienics arranged on the drawing board near the mattresses. Amongst the disarray

Collins noted a not insignificant quantity of laudanum, along with several political tracts and a few novels of a lurid nature.

Collins assembled these facts into a story of lust and avarice befitting the reading materials of the flat's inhabitants. It was clear Cutler had attempted to procure the volume from Mrs. Glennon, and that the pair obviously shared much more than a passing acquaintance. Not only had she cast a key to help remove the volume, she had filched enough of the bereaved family's own keepsakes to capitalize this venture. Worst of all, though, she had incriminated her student and charge – then dealt the punishment to the child herself!

Returning to our house, and ignoring Mrs. Glennon's protestations, Collins and my father once again interrogated me. When I attempted to say that Mrs. Glennon was a good woman, my father said he'd have no more lies from me.

I said I'd never seen her commit any wickedness. In the hours I was under her tutelage, I would see her come and go at admittedly odd intervals, but assured them her actions seemed benevolent. On the contrary, her brief separations seemed to reinvigorate her, and she returned to our studies with an improved demeanor, if less than full concentration and sobriety.

I told them, if I'd withheld this information from them, it was only because Mrs. Glennon had so insisted on pain of further lashings.

Inspector Collins had his constables roust Cutler from a local tavern and account for himself. He protested innocence, even agreeing to furnish samples of his handwriting. These would be identified as a match to the note found in the Glennons' living quarters.

Mr. Glennon admitted several of the products found in the flat were similar to those used by his wife. The pawnbroker produced a brooch belonging to my mother, an anniversary gift. The broker said a man roughly matching Cutler's description had pawned the bauble, well below its value, but the broker admitted he had trouble differentiating the specific facial features of gentiles.

Cutler accepted his sentence to hard labor, no doubt grateful he wasn't born a few years earlier, when forgery was a hanging offense. Mrs. Glennon was remanded to a women's' institute. While the scandal-mongerers presented them as desperate lovers, and Mrs. Glennon especially as a modern-day Black-Eyed Sue or Sweet Poll, to my knowledge they never exchanged so much as salutations.

145

I happily finished out my studies with the self-determination I so craved. What joy to set the chart and rudder of one's own voyage! Such freedom is priceless, desperately priceless, and all too rare.

When I began lecturing at the university several years later, I received a letter from Mrs. Glennon informing me that she'd been released. She'd found work in a hotel kitchen, and cheap lodging in a boarding-house in Southwark. She wrote that since the divorce, she'd entertained few visitors in her admittedly-shabby accommodations. Nevertheless, if I could tear myself away from my lectures for a fraction of an afternoon, I'd find myself welcome to join her for tea.

I've since made a rule never to consort with a known criminal, and never, for any reason, in that person's private quarters. Youthful arrogance! I sent her a reply indicating my pleasure to call on her.

The former Mrs. Glennon had aged severely, thinned out and grown sickly. We sat on a pair of carefully repaired cushionless chairs. Mrs. Glennon's unsteady hands poured out black tea from a battered service. No keepsakes of her prior life adorned her small apartment. Her quarters had the charm of a Dickensian orphan, and I informed her of such. She accepted the compliment graciously.

"I think you'll find," she said, "I've quite reformed. I practice nothing of the sort of activities I was accused of."

"A profitable way," I agreed, "to ensure one's happiness and liberty."

"Yes, one should confront what one has done, for by making peace with oneself, one makes peace with the world." I agreed with the sentiment for decorum's sake – who would wish to make peace with the world? Mrs. Glennon asked if I recognized the maxim's author.

"Cicero, I believe."

She shook her head but did not correct me.

"Coleridge? Swift, then."

"Margaret Ann Glennon," she said. "Something I made up just now. I was always quite gifted at coinings."

"An impressive trick," I said, "most useful for amusing a husband – beg your pardon."

"He saw education the same way," she said. "A parlor game, a diversion. I'm often glad my parents didn't share his sentiment. They valued *qua* knowledge, being devotees of Mrs. Wollstonecraft's inestimable volume. Knowledge is a lonely blessing, isn't it, James?"

I said nothing.

146

"I will admit, James, your infinite superiority in cunning and cleverness. I needed a year to deduce the authorship of your plot. Who could hold such a grudge against me, and to what end?" Her smile was not ironic. Sensing my hesitation, she added, "We're alone, I assure you, and I'm past the desire for retribution. But I would like to hear your reasons, as well as exactly how you accomplished my ruin." I indulged her – another weakness I have since attempted to correct.

She'd believed, erroneously, that I'd employed Cutler only to double-cross him. I explained that my accomplices numbered only two, and Cutler had not been among them. Rather, he had been part of the price for my partners' complicity.

"Yarborough," she exclaimed, speaking to herself as if validating a private theory.

"Indeed. The master felt a certain guilt for his apprentice's crimes, but nothing touching the infernal rage and humiliation of having his own works forged – and bettered, according to one cretinous critic."

I went on. "Yarborough himself forged the book; he did so twice, or more accurately, one and a half times. The volume first found in your room was a forgery – the best he could do without close scrutiny of the book. Luckily such scrutiny evaded my father as well. It resembled his precious volume enough to assure him of its authenticity."

"The volume which was returned to the case," Mrs. Glennon began.

"Stolen and traded with Mr. Yarborough's trusted servant, the forgery placed by your bed – yes, knowing it would be perhaps too spot-on at first, and my father's wrath would be incurred by me. But how much more on *you*, when he realized you'd deceived him, and acted as the instrument for the unfair punishment of his son?"

"A double blind," she marveled.

"Quite so." I was enjoying myself. Mrs. Glennon took the opportunity to refill our cups.

"Yarborough's servant helped me funnel several minor items out of the household. I'd drop them from my window to the garden below, or secret them during a walk. While delivering messages, the servant would retrieve them. Doubtless it was he who pawned the brooch, and arranged the room, resembling as he does Mr. Cutler in a very general way."

"And Cutler's note?"

"Included in Yarborough's correspondence – the old master outdid his pupil at forgery. When the time came, I broke the glass case and slipped the forged book into the garden in much the same way."

"Then the volume recovered from the apartment was the original?"

147

I smiled. "It is the one father still treasures in its case to this day. He is satisfied, and the profits of others with similar volumes are beyond his care."

"And Yarborough?"

"The old man died satisfied, happy to have outlived Cutler by several months. I understand prison weakens one's constitution – perhaps you could confirm this yourself. In any case, prison aged Mr. Cutler quite horribly."

"As it did me," she said. "Poor Mr. Cutler. Poor Yarborough, for that matter. A great deal of death."

I didn't respond.

"You remember, James, I spoke of the lonely blessing of knowledge? It is clear you have it. It would take the mind of Shakespeare to conceive a plot such as yours."

"Shakespeare nicked most of his plots from the Romans," I said. But I thanked her for the compliment.

"I apologize to you for my harshness as a governess," Mrs. Glennon said.

This I didn't expect. Stunned, I muttered my acceptance of her apology.

"I know well the feeling of being stifled, underestimated, underappreciated. All women know this, James, but my own education made me rather more sensitive to the issue. It is an English-man's world; a woman from the Hebrides has little place in it. I felt so fortunate your father chose me as your governess. How forward-thinking he was, to overlook class and race and gender! How I hoped to inculcate in you that same open-mindedness!"

"Mrs. Glennon," I began, but couldn't quite finish.

"James," she said, "I'm not long for this world, so permit me to play Cassandra to you – she was a prophetess whose words invariably fell on deaf ears."

"I know who she was," I snapped.

"I could have been an ally, James, even better, a friend. But your genius is singular. It brooks no competition, and therefore accepts no one as equal, no one as companion-worthy."

I shook my head, anger rising.

"You are a great man, young Mr. Moriarty – professor, I should say. A great man, and destined to make enemies of all those most able to understand you. If and when you are confronted with a true equal, rather than companionship, I suspect you'll find only mutual destruction. It's a

148

fall from grace, and one your young self has already taken. I wish I could pity you."

She prattled on; I took little heed of her MacBethian pronouncements. The passing years bore out my deafness. My wealth, my successes, my empire, stand in testament to the falsehood of her words.

In her way, Mrs. Glennon was a bright creature, perhaps at one time capable of overcoming the natural inferiority of her sex. To Professor James Moriarty, though, she would always be, merely, a woman.

The Adventure of the
Sleeping Cardinal
or
The Doctor's Case
by Jeremy Branton Holstein

My name is Watson, Doctor Watson, and it was my privilege to share the adventures of Sherlock Holmes. Throughout the many years I lived with Holmes in Baker Street, I came to know both his many gifts and his many faults. Chief among those faults was an intolerance of dull routine, an impatience that was often tested in the interim between clients when no new problems were available to challenge his active mind. It was during one such lull, in the summer of 1899, that my story begins.

It was early morning, and I was supping upon one of Mrs. Hudson's excellent breakfasts. Holmes, however, had declined the meal, and was instead pacing back and forth before the mantelpiece in our sitting room. Finally he threw up his hands and bellowed his frustration at the top of his lungs.

"Bah!" he cried. "This is interminable, Watson! Interminable!"

"What's that, Holmes?" I said, even though I knew the answer.

"This inactivity!" said Holmes. "Has the entire criminal population of London gone on holiday? Give me a case to solve, a problem to unravel! Anything but this endless boredom!"

"Calm down, Holmes," I said. "Something will turn up soon. Why don't you have some of Mrs. Hudson's breakfast?"

"I don't need food, Watson," said Holmes. "I need clients! I am a thinking machine, and my mind must be fed problems, lest it wither from languor."

"Perhaps there's something in the paper for your mind to chew on." I picked up the morning paper and leafed through the pages. "Ah," I said. "Here's an interesting item. They've found Henry Tuttle alive and in hiding! He'd faked his death to avoid his creditors."

"A cowardly act," said Holmes, "but far from interesting."

"I seem to recall you did much the same a few years back," I said.

"For entirely different reasons, Watson," said Holmes. "You know that."

I did my best to hide my smile. "If you say so." I turned another page, and a new article caught my eye "Ah, here's something. Apparently the *Sleeping Cardinal* has been put up for auction."

"The *Sleeping Cardinal*?" said Holmes. "Now that is interesting. I believe you were involved in the painting's recovery a few years back?"

"I played my part, yes," I said.

"Yet you've never told me the full story," said Holmes.

"It's never come up before."

"Well then, Doctor," said Holmes, "if the criminals of the present cannot challenge my mind, then perhaps the criminals of the past can. Tell me your tale."

"Are you, Sherlock Holmes, really asking me to tell you one of my stories? You usually dislike my writing in the *Strand Magazine*."

Holmes fixed me with the gravest of stares. "It's either your stories or the needle, Watson," he said. "I leave the decision to you."

"Very well," I said, and pushed my breakfast aside. "Where to begin?"

"You are the storyteller, Watson," said Holmes. "I place myself in your capable hands."

"I suppose," I began, "that the best place would be the summer of 1892. It had been over a year since your disappearance, Holmes, and some months before your reappearance in London. During the intervening time, I had left the world of criminal investigation behind, choosing instead to focus upon my medical practice and the health of my beloved wife Mary, God rest her soul."

"Indeed," said Holmes. "Pray continue."

I gathered my thoughts, and began.

It was a beastly hot summer, as I recall, and my list of clients had swelled as a result. I had just finished treating a patient for heat exhaustion over near Covent Garden when I, quite literally, ran into an old friend. I was walking home and so consumed with thoughts of my wife and her health that I didn't even see the gentleman until I had barreled into him.

"I beg your pardon, sir," I said.

The gentleman, however, did not want to give pardon and began to yell back at me. "Why don't you watch where you're . . . ." he began, but then stopped, his eyes widening in surprise and his mouth spreading into a grin. "Well, if that doesn't beat all," he said. "Is that you, Doctor Watson?"

My heart burst with joy at the sight of the man. "Why, it's Inspector Lestrade!" I said. "My dear fellow. It's good to see you."

"What brings you down to Covent Garden?" said Lestrade.

"Oh, I've just finished up with a patient," I said. "And you?"

"Business, I'm afraid."

"Ah!" I said. "A case?" I could not help but feel a tingle of the old excitement at the prospect.

"Still investigating crimes, Doctor?" said Lestrade.

"No, of course not. Not since Holmes's death at Reichenbach."

"Of course."

"I still follow crime in the paper, though," I said. "Try to puzzle them out as Holmes would have done."

Lestrade regarded me with a curious expression. "Actually," he said, "it's funny running into you like this. This robbery I'm looking into. It's exactly the sort of case your Mr. Holmes would have enjoyed."

"Really?" I said.

Lestrade considered me for a moment, and then said, "See here, Doctor, this is a bit irregular, but are you busy? I could use a fresh set of eyes on this one."

I smiled. "For old time's sake?" I said. "Why, Inspector, I'd be honored."

"Capital," said Lestrade. "Then follow me, and I'll outline the details of the case en-route."

"Lead the way," I said. "I'm your man."

We set off together down St. Martin's Lane, Lestrade talking as we walked.

"It's like this, Doctor," he said. "Last night, one Lady Margaret checks into the Hotel Metropole, carrying with her a very expensive painting, called . . ." Lestrade pulled a notebook from his pocket, and consulted his notes. ". . . *The Sleeping Cardinal*," he finished.

"I'm not familiar with it," I said.

"Neither was I before now," said Lestrade, "but they say it's a masterpiece and worth a king's ransom. Lady Margaret had brought the framed painting into town for an exhibition. Not wanting to leave it in her room, she asks the manager . . ." Lestrade checked his notebook again. ". . . one Patrick Pardman, if he'd store it in the hotel safe for the night. Mr. Pardman agrees, and locks the painting up in his office before heading home. You follow me so far?"

152

"Perfectly," I said.

"Well, Doctor," said Lestrade. "Imagine Pardman's surprise when he arrives the next morning, goes to open the safe, and finds the painting gone!"

"Stolen!" I said.

"One would think so, but there's no evidence of a break-in at all! The safe is stored in Pardman's office, a small room with no windows and only one entrance in or out, a door just behind the main desk of the hotel."

"And the desk was manned all night?" I asked.

Lestrade nodded. "They assure me it was. By one . . ." He checked his notebook again. ". . . James Ryder, I believe."

"James Ryder," I said. "I know that name from somewhere."

"Do you now?" said Lestrade. "Well, this Ryder claims no one else entered the office between the time Pardman left for the night and when he returned the next morning. So how did the painting disappear?"

"Was the office locked at night?" I asked. "Could someone have slipped in while Ryder wasn't looking? Or perhaps it could have even been Ryder himself?"

Lestrade shook his head. "Mr. Pardman assures me he locks the door when he leaves at night, and only unlocks it first thing in the morning."

"No sign of tampering, I suppose."

"None."

I thought about the problem as we walked. "This is a bit of a stretch," I said after a time, "but could Pardman himself have taken the painting?"

"Pardman was seen last night leaving the hotel by both Ryder and the porter," said Lestrade. "He wasn't even carrying a bag, let alone a framed painting."

"You're right, Lestrade," I said. "This is exactly the sort of case Holmes would have enjoyed."

"I thought as much," said Lestrade, "As you can imagine, Lady Margaret is quite distraught and demanding the hotel cover the value of her painting in currency. If we can't find the culprit and recover the *Sleeping Cardinal*, the hotel will find itself in quite a financial bind! Ah, here we are," he said, stopping on the street before the Hotel Metropole. "This way, Doctor," he said.

We entered into an opulent hotel lobby, empty save for a constable guarding three people by the main desk. The woman, who I took to be

Lady Margaret, for she was well dressed and ample, stood beside the two gentlemen who could not have looked more different from one another. One, who I soon learned was Patrick Pardman, was a tall, handsome fellow. The other, James Ryder, was short and rat-faced.

Lady Margaret wasted no time in pouncing upon Lestrade. "At last!" she said. "What took you so long?"

Lestrade was ever the professional. "My apologies, Lady Margaret," he said, impassively. "Yard business."

Lady Margaret huffed at this. "I don't understand what could possibly be more important than my compensation."

Lestrade ignored her indignation, and instead introduced me. "This is my colleague, Doctor Watson," he said. "He'll be assisting me with the investigation. Doctor, this is Lady Margaret, Patrick Pardman and James Ryder."

We all mumbled, "How do you do?" to each other.

"Excuse me," said Pardman, "but are you the same Doctor Watson who works with Sherlock Holmes?"

I considered correcting his grammatical tenses, but decided to let it pass. "I am," I said.

Pardman seized me by my hand and began to shake vigorously. "Bless me!" he said. "It's an honor sir. An honor."

"You've read my stories?" I asked.

Pardman let my hand go, somewhat sheepishly. "Well, not as such, no," he said. "But you're quite popular among the hotel guests. They're always chattering on about your friend's exploits. Is he here with you now? It would be a privilege to meet him."

"I'm afraid not, Mr. Pardman," I said. "Holmes is . . ." I paused, searching for the right word. ". . . away," I finished.

"If we can get back to the business at hand, please," said Lestrade, never one to let a sentimental moment remain uninterrupted. He pulled out his notebook yet again, and flipped open to an empty page. "Now, let's review the details for Doctor Watson's benefit. Lady Margaret. You checked in to the hotel last night around seven. Is that correct?

"Correct," said Lady Margaret.

Lestrade recorded this in his notebook. "And while checking in, you turned the painting over to Mr. Pardman for safe-keeping?"

"Well, of course!" said Lady Margaret. "I couldn't have such a priceless masterpiece of art lying around my room, now could I? You never know who works at these sorts of places."

154

"Madame," began Pardman, with the greatest indignity. "The Metropole is among the top hotels in London . . . ."

Lady Margaret interrupted him. "The top hotels in thievery, you mean."

"If I can continue?" said Lestrade, waving his notebook about for emphasis. "Now then. Lady Margaret, can you describe the painting in question?"

"Certainly," said Lady Margaret. "It is a particularly lovely piece of impressionistic artistry by the painter Flemming. With sublime brush strokes, Flemming depicting a priest at rest upon an altar . . . ."

Lestrade cut her off. "Just the size of the painting will do."

Lady Margaret looked as if she might explode, but she answered with even precision. "Two by three feet, Inspector, mounted in a mahogany frame."

Lestrade wrote this down in his notebook. "Thank you. Now, Mr. Pardman. You put the painting immediately into your safe, is that correct?"

"Immediately, sir," said Pardman. "Security is a top priority."

"And you locked the safe thereafter?" asked Lestrade.

"Of course," said Pardman. "I even double-checked the lock." His lip trembled at this, as some of his professional composure broke. "Oh, Inspector, how could this have happened?" he said. "I'll be out of a job!"

"Have some faith in the force, Mr. Pardman," said Lestrade. "We'll recover the painting, never fear. Now what time did you leave the hotel?"

"Just after eight that night," said Pardman. "Ryder had come on to work the desk shortly before Lady Margaret checked in, and I retired to my office to finish some paperwork. When I was done, I locked the office and bid Ryder good night."

"Ryder," said Lestrade, "can you confirm the time?"

Ryder, who had been very quiet up until now, nodded his head. "Indeed, sir," he said. "Eight o'clock."

"And you're absolutely certain," said Lestrade, "that no one entered the office between eight that evening and when Mr. Pardman arrived for work the next morning?"

"On my honor, sir," said Ryder. "It was a quiet evening, and I never left my post at the desk."

"Excuse me, Mr. Ryder," I asked, "but you look very familiar. Have we met before?"

"I don't believe so, sir," said Ryder, but he never met my eyes. I could tell he was lying.

155

Lestrade noticed none of this. "What time did Mr. Pardman return?" he asked.

"Around six this morning, I think," said Ryder.

"Six on the dot, sir," said Pardman. "Punctuality is my motto."

"And it was then you discovered the painting missing?" said Lestrade.

"Well," said Pardman, "not immediately. It wasn't until Lady Margaret came down and asked to check on her painting that I opened the safe. But when I did, the painting was gone!"

"No sign of a break-in?" said Lestrade.

Pardman shook his head. "None that I could see, sir."

"And Lady Margaret," said Lestrade. "What time did you come down?"

"Just past six-thirty," said Lady Margaret. "I'd had a bad dream, and woke up convinced something had happened to my painting!"

Lestrade rubbed his chin. "A dream, eh?" he said. "That's quite a coincidence."

"Mr. Pardman," I said, "could we have a look at this safe?"

"Of course," said Pardman. "Anything I can do to help. This way, gentlemen."

We left Lady Margaret and Ryder behind in the lobby as Pardman ushered us into a spartan office, devoid of any charm or character. No pictures adorned its windowless walls, and the only furniture was a single desk, two chairs and the large safe pushed into the far corner. The only luxury the room offered was its fireplace; a prize, I was sure, during the cold London winters.

"As you can see, gentlemen," said Pardman, "the door is the only way in or out."

Lestrade studied the safe. "I see no signs of tampering. What about you, Doctor?"

I studied the safe, looking for the scratches and dents that might indicate foul play. "None that I can see," I said at last. "Who knows the combination to the safe?"

"Only myself," said Pardman, "although I do keep it recorded on my desk ledger."

"Isn't that a security risk?" said Lestrade.

"Maybe," said Pardman, "but I've got a terrible memory, so it's better to have it written down than not. Besides, the office is locked at all times when I'm not here."

Lestrade turned away, whispering aside to me so that Pardman could not hear, "Little doubt how the thief got into the safe, is there Doctor?"

"Indeed, Inspector," I whispered back. "But there still remains the question of how he got into the office in the first place."

Lestrade turned back to Pardman. "Who all has the key to your office?" he asked.

"There's only one key, Inspector," said Pardman. "I keep it with me at all times." From his pocket he withdrew a keyring, singling one out.

"That's a rather unusual looking key, Mr. Pardman," I said.

"A Roman design, Doctor," said Pardman. "A trick for my memory to know which key fits my office lock."

"Now then, this Ryder," said Lestrade. "How long has he been with the hotel?"

"Less than a year," said Pardman, "but he came with references from the Hotel Cosmopolitan. I know the manager over there personally."

"And how long have you been with the Metropole, Mr. Pardman?" I asked.

"It'll be twenty years this January," said Pardman. "I'm second only to the hotel's owner, Mr. Saul."

I knew the name of Zacharias Saul very well. He was reputed to be one of the richest men in London.

I looked around the room, trying to think beyond the obvious, searching for any clues for how the thief might have entered the office. "This fireplace," I said. "Is it possible someone could have entered the office by the chimney?"

Lestrade shook his head. "I thought of that, Doctor," he said, "but if they had entered by the fireplace, they would have left traces in the ashes, and as you can see the ashes are undisturbed."

"Besides, the chimney's only a foot wide," said Pardman. He began to chuckle. "We joke about it around here. Say that it makes it very difficult for Father Christmas."

"What did you say?" I whispered.

"Father Christmas," said Pardman. "He's supposed to come down the chimney . . . ."

Memories rushed into my head. "Ryder!" I said. "James Ryder! Of course!"

I rushed out into the lobby, pointing my finger in accusation.

"Constable," I cried. "Seize that man!"

157

The constable seemed surprised, but did as he was told, seizing Ryder by him arm. Ryder struggled, but soon realized the constable was too much for him and his resistance evaporated into pitiful wails.

"Please, Doctor Watson!" he cried. "I haven't done anything this time! Have mercy!"

"Holmes gave you mercy once, Ryder," I said, "but he's not here to do it again."

Lestrade barged back into the Lobby, followed by Pardman. "Explain yourself, Doctor!" said Lestrade.

"Certainly," I said. "It was several Christmases past that Holmes and I investigated the theft of the Blue Carbuncle from the Hotel Cosmopolitan. Holmes's investigation determined the thief to be this man! James Ryder!"

Lestrade blinked in disbelief. "Ryder stole the Carbuncle?" he said. "And Holmes just let him go?"

"A thief!" cried Pardman with indignation. "A thief working the desk of my hotel!"

"Why'd you do it, Ryder?" I said. "You promised Holmes you'd flee the country and never steal again!"

Ryder stifled back a sob. "I tried to leave, Doctor Watson," he said, "but London's the only home I've ever known! I even tried to stick it out at the Cosmopolitan, but the manager came to suspect me, so I had to leave. I was trying to make a fresh start here at the Metropole. I didn't steal the painting! Honest I didn't!"

"We'll see about that," said Lestrade. "Constable, hold him tight while I search his pockets." Lestrade turned Ryder's pockets out, and searched through their meager contents. Unsatisfied, he looked about the lobby for more. "Where's his coat?"

"I believe I saw it behind the lobby desk, Inspector," said Pardman.

Lestrade strode around to the back of the lobby desk, seized the coat and raised it aloft like a prize. He thrust his hands deep into the pockets and fished about until he seized upon an object which he pulled out with a flourish of triumph. "Ah-hah!" he said. "What's this, then? Do you recognize this little beauty, Mr. Pardman?"

In Lestrade's hand was a metal key with the same distinctive Roman design we had seen only moments before.

"Of course I do," said Pardman. "That is a duplicate of the key to my office."

"I thought as much," said Lestrade. "James Ryder, you are under arrest for the theft of the *Sleeping Cardinal*!"

158

"But that key isn't mine!" said Ryder. "I've never seen it before in my life!"

"That's what they all say," said Lestrade, but then he began to laugh.

"What's so funny, Inspector?" I asked.

"It looks like your Mr. Holmes was finally wrong about something!" said Lestrade. "Letting a criminal go free like that. Mercy, indeed! Just goes to show you; once a thief, always a thief."

Despite Ryder's protests Lestrade led him away, assuring both Pardman and Lady Margaret that he would procure the painting's location during interrogation at the Yard. I watched Lestrade escort Ryder away down the Strand with the nagging suspicion that I had missed something, some detail that would turn this case around, but I couldn't then put my finger on it.

Holmes interrupted me, taking me away from my tale. "Leave the dramatics for your readers at the *Strand*, Watson," he said. "Please limit yourself to the facts.

"If you'd rather I stopped . . . ." I began.

"Oh, not at all, Doctor!" said Holmes. "While your prose may be overly colorful the problem is to my liking. Pray continue."

The following evening I spent in the manner which had become my custom: working on my memoirs in the company of my beloved wife. Mary was seated by my side reading the evening paper, and cried aloud as she came across something that sparked her interest.

"Did you see that you're in the paper tonight, John?"

"Hm?" I said, putting my pen aside. "No, I didn't. What does it say?"

Mary cleared her throat and began to read. "'Inspector Lestrade of Scotland Yard arrested James Ryder for the theft of the painting, the *Sleeping Cardinal*, from the Hotel Metropole. Assisting in the investigation was the long-time associate of Sherlock Holmes, Doctor John Watson!' My famous husband." She smiled at me, but that smile crumbled as a fit of coughing overwhelmed her.

I poured Mary some water, which she gratefully accepted. "Mary," I said as she drank, "you should get to bed. You know you aren't well."

"I'll be all right, John," she said, putting the water glass aside. "I'm just so happy for you. There's a sparkle in your eye when you're involved in a mystery. It's just like you used to say about Sherlock Holmes; you're happiest when there's a problem to unravel."

"Perhaps so," I said. "I just can't get this *Cardinal* business out of my mind. Something doesn't feel right about it."

"But you have the right man, surely!" said Mary. "Ryder's a thief twice over."

"He certainly had ample opportunity," I said. "Although the idea that he thought he'd be able to get away with it strikes me as incredible."

"If Scotland Yard is happy," said Mary, "then you should be too."

"I suppose you're right," I said. "But I'd be even happier if we can get you well again, Mary."

Mary put her arms around me. "I'd like nothing better, John."

I kissed her then, relieved that her coughing had, for the moment, subsided.

In the days following Lestrade was kind enough to keep me informed of his progress, or lack thereof, with the investigation. James Ryder continued to insist he was innocent, but Lestrade assured me it would only be a matter of time before he'd crack and give up the location of the painting. And that would likely have been the end of my involvement in the matter if not for a message that arrived at our doorstep a week later.

I was writing again in my study when I felt Mary's slender hand upon my shoulder. "John?" she said. "A telegram's arrived for you."

I lay down my pen. "Oh? Who's it from?"

"It doesn't say," answered Mary. "Just an initial at the bottom. The letter 'M'."

"M?" I said, excitement building within me, spurred by the possibilities of that initial. "Let me see that."

Mary handed me the telegram and I read it aloud.

WHERE IS THE PAINTING? CONSULT SHERLOCK'S CONTACTS. CONSIDER THE ASHES.

– M

I confess to being puzzled. "Consider the ashes . . . ?" I mused.

"What does it mean, John?" asked Mary. "Who are Sherlock's contacts?"

"Holmes kept numerous sources among London's criminal class," I said. "They helped him in his investigations."

"And you know these gentlemen?" I could hear the disapproval in her tone.

"A few of them." I saw no reason to scare my wife with the number of miscreants who I had come into acquaintance with during my time in Baker Street.

Mary was not fooled for a moment. "John," she said. "It might be dangerous."

"It might be at that."

Mary sighed. "But there's no stopping you, is there? I know that look in your eye. All right, John. Just be careful."

"I will, Mary," I said. "For your sake."

The telegram had reawakened the case in my mind. What had happened to the *Sleeping Cardinal*? There seemed two possibilities; either it had been hidden within the hotel prior to Ryder's arrest, or it had been secreted away from the hotel to be sold on the black market. Seeing as the police had conducted a thorough search of the hotel, I decided to pursue the second possibility. To that end, I sought out a man I only knew as 'Jones,' a shady sort I had seen frequently in our rooms at 221B Baker Street. His information had been instrumental in solving the Darlington substitution case several years ago.

I found him drinking in a disreputable pub in the lower-east end of London. I sidled up beside him at the bar.

"Is that you, Jones?" I said.

Jones looked askance at me. "Who wants to know?"

"My name is Doctor Watson. You might remember from the times you visited Sher – "

Jones clamped his hand over my mouth, silencing me mid-name. "Shhh! Shhh!" he said. "Not so loud! You want everyone in the pub to know who you is? Yeah, I remembers you, Doctor." He dropped his tone to a whisper. "Did Mr. H. send you? Haven't seen him around lately."

"No," I said. "Mr. H. is not in London at this time."

"Pity," said Jones, turning his attentions back to his drink. "He owes me money, he does."

"I'm looking for information," I said. "I was wondering if you can help me."

"Well, guv," said Jones, "help ain't cheap. It'll cost you."

"And just how much will it cost me?" I said.

"Depends on just how helpful you want me to be," said Jones.

161

"I'm looking for a painting."

Jones chuckled. "Oh! And not just any paintin'! You be lookin' for the *Sleepin' Cardinal* that got lifted out of the Metropole last week."

"Why, yes," I said, surprised. "How did you know that?"

"'Cause you ain't the only one," said Jones. "Scotland Yard's been down here lookin' for it too."

I felt a tinge of excitement. "You have it, then?"

"Good lord, no, guv!" said Jones. "You think I'm going to touch somethin' that hot?"

My excitement withered. "Then this has been a wasted journey," I moaned.

"Aw, cheer up, Doctor," said Jones. "I might not be able to help you find the paintin', but I might be able to give you a hint as to who took it." He looked around to make sure no one was listening, and then spoke to me in low tones. "There's this fellow, see?" he said. "Works at the Hotel Metropole, and he's in for some serious money with the local bookies. They say he likes the ponies and isn't the luckiest man in the world."

"Can you describe this fellow?" I said.

Jones smiled. "Course I can," he said. "But not until I see some coin."

"How much?"

Jones rubbed his chin, considering his options. "For information that valuable?" he said. "Well, now. Let me see. Five pounds might loosen my lips."

"Five pounds?" I cried. "That's outrageous!"

Jones shrugged. "Well, you think it over, Doctor," he said. "I'm not going anywhere. Not with it being so blasted hot outside."

I couldn't help but agree. "It certainly is that," I said. "It hasn't been this warm since . . . ." I broke off mid-sentence as something fell into place within my mind. "Good lord!" I said. "I have it!"

"What's that, then?" said Jones, sensing his fish had fallen off its hook.

"The ashes!" I cried. "Consider the ashes! I know who took the *Cardinal*!"

"Calm down there, Doctor," said Jones. "You're not makin' any sense."

"I have to go to Scotland Yard at once!" I said. I seized Jones by his hand, shaking it vigorously. "Thank you very much, Jones. You've been most helpful." I fished a coin from my pocket. "Here's a crown for your trouble."

Jones snatched the coin from my hand before I could even blink. "Why, thank you, Doctor." I turned to leave, and heard Jones call after me. "You're welcome!" he cried, followed by a mumbled, "I think . . . ?"

As I left the disreputable pub behind, my mind buzzed with excitement. I could see it all now; exactly who had taken the painting and how.

"Absolutely scintillating, Watson," said Holmes, who was pacing back and forth again within our sitting room. "You had of course noticed that the ashes . . . ."

I interrupted my friend before he could ruin my tale. "Holmes, please. Let me tell my own story."

"Of course," said Holmes. "Do forgive me, Doctor. Pray continue."

I rushed to Scotland Yard and sought out Lestrade. Together, we then made out way back to Covent Garden and were soon standing before a small set of rooms near the Hotel Metropole. We knocked at the door, and a tall, handsome man answered.

"Yes?" said Patrick Pardman. "Ah, Inspector. And Doctor Watson! What a surprise."

"May we come in?" asked Lestrade.

"Of course, of course," said Pardman.

He stepped aside, and ushered us within.

Pardman's quarters were spartan, devoid of the luxury the Hotel Metropole provided. It was a single room, with a small bed, a dresser and side table. A decanter, some bottles and glasses were perched on top of dresser, and Pardman poured himself a drink.

"May I offer you gentlemen some brandy?" asked Pardman.

Lestrade shook his head. "I'm afraid we're here on business."

"Oh?" said Pardman. "You have news of the *Sleeping Cardinal*?"

"We do," said Lestrade.

"Well, that is welcome news," said Pardman. "Mrs. Margaret is demanding her compensation by no later than noon tomorrow. Mr. Saul is most unhappy with the situation."

"I can imagine," I said.

"Then don't keep me in suspense, gentlemen," said Pardman. "Have you located the painting?"

"We have information that points us in a direction," said Lestrade.

"Well, that is encouraging!" said Pardman. "And where is the *Cardinal* presently?"

163

"That is what we've come to ask you, Mr. Pardman," I said.

Pardman blinked in surprise. "Me?" he said. "But it was Ryder who took the *Sleeping Cardinal*!"

"No," I said, "but that's what you wanted us to think."

"You knew of Ryder's suspected involvement in the disappearance of the Blue Carbuncle from your discussions with the manager of the Hotel Cosmopolitan," said Lestrade, "and knew he'd make a perfect scapegoat should a robbery ever occur at the Hotel Metropole."

"All you had to do was somehow mention Ryder's involvement with the Blue Carbuncle theft to the proper authorities," I said, "and Ryder's arrest for the new robbery would be almost assured. My appearance at the scene must have seemed an early Christmas to you. Why raise the affair of the Blue Carbuncle to the authorities when a known associate of Sherlock Holmes could do it for you?"

"The spare key was a nice touch in the frame-up," said Lestrade. "Only you made a small slip up there."

"Really," said Pardman.

"You said you never let the key of your sight," I said. "How then could Ryder have made a copy? I suspect if we were to check with locksmiths in the area of the hotel, they'd remember making a copy for you, Mr. Pardman, and not for Mr. Ryder."

"That proves nothing," said Pardman. "I have keys made for the hotel all the time."

"But the rest of the hotel uses standard keys," I said, "while the key to your office is Roman. Something with that unique a design is bound to stick out in a locksmith's mind."

"You slipped the duplicate into Ryder's coat so I could find it," said Lestrade, "which completed your frame-up. A very clever touch, but not clever enough for an officer of the Yard."

Pardman drained his glass, and regarded us calmly. "An entertaining tale, gentlemen," he said, "but you still haven't told me where the painting is."

"The painting's disappearance is really only a mystery if we assume it was ever in the safe to begin with," I said, "and we only have your word for that. If, however, the opposite were true and the painting were never in the safe, then the solution becomes obvious."

"You walked out of the Hotel Metropole that evening with the painting in hand," said Lestrade, "determined to sell it on the black market."

"That's ridiculous!" said Pardman. "How could I walk out with a painting that size and not be seen? The idea's ludicrous!"

"It is ludicrous," I said, "until you remember the ashes in your fireplace."

Pardman blinked at me in surprise. "I beg your pardon?" he said.

"Lestrade noted the ashes in your office as evidence that no one had snuck down the chimney," I said, "but what we should have been asking is why you were burning a fire at all during the hottest summer in recent memory? The answer is that you were burning the frame upon which the *Cardinal* was mounted!"

"With the frame removed, the painting was much easier to conceal beneath your coat," said Lestrade. "You wrapped the canvas around your body and walked out of the hotel, right in front of both Ryder and the porter, with neither the wiser."

"But this is madness!" cried Pardman. "Why should I do such a thing? I've been loyal to that hotel for twenty years! Ryder's your man! He's a thief, I tell you, a thief!"

"Yes," I said, "I wondered about that too. Why would you steal from your own hotel? But then I did some checking with Holmes's criminal contacts and discovered a very interesting fact."

"We know about the bookies," said Lestrade. "We know about the gambling, and we know how much you owe them. The game's up Pardman. Why don't you give us the canvas and be done with it?"

Pardman stared back at us in defeat. "Fine," he said at last. "You can have the blasted thing. No one's buying it anyway. They say it's too hot! But you have to protect me, Inspector! If I don't have the money by tomorrow, they'll kill me!"

"Then it's a good thing you're going to the safest place I know," said Lestrade. "A jail cell at the Yard."

Pardman retrieved the *Sleeping Cardinal* from its hiding place, and Lestrade took him away to an awaiting cell. That evening, with the painting in hand, Lestrade and I visited Lady Margaret to return her property. She seemed oddly cold to the *Cardinal's* recovery. In fact she hardly even bothered to thank us! But justice had been served, and I felt satisfied.

"And that, Holmes," I said, "is the story of how we recovered the *Sleeping Cardinal*."

Holmes, who had been smoking as he listened, opened his eyes and laid his calabash pipe on the mantle. "An entertaining tale, Doctor," he said. "I'm sure the readers of the *Strand Magazine* will enjoy it."

"Oh, I'll never write it up," I said. "It's your adventures they want, not mine."

Holmes smiled. "Ah, but perhaps I had more to do with the case than you realize."

"How do you figure, Holmes?"

"Did you never wonder who sent you the mysterious telegram?"

"Well," I said, "I had always assumed the message came from your brother, Mycroft."

"You are only partly correct," said Holmes. "The telegram was indeed from Mycroft. The message, on the other hand, was from me."

"You?" I said, astonished.

"I had requested that my brother keep tabs on you during my absence," said Holmes, "along with sending me full reports of your progress. When he sent me Lestrade's police report on your involvement with the robbery of the *Sleeping Cardinal*, I could not help but smile."

I sighed. "At how poorly I performed the investigation?"

"My dear fellow," said Holmes, "you underestimate yourself. You had the tenacity to question the obvious while Lestrade rushed toward the easiest conclusion. I knew if we provided you a small push in the right direction you would find the truth. No, I smiled as, despite my absence, you were still in the game."

"Ah," I said. "Well, thank you, Holmes."

"You did, however, miss one avenue of investigation."

"Oh? And what's that?"

"I find it difficult to believe," said Holmes, "that a woman who has just had her priceless painting stolen would immediately demand compensation rather than the canvas' recovery. I find it very probable that she planned the theft together with Mr. Pardman."

"Now, Holmes, that really is too much!"

"Consider the facts," said Holmes. "Consider that Pardman knew immediately how to smuggle the painting out of the hotel, almost as if he'd had advance warning. Consider that Lady Margaret chose not to store her painting in the gallery where it was to be exhibited, but instead to store it in a hotel safe. Consider also that she chose not to stay in a hotel near the exhibition, but instead a hotel owned by the richest man in London?"

"Good Lord," I said. "I have been blind all these years."

"Ah, but we shall never know for certain," said Holmes. "It was her estate sale you saw in the paper. Lady Margaret died last week. But cheer up, Watson. You did find the thief and recover the *Sleeping Cardinal*. As good an outcome as could be hoped for."

"Well," I said, "after your telegram provided a thread to follow, the solution was . . . er . . . ." I hesitated, wondering if I should dare.

"Go ahead and say it, Watson," said Holmes. "You've earned it."

"Why, it was elementary, my dear Holmes," I said. "Elementary."

The Case of the
Anarchist's Bomb
by Bill Crider

I have found but few joys in growing old. My great friend, Sherlock Holmes, no longer bids me to go adventuring, and spends his days keeping his apiary, while I, a superannuated physician, find that more and more often my afternoons are passed in looking over my notes on the many unrecorded cases that, for one reason or another, I failed to see into print in my younger and more enthusiastic years. There is, I confess, a bit of pleasure in recalling adventures long past, and for a moment I can almost hear Holmes's voice: "Come, Watson! The game's afoot!" Yet I know that in reality I am not likely to hear that voice again.

There is also a modicum of entertainment to be found in knowing that some portion of the public still takes the time on occasion to read one of my accounts of those long-gone days. Holmes often made light of those writings and sometimes resorted to what I considered ridicule; he would be quite amused, I am certain, to know that even now I receive an occasional letter about them, and that the letters often contain questions concerning what the writers consider serious discrepancies in the many stories, discrepancies in such things as the location of a certain wound caused by a Jezail bullet, or the precise order of various events in the lives of either me or Holmes or the both of us.

Having always thought that the answers to such questions were obvious, I have seldom bothered to respond to the letters, but perhaps that was boorish of me. I shall now state the obvious this one time only, and that will have to suffice for all who would ask about these things. I happily confess that the stories I set down, while accurate in most of their details, were perhaps not accurate in all. This is true for a number of reasons, some of which need not be mentioned, though the most prominent of them is simply that there are times when I am not certain myself of just where or when a certain event might have taken place. My notes are often jotted down in haste and present only the merest outline of events. Trying to set them in order at a later date is not always possible, thanks to the fallibility of human memory.

To take just one example, I know that it is generally considered true that Holmes returned to England in April, 1894, having been absent for quite some time after the regrettable incident at the Reichenbach Falls. It is possible, however, that the date is in error. As I said, I am not always certain about those things. Just why is hard to explain, but in perusing my notes for a specific case, I can see why I am necessarily unsure about things in that particular year. Perhaps if I put the incidents on paper, I will clarify matters for myself, if not for others.

It was February of 1894 when I received one evening a note from a man whom I did not know well, but with whom I had previously had dealings through Sherlock Holmes. The man was no less than Holmes's brother, Mycroft, and his note was a request for me to join him at the Diogenes Club for a conversation about a matter of extreme urgency.

I was, of course, puzzled by this, and wondered what Mycroft could possibly want of me. He is, beyond doubt, one of the oddest men in London, and one of the most intelligent. He had even on occasion given advice to Holmes about one or another of his cases, though that was not his main interest in life. He was a gatherer and an absorber of information, so much information, in fact, and so well ordered in the massive files of his mind, that he had made himself virtually indispensable to the government, and a word from him could establish or alter national policy. Holmes had done him a favor from time to time, and I had been involved to some extent, but merely as an assistant who acted when called upon and directed. All the ratiocination had been Holmes's.

My curiosity being aroused, I made myself ready and took a cab to the Diogenes Club, which is located in Pall Mall, along with many others. The Traveller's Club, the Athenaeum, and the Reform Club are well known. The Diogenes Club is not. It is as odd as Mycroft himself, being a haven for people who as a rule would never enter a club. It is understood that everyone who enters must be absolutely silent. No one must take any notice of anyone else. Those who do not obey the rules are summarily ejected.

It was a dank February evening, with a gray fog that slid along the streets and shrouded the stone buildings in dampness. Lights flickered dimly in the windows. I paid the cabbie and entered the club. I found myself in a long hallway paneled with glass through which I could see the club itself, its members sitting apart from one another, reading silently or simply staring off into space.

169

There is a small visitor's room just off the hallway where talking is permitted, and it was into this room that I directed my step. Mycroft was already there waiting for me, and my first impression was that he had grown even larger than he had been at our last encounter. He is quite the trencherman if one is to judge by his appearance, and Holmes had once told me that his brother's only exercise was the short walk between his rooms and the Diogenes Club. As a physician, I suppose I should have taken it upon myself to give Mycroft some advice on how to better care for himself, but he was not the sort of man who solicited advice or took it unsolicited, so I never broached the topic with him.

"Ah, Dr. Watson," said he as I entered the room. "Do have a seat. You'll pardon me if I don't rise."

"Of course," said I, removing my coat and hat and hanging them on a rack. It would have been difficult for him to rise, for he seemed to take up much of the small room with his bulk. The chair he sat in must have been especially made to accommodate him. I took a seat in the room's other chair, one of normal size.

Mycroft watched me settle myself with his peculiar light gray eyes. When I was comfortable, he said, "You have heard, I am sure, of this afternoon's sad affair of the Frenchman in Greenwich Park."

Indeed I had, but only because one of my patients had told me of it, for I, unlike Sherlock Holmes, was not a diligent reader of sensational newspaper articles. And this event had been quite sensational. A young Frenchman and known anarchist, Martial Bourdin, had fallen in Greenwich Park, and in doing so had exploded a bomb that he had in his possession. It had blown off his left hand and destroyed a goodly portion of his stomach.

"He was literally hoist by his own petard,'" said I, after asserting my knowledge of the affair. "An unfortunate fall."

"For Boudin, yes, but not for us," said Mycroft. "It is most fortunate that he did not reach his destination, for who knows what damage he might have done."

He paused and looked at me as if expecting me to speak. It was almost as if Holmes were in the room, for he often seemed to think I had the power to reason as he did. "You know my methods," he would say, and wait for me to bring forth some kind of response. Mycroft was fully his equal at waiting.

"What damage might that have been?" I asked after a while.

"Ah, that is the question," Mycroft said. "Or one of the questions, at any rate. Sherlock often said you had a way of getting to the heart of things, and I can see that he was correct."

I was flattered, though I should not have been, as I had no idea what he was talking about.

"You see," Mycroft continued, "we have no idea what Boudin's purpose was. Why did he have that bomb? Where was he going?"

"Surely he was going to the observatory," I answered. "He was a known anarchist and an associate of others of his stripe, possibly the leader of a gang of them. He had the intention of destroying the observatory."

"Highly unlikely," Mycroft said. "Think, Watson."

I thought, again trying to apply Holmes's methods. Eventually I thought I could see where Mycroft was aiming.

"A bomb large enough to destroy the observatory would not simply have blown away a man's hand and part of his stomach," I said. "It would have scattered him over a considerable area."

Mycroft smiled a thin smile. "You are correct. Therefore his intent was not to destroy the observatory. And there is more to the story. Bourdin was carrying a large sum of money. Where did the money come from? Boudin was a tailor, and he was not a rich man. Lately he had worked but little. He must have been given the money for some reason having to do with the bomb. Who gave him the money? Why? Bourdin lived long enough to tell us these things, but he refused to do so, and he soon died of his injuries. We need those answers."

It was a rare puzzle, indeed, but I still had no idea why Mycroft was discussing it with me. My association with Holmes may have sharpened my wits to some extent, but I was never his equal in the art of deduction. Mycroft was, of course, but he applied his powers to different ends, and besides, he could not be bothered to stir outside beyond his rooms or the Diogenes Club. With that thought, I began to see what need he might have of me, and he confirmed my suspicion with his next words.

"Within the hour," said he, "the police will raid the Autonomie Club, where Bourdin was a member. Perhaps you have heard of it."

"A notorious nest of anarchists," I replied.

Mycroft gave a minute nod. "So it is said. At any rate, I need a man among the police. There is no one I would trust as much as you to report what they find. You might also learn much of interest that they might miss. They are, after all, only the police, and no match for Sherlock Holmes."

171

"Nor am I a match for him," said I.

"You may surprise yourself," Mycroft said, and began to struggle to his feet.

I rose myself, still somewhat at a loss, and offered to assist him, but he managed to rise on his own.

"You will find a cab outside," he told me. "I have arranged for the driver to be at your disposal this evening and for as long as you need him. He will be your assistant in this matter."

Ah, if only Holmes could have been there. He would have much appreciated this game I was about to enter upon, and to tell the truth, I would have been much more comfortable as his assistant than in having an assistant of my own, much less some cabbie I had never met. Still, if he had Mycroft's recommendation, he must be a good man. I donned my coat and hat and told Mycroft that I would do as well as I could.

"And you will do admirably," said he. "But you must hurry, for the raid is scheduled for nine o'clock. You need to be at the club when it begins." He handed me a folded paper. "This letter is all you will need to show the police, should they ask for your bona fides. Keep it safe."

I slipped the letter into an inner pocket of my coat and bid Mycroft farewell.

When I emerged from the Diogenes Club, I discovered that the fog had thickened and that the evening had turned much colder. I drew my coat around me and looked for the cab that Mycroft had said would be there. I spied a hansom at the curb a short distance from the door and made my way to it. When I reached it, a man stepped out of the shadows beside it and said in a raspy voice, "Good evening, guv'nor. Do I have the honor of addressing Dr. John Watson?"

"You do," I responded. "And what is your name?"

"You can call me Albert, sir. It's an honor to be lending you a hand this evening. I hear of you and Sherlock Holmes everywhere, and I have read of your adventures."

Albert wore a dark slouch hat pulled down low on his forehead so that the brim covered his eyes, and I could not make out his features. He was slumped in his heavy coat so that I had difficulty judging his height, but I had the impression that he was taller than he appeared. In a way he looked vaguely familiar, but I had ridden in many cabs in London, and I might very well have had this driver before.

"I am flattered that you have read my transcriptions of the cases of Sherlock Holmes," I told him.

172

"There's just one thing, sir," said he, "if you'll pardon the impertinence. Are not those tales of yours a bit exaggerated?"

"Nothing of the sort," said I. "And now we must be off to the Autonomie Club. Do you know the way?"

"Certainly, sir," said he, without further comment, and as I climbed into the cab between the wooden-spoked wheels, he mounted to his outside seat above and behind me.

"Ready, sir?" he asked when he was seated, his voice coming through the small trap door that was situated to aid our communication.

"Indeed I am."

He clucked to his horse, and we were off, the cloppity sound of the horse's hooves on the street being muffled by the fog. The leather curtains in front of me were drawn closed in deference to the cold, and as there was nothing to see out the side windows, all being shrouded in the fog, I used the time to speculate about what Mycroft had told me. As I saw it, if I could find out who had given Boudin the money, the other answers to the other questions posed by Mycroft would be easier to find. Unfortunately, I had no idea of how to go about doing so, and nothing came to mind during our drive to the Autonomie Club.

"I believe I should stop here," Albert said when we were about a block from the club.

I peered out the window of the cab, and although the fog was a barrier to sight, I could see that a number of vehicles were stopped ahead of us and that policemen stood outside the door of the club. It appeared that they were arresting late-arriving members, who seemed astonished but cooperative, at least for the moment.

Others were there, as well, many of them carrying signs. I had read of these people in the newspapers. The signs they carried all expressed approximately the same sentiment, which could be boiled down to "anarchists go home," as they believed that all foreigners were anarchists and they wanted nothing to do with them. I myself had no sympathy for anarchists, but I knew quite a few immigrants who had no interest in anarchy at all.

"Yes," I said to Albert. "Stop here. We do not want to interfere with the police. Perhaps I should introduce myself to their commander and see what I can learn."

Albert got down to assist my exit from the cab, and when I was firmly on the pavement, he said, "Sir, might it not be better if we did not announce ourselves? The police do not welcome outsiders."

173

I thought about some of the Scotland Yard inspectors, who had no love for me and Sherlock Holmes, but they did not appear to be among the policemen here. Even at that, Albert's advice was sound. We might learn more if we were discreet.

I noticed that he had said "we" should not announce ourselves.

"Are you coming with me?" I asked.

"That was my commission from Mr. Mycroft Holmes," said he. "I am to accompany and assist you."

"Very well. Come along and we shall see what we can discover."

As we walked toward the club, I reached inside my coat to make sure that Mycroft's letter was still there, as indeed it was. I wanted to be sure to have it in case it became necessary to produce it. Already there seemed to be a bit of confusion at the club, however, and I thought that Albert's suggestion would prove to be the best approach.

Just as we arrived at the entrance to the club, one of the tardy members took serious offense at his arrest. He began to fling his arms about, striking several officers, while yelling in French. All the officers closed around him in an attempt to pin him to the wall. One of the other men tried to strike the Frenchman with his sign, and his companions began shouting. They appeared much more dangerous than the supposed anarchists who were being arrested, and were clearly intent on doing the Frenchman serious harm. The police found themselves very much occupied in sorting out the confusion, though they appeared to be getting the situation under control.

"A happy diversion," said Albert. "Follow me, Doctor."

It seemed that Albert had promoted himself from assistant to leader, but I chose not to argue. Instead, I followed him as he slipped past the busy policemen and entered the club, which was not nearly so luxurious as the Diogenes Club, nor was it as quiet. Men stood in small groups, talking in loud voices and various languages. There was no doorman, and I suppose anarchists would not approve of such a thing.

"Did you recognize any of those men outside?" Albert asked me.

"You mean the members of this club?" I responded.

"No. I mean among the others. The ones carrying the signs. It seemed to me that one of them was familiar."

I had often wished that I had the gift for faces that Sherlock Holmes possessed, but I did not. Still, I took a few moments to attempt to recall the men we had seen outside. The light had not been good, but I had glimpsed several of them. The one who had tried to strike the Frenchman with his sign did indeed look familiar, and after a several moments I remembered why.

"One of them was Henry Starnes," I said. "He is a leader of a group of nativists whose goal is to expel all foreigners, starting with those who have an anarchistic bent. I have seen his photograph in the newspapers. He is seeking a seat in parliament."

"I believe you are correct," Albert said, and then he sidled up to group of men in which the speakers were English, and I went along.

"The coppers will soon be coming in," Albert said when there was a lull in the talking and gesticulating. "Is there another way out?"

"Of course there is," said a big fellow with a red face and bristling hair. "But we shall not take it. We are not cowards. We have a right to assemble here and talk as we wish. And who are you, might I ask?"

"A friend of Martial Bourdin."

"Hah. The very rascal who's brought this raid upon us. Well, you might be seeking a cowardly way out, for the police will want to have more than mere words with you if you are his friend."

I had no idea what Albert could be up to, but he seemed to be quite comfortable in what he was doing.

"I do not fear the police," said he. "I do care about my friend."

"He was no friend of mine," the man said, and the others near him nodded as if to say he was not their friend, either. "Bourdin had few friends here."

"He must have had someone who cared enough about him to want to know the truth about what happened," said Albert.

"Perhaps Delebeck," said a short, stout man wearing spectacles. "He was Bourdin's landlord." He indicated a man in middle age with graying hair and a military carriage who stood alone near the wall opposite us.

"Thank you," said Albert. "Come, Doctor."

Once again, I followed. Albert had hidden depths.

Delebeck saw us coming, and while he did not appear eager to speak with us, neither did he flee. When we reached him, Albert nudged me in the ribs. Clearly he expected me to know what to do at this point, so I introduced myself.

"The very same Dr. John Watson who writes the amusing stories about his friend Sherlock Holmes?" Delebeck said. He looked at Albert. "And is this the great man himself?"

Albert and I chuckled. "No," said I, "this is Albert, who drives a cab, which we may be able to use, by the way."

175

"Use?" said Delebeck. "For what purpose? And for that matter, why are you here, Dr. Watson?"

"I am looking into the death of your boarder, Martial Bourdin."

"Indeed. In what capacity?"

"On behalf of Her Majesty's government," I thought to say as I reached for the letter from Mycroft, but then I remembered that Delebeck was an anarchist or at the very least an associate of anarchists. The letter would be more likely to anger him than to impress him.

"I am simply interested in the case," I said after a moment, trying to think what Holmes might say. "It has certain elements that intrigue me."

"I can understand why it might," Delebeck said. "I do not trust the police to find out anything about my friend's death. However, Dr. Watson, if your stories are not exaggerated, I believe I can trust you."

I tried not to take offense at his remark about the stories, though I thought I heard a low laugh from Albert.

"Your trust would not be misplaced," I told Delebeck.

"Then we should be leaving," Albert said. "For the police are now entering."

His hearing was sharper than mine, but I turned to see that he was correct and that the officers were now coming in through the front door.

"There is a back entrance, I believe," said I. "Let us take advantage of it."

We edged around the men grouped in the room and found a dark corridor that led to a stair going down to a door. We passed through the hall and then the doorway without hindrance and found ourselves in an odorous alleyway, enfolded in fog.

"Wait here," said Albert, "while I fetch the cab."

I was not happy to be left there, and I could see that Delebeck felt the same. However, we had little choice, as Albert walked away and was almost instantly lost in the fog.

While we stood there, I tried to think of the kind of questions that Holmes would be asking, were he standing beside me, and in that moment I missed him more keenly than ever. However, even as I wondered how he would have managed the situation, something occurred to me.

"Were you at home today when your boarder left?" I asked.

"I was, but you must know that I had nothing to do with this sad affair. I was entirely ignorant of anything concerning a bomb. While Martial and I both distrust the government and would like to be rid of it,

176

neither of us is violent in any way. We have made protests. We have agitated, but resort to violence? Never."

He sounded as if he were telling the truth, though one can never be certain about such things.

"Have the police searched Bourdin's rooms?" I asked.

"No, but I have been expecting them all day. Surely they must know by now where he lived."

Having experienced the methods of Inspector Lestrade, I was not so sure, and I was happy that we would have the first look at Bourdin's lodgings, even though my own search of them would never match one that Holmes would conduct.

"What about money?" I asked. "Was Bourdin quite rich?"

"Not at all. I have heard that he had a large sum with him when the bomb exploded, but I cannot say where the money came from."

"He did not have it with him when he left?"

"He may have," Delebeck said. "I broke my fast at the club this morning, and when I returned, he came out of his room and brushed past me without a word. That in itself was unusual. He had two parcels with him, but he was out the door before I could ask about them."

This was all interesting information, though I knew not what to make of it. I had no time to inquire further, as Albert came into the alley with the cab and stopped for us. He asked Delebeck where he lived, and Delebeck gave an address on Fitzroy Street. As soon as we were seated in the cab, Albert took us out of the alley and down the street at a sedate pace, turning away from the Autonomie Club and easily avoiding detection by the police, who by now were all occupied on the inside of the club. The men with the signs had all been sent on their way, and the foggy sidewalks were quiet.

I tapped on the small door between me and Albert, and he opened it at once. I smelled pipe smoke and heard him puffing away. On an impulse I did not quite understand, I conveyed to him what Delebeck had told me. He made no comment other than to say that we would do well to be careful of how we handled matters from this point forward, as it appeared that powerful forces were involved. I was about to ask his meaning, but he shut the door and cut off our communication.

"Have you and Bourdin talked often about the overthrow of the government?" I asked Delebeck. "In a theoretical way, of course."

"Of course. Naturally, we are opposed to the government. But we are also opposed to violence, Martial more than I. I cannot imagine him planning to use a bomb."

"Is it possible he would not have discussed such plans with you?"

"Yes, as he was a secretive sort, he might have kept it from me, especially knowing my nonviolent leanings. Yet I believe he would have told me of some plan to bomb the observatory."

Delebeck might have said more, but we had arrived at the address on Fitzroy Street. Albert stopped the cab, and Delebeck and I alighted. Delebeck let us into the house and showed us the rooms where Bourdin lived.

They were quite neat, and searching them would not take long, I presumed. There was something of an odd smell in the air, but it was so faint that I could not identify it. I could tell that Albert noticed it, too, though he said nothing. Delebeck seemed to be unaware of it.

I began my search by looking at the desk and its contents, I peered into the closets, into all the drawers, and even looked underneath the bed.

"Excellent work," Albert said when I was done. "I can see why Sherlock Holmes relies on you in all his investigations."

"Er, yes," I said, "but what exactly do you mean?"

Albert walked over to the desk and pointed to a book. "To begin with, this book. When you moved it, you revealed the rail schedule underneath it."

I had not moved the book much, merely pushed it aside, and I had not noticed the paper beneath it. But before I could mention that, Albert had picked up the rail schedule and walked to the wardrobe.

"And here," said he, "you discovered that the arrangement of clothes suggested that some of them were missing. No doubt they are in the valise you spied under the bed."

In truth, I had not spied the valise, as the dim light of the room hardly reached underneath the bed, but Albert had bent over and seen it. His eyesight must have been incredibly keen. He pocketed the rail schedule and pulled the valise from beneath the bed. Setting it on the bed, he opened it.

"Ah. Neatly packed," he said. He closed the valise.

"Did Bourdin mention travel plans?" I asked Delebeck, who had been watching the proceedings.

"No, but he did miss his home in France. He had traveled in America, and he liked it even less than he likes England."

"There is something more," Albert said. "Or something less. There is something missing."

"Missing?" Delebeck said.

178

"Yes," Albert said. "As Dr. Watson has so cleverly revealed to us by his search, there is nothing in this room, nothing at all, that could have been used to make a bomb. No plans and no chemicals."

I thought again about the smell I had noticed upon entering the room, but I could no longer detect it, so I made no mention of it.

"He could have made the bomb elsewhere," said I.

"Doubtful," said Albert, and he removed the rail schedule from his pocket. He opened it and laid it on the desk. "Look at this."

He placed his finger on the schedule. The times for departures to Dover were circled.

"Bourdin was going to France," I said.

"Excellent, Dr. Watson," Albert said, and I gave him a sharp glance. He had not removed his slouch hat, and it shadowed his face. I could not see his expression.

"He had money when he died," I said. "Along with the bomb."

"Yet we can infer that he had neither in his room until someone brought them here," said Albert. "He would not want to leave the money here, even though I am sure he trusted you, Mr. Delebeck."

"But who could have brought the money?" asked Delebeck.

"That is indeed the question," I said. "Perhaps we should convey our information to the authorities, Albert."

"Very well, sir," said Albert, and we prepared to leave.

As I passed through the doorway, I brushed the jamb with the sleeve of my coat.

"Ah!" cried Albert. "Dr. Watson, you have done it again!"

"I have?"

Albert pointed to a spot or stain of some kind on the door jamb about level with my elbow. Otherwise the wood was quite clean.

"See here," said he, looking at the spot. "As you have indicated, Dr. Watson, it is likely to be of importance. Do you have an envelope?"

"Er, no, I do not."

"Never mind," Albert said, producing one from a coat pocket. "I happen to have one."

He carefully scraped a bit of the stain from the wood into the envelope. When he was done, he sealed the envelope and handed it to me.

"Keep it safe," he said, and I told him that I would.

"Good," he said with a satisfied air. "Now, is there anything more, Doctor?"

"I . . . do not believe so," said I.

179

I was not even certain about what we had, so after we had thanked Delebeck for his help and departed, I sat in the cab and tried to put things together as Holmes might have done. I had hardly begun my cogitations when Albert tapped on the communicating door.

"Have you reached any conclusions, Doctor?" he asked when I opened the door.

"Not yet," I replied. "It seems that we have a good bit of evidence, but where does it lead us?"

"What would your friend Sherlock Holmes say?"

Again I tried to apply myself to a solution. I wanted to begin at the beginning of things and move forward, but where to begin?

"The rail schedule tells us that Bourdin seemed to be planning a return to France," I said at length. "For that he needed money."

"How would he obtain it?" Albert asked. "By performing some sort of dangerous task, perhaps?"

"The bomb," said I. "Of course. He was not a violent person, according to Delebeck, but he might have resorted to placing a bomb for someone if the payment were sufficient."

"And who might have a motive to pay a known anarchist to place a bomb at the observatory?"

The horse plodded along. The cold damp air invaded the cab, and it seemed to clarify my thoughts.

"Someone who could gain something or advance his cause," I said. "Or both."

"Someone like Henry Starnes?" Albert asked.

"Yes. This incident will cause many more people in England to turn against all anarchists, but especially those from other countries. Starnes and his nativists will certainly gain a greater voice in politics. His seat in parliament would be assured."

"Very sound, Doctor," said Albert. "And if Starnes wanted to cause a commotion rather than do real damage, the observatory would be a sufficient target. Well known, but not essential to the nation's business."

"The death of Bourdin, though. He could not have predicted that."

"No. It must have been accidental. Perhaps Bourdin fell and activated the bomb prematurely, thus bringing about his own demise."

"It sounds very likely," said I, "but we have no proof."

"I think we do," said Albert. "Did you not notice a certain smell in Bourdin's rooms?"

"Yes, but I could not put a name to it. It was faint and had soon faded away completely."

"As if it might have been brought there on someone's clothing," Albert said. "Like whatever stained the doorframe."

Suddenly it came to me. "Paint," I said. "The smell was oil paint."

"Such as might be used to paint a sign," Albert said. "I believe that if the sample in the envelope were to be compared to the signs of Starnes's group, it would be the same."

I was momentarily elated, but something occurred to me. "Many people might have used that paint. We have no proof that it was Starnes."

"Mycroft Holmes will soon find out by examining his clothing," said Albert. "And he will question everyone along Fitzroy Street. Someone will have seen Starnes there."

He was correct, and I felt sure that now I had solved the problem Mycroft had set me.

"We have arrived at the Diogenes Club," Albert said.

The cab came to a stop, and I made my exit without assistance. I stood on the sidewalk, waiting for Albert to join me, but he clucked to the horse and the cab moved away.

"Wait," I called. "You must come in and speak to Mycroft with me."

"You have no further need of my assistance, Doctor. You have done a wonderful job on your own."

"It was not entirely on my own," said I, but he appeared not to hear me as the cab moved away and was swallowed up by the fog. I looked after him for a moment and then went inside the club to present my findings to Mycroft.

Perhaps now my readers are aware of why I have some misgivings about dating the return of Holmes to England as late as April of 1894. He was a clever man when it came to disguise, and during his career he fooled everyone, including me, more times than I care to enumerate. Could he have done it once again? If so, he never mentioned it after his recognized return. But now, after the passage of many years, most especially on cold winter nights when the fog settles over all, I still wonder about the case of the anarchist's bomb and just who was helping whom.

181

The Riddle of the
Rideau Rifles
by Peter Calamai

As I write these lines, a dreadful darkness is descending over the civilized world. In Europe, only Britain, Ireland, and neutral Sweden and Switzerland remain free from the Nazis, and yet the United States of America remains on the sidelines as Herr Hitler extends his mailed grip around the Mediterranean and North Africa. Canada and the other self-governing Dominions are doing all they can to help our Mother Country. But without the industrial and military might of America on our side soon, I fear for the future of humanity.

This is not a propitious time to make public the tale which I recount here. Its publication now could arouse further those isolationist and anti-war sentiments already too evident among our neighbours to the south. But it is a story which the world should hear someday, and while I am still able I must record how brilliant detective work averted what would have been a calamitous international incident between Canada and the United States.

Yet I am getting ahead of myself. In writing this narrative I have drawn upon my personal diaries and other original documents in my possession. Once I completed my task I destroyed those documents, lest others reveal matters that I believe must remain forever secret. To my nephew Jonathan – or indeed to his progeny – I leave the decision about when to publish this account of the wisest man I have ever known.

Bartholomew Evans
Ottawa, November, 1940.

The little water remaining in the Rideau Canal was still frozen solid that March Tuesday in 1894 when the Private Secretary informed me that the Prime Minister, Sir John Thompson, wished to see me. I hurried along the corridor in the Centre Block where I, a very junior aide, was privileged to share a cramped office with several other young men. To my surprise, I was instantly ushered into the Prime Minister's office.

"Evans, I have an important task for you," Sir John said without preamble. "Read these."

From a pile on his desk, the Prime Minister handed me what I recognized, even at that early stage of my career, as a sheaf of state papers. Or more precisely, fair copies of those papers. They revealed an astonishing development.

That great Liberal, William Gladstone, then Prime Minister of Great Britain for the fourth (and final) time, had written my Prime Minister, soliciting his support publicly for a movement called the Anglo-American reunion, which sought the ultimate federation of the entire English-speaking world.

"We would thus repair the ruction with America caused by the folly of George III and the blundering of Lord North," Gladstone wrote.

Sir John had replied (no doubt also by diplomatic bag) that he was well disposed toward the idea, but domestic circumstances forbade any public show of support. His letter then marshalled facts of which I had been utterly unaware.

My Prime Minister said mysterious elements in Ottawa had begun fomenting anti-American sentiment within the past year, and their machinations had found favour in his own caucus and, indeed, even within his cabinet. Despite discreet yet concerted inquiries by Colonel Arthur Percy Sherwood of the Dominion Police, the source of this campaign remained unidentified.

"Until it is known and scotched, my hands are tied and I dare not act as you request," Thompson had written.

The third and last letter was the response from Gladstone. He well understood Thompson's predicament, he wrote, and had a possible solution to offer. With our approval, the British Prime Minister would dispatch a personal representative to investigate the anti-American phenomenon. Although the investigator was as yet unknown to the wider world, his detecting talents were highly recommended by Mr. Gladstone's closest advisor, a man who sometimes constituted the entire British government because of his unparalleled knowledge of every portfolio.

"I agreed, of course, Evans. What else could I do? I have just had a cable saying that this man is arriving by train in an hour. Apparently his name is Sigerson. Your task is to offer him every assistance, acting with my full authority. But keep me informed as well."

So overwhelmed was I by this sudden revelation of domestic unrest and secret prime ministerial investigations that it was all I could manage to stammer my assent and retreat from Sir John's presence, clutching the sheaf of papers. A quick consultation with the Private Secretary revealed that a suite of rooms had been booked at the Russell Hotel for Mr. Sigerson.

I met Gladstone's representative at the station what seemed like mere minutes later. My first impressions were favourable. Mr. Sigerson carried himself with a quiet authority beyond his years, which I judged to be about forty. Spaced widely above an aquiline nose, his grey eyes darted constantly, taking in details. When we shook hands his grip was firm, and his figure, while slight, was wiry. He stood perhaps an inch or more taller than my five-foot-ten. I judged that Mr. Sigerson would be a good fellow to have beside you in an altercation, should our mission come to that. Just as I completed this surveillance, he spoke:

"I am going to address you as Evans and you should call me Sigerson, now that you've taken my measure," he said with a wry smile. "Our first order of business must be to gather data. I cannot make bricks without straw."

I was to discover in our short time together that Sigerson (as I indeed came to call him) was given to uttering such homilies leaning heavily toward Biblical and classical allusions. From this habit and his precise manner of speaking, I judged that he was a university man like myself, although a product of the English system and a decade my senior. Yet I failed utterly during the next few days to draw from him whether he had attended Oxford or Cambridge.

My own university connections from Queen's, however, could serve us well for this sensitive mission. Many of my fellows were now placed within the federal government as I was, not yet exercising great authority, but in positions where their fingers rested on many quivering strands of information.

We agreed that we would conceal Sigerson's real mission in Ottawa, telling people instead that he was an academic from Norway making a study of Canada-U.S. relations as a possible parallel to Scandinavia. We left his bags at the Russell and took the chance of calling on two of my Queen's connections without making appointments.

In the first of what turned out to be continual surprises, not only did Sigerson immediately begin to speak English with what sounded to my ears like a Norwegian lilt, but he also somehow contrived to *appear* Scandinavian, if not actually Norwegian.

Unfortunately, the first interview with a university contemporary elicited little more than some embarrassing sobriquets by which I had been known in certain undergraduate circles. The second classmate, however, suggested it might be worthwhile for us to talk with a friend of his, Jack Wells, who was with the detective service of the Ottawa city police.

"I will send a note saying that you will call this afternoon. If there have been any day-to-day incidents arising from tensions between Canada and the U.S., Jack is the fellow to know," said my classmate.

After a modest lunch, we walked to the police station and were quickly shown into the office of Detective Inspector Jack Wells. Events intervened even as we took our seats.

"I apologize if I seem somewhat distracted, gentlemen, but I received information of the most distressing nature only hours ago," said Wells. A few questions from Sigerson drew out the whole story.

A promising young detective constable named O'Reilly had been killed in a fall early that morning, apparently after a bar room brawl. His battered body, reeking of liquor, had been found on the stone bottom of a drained lock of the Rideau Canal, adjacent to an old government building known as the Commissariat.

"It's a black eye for the force, sure enough, but worse than that, his family won't be eligible for any pension because he wasn't on duty when he died. And the wife has two small children to rear by herself."

"What ought O'Reilly to have been investigating, Inspector?" I asked.

"Smuggling, Mr. Evans. We have reason to believe that someone is attempting to smuggle explosives into Canada. It could be some latter-day remnants of the Fenians."

I quickly informed Sigerson about the rag-tag Irish-American nationalists who had sought thirty years earlier to "capture" Canada and hold it hostage until Britain granted independence to Ireland. With the exception of one raid, their military forays into Canada had been failures and, by the early 1870's, the Fenian Brotherhood had vanished.

"I should like to examine the constable's body," Sigerson said without preamble. "My knowledge of advanced forensic techniques has proven useful to authorities in the past."

Wells replied, "I don't see that any harm can arise from that. We will do anything to get to the bottom of this tragedy."

In the station's basement mortuary, Sigerson drew from an inner coat pocket a magnificent brass-bound magnifying glass. Not that one was needed to see the terrible bruises, mottled yellow and purple, which covered almost every part of the constable's body. Instead, Sigerson studiously applied his glass to the man's hands, wrists, forearms and ankles. From one wrist he plucked something with a pair of tweezers,

185

placing it in a small envelope. He did the same with a scraping from the sole of one of the constable's shoes.

"Your constable didn't die as a result of a bar room brawl or even a tumble onto the lock bottom, Inspector," Sigerson announced as we mounted the station stairs. "He was beaten to death by several men who used clubs and also their feet, and they delivered the fatal blows when he was bound and unable to defend himself. It was homicide, likely deliberate murder."

"You astonish me, Mr. Sigerson. How can you possibly know this?" asked Wells.

"Because the constable himself told me, or rather the evidence of his body did. The backs of his hands and forearms are cut and battered, the classic wounds suffered by someone trying to defend himself against a superior force which overwhelmed him in an initial assault.

"Rope burns around his ankles and wrists indicate he was struggling against restraints. I would hypothesize that he was beaten while bound in an attempt to extract some information. When your police surgeon performs an autopsy, he will likely discover many broken ribs, and possibly tibia and fibula as well. Those would not result from your standard drunken brawl."

The Inspector was beside himself with excitement.

"If this is true, it will be a capital piece of good news in this sorry affair, Mr. Sigerson. Not only would it remove the stain from the constable's character, and from the force's, but it would go a long way toward convincing the commissioners to award a service pension to O'Reilly's widow. Is there no way to obtain some evidentiary proof?"

Sigerson replied: "I took the liberty of removing a small sample of the rope fibre that was adhering to the constable's skin. With access to a dark-field microscope, I expect to identify its origin. I have written a small monograph about distinguishing fibres of the seventy-three most common ropes."

As luck would have it, another of my Queen's contemporaries had recently been seconded as an assistant to George M. Dawson, the second-in-command of the Geological Survey of Canada, which was Canada's oldest scientific agency. The survey was housed in a former hotel on Sussex Street and would have the latest in microscopes. I undertook to get in touch with my colleague and arrange access to the specialized equipment for a "distinguished scientific visitor from Norway." Sigerson and I agreed to reconvene Wednesday at the hotel.

That morning we called first upon Jephro Clarke, also a friend from college. He turned out to possess an ample supply of the sort of "straw" sought by the British/Norwegian investigator to form the "bricks" of his case.

"Yes, I myself have noticed anti-American sentiments about town, and not just the letters to the editor in the *Free Press*, *Journal*, and *Citizen*. They are particularly strong in a society to which I belong," Clarke confided.

"Pray tell us more, Mr. Clarke. Omit no detail, no matter how trivial it may seem to you," Sigerson urged.

"There is not much to relate, Mr. Sigerson. I am a member of the Hibernian Debating Society, an assemblage of good fellows who convene every Thursday evening for invigorating discourse about matters of topical concern. We normally gather in a meeting room of an inn on Duke Street and then adjourn downstairs afterwards to the public bar where the discussion continues, usually becoming somewhat more animated.

"Yet animus has never been a feature of our discussions, at least not until these past months. A few members began voicing opinions antagonistic towards our American neighbours, and the sentiment seems to have gained a hold, certainly among some of the more vocal members."

"Is there anything which distinguishes these particular men?" I asked. Sigerson shot me what I imagined was a look of approval.

"Not really, Bart. They're relatively new here in town but mostly from up the Valley, so there's the usual touch of Irish somewhere in their background. You hear traces of it when they talk. But they're solid fellows. I had occasion to recommend two of them, a father and son, to my superior for employment when we were faced with a sudden double vacancy at the Commissariat."

At the second mention in two days of this building, Sigerson raised a quizzical eyebrow, and Clarke elaborated. Like me, he was a personal aide, in his case to the Deputy Minister of Militia and Defence. The department was responsible for the Commissariat Building, a substantial stone edifice beside the lowermost locks of the Rideau Canal. Dating from 1827, the building had originally stored tools and equipment during the canal construction. For the past four decades, it had served as a storehouse for military goods, with an armourer and carpenter actually living on the premises. The current holders of those posts had been recruited from the Hibernia membership after the previous incumbents

187

were discharged by the Clerk of Military Stores, the official with day-to-day responsibility for the building.

"I am heading over that way myself on a small errand, gentlemen. If you would like to accompany me I can show you around and introduce you to the Pattersons, father and son."

It was but a short walk to the west side of the locks and a gentle descent from Parliament Hill (formerly Barrack Hill) to the Commissariat. Somewhat to my surprise, Sigerson cross-questioned Clarke about the changing uses of the building and the various structural additions and subtractions. This inquisition continued as we toured the three floors, with Clarke throwing open doors to reveal stores of tunics, boots, infantry greatcoats, serge trousers, forage caps, braces, brushes for hair, shoes and cloth, button sticks, eating utensils, and all else necessary to keep a battalion of soldiers well shod, well clothed and well fed.

On the second floor, Sigerson opened one door himself. "This is far neater than I would have expected," he murmured.

"I believe that room is used for training purposes," responded Clarke, who did not look in. My quick glance revealed a dozen or so unmatched wooden chairs arrayed around three walls, while windows in the fourth gave a view out to the Ottawa River. Several coils of heavy rope were piled in a corner, leaving most of the floor unobstructed, probably for training demonstrations as Clarke had said. This interpretation was reinforced by the spotless nature of the floorboards, which were obviously scoured regularly.

On the main floor, a storeroom held rows of wooden crates of Snider and Martini-Henry breech-loading rifles, plus metal ammunition cases. Here Sigerson again withdrew his magnifying glass and proceeded to examine the rifle crates minutely, even dropping down onto the floor to look more closely at some detail.

He paid the same close attention to the work spaces used by the armourer and carpenter. As he was finishing that inspection, the Pattersons walked in and were introduced by Clarke. He and I moved off a few paces as Sigerson engaged the father and son in animated conversation.

"Well that was two hours very profitably spent," Sigerson said, rejoining us.

As we climbed back to street level, I informed Sigerson that he could call at the Geological Survey at his convenience to use the microscope, and he decided to go at once.

Meanwhile, I pursued my own line of inquiry. At Sigerson's request, I was to uncover everything I could about the Clerk of Military Stores, the official who had summarily dismissed the previous armourer and carpenter at the Commissariat.

This proved a more difficult task than I had imagined. Ottawa was then (and is even now) really a very small town, despite being the national capital. All persons of note are known to one another and information circulates quickly about their character and any particular foibles. But although several of my coterie could name this shadowy figure as Benjamin Saunders, none could provide any other details. Finally, through the friend of a friend of a friend, I was able to glimpse the personnel file of the man who effectively commanded the Commissariat and maintained an office there. Brimming with fresh information, I rushed back to the Russell Hotel.

Sigerson was curled comfortably into a basket chair in front of the blazing hearth in his sitting room, a darkened cherrywood pipe in one hand. From the opacity of the room's air, I hazarded that he had smoked more than one pipe.

"Yes, this is fully a three-pipe problem, my good Evans. Please tell what your inquiries have uncovered."

Restraining my excitement I marshalled and summarized the facts as logically as I knew how, for Sigerson seemed to prize ratiocination above all other virtues.

"The Clerk of Military Stores is Benjamin Saunders, although perhaps I should say Colonel Saunders, for it was his military service in the British Army which secured him the post only last year. One of his letters of recommendation came from his superior, the commanding officer of the Irish Guards.

"But the most interesting fact lies in Colonel Saunders' outside activities. My friend Clarke confirms that the clerk is an active member of the Hibernian Debating Society. Clarke also now recollects that it was Saunders who first drew the Pattersons to his attention as possible replacement artisans at the Commissariat, whose hiring Clarke in turn recommended to his Deputy Minister."

"Did you discover anything further about the two men who left so precipitately?" Sigerson asked casually, blowing out a smoke ring.

"They have disappeared from town so I could not talk with them. But from all accounts, they had given satisfaction right up to the time when they were summarily dismissed by Saunders."

189

Sigerson appeared to be digesting this information and for a minute his eyes strayed toward a violin case on the window sill. With a shrug, he turned again to me.

"My own inquiries were also productive, Evans. The Survey indeed possessed the requisite microscope and I was able to identify the fibres which I took from Constable O'Reilly's wrist. They come from a particular type of tarred rope manufactured exclusively for the Royal Navy, although it is sometimes also supplied to Britain's colonies if they are raising their own fleets, as I understand Canada is.

"Making use of this information requires us to have been especially observant. Would you please provide me with a description of the empty room we saw at the Commissariat, my dear Evans?"

It was a test, and I strove to come up to the mark, repeating the details mentioned earlier.

"Have I missed anything of importance, Sigerson," I inquired.

"Only everything," he replied with a sigh. "You see, Evans, but you do not observe. In contrast, I immediately noticed a ladderback chair along the west wall which showed rope wear on the lower portion of the front legs. And in that pile of ropes, the top coil was a tarred hemp which I wager will match the fibres from the constable's wrists.

"As well, the spotless nature of the floor is suspicious in a room devoted to training. I fear the floor had been only recently scrubbed to remove blood stains, and that it was in that room that Constable O'Reilly received his fatal final beating. Despite poisoning myself with three pipes, however, I am no closer to understanding how he got there and why someone thought his death was necessary."

I was beginning to lose patience with this self-indulgent performance. "Is there anything else I should have noticed at the Commissariat, Mr. Sigerson?" I asked with some asperity.

"I draw your attention to the curious use of nails in the end pieces of the gun crates. Also worth a second look are the stocks of wooden dowels beside the carpenter's bench."

He could not be drawn further on that point. Over dinner in the hotel dining room, he instead expounded knowledgeably about an astonishing range of subjects, from the bimetallic question of Montreal to the great herd of bisons of the fertile plains and the breeding cycle of the stormy petrels of British Columbia.

"I have some private inquiries to make during the day tomorrow, so perhaps we can meet here in the late afternoon and partake of some more of the hotel's excellent cooking. As well, it would be best if you could acquire a set of clothes suitable for a labourer."

"What sort of labourer?"

"Oh, nothing too exotic, someone along the lines of a beamster, wheel tapper, drayman, pot burner, or knacker. Even a guard lacer would do, although it might be too early in the year for their activity."

I am positive that Sigerson was hiding a smile behind his hand as he ran through this list of occupations, still common then toward the end of the Victorian era but likely unknown to many as I write.

Late the following afternoon, dressed as a drayman, I called at Sigerson's rooms. Instead of the investigator, I was greeted by a fellow of coarse appearance, the lower part of his face obscured by a black beard and his stout body contorted from some sort of arthritic condition. His blackened fingers and stained vest front suggested daily toil with greasy machinery.

"Do you think I will pass as a plate-maker, Evans?" the apparition asked. His accent sounded like a kinsman to the Pattersons, father and son.

I was so completely deceived by Sigerson's disguise that it was some few seconds before I replied in the affirmative.

"We are bound for the Couillard Hotel, an establishment in one of the less salubrious parts of your nation's capital, an area called LeBreton Flats, I believe. The Hibernian Debating Society will be holding its weekly discussions upstairs and then adjourn to the public bar. We will watch them from a quiet corner. If there is any talking to be done, pray let me do it. As you may have noticed, I have some small facility with accents and dialects."

The new Ottawa Electric Railway did not yet service that area, so we took a hack and had the driver let us off a short distance from the Duke Street location. As local residents, a drayman and a plate-maker obviously would arrive on foot. There was time only to settle ourselves at a secluded table with our pints before a dozen or so men descended the stairs. Among that number were the Pattersons and Colonel Saunders, but not my friend Clarke. Equally fortunate, I had been in the background when Sigerson spoke with the Pattersons at the Commissariat.

Just as I was congratulating myself on the success of our covert observations, Sigerson poured the remains of his bitter into my glass and approached the bar for a refill. While there, he made a point of talking with the Pattersons, who seemed to have no inkling of his true identity.

"Well, Evans, at last I am beginning to see the light," he said as he returned.

"I fear the case is still all dark to me," I replied.

"It is not my custom to divulge the outcome of my investigations until they are complete, a practice which sometimes causes distress to a regular companion in London." Sigerson paused and gazed briefly into the distance. A smile flickered across his bushy face.

"But matters stand differently with you, who have not had the opportunity to become inured to my difficult moods. So I will tell you the key to the whole puzzle. Those men are not, as you think from their speech, natives of the Ottawa Valley. They are in fact Irish Americans."

Not another word of explanation could I wrest from him that evening, as we sat and watched for another two hours until all the Society members had departed. As we stepped outside, Sigerson gave a triumphal cry and bent down to scoop up a finger's worth of the muddy clay protruding beside the boardwalk.

"The last piece of the puzzle," he ejaculated in triumph.

All I learned, however, was that I was to call at his rooms the next morning and also arrange through my friend Clarke for a ten o'clock rendezvous at the Commissariat to include the Pattersons, Colonel Saunders, and Clarke himself.

I remember that I did not get much sleep that night and called so early that Sigerson had only just completed his toilet. He insisted on ringing for breakfast, and shortly we were joined by Detective Inspector Wells. Yet Sigerson's only reference to the case was to ensure that three constables from the Ottawa force would be present at the Commissariat.

On our walk to the Canal, he spoke of Archibald Lampman, a poet who was a public servant in Ottawa and whose work appeared in *Atlantic Monthly*, *Harper's*, and *Scribner's*. Both the Inspector and I confessed that we had never heard of Lampman or his book, *Among the Millet*. But Sigerson was an admirer and had called upon the young poet at the Post Office Department, offering praise and encouragement.

"Art in the blood is liable to take the strangest forms," he remarked enigmatically.

At the Commissariat, a choleric Colonel Saunders and a brace of truculent Pattersons awaited us.

"What is the meaning of this? Why am I being mustered like this on the say-so of some pettifogging youngster," the Colonel demanded, glaring at Clarke and then at the three uniformed constables hovering in the background.

Sigerson took charge masterfully, abandoning his Norwegian persona. He led the group to the room containing the workbenches and crates of rifles. There he explained that he was acting on behalf of Sir John Thompson, and indicated me as the Prime Minister's private secretary (a post I would, in fact, occupy later but with a different man.) His remit was to investigate the origin of recent anti-American feeling and discover how deep it went.

"And I can now answer those questions," he announced in a restrained tone. "The anti-Americanism is an elaborate hoax, a ploy to camouflage a much more sinister purpose. That goal was to stage an inconsequential armed attack against the United States, one in which no one was harmed, which would appear to have been carried out by forces from Canada, acting with official sanction. And the Commissariat served as the planning and training centre for all this."

Bedlam erupted. Who was behind such a plot? What was the intention? When would it be carried out? How? And did he have any evidence for this fantastical suggestion?

"You are looking at it," said Sigerson, pointing to a crate labelled as containing a dozen Martini-Henry rifles. "Rifles have been removed and cached for the putative assault, after which they will be abandoned as evidence of Canadian involvement."

"This is preposterous," Colonel Saunders exclaimed, stepping forward. "Try to lift that crate with the rope handles on the ends, and the weight will prove the rifles are there."

Sigerson continued in the same quiet voice. "Yes, I concede that the crate feels heavy enough to suggest nothing is amiss. The men behind this plot, although in my opinion seriously deluded, are at least cunning. Yet they were undone, as in that old adage, by something as common as a nail."

He tapped the end of the crate with his walking stick.

"I tried to draw Mr. Evans' attention to the peculiar nails in these endpieces. They are of a larger size than the nails used elsewhere in the crates. That is because the original nails have been extracted to remove the endpieces, which were modified and replaced. If you look carefully, you will also notice a few holes from the original nails in which someone failed to properly place the larger nails."

Sigerson offered his magnifying glass and the Inspector took a look.

"I dare say you are correct, Mr. Sigerson, but I don't see how this proves the rifles are missing, much less the serious plot you have alleged," he said.

193

"You have to ask yourself, Inspector, why nails were substituted in the endpieces. The most rational explanation is that longer nails were necessary to contain something extra added to the ends of the crates. My surmise is that this something extra is lead which Patterson senior, the armourer, crafted in sheets to fit. This additional weight was necessary to compensate for rifles which had been removed."

At this repeated allegation, Colonel Saunders erupted.

"This is a farrago of absurd suppositions and theories and I intend to expose it. Patterson, open this crate at once," he ordered the carpenter.

"Yes, please do," added Sigerson.

The cover was quickly off, revealing a top layer of three neatly arranged bundles. Despite the thick cloth swaddling, we could discern the tell-tale shape of a rifle.

"Go ahead, take one out and unwrap it for this gentleman," the Colonel told Patterson.

In a moment, the young man held out for inspection a Martini-Henry rifle still shiny with protective grease from the factory.

Sigerson stepped forward. "Mr. Clarke, would you be so kind as to remove a bundle from the second layer and unwrap it for us."

The Colonel moved so quickly that he eluded the outstretched arms of the Inspector and two constables. The third brought him down with a classic rugby tackle. When we looked round, Clarke was holding out a wooden replica of a Martini-Henry. Further investigation revealed that the crate had contained three actual rifles, nine replicas and sheets of lead in the endpieces.

"Copying the rifle stock in pine was a simple matter for a carpenter," Sigerson said. "But he needed something ready-made in the shape of a barrel. I attempted without success to interest Mr. Evans in the absurdly large supply of wooden dowelling here."

Inspector Wells was motioning his constables to take away the Pattersons and Colonel Saunders. "We will get the details of this plot from them back at the station, Mr. Sigerson."

"I have no doubt that you will, Inspector. But there is something much more serious about which you will also want to question these men than theft and this half-baked plot, as it would be called in Devon."

Without another word, Sigerson then led the entire company to that mostly empty drill practice room on the next floor.

"Here is where Constable O'Reilly was beaten to death, and these are some of the men who did it," he announced with more emotion than he had shown previously. This was the story he then unfolded.

194

The constable was indeed on the job Monday night and he had followed one of his smuggling suspects to the Couillard Hotel. Sigerson matched soil from O'Reilly's boot to the mud sample from outside the inn. ("I have written a small monograph about soil identification," he said.) Somehow the "Society" members drinking there concluded, erroneously, that the constable had tumbled to their plot. They overpowered him and took him to the Commissariat, where they roused the Pattersons in their living quarters.

Sigerson walked over to the wall and lifted out a ladderback chair. Then he gathered the top coil of rope from the corner.

"The constable was tied to this chair with that rope and systemically beaten to discover how much he knew. But it was all a terrible mistake. By the time the conspirators realized O'Reilly was following another trail altogether, it was too late. He now knew they were up to something even more diabolical. They felt they must kill him, which they did with blows to the head. They then doused his body with liquor to make it look as if he had been in a bar room brawl. After that they dropped him head-first onto the stones on the bottom of the empty lock in an attempt to conceal the true cause of the fatal head injuries. The inference would be that O'Reilly had stumbled into the lock in a drunken stupor – which is in fact the conclusion leapt to by his superiors."

From the looks the constables gave the Colonel and the Pattersons, I feared it would go much harder for them now back at the station.

Before going our separate ways, we had agreed to meet later for a final summing-up. It was a sombre group which gathered that afternoon in a conference room attached to the Prime Minister's office.

Sir John himself was present and listened with great attention as Sigerson recounted the events at the Commissariat and explained his deductive trail. Inspector Wells then reported that three other crates of rifles had been similarly tampered with, and that the missing rifles, along with numerous articles of official Canadian army gear and uniforms, had been recovered from a cache. Under vigorous questioning, the three men had confessed their participation in the plot and implicated others, including many members of the Hibernian Debating Society.

All but a few were American citizens, of Irish ancestry, who had been posing as Canadians from the Ottawa Valley. Colonel Saunders, however, insisted he was British, although of Irish sympathies, and denied any part in the fatal beating of Constable O'Reilly.

"I still can't quite fathom what they hoped to accomplish by all this," said the Prime Minister.

"Their plan contained far more passion than reason," Sigerson replied. "As latter-day Fenians, they were looking to thwart Britain at every turn. A strong federation of English-speaking people could only delay Irish independence, in their perverted view. So they came to Canada a year ago and began what amounted to a whispering campaign to make it seem that Canadians were becoming increasingly anti-American. The raid across the border would be the culmination, with your army's rifles and uniforms abandoned to implicate the Canadian government. No matter how strenuous the denials, there would be no way that the American public would accept stronger ties between our two countries under the guise of the proposed federation."

"What first alerted you to this plot, Mr. Sigerson?" asked the Prime Minister.

"The Pattersons' accents. It was obvious at once to my trained ear that the overlay on their Irish background was American, likely Eastern Seaboard, not from the Ottawa Valley. That started me along the line of investigating why Irish Americans might be trying to pass themselves off as Irish Canadians."

"I assume you will be heading back to London to report."

"Not for a few weeks, Prime Minister. My report to Sir William will be sent by diplomatic pouch. I have a good acquaintance who suggested that I visit his farm out West. But first I must stop in Toronto."

"Why is that, Mr. Sigerson," asked the Prime Minister as he rose.

"My acquaintance urged me to get shod there. His bootmaker is Meyers. Perhaps you've heard of his establishment?"

Postscript

It was to be seven more years before Meyers the Bootmaker achieved immortality through publication in 1901 of The Hound of the Baskervilles, *an adventure that actually took place in 1889, five years before our Ottawa story, according to Dr. John Watson's account. A reader of this tale today may well marvel how I could not have recognized an investigator who spoke of a "three-pipe problem", yearned to play the violin, employed a magnifying glass to such effect, and appeared to have written monographs on every aspect of criminal deduction.*

In my own defence, all I can say is that the whole world believed that the Master Detective had died that terrible day in May 1891 when he plunged over Reichenbach Falls in a fatal embrace with his arch-

enemy Professor Moriarty. In reality, he was to reappear to Watson's astonished eyes the month after the visit to Ottawa, but his return did not become general knowledge until October 1903, when The Strand *magazine published a story entitled* "The Empty House."

You can imagine my astonishment while reading that tale to learn that while Sherlock Holmes roamed the globe between May 1891 and April 1894, he often assumed the persona of a Norwegian explorer named Sigerson.

Ottawa References

- *The Dominion Police* – Organized around 1870 to monitor and infiltrate the Fenian movement and protect cabinet ministers. Later responsible for security on Parliament Hill and for most federal policing services east of Lake Superior. Colonel Arthur Percy Sherwood became head in 1885 and held that post for a generation. In 1919, the force was merged with the Royal North West Mounted Police to form the RCMP.
- *Russell Hotel* – Built in 1865 on the east side of Elgin at Sparks, the Russell was the fashionable hotel in Ottawa until the Chateau Laurier opened in 1912. It was first building in the city to boast bathrooms and steam heat. Prime Ministers John A. Macdonald, Charles Tupper and Wilfrid Laurier all lived at the Russell during their terms in office. The hotel suffered a fire in 1901, was rebuilt, but closed in 1925. It stood derelict until April 14, 1928, when another fire gutted the building and the land was cleared for the War Memorial.
- *George M. Dawson* – Director of the Geological Survey from 1895 until his sudden death in 1901.
- *An inn on Duke Street* – The Duke Hotel, later the venerable Couillard, was at 101 Duke Street.
- *Commissariat Building* – Now houses the Bytown Museum.
- *Beamster, wheel tapper, drayman, pot burner, knacker, guard lacer, plate-maker* – Tannery worker, railway worker who checked the wheels of locomotives, goods carrier by horse cart, pottery worker, dealer in old/dead horses, someone who laces up ladies' bicycles to prevent dresses getting caught in the mechanism, engraver of printing block plates.

197

Sherlockian References

- *Sometimes constituted the entire British government* – The phrase "sometimes the British government" was applied to Mycroft Holmes, older brother to Sherlock and a senior public servant.
- *Attended Oxford or Cambridge* – A contentious and unresolved issue in Sherlockian scholarship.
- *Have written a small monograph* – Holmes wrote monographs about the identification of tobacco ashes, tattoo marks, the tracing of footsteps, ear shapes, the effect of trades upon hands, and ciphers. He planned ones about the use of dogs in detection, malingering and the typewriter in crime.
- *You see, Evans, but you do not observe* – A recrimination Holmes directs at Dr. Watson more than once.
- *A three-pipe problem* – A classic Sherlockian description.
- *The bimetallic question, the great herd of bisons of the fertile plains*, and *the stormy petrels* – The names of three Sherlockian scion societies in Canada.
- *Meyers* – The title given to the leader of Canada's premier Sherlockian society, the Bootmakers of Toronto.

ACKNOWLEDGEMENTS: This story could not have been written without the plot advice and editing skills of J.A. ("Sandy") McFarlane. Valuable assistance was also provided by librarians in the Ottawa Room of the Ottawa Public Library, Gideon Hill, BSI, and Rideau Canal enthusiast Ken Watson.

The Adventure of the Willow Basket
by Lyndsay Faye

"An artisan of considerable artistic skill," Sherlock Holmes answered in reply to my latest challenge, pulling a thin cigarette from his case. "A glass-blower to be specific, although I nearly fell into the rash error of supposing him a professional musician. Shocking, the way the mind slips into such appalling laxity after a full meal – I'll be forced to fast entirely tomorrow in case my wits should happen to be called upon."

Staring, I marvelled at the man before me, who scowled at his now-exhausted supply.

"Dear me, I shall have to stop for tobacco on our – "

"No, I won't have it!" I lightly slapped the white linen tablecloth between us, causing our whiskys to shiver with a sympathetic happy thrill. "Eight in a row is quite too many, Holmes! Even you cannot pretend to clairvoyance."

"You wound me, my boy." He lit the cigarette, suppressing an impish expression. "I have never pretended to clairvoyance in my life, though I have placed eleven such repellent creatures in the dock for swindling the credible out of their hard-earned savings. One, a Mr. Erasmus Drake, defrauded over a dozen widows using only a mirror, a pennywhistle, and a cunning preparation of coloured Chinese gunpowder. He won't be free to roam the streets for another three years, come to think of it."

"Well, well, never mind clairvoyance then, but you have just identified the professions of eight individuals at a single glance! I shall have to commence approaching complete strangers and demanding they give us a full report of their lives and habits in order to corroborate your claims."

"My dear fellow, surely you know by now that you needn't trouble yourself."

"All right – how do you know he is a glass-blower?"

The detective's eyes glinted as brightly as the silver case which he returned to his inner coat pocket. We sat at our preferred table in the front of Simpson's, before the ground-glass windows where we so often

199

watched the passersby; but despite the glow bestowed upon London minutes before by her army of gas-lighters, the illumination beyond the wavering panes no longer sufficed for even my friend's keen gaze to pick out those details by which he had built his reputation, and thus we had shifted in our seats to examine the restaurant patrons instead. Holmes's turbot and my leg of mutton had long since been whisked away following our early repast, and we sat in a small pool of quiet amidst the throng of hungry journalists and eager young chess players, their sights fixed upon sliced beef in the dining room or cigars and chequered boards up the familiar staircase. There seemed not a man among them my friend could not pin with the exactitude of a lepidopterist with a butterfly; and, while his remarkable faculty always gives me as much pleasure as it does him, on that evening we reposed with the more luxurious complacency of two intimate companions who had nothing more pressing to do than to order another set of whiskys.

"I know he is a professional glass-blower because he is not a professional trumpet player," Holmes drawled, gesturing with slight flicks of his index finger. "His clothing is of excellent quality, only a bit less so than yours or mine, suggesting he is neither an aristocrat nor a mean labourer, but rather a respectable chap with a vocation. His cheeks are sunken, but the musculature of his jaw is strongly developed, overly so, and there are slight indications of varicose veins surrounding his lips. His lungs are powerful – I don't know if you heard him cough ten minutes ago, but I feared for the crystal. He has been expelling air from them, with great strength and frequency. At first I nearly fell into the callow error of supposing him an aficionado with some brass instrument, possibly playing for an orchestra or one of the better music halls, for which failing I blame the exquisite quality of Simpson's seafood preparations. However, when I glimpsed his hands, I instantly corrected my mistake – his finger-ends display no sign of flattening from depressing the valves, but they do evince a number of slight burn scars. Ergo, he is a glass blower, one I would wager ten quid owns a private shop attached to his studio if the cost of his watch chain does not mislead me, and you need not disturb his repast, friend Watson."

I was already softly applauding, shaking with laughter. "My abject apologies. I was a fool to doubt you."

"Skepticism is widely considered healthy," Holmes demurred, but the immediate lift of his narrow lips betrayed his pleasure at the compliment. My friend is nothing if not gratified by honest appreciation of his prodigious talents.

200

For some forty minutes and another set of whiskys longer, we lingered, speaking or not speaking as best suited our pleasure, and I admit that I relished the time. My friend was in a rare mood – for, while he is tensely frenetic with work to energise him, he is often brooding and silent without it. The extremities of his nature can be taxing for a fellow lodger and worrying for a friend, though I suspect not more so than they are burdensome for Holmes himself. It was a pleasure to see the great criminologist at his ease for once, neither in motion nor plastered to the settee in silent protest against the dullness of the world around him.

I was just about to suggest that we walk back to Baker Street when we wearied of Simpsons's rather than flag a hansom, for it was mid-June and the spring air yet hung blessedly warm and weightless before the advent of summer's stifling fug, when my friend's face changed. The languid half-lidded eyes focused, and the slack draught he had been taking from his cigarette tightened into a harder purse.

"What is it?" I asked, already half-turning.

"Trouble, friend Watson. Let us hope it is the stimulating and not the unpleasant variety."

It was then I spied our friend Inspector Lestrade casting his dark, glittering eyes around the dining room, turning his neatly brushed bowler anxiously in his hands. His sharp features betrayed no hint of their usual smugness, and his frame, already small, seemed to have shrunk still further within his light duster. When I raised a hand, he darted towards our table with his head down like a terrier on the scent.

"By Jove, there's been a murder done!" Holmes exclaimed, as usual failing to sound entirely displeased by this development. "Lestrade, pull up a chair. There's coffee if you like, and – "

"No time for coffee," Lestrade huffed as he seated himself.

Holmes blinked in urbane surprise, and I could not blame him. I, too, suspected that beneath the inspector's obvious anxiety lurked another irritant – while Lestrade is often officious, he is never curt, and he had not bothered to greet either one of us.

Musing, I took in the regular Yarder's rigid spine and brittle countenance. My examinations drew a blank, save for the obvious conclusion that his nerves had been somehow jangled. I could not imagine what the matter might be, for the year was 1894 and I had not seen the inspector since April and the arrest of Colonel Sebastian Moran, a dramatic event indeed, but one which paled significantly in comparison to the fact of Sherlock Holmes being alive at all. Following my friend's return from his supposed death at the grim plunge of Reichenbach Falls,

I had wrestled briefly with powerful conflicting emotions, the pain of abandonment and the joy of an unlooked-for miracle foremost among them – but by June of that year, the occasional haunted, hunted looks in Holmes's eyes, which even he could not conceal, combined with the rueful courtesies he showed me when his natural impatience ought to have driven such considerations clean from his vast mind, had convinced me he could not have done otherwise than he did. Excluding the deep pangs caused by my recent marital heartbreak, I felt as ebullient as any shipwreck survivor, and only wished our old friend Lestrade the same felicity.

"Tell me about the murder," Holmes requested, "since you decline to be distracted by coffee."

"Beg pardon?" Lestrade growled, for he had fallen into a reverie with his fingertips pressing his temples.

"Report to me the facts of the homicide, since you refuse the stimulating effects of the roasted coffee berry."

"I do speak English, Mr. Holmes." Lestrade tugged at his cuffs in fastidious annoyance, recovering himself. "It's a bad business, gentlemen, a very bad business indeed, or I should not have troubled you. I applied at Baker Street, and Mrs. Hudson said you were dining here."

"That much I have deduced by your – "

"Shall we skip the parlour tricks, Mr. Holmes?" Lestrade proposed with unusual asperity.

Holmes's black brows rose to lofty heights indeed, as did mine, but he appeared more curious than offended. As I had not observed the pair interact other than a terse welcome back to London from Lestrade at Camden House in April, followed by some professional discussion of the charges Colonel Moran would face, I sat back against the horsehair-stuffed chair in bemusement which verged upon discomfort.

"It is a murder," Lestrade admitted, clearing his throat. "Mr. John Wiltshire was discovered in his bedroom in Battersea this late morning, stone dead, without a trace of any known poison in his corpse, nor a single wound upon his body to suggest that harm had been done to him."

"Remarkable, in that case, that you claim a murder has been committed."

"He was drained of blood, Mr. Holmes. His body was nearly free of it." Lestrade suppressed a shudder. "It disappeared."

A chill passed down my spine. As it has been elsewhere mentioned in these chaotic memoirs that Holmes rather admires than abhors the

202

macabre, I shall not elaborate upon this quirk of his nature – I must mention, however, that Holmes's entire frame snapped into rapt attention, while Lestrade's bristled in what I can only describe as animosity.

"There's some who would think that horrible, but you're not to be named among them, I suppose." The inspector levelled a challenging stare at Sherlock Holmes.

"I readily admit to thinking it varying degrees of horrible based upon the character of the deceased," Holmes replied with a yawn, reverting to his typical supercilious character. "The facts, if you would be so kind."

"The facts as I have them in hand are these: Mr. John Wiltshire dined with his wife and an old friend on the night of his death, and later Mrs. Helen Wiltshire called for a bath to be drawn for her husband. The housekeeper asserts that the ring occurred, the water was heated, and nothing else of note took place. The upper housemaids all confirm that Mrs. Wiltshire slept in her own room that night, afraid to upset her husband's apparent need for quiet and solitude. Other than the fact a man has apparently been bled to death by magic, you'd not find me disturbing your supper."

"You know very well that we would hasten to come whenever you have need of Holmes," I asserted, only noting in retrospect my grammatical error.

A glass of whisky appeared before the inspector. Nodding subtle thanks to the jacketed waiter, Holmes ordered, "Do have a sip – it seems as though the circumstances merit it."

Lestrade's countenance dissolved into what might – save for his own restraint – have been a sneer even as he tasted the drink. "Another deduction?"

"You have clearly been much taxed," said Holmes, as dismissive as ever. "Pray, what would you have us do? I require an invitation or a client, and presently I have neither. Shall I look up *vampires* in my commonplace book and wire you upon the subject, or test your patience so far as to accompany you to the crime scene? Has the body been moved?"

"No. I came straight to you," Lestrade retorted, taking another swallow, "whether I liked it or not."

My mouth fell open, and Holmes's deep-set eyes widened fractionally. I fully expected a scathing retort to follow close upon this subtle hint of dismay. To my great surprise, he merely rose, however, nodding at the quaint tobacconist's shop nestled inside the restaurant, and said coldly, "I am at your disposal, Lestrade, after buying more cigarettes. You are giving me the distinct impression I shall have need of them. Watson, settle the bill if you would be so good."

Never will I forget that crime scene, for it occurred after what had been so casually glad a day for me, and the shift into horror was as swift as our cab ride. John Wiltshire lay dead in his tastefully appointed bedchamber, its heavy emerald draperies thrown wide to let in the sunlight and now forgot under the shrouded gaze of invisible stars. He reclined in a bath over which a muslin cloth had been draped, the atmosphere in the room stale with police traffic and tense with revulsion, and a still-damp rubber tarp on the rug nearby informed me he had been examined by the coroner and then returned to his original attitude. Mr. Wiltshire's head and upper torso were visible, his mouth slack and lips white as chalk. The setting and the centerpiece were utterly jarring, with the stately furnishings surrounding a body that appeared horribly – nay, obscenely – withered. Should I have reached out and touched the late Mr. Wiltshire's skin, I could picture it crumbling to dust like paper left to desiccate for centuries. He had in life been a slender man, with deep pouches beneath his eyes and a thin, downturned mouth.

The coroner was finishing his notes wearing a grim expression and, after a gesture from Lestrade, he stepped aside to allow Holmes and myself to view the deceased. My friend whistled appreciatively, which garnered a dark look from Lestrade.

"Skin white as that cloth and utterly parched, vessels drained, form shrunken, as if he had shriveled into a husk," I summarised. "But are we *certain* there were no epidermal wounds inflicted which could have caused this? He was examined on this tarp, I take it."

"Indeed, Doctor. A minute examination was made in this room, but Inspector Lestrade insisted the deceased be replaced lest his original positioning or the water itself provide a clue for Mr. Holmes here," the coroner answered, nodding politely.

"By the Lord," Holmes said mildly, "and here I supposed the circumstances of the killing itself the only miracle which took place today. Admirable, Lestrade."

My friend appeared to be getting a bit of his own back at last, and the official detective ground his teeth as Holmes dipped his torso towards the bath. Avid as the most passionate connoisseur, he lifted the dead man's dripping hand from the water and examined the ivory cuticles, checked the underside of the limb draped over the lip, made a minute study of his dark hair and his unmarked scalp, even lifted the wizened eyelids to reveal his unseeing pupils. I watched, eager to help if I could, but all I beheld seemed the stuff of nightmare and not medicine. Holmes next drew his delicate fingertips along the copper rim of the tub, going so far as to touch the now-tepid water and bring it to his nose.

"For heaven's sake," Lestrade muttered in my ear – but at me there was directed no pique, merely the casual camaraderie of old.

I half-drew a hand over my moustache to hide a smile, but added under my breath, "If Holmes weren't the most thorough investigator the world has ever known, I doubt he would be here."

"More's the pity," Lestrade sighed as my companion pushed upright again.

"I have exceptionally keen hearing, you realise," Holmes mentioned tartly. "Fascinating. As I happen to trust in your thoroughness, coroner – Adams, was it? Yes, Mr. Adams, I suppose you correct in stating that the body lacks superficial wounds. They should have bled into the water if he was killed here, in any event, and this liquid is far too pure to indicate a man's entire life-force could have possibly been drained into it. I can see no trace of blood at all. Testing it for minute traces may prove necessary, and I have that ability, but more urgent matters demand our attention, supposing we can keep this evidence intact? Very good. I detect no more sign of poison than you do, but anyhow poisoning is a medically impossible means of sapping a fellow's blood, unless we are dealing with a substance altogether unknown to science. So here we have a man whose blood was somehow siphoned, and the water is clear. Supposing the corpse had been moved, that would have proven nothing whatsoever, but . . . ."

"But the corpse was not moved," Mr. Adams obliged when Holmes paused expectantly, "because the deep depressions upon the back of his neck and the other on his forearm – there, where it was resting – indicate he was robbed of his blood here somehow, and left to die."

"Capital!" Holmes exclaimed.

"Yes, we worked that one out on our own, Mr. Holmes," Lestrade groused.

Sherlock Holmes did not deign to reply, instead turning his attention to the crime scene as Mr. Adams excused himself, intending to help the constables make arrangements to remove the remains. Holmes made every effort, as he always does, diving into corners and walking with his slender hands hovering before him, seeking any aberration which might bring light where all was dark. After some fifteen minutes of studying carpeting, framed photographs, a mahogany bedstead, and every crevice of every object in the room, however, he tapped his fist against his lips and turned back to Lestrade.

"Will you be so good as to deliver me this unfortunate fellow's biography?"

"Readily, Mr. Holmes. Mr. Wiltshire is employed at a banking firm in the City and has been for some six years hence. We've had scant enough time to question anyone, but this afternoon his direct superior sent me a good report of him. The servants seem to think him a somber man, but altogether a satisfactory employer. He has no outstanding debts and no known enemies – he lives in a quiet fashion with his wife, Mrs. Helen – "

Holmes snapped his fingers. "I hadn't forgot the detail, but was admittedly distracted by so very dramatic a corpse. They entertained an old friend last night – the wife, take me to the wife," he commanded, and quit the room.

Lestrade followed, and I matched my stride to the shorter man's. "I cannot help but sense that our presence on this occasion distresses you, Inspector."

He glanced backwards in surprise. "Oh, I could never be distressed by your help, Doctor. It's always a pleasure to see you. It's merely that Mr. Holmes – well, never mind, Mr. Holmes has never cared a fig what I think, and I don't see why he should start now, so I'll say no more. He'll be waiting for us, and he's right to want interviews at this stage. There *was* a visitor, and it was the wife who rang for the bath to be drawn. I've not been able to question Mrs. Wiltshire yet – she fainted dead away at the sight of her husband and only recovered whilst I was fetching you. Never mind Mr. Holmes's quirks when there's a murderer to run to ground, I always tell myself."

Still mystified for multiple reasons, I could do nothing save accompany him downstairs. We waited in a pretty parlour with all the lamps blazing, a room full of light and colourful decorative china, its walls masked by potted greenery. Something about its coziness unnerved me, and the chamber seemed all the more garishly cheerful when my imagination flashed upon the ghastly events doubtless taking place upstairs, as the shrunken rind which had once been a man was taken out the back through the servants' entrance and at last to the morgue.

When Mrs. Helen Wiltshire entered, she naturally appeared greatly disturbed in mind – her comely complexion was ashen with dismay, her full lips a-tremble, her green eyes red at the edges, her pale blonde hair disarrayed from clutching it in the extremity of her emotion. She was of an age with her late husband, midway between thirty and forty, and was a lovely woman despite her distress. My friend was up in an instant and led her with easy courtesy to the settee, where she perched as if about to take flight.

Holmes smiled gently as he regained his own chair, displaying the almost mesmeric softness he only ever expends upon the fair sex, and only when he desires information from them; but then, I am not being quite just when I say so. My friend may not seek the company of women, but he genuinely abhors seeing them harmed.

"Are you quite comfortable, madam? Should you like a little refreshment to strengthen you? My friend here is a doctor, and he will be happy to locate something fortifying."

"I . . . I don't think that would be . . . ." Mrs. Wiltshire shifted, attempting to smile with little success. She was silent for so long that Sherlock Holmes continued, face alive with encouragement.

"You are of Scottish origins, I observe. In the vicinity of Paisley, Renfrewshire, unless my ears deceive me."

A wash of colour infused Mrs. Wiltshire's dulled cheeks. "Aye, Mr. Holmes, though I've lost a good deal of that manner of speaking."

"Yes, it's extremely subtle. You went on a long stroll this morning, Mrs. Wiltshire? It must be pleasant, living so close to Battersea Park and its walkways, especially at this time of the year – though I discern from your boots that you wandered alongside the Thames on this occasion."

She glanced up, twisting her fingers in her coral skirts. "Why, yes, Mr. Holmes. I was out walking. That is the reason I only learned at around noon that – oh, I can't, I can't," she said upon a small sob. "I very often take long constitutionals. I've never regretted the habit so much as I did this afternoon, when I arrived home and discovered the house was in an uproar and the police had already been summoned over . . . over . . . ."

"Quite."

"I was most unwell afterward. I've only just found a tiny store of strength – I hope you will forgive my weakness, but . . . ."

Again she trailed off, and again Holmes continued. "Will you please tell me about your caller of last night?"

Helen Wiltshire nodded, more tears forming. "His name is Horatio Swann, an explorer of some note."

207

"Indeed!" Holmes exclaimed. "Yes, I have heard of him. He has made quite the name for himself in scholarly monographs."

"Yes, that is the man," she agreed with another weak twitch of her lips. "My husband and he were acquainted years ago, but Mr. Swann has been traveling in Siam, studying indigenous wildlife. We passed a most pleasant meal, and afterward John seemed fatigued at having spent so much time over vigourous conversation and plentiful claret. I ordered him a bath and left him to himself. He could grow . . . melancholy at times, Mr. Holmes. But for such a fate to befall him . . . ."

Mrs. Wiltshire at this point dissolved entirely and ran from the room.

Lestrade exchanged a glance with Holmes, all pique forgotten in the peculiarity of the moment. He leant forward with his elbows on his knees. "She must have been quite devoted to him."

"It would seem so," Holmes replied without inflection.

"The poor woman must be wrought to her highest pitch of nerves over such a ghastly shock. We must seek out this Horatio Swann," I conjectured, "and ascertain whether he has anything to do with the affair."

"As usual, Watson, you have hit upon the obvious with uncanny accuracy," said Holmes dryly. "But I wonder . . . well, there may be nothing in it after all."

"Nothing in what, Mr. Holmes?" Lestrade questioned, a furrow forming above his narrow nose.

"It's only a whim of mine, perhaps a trivial one at that. But why one should walk along the Thames, noisome as it is, when one could walk through Battersea Park?" Holmes mused, rising and ringing the bell.

A maid appeared within seconds. "Show in the housekeeper, please – what is her name?" Holmes inquired.

"Mrs. Stubbs, sir."

"Mrs. Stubbs, then. Thank you."

Lestrade nodded absently, stretching his legs out before him as if in agreement over Holmes's choice of witness, and I dared to hope that whatever mood had plagued him had been a fluke, and that all would henceforth be well again. Mrs. Stubbs, when she entered, proved a broad woman with neatly arranged curls, the flinty spark of extreme practicality in her eyes, and a direct manner. She stood upon the Turkey carpet with her hands clasped placidly before her, the slight slump of her shoulders the only indication she had been sorely tried that day.

"Yes, gentlemen?"

"Mrs. Stubbs." Holmes remained standing, pacing as he questioned. "My name is Sherlock Holmes, this is my friend and colleague, Dr. John Watson, and this is Inspector Lestrade of Scotland Yard. We wonder whether you might help us in clearing this matter up. You have been the housekeeper for how long?"

"Six years, sir. As long as the Wiltshires have lived in Battersea."

"You find the position amenable?"

"I do."

"Would you describe for me the nature of your late employer?"

"John Wiltshire was a good provider, and I hadn't much cause to speak with him. At times, he seemed a bit wistful perhaps, but he never lashed out or gave me the impression such spells were anything more serious than fatigue."

"Then you would say Mr. and Mrs. Wiltshire were happy together?" Holmes pressed, selecting a cigarette.

Mrs. Stubbs sniffed, seeming more impatient than offended. "As happy as anyone, I hope. They never quarreled, and when banking cost him long hours away, she never begrudged him the time."

"Did she not?" Holmes threw the spent Vesta in the fireplace. "Have you any theory as to what happened last night?"

This at last seemed to move her, but she maintained a neutral expression, swallowing. "That'll be for you gentlemen to decide, I'm sure."

"Was there sign of any intruders this morning?" Lestrade put in.

"No, sir. Well, not precisely."

Both Holmes and Lestrade paused at this, tensing. "What do you mean by 'not precisely,' Mrs. Stubbs?" Lestrade urged.

"It's a silly thing, but the new scullery maid has misplaced the marketing basket." Mrs. Stubbs shrugged. "She's more than a bit simple, and everything is so tospy-turvy today – I'm sure it will turn up. Last week she managed to put the cheese wheel in the breadbox after clearing the servants' supper."

Lestrade sagged, disappointed.

"Would you describe this basket, Mrs. Stubbs?" Holmes requested.

Our eyes flashed to the detective in disbelief.

"It's a plain split willow basket, about a foot-and-a-half long though not so wide, with a handle for the shoulder, lined with a cotton kitchen towel," Mrs. Stubbs answered readily, though her tone was skeptical.

"Thank you," said Holmes, whirling a bit as he strode in tight loops before the fireplace. "One question more, I beg. What was Mr. Wiltshire's mood like after Mr. Horatio Swann had departed?"

"Morose, sir," the housekeeper replied flatly.

Sherlock Holmes stopped, quirking an agile brow. "The usual affliction?"

"Worse, sir. Perhaps he'd a premonition." Mrs. Stubbs set her lips grimly. "To die in such a way . . . God knows he deserved warning of it. Do call for me if you need aught else, but I've plentiful extra tasks to see to and would fain take my leave," she concluded.

When she had departed, Lestrade slapped his knees and hopped to his feet, his unexplained ire fully returned. "This is a serious investigation, Mr. Holmes!"

Holmes swiveled to face the inspector, his high cheekbones dusted with colour, for the first time visibly vexed at the criticism. "I assure you I am treating it as such."

"Oh, yes, I'm sure the *exact* description of this misplaced potato basket is going to greatly assist us in tracking down the killer! Why don't *you* solve that mystery – question the scullery maid, that'll be a good start – and *I'll* catch a murderer. I need to see whether my men have finished," Lestrade growled, storming out.

"What on earth can be the matter with him?" I wondered, regarding Holmes in amazement.

My friend pulled in smoke with a vengeance before crushing the cigarette in a tray for the purpose and shaking his dark head. "I had six theories at the beginning of the evening. I've eliminated five of them," he confessed, striding in the direction of the outer hallway.

"Then what is wrong?" I repeated as we donned hats and gloves.

"A conundrum even I cannot solve."

I opened my lips to protest but found Sherlock Holmes's face as stony as I had ever seen it; he pivoted away from me, thrusting his hands into his pockets as we made to quit the blighted Wiltshire residence.

"But the murder, Holmes! Hadn't you better question more of the ser – "

"That conundrum I *can* solve," Holmes interrupted me. "As a matter of fact, I just did solve it, about five minutes ago. There was never any difficulty in the matter. Come, Watson. We must see what Mr. Horatio Swann has to say."

As circumstances had it, we could not call upon Mr. Horatio Swann until the next morning, as Lestrade had not found us at Simpson's until well past seven after travelling from Battersea and stopping at Baker Street, and Mr. Swann lived some miles distant, in a grand house near to Walthamstow. Lestrade supplied us with a four-wheeler and a pair of constables lest matters take a dark turn, and the journey would have been pleasant enough, passing through the small brick towns with their peacefully crumbling churches and snowlike dusting of white petals from the blooming Hawthorne bushes, had the inspector not been sullen and Holmes coolly silent. I, meanwhile, was abuzz with anticipation, desperately eager to discover what my friend had made of the dreadful affair.

When we three at last stood before the stately structure in question – walled round with charming grey stone, a little lane leading up to a curved set of steps, mullioned windows all sparkling as they reflected the dancing shadows of the white willow branches – Holmes hesitated upon the gravel. Lestrade and I by habit likewise slowed to see whether he would deign to share any of his thoughts.

Then Holmes froze entirely, his spine quivering. We waited, with bated breath, for him to speak – or at least I did.

"Well, what the deuce is the matter?" Lestrade queried, every bit as waspishly annoyed at my friend as previous.

Holmes chuckled, rubbing his hands together. "It's all too perfect. I told you I had heard of Mr. Horatio Swann yesterday, did I not? I have followed a few of his monographs upon the subject of certain freshwater wildlife with particular care."

"And what of it?" Lestrade demanded, exasperated.

"Rather an outlandish residence for a scientist, wouldn't you say?" Holmes replied, winking. "Call for the constables. We'll want them."

Brown eyes widening in astonishment, Lestrade at once did as he was bid, returning a few yards up the lane and gesturing for the Bobbies to follow. By the time they had done so, Holmes had cheerily knocked upon the door and been admitted, I at his heels.

The taciturn butler led us – and, after some persuasion, the Yarders – into Mr. Swann's study. From the instant I entered it, my eyes knew not where to light; the place was a splendidly outfitted gentleman's laboratory, replete with chemical apparatus and walls of gilt-stamped leather books and specimen jars. Of these last, there were dozens upon dozens, lining the shelves like so many petrified soldiers at attention. When my friend saw them, he smiled still wider.

Mr. Swann, surprised, emerged from behind his desk. He was a strongly built man, with a shock of ruddy hair and a ruggedly handsome visage, still wearing a dressing gown and house slippers, as we had begun our journey as early as possible. He appeared merely intrigued at the sight of Holmes and myself – but when he glimpsed the uniformed constables behind Lestrade, his expression shifted to a grimace of pure rage.

"Gentlemen, allow me to introduce Mr. Charles Cutmore, the mastermind behind the infamous Drummonds Bank robbery which so confounded the Scottish authorities, the renowned author of no less than twenty scientific articles of note, and likewise the cunning author of the murder of Mr. John Wiltshire – whose name is actually Michael Crosby, by the by, and who some seven years ago aided this man in making off with six thousand pounds sterling. The pair of them had a female accomplice, to whom you have been introduced under the alias of Mrs. Helen Wiltshire. A pretty little bow to top this strange affair, would you not say so, Lestrade?" Holmes rejoiced.

The inspector stood there stunned for an instant; but a howl of fury and a charge for the door on the part of Mr. Charles Cutmore ceased all rumination. The set of brawny constables hurtled headlong into action, and the pair wrestled their frenzied captive into a set of derbies.

"You've no right!" Charles Cutmore spat at us. "After all o' this time, by God, how d'ye think ye've the *right*?"

"Precisely my question, Mr. Cutmore," said Holmes. "After all of this time safe in Siam with your plunder, why return?"

A steely shutter closed over the bank robber's face even as he renewed his violent efforts to break free. He was dragged, spitting curses at the lot of us, into the adjoining parlour as the men awaited instructions.

"What the devil was that?" Lestrade cried. "A clearer confession I've never heard, but that doesn't explain – "

"No, but this does," Holmes said almost reverently, turning as he lifted one of the glass jars from its shelf.

A miniscule red creature swam within, suspended in pale green-tinged water. It was no bigger than my thumbnail, and the shape of a repulsive maggotlike larvae. I felt my skin tingle with disgust when I saw that, though eyeless, one end of the tiny worm was equipped with a gaping sucker-like mouth.

"Behold the Siamese red leech," Holmes declaimed grandly, presenting it to us. "Not our murder weapon, Lestrade, but one of its kindred. Some of my own studies regarding blood led to a side interest in leeches, and this is one of the only deadly specimens in the known world. It possesses biochemical enzymes in its mouth which render its victims numb and dazed when attacked – and, after having bloated itself upon its unsuspecting meal, expanding to hundreds of times its size when unfed, the same chemicals shrink the wound until it is practically invisible."

"My God, that's hideous!" the inspector breathed, echoing my own thoughts. "But how did you – "

"Charles Cutmore and Michael Crosby were known to be the culprits in the Drummonds affair, but they went deep underground," my friend explained, setting down the deadly specimen. "Crosby had never been photographed, though his description was circulated – he was the faceless banker who enabled the inside job to take place at all – but Cutmore was already making advances in his studies of marine animals, marsh grasses, freshwater habitats, and the like when the theft was discovered, and his photograph was published by the Scottish authorities, which is how I came to know of him. The pair were at school together in Edinburgh. Much more was known about Cutmore than Crosby and, at the time of the robbery seven years ago, Cutmore was affianced to one Helen Ainsley, with whom we spoke. I never dreamed that Charles Cutmore and Horatio Swann were the same biologist until yesterday."

"It still isn't clear to me," I interjected. "You yourself asked him why he returned. Whyever should Cutmore murder Crosby, and after all this time?"

"There we enter the realm of conjecture," Holmes admitted, "and shall only know all after Cutmore is questioned. But here is what I propose: after the robbery, Cutmore made off with considerably more than his share of the profits – note comparatively the residences of the conspirators, after all. So. Cutmore fled to Siam, publishing under an alias and waiting until such time as he could return to the British Isles without his features being so recognisable. Crosby, meanwhile, disappeared into the great cesspool of London and took Helen Ainsley with him, marrying her in Cutmore's absence and continuing to practice banking, from time to time mourning his lost fortune. They may well have believed that the man who betrayed them would never return. But suppose that Cutmore still harboured affections for Helen Ainsley and regretted the loss of her? The reunion last night may have purported to be a friendly one, and Cutmore may even have vowed to restore what he owed them – we have seen the results, however."

"You think this was a crime of passion?" Lestrade drew nearer, glowering.

"Of a sort. Of a very premeditated sort. You have met Charles Cutmore," Holmes reminded him, half-sitting on the desk. "He and Mrs. Wiltmore were once engaged. He does not seem to me the type to remain in hiding forever, supposing he desires to return to someplace, or someone for that matter."

"But what of her husband?"

"Surely you can see that her marriage to the man calling himself John Wiltmore was a matter of expediency – they knew one another's worst secrets and were very much thrown together. I do not claim to have any practical knowledge of the matter, but who ever heard of a married couple who *never* fought, as Mrs. Stubbs claimed? If they seldom fought, I should only have suspected a happy union, and the same goes for an unhappy one if they fought often. But never? It wasn't a union at all. In fact, I should lose no time arresting her."

"On what charge?" Lestrade demanded.

"That of ordering a bath for her freshly unsettled husband and placing a Siamese red leech in it," Holmes replied, his piercing tenor grown grave. "You don't suppose that Charles Cutmore marched up the stairs and dropped it in unnoticed? When I asked him why he returned, he refused to answer, though he had already given himself away – he was trying to shield his former fiancée. The urge was an honourable one, though she shan't escape the law. I haven't evidence enough lacking her confession to prove my findings in the mystery of the missing willow basket, but judging by her behavior at the house, she'll crack on her own once Cutmore is charged. The pair of them have been in contact for far longer than a day, I believe, probably since shortly after his return to England and his purchase of this estate."

"The missing willow basket? Make some sense, by George!"

"Where is the leech now, Lestrade?" Holmes spread his hands in a dramatic show of longsuffering.

"Good heavens," I gasped. "Holmes, you're right – you must be. They planned it together. You said she had been walking by the Thames and not in the park. She took the leech, wrapped it in the cloth, and made off with it in the marketing basket. It must be in the river now."

"Managing to make the most disgusting body of water in the history of mankind still more repugnant." Holmes chuckled, clapping once. "Well done, my dear fellow."

"To think that he left Helen Ainsley behind and then never forgot her, only to lose her again," I reflected. "It's a terrible story."

"And you claim," Lestrade hissed, advancing still further on my friend, "that you knew all this *yesterday*?"

Holmes glared down his hawklike nose at the inspector. "Can you be serious? Are you suggesting you would have believed me if I told you last night that John Wiltmore was killed by a Siamese leech?"

"I might have believed you."

"You might have laughed in my face. This relentless persecution grows tedious, Lestrade."

"Persecution?" Lestrade snarled. "I'm persecuting *you*? Oh, that's rich, Mr. Holmes. Very funny."

"Oddly, I don't find it the slightest bit amusing."

"Gentlemen – " I began.

"Let's have it out in the open then, shall we? Man to man?" Lestrade's shoulders hunched above his clenched hands as if he longed to express his emotions with pugilism.

"By Jove, yes, let's," my friend hissed, standing to his full height.

"Perhaps I had better give you some privacy." Fearing nothing for my friend's safety but feeling dreadfully awkward, I took a step backwards only to find that Lestrade was pointing at me furiously.

"That man," Lestrade snapped, "would – no, don't leave, Dr. Watson, you'd best hear my mind on the subject. That man there, Mr. Holmes, would have taken a bullet for you, I'd stake my own life on it."

Holmes said nothing as I gaped at them.

"And what do you do?" Lestrade was turning crimson with fury. "Instead of seeing it through together, you leave the doctor out entirely, and then you make him think you were *dead.* You stood up there at the altar with him on his *wedding day,* for the love of all that's decent, and do you suppose he enjoyed being written out of the picture? For that matter, how do you suppose *I* felt when I learnt about your demise from a common news hawker? Or when I discovered down at the Yard that Inspector *Patterson* was dashing about rounding up the scoundrels you had apparently been trying to capture for three long months? I should have thought we deserved better from you, Mr. Holmes, and you ought to know it."

Sherlock Holmes, always remarkably pale-complected, had turned absolutely pallid during this speech, though his face betrayed no expression whatsoever otherwise. Meanwhile, my heart was in my throat. I had hardly begun to speak when Holmes held up a perfectly steady

215

hand demanding my silence and said frostily, "You want to know why I left the papers needed to destroy the Moriarty network with Patterson and not with you?"

"I'd find the subject of interest, yes," the small inspector seethed.

Holmes towered over him with that air of aristocratic mastery only he can assume. "I selected Patterson for the task because he *was not* you."

"Of all the . . . ." Lestrade spluttered in outrage.

My friend commenced idly examining his fingernails. "Professor Moriarty was proven to be directly or indirectly responsible for the murder of no less than forty persons, though I suspect the true death count to be fifty-two. Patterson is above the common herd, for a Yarder anyhow, but I had previously worked with him twice. You and I, Inspector," he continued, pretending to struggle for the exact accounting, "have worked together on . . . let me think, dear me, thirty-eight cases, today marking the thirty-ninth. Now, I realise that so many figures in a row must be difficult for a man of your acumen to grapple with, but I shall add one more and have done. Ask me how many times I was shot at during the course of this very interesting little problem we are discussing."

"How many?" Lestrade inquired rather faintly.

"Nineteen," my friend reported, though this time fire underlay the ice of his tone. "And if you think I am not aware of the fact *that man*, as you referred to him, would take a bullet for me, then you are still denser than I had previously supposed."

So saying, Holmes checked the time on his pocket watch and swept out of the room.

We were silent for a moment.

"Oh, good lord," Lestrade groaned, rubbing his hand over his prim features. "I'm the biggest fool in Christendom. That was . . . God help me."

"I'm going to . . . ." said I, gesturing helplessly.

"Yes, yes, go!" the inspector urged, pushing my shoulder. "I'll just confer with the constables while I reflect on the fact that Mr. Holmes is right to call me dense. Go on, quick march."

Hastily, I gave chase. Not imagining my highly reserved friend had any wish to remain in a house where such a scene had just been enacted, as his levels of detachment border upon the mechanical, I dove for the entryway and the faintly blue atmosphere of the mild spring morning beyond.

216

I found Sherlock Holmes some thirty yards distant, leaning against the ivy-draped stone wall. He seemingly awaited my arrival, although he confined his eyes to the smoke drifting skyward from his cigarette. When I had reached him, I halted the words which threatened to leap from my tongue, knowing this situation required more careful handling. Several tacks were considered before I settled on the one likeliest to succeed without causing further harm, and immediately, I breathed easier.

"Well, my dear fellow?" Holmes prompted in a strained voice when I said nothing. Crossing his sinewy limbs, he lifted a single eyebrow although he still failed to look at me. "Have you any salient remarks to add to this topic? Come, come, I am eager for all relevant opinions upon – "

"Holmes," said I, gripping him warmly by the forearm. "Everything I have to say has already crossed your mind."

He did peer at me then, searching my face with the sort of razor focus he ordinarily devotes to outlandishly complex and inexplicable crime scenes. After what seemed an age of this scrutiny, a sorrowful smile crept over the edges of his mouth.

"Then possibly my answer has crossed yours," he continued to quote in an undertone. "You stand fast?"

"Absolutely," I vowed.

A flinch no one save I would ever have caught twitched across his aquiline features; he then clapped my hand which still grasped his arm and broke away to stub his cigarette out against the wall.

"The inspector is sorry over – "

"He needn't be. As Charles Cutmore seems to have learnt to his detriment, the returning can be harder than the leaving."

"Holmes – "

"Do you know, as many features of interest as this case held, I find I tire of it dreadfully, my dear Watson," he announced, wholly returned to his proud and practical self. "A ride back to London with our friend Lestrade and his men and our quarry I think is in order, then a pot of tea at Baker Street and a complete perusal of the morning editions on my part, whilst you work upon whatever grotesquely embellished account of our exploits you plan to inflict on the world next, followed by a change of collar and an oyster supper before Massenet's *Manon* at eight."

So it came about that the good Inspector Lestrade, whose opinion of Holmes's dramatic demise had been such a low one, came to look upon the matter in another light. Whether he ever again spoke to my friend of that impassioned conversation, neither man was gregarious enough to inform me; I highly doubt they broached the topic afterwards. To this very day, however, when Holmes requires a stout colleague or Lestrade has need of England's greatest detective, they call upon one another without hesitation. The horrible death of Crosby the banker was determined a murder by the Assizes and will be tried as such; though the fates of Charles Cutmore and Helen Ainsley have not yet been determined, they belong to that enormous criminal fraternity who have such ample cause to bemoan the existence of my fast friend, the incomparable Mr. Sherlock Holmes.

The Onion Vendor's Secret
by Marcia Wilson

"I suppose," said Sherlock Holmes, "you may as well write it up. It will keep you occupied for a few days. More, if you persist in supporting the sentimentalism that is infecting the common taste."

This prickly observation was finalised with a loud cough, and the Great Detective once again reclined upon his sick-bed, with his wrist over his eyes in the very picture of ailing petulance against the backdrop of his bedroom window and its view of his bees devouring a stand of blue tansy.

"My dear Holmes!" I exclaimed. "I was not even asking for such a thing – and my thoughts are more upon your health, which you have severely neglected."

"Neglect – what of it? The war is over, Watson and to that end I have funneled my energies. Now I rest as the world muses – give them something to celebrate over and perhaps they will leave me in peace!" He sniffed and added, "If you keep to the facts and not the window-dressing, you ought to finish before our guest arrives with Tuesday's milk-cart."

Although his tone and wording was strident, I understood the warmth of his feelings. The Great Game, which he had played so well, had cumulated with the Great War, and now he and the world were equally spent. They had both shared the miserable truth that large emergencies do not remove the smaller ones. That he was still alive was a wonderment to me, I who have felt this astonishment far too much in my life.

As I write with my pen in the past and my eyes upon the future, it occurs to me what an extraordinary life it has been to share it with such a friend as Sherlock Holmes. Long gone are the days when I was a shattered veteran of the desert, and he a young consultant on the verge of becoming an active force for justice. I have no regrets save in general: that of each case my readers saw, there were at least twenty left silent and unseen. Some patiently await their day in the vaults of Cox; some were remarkable for only a day – and became un-remarkable just as quickly. These "Mayfly Cases", as Holmes once described them, were important for the intellectual exercise, and he viewed them with the absent respect a master musician gave to the importance of his warm-up scales. The most beloved of these must surely be that of the gentleman's hat, which led to the discovery of a precious stone within a goose.

But some cases fall into a category where they have taken on veritable lives of their own in the imagination of the public. These are what may arguably be termed "the immortal ones" for their continued attention and fascination. They remain as talked-about as they were upon the day they were emergent news. Most are our shorter adventures, such as the matter with the repulsive Roylott, and I have it on good authority that not a single British jeweler can pass the year without someone asking for a stone to emulate the aforementioned Blue Carbuncle. If Holmes bemoans my florid style, I admit that I am equally baffled by the never-ending pleas from my publisher, his wife, and even the random acquaintance upon the street, for these immortal tales.

By now my reader has suspected my intention: I am permitted at long last to break silence and offer them what they have so often begged to read – A return to Dartmoor.

I apologise now, for I will not satisfy the countless pleas for the impossible return of Jack Stapleton from a watery grave, or the marriage of his widow to Sir Henry, and it is certainly not about a return of a devilish hound. But I beg the reader's pardon one last time, and suspend judgment until they have read the tale through. Crime has been the livelihood of Sherlock Holmes with all the necessity of a knot into a skein, and some knots need time to untangle.

"Halloa!" exclaimed Sherlock Holmes, his interest sharp and his enunciation perfectly clear as he held his favoured cherrywood between his teeth. I looked up from my breakfast in time to see him leap from the table to the window to peer down his nose at the street below. "Now this is no light thing," he observed to me without looking away. "Onion Johnny is about to pay us a visit."

My old wounds were paining me, but I threw down my napkin and went to see this marvel for myself. This time of day, the city was choked with early news-chaunters, messenger boys, and rented cabs as the public strove to move between train stations. Against the swarm of obstreperous humanity, a little Frenchman stumbled with an exaggerated, uneven stride we knew well. Like all of his kind, he stood out by the unmistakable costume of his profession as an *oignon vendeur*: A short coat over his striped shirt matched a navy beret upon his dark head. Like a tiny fisherman's float in a great sea, he bobbed in and out of the confusion. He was hardly a prepossessing size to manage for himself, but he held a stout stick upon his shoulders, and upon that stick depended heavy braids of French onion, which slowly swung back and forth and encouraged others to make way.

"I believe this is a first, Holmes. I've never seen him at Baker Street before the end of his work-day."

"To be sure he has from time to time, but he is not unlike a pony in a coal-mine. If he deviates from his schedule we may blame the path, for he lacks the imagination to wander off it himself. His world is shaped by clocks and blinkers."

I studied the heavy weight of his cargo again, and attempted to use Holmes's methods. "He must have stopped selling his wares to come here." For it was clear that he was desperately making his way to us; his face kept turning up to reassure himself that our rooms had not vanished in the curling fog, and I was certain it was relief in his dark little face to glimpse our forms behind the glass. For all his efforts, he was stymied by the slow march of brick-carters that blocked his crossing. Despite the anxiety of his situation, we had to smile as he stamped his foot.

"And which of my methods have you used to determine this, Watson?" Holmes smiled around his pipe-stem and puffed cold vapours.

"It is the meagrest of observations, I fear. I remember he told you once that his bundles weigh up to two-hundred-and-twenty pounds, and it would seem he has nearly that much to carry."

"A simple observation is often the correct one, Watson. Bravo! And bravo, Johnny!" For the little man had abruptly nipped down the street in order to get around the parade faster. "He shows initiative today! Well, Watson! At the very least we can say our breakfast-time has proven diverting."

Before long, our guest was gasping by our low fire. His wares had been abandoned for safe-keeping in Mrs. Hudson's kitchen, and he strode in with his sun-darkened face flushed from exertion. A chapelet of the pink two-pound Roscoff onions swayed easily in his hand. Not for the first time I marvelled at how of a type he was. With his sharp-chiselled face and sable hair with piercing dark eyes, he could have been any man from the coast of France, all the way to the south of England.

Unlike the usual *vendeur*, ours was well-versed in the English tongue, and he often used it to good effect.

"I am aware that I am hours too early, *Messieurs*," he began with his beret twisting in his hands. "But a sorry matter has come to my attention and I have in turn come to you on behalf of my brothers in trade."

"Come, come." Holmes proclaimed generously. "The onions will keep. We are always glad to see you, regardless of the circumstances." He lifted his pipe to the mantle. "There is a bit of tobacco which you may enjoy if it helps your blood cool from your travels."

"Ah, and I thank you both, but my duties keep and must be on my way. There are many Captain's Heads that need their crew and I am to supervise the fleet." Johnny flashed a quick grin of teeth and tapped his rope of onions. "I promised to make a matter known to you, and I must keep my word."

"By all means, Johnny." Holmes smiled and leaned back, pressing his fingertips together. I have witnessed his management of the many different guests to his office, but Onion Johnny was a guarantee to put him in good cheer.

"Sir Henry Baskerville is paying penance for the lost soul that was his relative."

"That is hardly news, Johnny." Holmes said mildly. "It has coloured the papers and the gossip-halls since he returned from his constitutional."

"I know, Messieurs," he nodded to us both, "and we have heard how he has given a new well to that Boys' School, and money to the Madame Beryl's family. I am speaking of the four burglaries of your West Country, where my brothers sell their onions."

"Hum." Holmes opened his eyes and tapped his fingers. "As I recall from the news, Sir Henry prudently hired a detective for each of the burglaries to prove the culpability of the unlamented late Stapleton. All of them men of the law who can be trusted with such cases."

"It is Folkestone Court that concerns us." Johnny lifted his heavy weight of onions in his agitation. "And Sir Henry has hired that Lestrade to solve this one. But the damages, sir, and the damages are only for the loss of property, and no one is thinking of the little page coldly pistoled by the thief."

Holmes exclaimed in surprise. "Well, this is most unusual. Surely a loss of life would be part and parcel of the damages incurred!"

"The conversation was heard clearly by my kinfolk." Our guest insisted.

"Do continue."

"I cannot explain but if you were to go and see, we will pay you." Before anyone could protest, the little man had a purse out and slapped it upon the table with his rope of onion, cheeks bright with high colour in his Gallic fervor.

"You needn't worry about the fee, Johnny. My rates are fixed, and you have given Mrs. Hudson as well as the Irregulars your excellent onions on credit," Holmes murmured. "If you say I ought to go speak with Friend Lestrade, then I certainly can find the time."

"You must speak soon!" Johnny persisted. His urgency had not been appeased by this peace-making. He turned to go, and then stopped to wag a scolding finger upon my friend.

"And do not again use my onions for your mischief! The Roscoff is a sweet onion. The next time you make a plaster, use one of those rude Spanish friars!"

When we were alone we burst out laughing. "Rude Spanish onions!" I wiped my eyes. "So he reads Dickens?"

"Many do, even the French." Holmes had recovered his breath and was lifting the chapelet to test its weight. "Thirty pounds! This may be diverting. Crime has been very un-imaginative of late, and while this promises to be no different, at least we can be in the open air." He chuckled. "Perhaps I owe our little friend recompense for offending his vegetables. Never argue onions with a Continental, Watson. Their proverbs centre on peeling away problems even as they weep for them."

"Anstruther has my practice while I recuperate," I consulted the Bradshaw. "There is a train at two o'clock."

"Well, well. We have been cooped up like chickens in a rather dull London. A minor diversion in the open air with the famous Folkestone butter will be to our improvement." Holmes examined the onion rope in his long fingers. "Not a single blemish. And what a fine head is this captain!" He prodded the crackly bottom bulb, which was markedly larger than the rest. "The captain suits this crew. Remarkable, is it not, Watson? The secret to so much fine British cooking rests within Roscovite soil where Mary, Queen of Scots once set her contrary feet. One can hardly imagine England without these little entrepreneurs, and yet they are a new pigment on the bright canvas of our country."

Holmes's loquacity advertised a fine mood, which in turn led me to suspect this case may be more than a seeming plea to Lestrade on behalf of a legal fine-point. In this I wisely bowed to his instincts, for I would not go against the observations of the expert any more than Holmes would deny my diagnosis as a physician.

We soon ticketed ourselves to the west. The London fogs cleared under a blue summer sky, and the city melted to silvery streams trickling across sloping greens by which droves of men and women drove flocks of geese to Leadenhall. I asked myself if Holmes expected the matter to stimulate his intellect in some way, for I knew nothing appealed to my friend so much as a thorny problem. After tucking the onions away to Mrs. Hudson's kitchen, he had fallen into a brief stupor of concentration from which I knew better than to intrude.

I distracted myself from the aches and pains aggravated by the train's movement by pondering our visit. "I confess I have been puzzled about the news, Holmes. Why did Sir Henry employ Lestrade for one of the cases? It cannot be because they know each other."

"You are correct. It is because of the current owner of Folkestone Court, Abraham Quantock, wants redress for Stapleton's burglary."

"The name means little to me."

"Did you glean nothing of him in the many newspapers, Watson?"

"Holmes! I have read the exact same articles as yourself, and none have said more than the fact that he is a retired expert in properties from London."

"The absence of news can be the most illuminating. He originally served the nobility, but greed created too many compromises, and he is retired for the betterment of all to Folkestone Court, owned by his Aunt Oriana Quantock, a sensible dame. Alas, the shock of Stapleton's attack contributed to her death, and this charming nephew took the estate.

"Hypocritically, he demands the highest conduct from all, as though he were as worthy as his clients. One false step in his presence and vituperative violence is his reaction. I had the delight of the man whilst solving one or two small matters for my brother." Holmes chuckled. "No doubt he thinks the title of baronet is still a young and upstart one, a purchased billet into the presence of his betters."

"Is Lestrade a bridge between Sir Henry and this fellow?"

"There is some *finesse* in the baronet. Quantock must be wondering with every ounce of his ferocious will if Lestrade is secretly conducting business for the Foreign Office – for they are not without their extensive spies, and his former office employed them heavily."

"You do not paint a rosy picture. I begin to feel sorry for Lestrade."

"By now Quantock knows why Sir Henry employed Lestrade: Our unimaginative friend has no fear of living man. He will not concede to a title nor flinch at a powerful name. No, Watson, Lestrade is an *excellent* bridge between the two opposing poles of Baronet and Buffoon. He may trust our assistance if he so needs it. For all his flaws, he is honest enough to admit them."

"It all seems peculiar. Sir Henry restores the honour of his family name by making restitution for Stapleton's crimes. Wouldn't Quantock reciprocate by only asking for the value of his lost property?"

"And that is the question that begs." In his lap rested his collection of newspaper clippings. "If one relishes irony, here is a feast. You will never see a province so charming and rich with creameries as Folkestone, where it is said the native-born cannot swallow his tea without butter. Quantock is as cold and thin as the lands are fat. He is pure puffery, Watson! Folkestone Court is respectable only by age and history. The family money begat itself in the Navy, but you will find this Quantock's feet high and dry. He would imply that the house and its holdings has always been his, but in truth he received it in exactly the same way as Sir Henry did Baskerville: there was no-one left to inherit. Here, Watson. What do you think?" He placed the open book in my lap.

On the collected front page rested the proud face of our friend the baronet, standing before seemingly endless rows of winged insects in tight glass frames. By coincidence or design, a small speckled moth matching his necktie sat on the wall behind his shoulder.

SIR HENRY RESCUES RARE COLLECTION FOR SCIENCE

The article itself was dull and rambled to tangents, but the gist was plain: As the owners of Merripit House had suffered for tenants after the scandal of the Stapletons, and Beryl Stapleton wanting nothing from her former life, Sir Henry had purchased the property. His first act was to rescue the collection of insects, for they were fragile in an unheated house.

The article included a quote from MRCS Mortimer, who was pleased that science would benefit. All that was left, he assured the readers, was the appropriate place for the collection.

Almost hidden in the far corner was a tiny legal missive: Sir Henry had successfully applied to have one Jack Stapleton recognised permanently as Jack Stapleton, and *not* as his former identity of Rodger Baskerville. The law agreed that it was highly unusual to change the name of a dead man, but as he had willfully changed it in life, they saw no reason not to accept Sir Henry's plea. As easily as that, the line of Rodger Baskerville vanished from the Baskerville records.

"I see nothing more than I did when I first read this."

"Exactly."

Holmes pulled back his book and wasted no time in raining copious notes upon the pages. I left him to it and amused myself in the countryside.

Our stops grew further apart as industry dissolved to agriculture. By the time we eased into Folkestone, there was little more to see than lazy slopes of rich green meads and herds of Folkestone's legendary White Cattle, peppered with small stone shelters freckling the greensward amongst ancient standing stones. The hedgerows were cleverly sculpted of ancient blackberry under bloom as white as the cattle itself. The scene was breathtaking.

Holmes prodded my arm. "That would be Folkestone Court."

I followed his gaze up the tallest of the gentle rises to see what I had presumed a large standing granite was actually a creaky stone lump of windows and bottle chimneys. Long ago its high rock walls must have been impressive; now it was an ageing dowager refusing to conform to her age, and clutching the pearls at her throat in the form of the strings of white cattle lowing upon the hill.

A herd of these cows browsed behind a lively country market against our stop. Under their placid eyes, two Johnnies laced their onions upon sturdy bicycles and took off, wobbling under the weight of their chaplets. A third held office before a swarm of sharp-eyed country cooks as a boy chalked the transactions on a blade of slate.

Before long we saw Lestrade, smartly dressed with a walking-stick under his arm. His lean face twitched, and his sly dark eyes glittered in amusement.

"Pale as a mushroom, Lestrade." Holmes scolded. "Of what use is country air if you cannot breathe it?"

The little Yarder drew himself to his full height and looked up at Holmes. "Easy for you to say," he complained. "I've been indoors!" He sighed and glanced about. "I got your wire just in time. Come. I've rooms."

"By all means. We look forward to an illuminating conversation."

The little professional whistled up a waggonette. "The Candlebat Inn," Lestrade instructed. To us he muttered: "Abraham Quantock is possibly failing in his senses. He is obsessed with getting full value of damages from the theft that we believe Stapleton committed upon him, but his notion of reparation is . . . ." He glanced about him, though by now there was no one to hear. "It was you who first suspected he was behind the Folkestone Court murder and theft."

226

"I still do."

"Well, Sir Henry agrees, and it should be a simple case of collecting the testimony of the damages incurred by Stapleton. But here Mr. Quantock wants the damages of the page's death to go to *him*, not the grieving family! He claims that as the page – Artie Baldwin – was in his employ, thus *he* is the one with reparations, as he had to do without a page thanks to Stapleton."

Lestrade rested his chin on his hand and we could see for the first time the hours of sleepless duty upon his face. "He refuses reason, Holmes, and swears if he is not satisfied he will sell and move to London, and the very thought has panicked the people. Quantock is the lifeblood of these people." Oddly as he said this, his eye fell upon a watching herder and he frowned.

"Does he own the cattle?" I asked.

"He rents the *land* for the cattle and the land is vital for the milk that makes their famous butter. The dairies need the wild grazing. Everything here is bound to the cows! It is the only reason why the train even stops here on the way to Coombe Tracey."

"This is indeed a problem. What of the page's family?"

Lestrade groaned. "The father is Charlie Baldwin, a retired seaman and an outsider, but well-liked for all of that. His mother's needlework at Court got Artie the post. They relied on his small income as a page, but upon his death the pressure is on to bow to let Quantock have all of the restitution . . . even though they are close to being evicted for their struggle to pay rent, because it was all on their head to pay for Young Artie's funeral!"

"Perhaps you could explain Sir Henry's instructions."

"The baronet is leery of Quantock. He will pay full value to Folkestone Court all damages proven wrought by that wretched Stapleton, which is estimated at £3,000 and no more. He is content to pay for the glazier's time in the repair of the cut window used to gain entrance, you see, but not for the glass itself, which Quantock picked up and threw to the floor in his rage. Mr. Mortimer is the one who sewed him up when the shard caught his cheek."

"Forever charming." Holmes murmured. Although the news was sensational, I could not understand why he was in deep thought. Clearly there were facets of this case that escaped me, and I could only wait for the outcome. "Is Mortimer available?"

"He is at a dig on Lewis. I could try to contact him for you."

"Perhaps later. Would it be difficult to see this scene of old crime?"

"Quantock is expecting a final meeting of the scene tomorrow morning. And here we are."

We could now see the inn. It was a large cube built alongside a skeleton-thin road that by neglect had worn down to little more than ribbons in the grass. A broad man with a wooden peg-leg scattered barley for a flock of hens beneath a large painted sign of white moths before a lantern – the "candlebats" of the Inn.

"It looks pleasant." I offered.

"Be careful outside it. There are many ears." Lestrade murmured. His gaze, we saw, had never completely left off from watching the solitary herder in the fields.

Holmes left for a walk. My old wounds had drained me, so I spent the time jotting down my impressions and the facts of the case as I knew them. A stately country dame brought a tea tray, and even the skimmed milk held lumps of butter. Stories of the White Cattle were not exaggerated.

It was a pleasant place, not unlike Coombe Tracy. The thick Dartmoor mists were but weak wisps, easily taken by the fresh sunlight and the touch of the sea-breeze from the south. Instead of wild ponies and crags, I saw tame bovine and stone crosses. I knew Holmes saw the countryside as silent wells of horror, but here it was hard to imagine anything more violent than the inn's moths flying into the lantern.

Lestrade and Holmes returned and fell upon their portions. Afterwards, Holmes settled back upon the bed with his knees drawn to his chest, unconscious of anything but his pipe and the occasional question. I opened the window, and Lestrade filled me in on pertinent details that I would not have found without weeks of gossip: Quantock's anxiety over money, he assured me, was rooted in his purse.

"It isn't cheap to own a monster like the Court," he said over his own buttery coffee. "All that history means freezing rooms and tons of coal burning nonstop to keep the frost off the floor. It smokes like London year-round! Why, I'm certain he has a full staff just to keep down the mold. The Quantock fortune is bound up in legal knots, and he can't get at it or raise any rents."

"We are alone now. What else do you know about the Baldwins?"

"They rent this inn, and they are afraid to be seen talking to anyone," Lestrade said into his cup. By his actions, my friend had as much proclaimed his loyalty to the Baldwins. "Charlie is joked about as Folkestone's last Catholic. He met and married Miss Fern Runston when

228

he was reduced from ferrying Onion Johnnies from Brittany into becoming one himself. Artie was their only son, but another has arrived since. Injuries keep Charlie from putting in a full day, but he is clever and makes string bags to sell to the dairies to carry the small tubs of butter. His style of stringing has become part of the signature of the area, and they would all grieve if the family had to leave."

"Something puzzles me . . . Mortimer knows Quantock?"

"He knows the Court's collection." Lestrade shuddered. "Simply all sorts of dead things on every wall – bones, skulls, feathers, stuffed and mounted beasts. The late Oriana was like most Quantocks and collected. Lichens and insects. Before the murder, her frames took up the entire library wall! The servants say Abraham is not a collector, unless one counts coins."

"If there are bones, Mortimer would visit. It sounds like a museum."

"It is! Do you remember when Ellen Terry played Lady Macbeth at the Lyceum back in '88?"

I said that was six years ago, but no one who had seen the fire-haired Queen of Theatre could forget her in her glittering green dress of a thousand wings of the Jewel Beetle.

"Miss Oriana was consulted for the dress design because she knew beetles so well. Discreetly of course – her people wouldn't like any connexion with actresses living arrears."

"How did you learn this?"

"Miss Oriana was the consultant, but Mrs. Baldwin's needle made the samples."

"I see."

"Miss Oriana hoped to make the Court a private museum. Folkestone approved because it would encourage the sort they like – moneyed temporary visitors who gad about with their nets and jars, breeze in and breeze out. The subscriptions would have modernized the Court and, of course, the butter would be sold on-site without the added expense of shipping it off to the city. But now it is all going to go to waste." Lestrade morosely toyed with his gloves. "And suddenly . . . Mr. Quantock has recently claimed the only that thing will satisfy this affair is the deed to Merripit House."

Sherlock Holmes had been calmly smoking, but at this news he sat bolt upright. "That is very odd, Lestrade!" His grey eyes glittered with a feverish excitement that I did not understand.

"The house is an eyesore, but would improve with a grazier, and the orchard comes with twenty hives of black bees. Lastly, the well has

229

never dried up, and you know how valuable that is. Sir Henry may easily profit after a little work on it."

"There is something about this that tastes bad." I ventured. "I cannot quite put my finger on it."

"I know. Strangest of all is Quantock's insistence that Sir Henry *not* improve the House. He wants it as Stapleton had left it, in order not to 'ask more than his fair share!'" He scowled, and his dark eyes suddenly looked quite angry. "I can't prove it or provide an explanation to any court of law, Mr. Holmes, but Quantock's fiddling about was driving us mad. Yet, as soon as Sir Henry received the copy of Merripit's Deed on his desk . . . he changes his offer yet again, only instead of half-a-hundred itemised damages, it is just one thing – Merripit House, which is currently valued at less than half of the damages at the Court. For that matter, the rental properties are out of proportion; seven per-cent of all the land is hedge! Wasteful, except here, where it is part of the key to the grazing that maintains the health of the cows. Rent has been fixed at 1.23/acre for fifty years. Quantock can't even pay his own tailor!"

"You are out of your depth, Lestrade. You should have summoned me."

"I am being watched." Lestrade said with grave dignity. "Poor folk, desperate and afraid to see the end of their livelihoods. I hold them no grudge, but I wish for restitution of my own."

"I daresay you will get your wish. And you will see Quantock tomorrow?"

"Early on."

"Sir Henry?"

"He said it is a low thing to be predictable to one's enemies. He has authorized me with full powers of decision if I must." Lestrade produced the necessary letter from the baronet.

"Sir Henry is a cunning fox." Holmes admired. "Very well. The three of us will venture out and gird this cave-lion in his draughty den."

"You should not mention the smuggling, Watson. It would not be in the best interests of the people in your sensationalist writings."

I set down my pen. "And I will not, I assure you."

"You practically have, my good Watson. A lantern painted on the Inn-sign! The proximity to Plymouth! The use of Bretons! The stone manse!"

"I did not mention the old shipwreck's lookout, or the unanswered questions about the root cause of the Quantock's <u>original</u> wealth,

Holmes. I could not mention any of these things without being forced to comment on the local's surreptitious form of income."

"We are in agreement." Holmes riposted pettishly. Being feverish never helped his temper, and I ignored it. It was better to encourage him to health. "And do not put Lestrade in the ending."

"I would not dream of it."

"Do not be overly descriptive of Quantock. Put him down as the world's scrawniest toad and leave it at that."

"I am not sure that is possible, Holmes. There is no such thing as a lean toad."

"I was referring to his complexion."

"Holmes, you may read this for yourself when I am finished."

"Must I?"

Abraham Quantock allowed us entrance to his private study that was so poorly lit it gave him the impression of a lean toad. His flat, moist blue eyes glimmered at Holmes, who was the only one tall enough to meet his gaze, and he spared Lestrade an icy glare. Myself he dismissed as irrelevant.

Holmes found a corner by the window and puffed on the pipe he had carried with him on our journey to the Court. Every inch of his lanky form exuded the boredom of a man who must be present for the sake of appearances but nothing more. As I watched, Lestrade struggled more and more for calm as Quantock's ugly amusement grew at Lestrade's expense.

For my part, I knew Holmes was often unfathomable, but there was no sense in trying to draw him out. He would speak when ready and not before, and Lestrade knew this as well as I. But the little professional was baffled at the seeming loss of his ally.

"My terms are clear." Quantock said coldly. "Sir Henry cannot disagree that it is against restitution if I am left the poorer from it. I only wish Merripit House."

"You wish to own it in its original condition," Lestrade countered doggedly. "That is not to put too fine of a point on it. The house needs work. Stapleton was more interested in netting butterflies than keeping it up. You could have purchased it at any time, but you waited until after Sir Henry bought it."

"My reasons are my own."

"And my duty is clear. I will accept your statement and personally deliver it to Sir Henry, but I cannot give you the guarantee that you desire."

"You shall remind your baronet those are my only terms."

"I will, but it would go well with you if I had some reason for your decision."

"No more than it was my Aunt's dream to open Folkestone to naturalists and collectors like herself. Stapleton damaged her original collection and contributed to her untimely passing; it is fitting that her memory receive the benefit of his residence." Quantock grew agitated with the force of his own words and rose up. "Merripit is ideal for the scientist with the desire to do more than take a pleasant stroll among the trout-streams. It is close to the wands planted for safe passage and one less burden I would have on my family's name."

"Not to mention your soul," Lestrade said, in one of his rare examples of dry wit. "You would need to maintain the property, Mr. Quantock. Sir Henry would not let you beggar yourself. Can you afford such a thing?"

"I would own Merripit House only long enough to restore it to fine condition, and then offer it free and clear to the Baldwins, on the understanding that they would host any visitors who come to visit the Moor."

Lestrade was as speechless as myself. He looked at Holmes, who continued smoking with a bored air, as though this were all a trivial affair. He looked back to Quantock and found his voice. "Is *this* your final word, sir?"

"It is."

"Then I will explain your position to Sir Henry immediately, but it would help if you also wrote your wishes down on paper, which I and any of these gentlemen would be content to sign."

"That we would," I said firmly.

Holmes shrugged. "Oh, I suppose if it pleases you," he drawled.

Quantock sniffed. "It will do."

In short time, Quantock drafted a terse statement and we all signed it. Lestrade let no emotions escape his face, but I could tell he was simmering with rage under his calm mask. It was not until we were well outside shouting-distance from the Court that he finally opened his mouth.

"I've talked to brick walls with more sense!" he roared. "And if that man ever gave anything to anyone 'free and clear' it was a germ!"

Holmes was so overcome with hilarity he was unable to regain his composure for some minutes, during which he clapped the little Yarder on the back and leaned upon his shoulder. I thought it a rare sight, with long and lean Holmes bent over the small police detective.

"Be calm, Lestrade!" he cried. "Rest assured, you have done your duty. You saw my lackadaisical performance and responded beautifully to my rudeness, which delighted Quantock so well he assumed he had the upper hand in the debate. Now we shall make haste and inform Sir Henry of the latest development."

Sir Henry's promised electric lights perched like soldiers down the drive of Baskerville Hall, and the ragged greensward was neatened by the thrifty use of white-faced sheep. Small ponds cunningly crafted from the native stone dotted the landscape, shimmering like mirrors and populated by many gossiping birds.

What we took for a gardener proved to be Sir Henry himself, dressed for digging with a large straw hat. He grinned as he waved us over to the edge of a large, shallow circle sliced into the sod, barely more than two inches deep and filled to the brim with clear water.

"Just in time for dinner!" He laughed. "Come and see my dewpond – a real marvel, eh?" The Neolithic collection-pool was a testimony to the skill of Dartmoor's early forbearers, and the convenience of sweet water lured the wild ponies from an early death in the Mire.

"That, and my new mares," the baronet told us. "I've been improving the bloodstock." He turned to Lestrade with his hands on his hips. "I expect you have news for me. Come in and let's talk over a drink."

Lestrade sadly gave a summary as we walked inside the Hall. Stapleton's impressive collection of butterflies hung on the walls, but even I could tell Sir Henry planned to move them out as soon as he could.

Sir Henry was startled. "I knew he was contrary, but . . . Mr. Holmes, can you riddle this?"

"Perhaps. A separate party hired me to facilitate an equitable solution for all involved. Can you add anything?"

The baronet shuddered. "I've dealt with enough snakes that I can't help but respect them for being good at a job no-one else in Creation wants. But this . . . ." He rose to serve a strong rye bourbon. "This out-Herods Herod, by thunder!" With a troubled air, the young baronet turned to Lestrade. "I thought I was giving you a straight job, not a wild goose chase."

"Lestrade is capable of fulfilling his duty, Sir Henry," Holmes assured them both. "And the matter can still be resolved cleanly."

"I'll believe you, Mr. Holmes, but I wouldn't believe anyone else." Lestrade rubbed at his brow.

"No-one need believe. Simply tell Quantock to come here tomorrow to sign the agreement. Watson is a splendid fellow in a pinch, and he can be trusted to add his signature of witness to the agreement, am I correct?"

"Indeed," I said stoutly. "Although I have no more an idea of what you wish than Lestrade."

"Or me." Sir Henry lifted his hand like a boy in a schoolroom. "But I'll be ready for anything!" He grinned. "And I'll be glad to see this through!"

"Excellent!" And without further warning, Holmes turned and dashed down the Hall with the speed of a schoolboy, stopping by turns to peer up the walls and skipping down again. The three of us gaped, but at the very end we saw him grab something in the murk and run back with the object under his arm. It was the light-speckled moth next to the baronet's elbow in the newspaper clipping.

"Your job will be simplicity itself, Lestrade!" Holmes declared. "Merely place this on Sir Henry's desk like so – there! Right next to where the deed shall rest. A delightful conversation piece, is it not?" He beamed with his hands on his hips and admired his handiwork as we again looked at each other, baffled.

"This is one of your tricks, is it not, Mr. Holmes?" Lestrade asked in resignation.

"Not at all, Lestrade. Simply remember," he lifted his hand, "'I swear to you that The Merripit House Collection is complete!' Every specimen that rightfully belonged to Jack Stapleton will be returned to its walls so that Mr. Quantock can accept the deed on his terms. Mr. Quantock agreed before witnesses that he would personally repair Merripit as part of his concession to the plight of the Baldwins."

"Why am I thinking of a pony and a potato right now?" Sir Henry muttered with smile upon Holmes. "I've seen your look in a man's eye before, friend, and it was always right before someone got their comeuppance."

"You give me too much credit, Sir Henry." Holmes pursed his lips. "And now, you spoke of dinner?"

Here my pen falters, for though I have often devoted my thoughts to this crucial scene, I still cannot give full description to how Quantock strode proudly into Baskerville Hall, only for his swagger to crumble like sand under rain as his eye fell upon Sir Henry's desk. He paled before our eyes, and his greeting quivered in his throat.

"Good morning, Mr. Quantock," the baronet said. With his fingers laced together upon the blotting-paper, and his large hazel eyes unblinking upon the newcomer, our friend smiled. "I believe you wished to own Merripit House?"

With a shaking hand, Quantock signed his agreement to Sir Henry, and Lestrade, Holmes and I added our witness. Merripit House thus passed from Baskerville Hall to Folkestone Court, and Quantock was promptly beggared in the repairwork that was past his means. He was close to penniless when he passed the house to the Baldwins. That good couple promptly sold it back to Sir Henry for no more than the value of the Candlebat Inn, and reside comfortably there to this day. It was a far better fate than Quantock's, for he soon was forced by penury to do as he had sworn in revenge, and had to sell what he could and return to London. Allow me to say that the purchaser would have made Miss Oriana proud, for they thought her dream of a Museum a sensible one, and Folkestone breathed fresh relief at a new source of money.

"Sentimentalism, Watson!" Holmes protested. "And of the basest kind. You would have them think it was purchased out of the kindness of the heart!"

"I doubt the Foreign Office would like it if I mentioned their interest in the property, Holmes. They do like to keep their eyes on private entrepreneurs."

"Bah," Holmes sneered. "In any case, your tale is missing large chunks. You will have to splice in a build-up of atmosphere with our journey to Folkestone and keep up an over-inflated account of my behavior to unsettle Lestrade."

"I thought to put that in later. Tuesday is almost upon us."

"At least there will be fresh milk."

"All right, Mr. Holmes." Sir Henry had gathered us all before the fireplace, for even summer in Dartmoor is chilly. He gnawed on the stem of a new pipe in a seeming picture of content. Only the gleam in his eyes and the smile on his lips said otherwise. "You played a long game, and you came out on top again, but it is done and time for the magician to spill his tricks."

Holmes bowed with a pleased mien to be compared to a magician, and bowed again as Lestrade and I leaned forward.

"Quantock only pretended to be callous of his Aunt's work. In reality, he was quietly replacing choice specimens and selling the originals. He could do this because of her failing eyesight, and he started with the pieces high up, knowing she would be content with examining her paintings and sketches. But the real plum, the prize specimen, was the Vandeleur Moth, which you so kindly placed on Sir Henry's desk, Lestrade."

"What!" Sir Henry stared wildly at the silent moth. "You mean that Moth named after Stapleton back when he was passing as Vandeleur?"

"The same."

"By thunder!"

"Yes. I asked myself if it was indeed that worthy moth, but although my suspicions were strong, I had no confirmation until Lestrade gave me the proof I needed with the news of Quantock's sudden desire for Merripit House.

"Stapleton knew from his friendship with Mortimer that the Folkestone Collection was worthy of a visit, and one day he did just that. He must have felt as though his secret days were numbered when he saw the very moth credited with his old name from East Yorkshire was under glass! If its presence became common knowledge, eventually a Yorkshire expert would come to visit, and his disguise would be circumspect. He did not think that his distinct hobby was already a danger to his identity, but we have established his 'hazy thinking' in the past. Naturally he had to have the moth, but he could not ask overtly – Miss Quantock's dream of a museum was public. No, he had to recover this specimen covertly.

"Thieving was on his mind that fateful May, but not just for the silver. The moth was his true goal, though he was already dangerous with his need for money. Little Artie may have seen him take down the case; we will never know. He shot him down in cold blood and fled with silver and moth, leaving behind a wreck of the specimens on the wall.

"What with the loss of her closest confidant's son, which Miss Oriana felt responsible for by securing the child's post, and the devastation of her beloved collection, she was not far from the grave. Stapleton must have thought himself safe, for even he had no idea

236

Abraham Quantock was a savvy moth-man, chafing at the believed destruction of the rare moth.

"For this *was* a very rare moth indeed with reverse-patterned wings. This happens less than three times in five thousand specimens – which Stapleton had estimated but had never been able to personally collect."

"I still can't imagine it." Sir Henry's expressive face was clouded. "All of this for a little moth."

"Do you know the root of entomology, Sir Henry? From the Greek *entomos*, 'that which is cut in pieces.' The entomological world is as complex as the creatures they study. The fanciers of moths alone will guarantee you a fair share of rivalries, destroyed careers, and thefts of far more than specimens.

"Sadly for Mrs. Baldwin, in helping restore the room of her son's murder, she discovered the forgeries within the cases. With Miss Oriana's failing health, she had taken over for her mistress more than anyone could guess. She knew it could have only been the nephew's work. But what could she do? The shock of learning her Abraham was a thief would surely reduce the old lady's life further. In miserable silence, this poor woman kept watch over her friend, but grief is difficult to mask, and Abraham not only learned she had his secret, but that she was very easily bullied into submission. It was the work of a minute to remind her of the slender financial thread upon which their livelihood hung at the Inn. It took only a minute more to force her to swear to silence. And so this sad affair continued through Miss Oriana's decline into death. Unable to bear the strain, Mrs. Baldwin consciously cut her income by moving back to the Inn, and Quantock's greedy soul must have thrilled that she had by choice ran away. She had sworn never to speak, and he firmly believed in the superstition of the peasant against breaking their word.

"Alas for his schemes! Stapleton's perfidy was exposed the moment Quantock saw the newspaper photo of Sir Henry by the rescued Merripit Collection! For there by his arm was his aunt's Vandeleur Moth, a spectre from the past! In a single stroke, Quantock thus gasped Stapleton's blow and plotted frantically to get the moth back.

"Quantock hit upon the idea of using Sir Henry's need to clean Stapleton's stain from Baskerville honour by ploy of Merripit House. If he had the full collection of Stapleton's plunder, he would have the precious Vandeleur again, sell it, and easily do as he vowed in repairing Merripit. But he dare not tell Sir Henry his true goal, for his greedy soul could not imagine so much honour in a baronet. His need for the moth

237

and its verified price on the market was twenty times that of Merripit House, and almost equal to that of Folkestone."

Sir Henry exploded. "I wouldn't sell him his own family's moth back to him!"

"Be calm, Sir Henry. It is no slur on you that a morally destitute man viewed you with his own limited lens." Holmes soothed. "One may very well ask an ant's opinion of a pine tree."

"Maybe so, but all this effort to lie when they could have just kept to the truth!" But the baronet quieted, his fists thrust into his pockets as he listened.

Holmes continued his explanation. "His foggy scheme, which is only slightly better contrived than Stapleton's theft, would have been successful had he remembered Mrs. Baldwin. Her sense of duty was no less as strong as a Ghurka's, and when she saw the same newspaper article, she recognised the moth for what it was. Suddenly there was a shard of her beloved lady's legacy – survived! She had to protect, and so she *wrote* her grief to her husband, circumventing her oath to never talk. Together they hatched a clever plan to avoid Quantock's spies using the Onion Johnnies.

"The Onion Johnnies are a stout brotherhood, and word passed amongst the ranks in their Breton tongue until they found a rather clever one with the idea of directly appealing to Sherlock Holmes." Holmes paused for a moment, his grey eyes twinkling, and we saw Lestrade straighten in surprise. "I was soon on my way to Folkestone. The Johnny did not need to know much. He was simply an Onion Seller who happened to know a consultant able enough to go where Sir Henry and Mr. Lestrade could not. It was a moment's work for the Baldwins to slip a detailed confession to me within the head of the largest onion – the Captain's Head, as it is called in the vernacular, and according to the proverbs of these folk, *the Head keeps all secrets*. By these means, I was able to learn of the Baldwins' plight without anyone else the wiser."

"I was certainly not the wiser!" I breathed. "I heard a crackle when you lifted the onions up, and thought it was only the papery skins! It was the message, wasn't it?"

Holmes bowed again.

"All this made possible by an Onion Johnny!" Sir Henry whistled. "Well, I knew I liked the fellows for a reason. Good with delivering mail when you need them to, and honest to a fault."

"So I've heard," Lestrade agreed evenly, and it was all Holmes and I could do to keep our countenance intact. "Mister Holmes, this is one of your queerest cases yet, but it seems to be what you excel at. Still, solving a case backwards is amazing even for you."

"Why, thank you, Lestrade." Holmes glanced at his watch. "But I fear the congratulations must be cut short. We have just enough time to return to the Inn and pack before the next train leaves Folkestone."

And here I have paused. Holmes is finally asleep. I do not pretend I aided this step to recovery; doing nothing is worse for him than doing too much, and keeping him occupied with my poor writings has served this cause before. He rests when he is busy, and frets when he is not.

But it is my sincere hope that with this sleep he will overcome his illness and rise up, as our equally weary England struggles to rise from her sick-bed. I do not lie when I say my friend is indistinguishable from England.

But I must stop now. I can hear the milk-cart rattling up the shell drive, and with it our long-awaited guest . . . .

"Halloa the house!" A familiar cry makes me smile. As I limp outside with my cane on the uneven earth, the milk-man hurries his cargo to the cool-room for the housekeeper. Our guest is lowering a small bag to the earth, and despite his considerably advanced years compared to mine, he remains as stubbornly spry and active as ever. Only the bright silver wings sweeping from his temples suggest his age, and a jaunty beret perches upon his touseled head.

I cannot but laugh to see an Onion Johnny here in the Sussex Downs, but they seem to be everywhere, now that there has been just barely enough time for the first crops since the War. And the Bretons will not choose in their loyalties of England or France – it is like asking a child to say which parent they love the most.

He limps unevenly to me, and his own stick is no longer for show. A chapelet of Roscoff's finest droops over his shoulder.

"What is this?" I exclaim. "I thought you had retired!"

*"*Lestrade *has retired, Doctor Watson!" is my response. "But* Onion Johnny *still works."*

I laugh out loud and take the chapelet. "For himself or for the Foreign Office?"

"They are much the same." This old friend reassures me. "You are looking better! I take it Holmes finally gave you permission to write about that last mess with the moth? Why else would he 'put in an order' for onions?"

239

And the truth strikes: I had thought I was seeing to Holmes's health, but all this time he was seeing to mine. He kept me from fretting over him and the wake of the War by concentrating on a long-awaited tale.

"I had thought to hide my health from him, since his was so much worse."

"Hum." Lestrade snaps a cigarillo alight between his lips. "Well, anything I can do to help?"

"Only answer how you could turn from browned Johnny in London to pale Inspector in Folkestone so quickly."

"No great secret. Most stains come right off, but it was a bit close. I took the chance. People were watching a late-napping Inspector Lestrade, not the in-and-out Johnnies at the inn."

"I am glad."

"As am I." We pass the tobacco between us and nod to the departing milk-cart. "Come. Holmes will wake soon, and if he hasn't improved, I am making him a plaster!"

"Not from my onions, you won't!"

"Certainly not. There is always a rude friar in the kitchen . . . ."

240

The Case of the
Murderous Numismatist
by Jack Grochot

After I sold my medical practice in Kensington to Dr. Verner and returned to Baker Street to share rooms again with my friend Sherlock Holmes, life in the summer of 1894 became hectic. I had re-joined Holmes at a time when he was juggling three or four cases at once. Consequently, my own erratic schedule, to say the least, took me hither and yon unprepared, for I usually accompanied Holmes on his adventures, but now I was writing down notes of his movements or encounters haphazardly, with the hope that my memory of events would not fail me when I sat at our dining table to compose a magazine article about the ingenious methods and mind-numbing accomplishments of this peripatetic consulting detective. What follows is an example of my remembrance combined with those sketchy notes:

One day at lunch in our flat – a meal of turkey pot pies served graciously by our landlady, Mrs. Hudson – Holmes flipped a coin onto the tabletop and watched it twirl noisily until it came to a stop.

"What can you tell me about this piece, Watson?" he wanted to know.

I picked it up, examined it, and told Holmes the date the crown was minted, 1707, the very year it was introduced as currency to commemorate the Union of the kingdoms of England and Scotland.

"Is that all there is to it?" Holmes persisted, as if to entertain himself.

"Only that this is a rare coin, a collector's item," I added.

"Wrong on all counts, as I anticipated," he blurted with an exaggerated wink.

"Wrong? How can you allege it?" I insisted.

"This is not a genuine crown. It is counterfeit," Holmes revealed, surprising me. "It is not solid silver, it is silver-plated and made of lead, weighing approximately a half ounce more than it should."

"Where did you get it?" I quizzed.

"From a new client, or I should say a group of clients," he answered. "Here is a letter from them that arrived in yesterday's post, along with the spurious coin." He unfolded a sheet of correspondence that was in his jacket pocket, then tossed it over to me, and I read it aloud:

"We, the undersigned, represent the Society of American Coin Traders, an organization of more than two hundred members," the message began. "One of us, one whose identity will remain anonymous, purchased this coin by mail from a London dealer, a Joseph Smisky, for the sum of ninety dollars. This specimen is worthless, for it is a fake.

"We have sent a telegraph to Mr. Smisky to demand that the money be returned, and he has ignored our plea. Instead, he has continued to advertise in the newspapers that he possesses a 1707 crown for sale in mint condition. We suspect he actually possesses several reproductions of this valuable coin.

"We urge you to bring an end to his fraudulent scheme and to intercede for us with your Scotland Yard contacts to see that justice is served. We shall reward you with a fee in whatever amount you deem sufficient under the circumstances, providing, of course, that it is reasonable."

The letter gave the impression Holmes's task was a simple one, but he informed me otherwise. "If Mr. Smisky is to be prosecuted, it must be proven that he not only peddled a counterfeit, but that he knew it was counterfeit when he did so," Holmes advised. "Thus, the sticky wicket."

"How do you intend to establish he knowingly sold a bogus collectable?" I wondered with skepticism. "What was in his mind is hardly possible to decipher."

"My plan – " Holmes started to say, but a knock at the door interrupted him.

"It is only I, here to collect the dirty dishes," said Mrs. Hudson cheerily, letting herself in and directing a comment toward Holmes. "That pot pie should help put meat on your bones. The way you have been running about at all hours takes a toll on the frame, and you can't stand to lose any more than you have already."

"It was delicious and abundant, my lady, and no doubt it will amount to as much as a pound on my sorry frame," he responded, then charmed her with a compliment about her hair.

"Oh, Mr. Holmes, I didn't think anyone would notice how I did it up differently this morning," she giggled, blushing. "I'll be out of your way in a jiffy. You gentlemen have more important things to discuss besides my appearance. You approve though, eh?"

242

"It becomes you, Mrs. Hudson," I piped up. "No need for you to hurry off."

"All the same, I best get going, because I am expecting a gentleman caller," she disclosed, stepping away with the dishes in a rush.

"The word romance never would have occurred to me in a conversation about Mrs. Hudson," Holmes jested in a low voice after we heard her lively footsteps on the stairs.

"You were about to tell me your plan when she came in abruptly," I prodded, expecting Holmes to resume our discussion.

"Better yet, Watson, you can enthrall your readers even more so if you witness my stratagem unfolding, rather than listening to me explain it," he contended. "Come with me to Gravesend, where I shall acquaint you with a female constable who is also an amateur stage actress in her off-hours. Gertie Evans is the key to my grand design and its shocking aftermath for the likes of Mr. Smisky."

"Grand design? Shocking aftermath? What on earth?" I marveled.

"I suppose I should confide in you my ulterior motives for accepting this case, my good man. The investigation of a counterfeit coin is a means to an end. Dealing dishonestly in rare coins is but a minor crime for the nefarious Mr. Smisky, a commonplace infraction ordinarily not worthy of my attention. The fact of the matter is that I have another client, The British Fire and Casualty Company, which has its sights set on Smisky for a heinous insurance swindle. The company has engaged me to probe his responsibility in the destruction of a tenement he owned in the East End. A tremendous explosion and conflagration leveled the structure last April, killing six occupants and injuring a multitude of others."

"I recall reading about it, Holmes, but if I remember correctly, the police blamed a faulty gas valve for the tragedy," I interjected.

"The police suspect sabotage, but they didn't say as much to the newspapers to avoid arousing interest on the part of Smisky or the professional arsonist he employed," Holmes stated categorically. "Unfortunately, the authorities have been unable to assemble any evidence of a deliberate act. The insurance firm has come to me, therefore, to solve the puzzle so it can deny Smisky a settlement of fifty thousand pounds."

"Good heavens, he committed six murders, for money. How disgraceful and malicious," I remarked scornfully. "His malevolence is unparalleled."

"As is my ambition to see him hang," Sherlock Holmes threatened. "Shall we go now?"

"I am as eager as you," I assured him, donning my bowler.

The afternoon sun was intense, so we rode in a hansom to Charing-Cross, where we boarded a train to Gravesend, down by the great river. On the train, Holmes spoke not a word, but tapped his toes to the rhythm of a song in his head and drummed his bony fingertips on his knees, his close-fitting cloth cap pushed forward onto the bridge of his hawk-like nose. When we reached our destination, he cautioned me on the platform not to let on in public that I knew Gertie Evans was a police official. "She works surreptitiously and wears no uniform," he observed, "and she is very careful to protect her true identity."

We met Gertie at the Boar's Head Pub, a raucous establishment on the waterfront with sawdust on the floor and medieval armour hanging on the walls. She waved warmly to Holmes from a corner table occupied by three surly men competing for her attention, one a sailor, another a businessman, and the third a football player wearing his colours. Gertie, aged about thirty, looked lovely in a dark blue dress and yellow blouse with ruffles around the neck and on the ends of her sleeves. Her auburn hair was done in large curls that draped over her shoulders and back, accenting a youthful, angelic face. As Holmes and I approached, she ordered the three suitors to "take a powder, boys, I have private business to discuss with these two gents." Grumbling, the men strolled to the bar.

"So this is your deputy and biographer, Dr. Watson," she said coquettishly to Holmes, who stood at the table until she motioned for us to sit. "It is my pleasure to see you in the flesh, Doctor, because I have admired your writings from afar," Gertie crowed. "And Mr. Holmes, I consider it an honour to collabourate with you once more." A waitress took down our preferences for refreshments and Gertie wasted no additional time getting to the matter at hand.

Speaking barely above a whisper in the din of the pub, Gertie outlined the step she had taken on her own. "My sergeant is a numismatist, and he loaned me five rare coins from his collection to offer them to Smisky for the right price. Give me the imitation crown and I'll put it with them."

Holmes produced the counterfeit, which she inserted into a small paraffin paper jacket and dropped into her reticule. "Your plan will fall apart if Smisky buys back this hunk of junk," she frowned. "I'll memorise his words when he lays eyes on it. Now let's see what happens." We departed the pub together, Gertie hailing one cab while

Holmes and I summoned another to take us to the railway station. "Best we're not seen together until this is over," Holmes theorised when we boarded separate cars for the trip to Saxe-Coburg Square, the location of Smisky's coin shop. Once in the vicinity, Gertie walked alone the two city blocks to the shop, with Holmes and me trailing about twenty paces behind. As she went in, we plopped down on a bench near the entrance so we could hear the banter between Gertie and Smisky, close enough to intervene in the event there was trouble.

"I wish to speak to the owner," she notified the muscular man with a handlebar moustache behind the counter.

"You're lookin' at him, lady," he snickered.

"Do you buy rare coins at a fair price?" she asked.

"What price I pay will beat any competitor's, so help me God," he swore.

"Well, then, I have six to sell. My dear father passed away and left me his collection. Before he went on to his reward, he told me which ones to part with if I fell onto hard times."

"I won't take advantage of you, miss," he pledged. "Let's see what you have."

Gertie reached into her handbag and displayed the coins on the glass countertop.

"Hmmm," Smisky hummed, examining each one and replacing them into a row. "This one is worth five pounds to me, this one a little more, and the rest about ten pounds apiece – except this one," he scowled, manipulating the counterfeit 1707 crown between his fingers, flipping it into the air with his thumb and forefinger, then catching it in the palm of his stubby right hand. "This one is worth nothing, not even face value," he claimed.

"What in heaven's name do you mean by that?" Gertie ejaculated, pretending to be stunned.

"It's too heavy. It's a replica, not the genuine article," Smisky laughed.

"We'll see about that," Gertie snapped. "I'm taking it back, in fact all of them – I shan't do business with a scoundrel."

"Suit yourself for today, miss, but I'll gamble that when you find I've been truthful I'll see you again," Smisky concluded arrogantly.

"You can bet your life on that," Gertie mumbled to herself quietly as she stomped out of the shop.

"A marvelous, convincing performance; I believed you myself," Holmes beamed, complimenting her at the train station. "Mr. Smisky is one notch closer to the gallows."

"I was tempted to clamp the irons on his wrists right then and there," Gertie admitted, "but I realised that would interfere with your plan, Mr. Holmes."

Gertie returned to the constabulary in Gravesend, while Holmes and I rode on to the Strand for a dinner at Simpson's, our usual Wednesday evening habit.

That night, dressed as an Episcopalian cleric with a grey beard and frizzy white hair, Holmes went on the prowl in the West End, searching the streets for Gunther Williams, a clever and stealthy informant who once served time in Dartmoor Penitentiary for a series of burglaries, and who was known in the underworld as Hobo Willie. Holmes, who had been instrumental in the convict's early release from prison, based upon testimony that he financially supported the orphanage where he was raised, came across Williams at midnight outside a cafe famous for its coffee and fresh-fried donuts.

"I have a job for you, Gunther," Holmes began.

"And who might you be with a job for me?" Williams retorted.

"It is I, Sherlock Holmes, your benefactor," Holmes replied.

"By Jove! If it isn't you, Mr. Holmes. Preaching the gospel, are you?" a startled Williams quaked, to which Holmes responded with this quote from *Oliver Twist*:

"Yes, I'm preaching the gospel according to Charles Dickens: 'To do a great right, you may do a little wrong; and you may take any means which the end to be attained will justify.'"

"You want me to do something underhanded, then," the corpulent Williams predicted, stroking the fleshy portion of his double-chin.

"Skullduggery is more like it, Gunther," Holmes corrected. "There is a coin dealer in Saxe-Coburn Square who paid what the Americans call a torch to set an apartment building ablaze in the East End, where six people were burned alive and many others scorched. I want you to make a friend of him and learn the identity of the culprit who destroyed the building."

"That's an easy assignment, Mr. Holmes," Williams boasted. "I know the man, Joe Smisky, and he is a hard case, but I am more brainy. I'll betray him to you, yet never to the coppers, though. They would make me go to court and expose myself as a snitch."

"I shall protect your role in this, Gunther, rest assured," Holmes promised.

"Your word is your bond, I know that for a fact," Williams conceded, then was ready to disappear into the darkness until Holmes delayed him with the story of Gertie Evans and the counterfeit 1707 crown. Holmes also gave Williams explicit instructions on how to prompt Smisky to name the arsonist. "I'll sleep on all this and give you my report tomorrow before suppertime, Mr. Holmes," Hobo Willie vowed.

Holmes arrived back at Baker Street in the wee hours of the morning and devoted much of the time thereafter poring over his Index of criminals or pacing the floor of our sitting-room in his purple dressing gown, smoking his bent-billiard, briar-root pipe.

I awoke at dawn to the sound of his brewing the strong coffee that he favoured, which gave off a pleasant aroma that circulated upstairs to my bedroom. Groggy, I stumbled down to the table and helped myself to a cup while Holmes was sipping his as he scribbled a long message to Inspector Lestrade of Scotland Yard.

"Watson," he muttered without looking up from the stationery, "I have deduced the identity of the arsonist and will receive confirmation of my finding today from my informant, Gunther Williams, if he follows my script." Then, staring into my bleary eyes, Holmes warned: "Tonight will be a dangerous time. I must be off now to bait the trap."

While he was gone, Williams was fulfilling his commitment to Holmes, rapping on the door to Smisky's coin shop about eight o'clock to roust him out of bed in a back room. Drowsy from a deep slumber and in a foul mood, Smisky unlocked the door and opened it a crack. "Well, Hobo Willie, what do you want at this ungodly hour?" he sneered.

"Let me in, Joe, I have something to sell," Williams pleaded.

Opening the door wider and motioning with his head for his visitor to come inside, Smisky greeted him with an insult. "Something to sell? From one of your sticky finger endeavours?"

"No, Joe, it's information I'm pitching," came the answer.

"I'm not buying. I have all the information I can use," Smisky growled.

"This is about you and your future in the labour camp, or maybe even at the end of a rope," Williams enticed. "What's that worth to you?"

"It's not worth one pence so far. Are you out of your mind?" Smisky, now curious, said to lead Hobo Willie on. "I see you're all spruced up, shaved, hair trimmed, and in a new suit of clothes. Come into some money, have you?"

"Yes, I've been working, and these are my working clothes," Williams lied.

"Working at what, you tramp?" Smisky cackled.

"I've been working with Sherlock Holmes, the renowned detective, and he has the goods on you, Joe," Williams revealed.

"Has the goods on me? For what?" Smisky clamoured.

"That's what I have for sale, the whole picture," Williams professed. "I can give you information that will save your bacon."

"You're doing your pandering behind Holmes's back, then, for a bit of extra cash?" Smisky wanted to learn.

"You could say that, Joe, but it's more like I'm sharing what I know with a friend," Williams continued.

"Let me hear what you have to tell, and then I'll decide if you get anything from me for it," Smisky specified.

"Doesn't happen that way, Joe. First, you make an offer, and, second, I make the decision if the price is right," Williams bargained.

"Ten shillings, then, is that enough?" Smisky acquiesced.

"Not for what I have," Williams spouted.

"How much do you want, you little crook?" Smisky smirked.

"A five-pound note will buy everything you need to know," Williams boldly stated.

"Five pounds! Do you think I'm made of money?" Smisky protested, his face flushing.

"That's my price, take it or leave it," Williams countered.

"I'll take it, but this better be good, you blackmailing bastard," Smisky cursed.

"Good. By the way, Joe, this is extortion, not blackmail. There is a distinction in the law. Put the money where I can see it and I'll not touch it until you're satisfied I sang like a bird," said Williams confidently.

Smisky, moaning, went into the back room and emerged with a five-pound note, which he laid on the counter between himself and Hobo Willie. "Now sing your song," he demanded.

"I'll start with how you cooked your own goose yesterday," Williams began. "The young woman who came here with rare coins to sell was in league with Sherlock Holmes. All they wanted was for you to show them you knew a 1707 crown was a phony. You did just that, which made the case against you for transacting in counterfeit. That'll probably get you a three or four-year stretch. Now for the bad news.

Holmes has tracked down the party who burned your building in the East End, and the man has confessed, with the prospect of escaping the gallows if he testifies against you and the others who paid him to set fires. He told Holmes how he did them all, by rigging the gas valves. Now if he goes to court and fingers you, that could mean you'll swing from Old Bailey."

"I don't believe it," Smisky bellowed. "Frank Kiefer is smarter than any private detective. He wouldn't spill his guts if his life depended on it."

"His life did depend on it, Joe," Williams argued. "Sherlock Holmes caught him in the act of doing another job."

"T-t-this is terrible," Smisky stammered. "Has he gone to the police with his evidence?"

"Not yet, because he hasn't wrapped up the package in a neat bundle, at least not until he persuades you to confess, too," Williams informed Smisky. "Besides, he isn't working for the police. His client is an insurance company."

"I have some time, then. I can still do something about this meddlesome busybody," Smisky surmised. "Where can I find him?"

"He's pounding the bricks, he's on the street right now," Williams advised. "But I know where he'll be at seven o'clock tonight – having dinner at Simpson's in the Strand with a witness on another case."

"What's he look like?" Smisky questioned. "I think I'll have dinner with him."

Hobo Willie described Holmes down to the clothing he would be wearing that day, picked up the five-pound note, wished Smisky good luck, and departed in a jolly frame of mind, mission accomplished. He would make his report of a successful effort to Holmes at Baker Street in the afternoon, as he had prophesied.

Meantime, Holmes was experiencing success as well. He had traced Frank Kiefer to a brothel and opium den he owned in the sleazy Limehouse district.

"Frank, I am a friend of Joe Smisky, who says you can make gravel burn," Holmes exaggerated by way of introduction. "My name is Matthew McKinney, and I am a businessman from Baker Street, where my haberdashery is located. I have lost all my savings on the poker tables and I am in debt to the gamblers. I need you to arrange a gas leak."

"I can do that easily enough, but the cost to you will be severe," Kiefer foretold. "Joe had to triple the coverage on his apartment building to accommodate me and make a tidy profit at the same time. He was

249

pleased with the results, though. The job turned out beautiful. What a sight it was! Oooo, the flames were magnificent. Too bad so many people had to die and get hurt, but, like Joe said, they were the scum of the earth. How much insurance do you have?"

"Ten thousand pounds. How much do you want for the job?" Holmes asked.

"Ten thousand is my price," Kiefer allowed. "You'll have to do the same thing Joe did, double or triple the coverage, depending on how much you owe the sharks. What kind of building is it – what's it made of?"

"It's brick on the ground floor and wood frame on the floor above," Holmes related.

"Brick, you say?" Kiefer said hesitantly. "That will add a thousand pounds to the price. Brick needs a powerful blast. I'll come take a look at it tomorrow afternoon – be there at two o'clock. What's the address?"

"It's 221 Baker Street in the West End," Holmes told him. "Will you come alone?"

"My understudy, Donald Bonsal, will be with me," Kiefer disclosed. "He is my right arm, ever since I lost mine in an explosion three years ago. I was chopping holes in the roof of a club for ventilation when my ax struck a steel beam and created a spark. That was enough to ignite the gas. The vapors are volatile. I charge a lot of money for my work because it is so hazardous. But I guarantee the results and leave the coppers scratching their heads. When Frank Kiefer finishes a job, they can't prove a thing."

Stunned by Kiefer's callous attitude, Holmes made an excuse to exit after declining the arsonist's invitation to stay for a smoke in his opium room. Upon his return to our diggings, Holmes rubbed his sinewy hands together and fished half a cigar from the coal scuttle, lit it, inhaled, and repeated for me the incriminating chat he had with Kiefer.

"He is an amoral slouch with a haughty indifference toward the lives of the impoverished, as is Smisky," said Holmes to preface his rendition of the dialogue. "Society will be better off with those two reprobates in their graves. And I have the material to put them there."

Just as he completed his version of the event, Mrs. Hudson appeared on our threshold to announce that a Gunther Williams was in the foyer asking for Mr. Sherlock Holmes.

"Send him up with dispatch, Mrs. Hudson," Holmes directed her.

"It's uncanny, Mr. Holmes, but you were on target with what you said would happen," Williams praised. "He fell for it hook, line, and sinker. The name of the arsonist is –"

"Let me guess, Gunther, it's Frank Kiefer," Holmes butted in.

"If you knew that, why did you put me through –" the informant went on.

"I am sorry, but it was because I needed confirmation, Gunther," Holmes apologised. "I only had a suspicion it was Kiefer when I read in my Index at four o'clock this morning about the one-armed arsonist who was an expert with the properties of natural coal gas. Tell me more of your encounter, Gunther."

"Well, Smisky is planning something, probably to harm you fatally," Williams postulated. "Like you told me to say, I mentioned that you would be having dinner at seven o'clock at Simpson's. He asked me to describe you and said he might join you."

"Excellent, Gunther!" Holmes extolled. "Here are three guineas for your trouble. Let us fix you a ham and cheese sandwich, for I am certain you've had no lunch."

"Oh, thank you, Mr. Holmes, I am awfully hungry," Hobo Willie admitted. "I'll take it with me and eat it on the way home – in a cab, no less, now that I have the fare."

"Wait! Before you leave, Gunther," Holmes boomed with concern, "I feel obligated to warn you to keep a low profile for a day or so – don't patronise your usual haunts, don't follow your usual pattern. Smisky is sharp and he could smell a rat, meaning you. He is capable of violence against you, too."

"He is an idiot and a weasel, Mr. Holmes, and he'll never think to suspect me," Williams quarreled. "He is the least of my worries."

As Williams left, devouring the sandwich, an incensed Joseph Smisky was standing at the entrance to Frank Kiefer's brothel and opium den in the Limehouse district, summoning up the courage to do what he had come to do: eliminate the threat of a hardened criminal testifying against him at a trial that surely would spell his doom. He would silence Kiefer before he had the chance to speak under oath the words that would sway a jury to find the coin dealer guilty and send him to the gallows.

Smisky burst through the door and was immediately confronted by a Chinese attendant, who asked him in broken English if he wanted a girl, a smoking room, or both.

"I'm here to see Frank, that's all," Smisky barked.

"I fetch Master Frank, you sit," ordered the Chinaman, sensing an altercation. He climbed a stairway and opened a door.

"Master Frank, angry man downstairs to see you, very mad," said the agitated Chinaman.

Kiefer retrieved a six-shot revolver from a drawer and leveled it at his waist, then went to the bottom of the staircase and saw Smisky stewing on the sofa.

"Joe!" he hollered. "Yung-se says you're upset. Excuse the pistol. What's the matter?"

"I came here to choke you to death, Frank," Smisky acknowledged. "What's this I hear about you cooperating with Sherlock Holmes?"

"With who? Never met the man," Kiefer insisted. "But I did meet a friend of yours today, Matthew McKinney, who wants me to pulverise his haberdashery."

"A friend of mine? I don't know the name. What did he say about me?" Smisky queried.

"He said you recommended me to him. He knew I took care of business for you," Kiefer informed a puzzled Smisky.

"What did this McKinney look like?" Smisky asked.

"He was tall, skinny, a bird's beak for a nose, piercing eyes, with dark hair that was perfectly combed," Kiefer recalled.

"That was no Matthew McKinney. That was Sherlock Holmes," Smisky wailed.

"Who is Sherlock Holmes anyway?" Kiefer wanted to know.

"He's a beastly private detective who is investigating us for the fire," Smisky said to enlighten him.

"That evil rodent! Let's take care of him before he can do us in!" Kiefer roared.

"He'll be at Simpson's in the Strand at seven o'clock. We'll kill him there," Smisky agreed. "We'll make minced meat of him. But there's somebody I want to dust before him, Hobo Willie. He set me up for Holmes. Lend me a gun and twelve rounds of ammunition."

Smisky and Kiefer made plans for the murder at Simpson's, then Smisky left to hunt down Gunther Williams.

Finding him at the same cafe where Holmes ran across him, Smisky sneaked up behind him as he drank coffee on a stool, knocked the cup out of his hand, pointed the muzzle of the weapon in his pocket at Williams's ample belly, and coldly instructed him to walk outside. From there he escourted the victim to an alley, where he accused him of a double-cross.

"You are a traitor, and traitors are shot!" Smisky howled, then pulled the trigger six times, pumping Hobo Willie full of lead even after he was dead. "Let that be a final lesson to you, you maggot," Smisky seethed with abject bitterness, hovering over the corpse, "I'll see you in hell."

Word of Gunther Williams's demise would not reach Holmes that day, for the newspapers already had published their late afternoon editions, and the body was not discovered by constables until their evening rounds.

Holmes was pensive, fiddling with his chemicals at the deal-top table, stroking his violin aimlessly, checking the firearm in his shoulder holster to make sure it was loaded, asking me twice if I had examined mine, talking idly about the theatre and concerts, and, ultimately, about what Smisky might be intending and how. The minutes until seven o'clock ticked away.

When the timepiece on the mantel struck six-thirty, we donned our jackets, ventured casually out the door past Mrs. Hudson in the kitchen – "Enjoy your night out," she called to us – and stepped onto the pavement to flag down a hansom at the corner.

"Where to?" the driver sputtered, and Holmes gave him a light-hearted answer: "Simpson's in the Strand beckons us for a delightful meal." I boarded the vehicle first, and Holmes, ever vigilant, glanced in all directions before following me up into the seat. The horse moved forward and trotted through Cavendish Square, then beyond Regent Street near the intersection of Oxford Street, where Holmes raised up and surveyed the avenue behind us to determine if we were being stalked. "It looks clear, save for one cab about fifty yards to the rear," he observed, almost under his breath.

When we reached the Strand, my careful friend told the driver to pull to the curb around a bend in the road. "We'll walk the rest of the way," he apprised the driver. "Here is an extra two shillings if you continue on to Simpson's and stop in front for a minute until the cab behind us passes you by."

"Will do, guv'nor, whatever you say. Appreciate the tip," the driver concurred.

We strolled briskly toward the restaurant past the familiar shops and hotels until we were within sight of our destination. I checked my pocket watch and noted to Holmes that the time was six-fifty. "Avert the front door, Watson – we'll go in through the back and into the kitchen,"

Holmes advised. "Keep your eyes peeled, Watson. Remember, he's the stout fellow with a handlebar moustache."

"I would never forget that face, be certain," I assured my companion.

We emerged from the busy kitchen and into the crowded dining area, where an astonished *maître-de*, Oswald, excitedly encountered us. "Good gracious, Mr. Holmes, Dr. Watson, I never expected an entrance like this!" he cried. "Nonetheless, your table is ready."

We trailed after him to a setting in the centre of the room, seated ourselves, and scoured the faces of the patrons to see if the assassin had already arrived. There was no sign of Smisky, so we asked the waiter to bring us two glasses of dry sherry. It was seven o'clock.

Our drinks were served and Holmes proposed a toast. "May the dinner be succulent, uneventful, and safe," he prayed, "and may Joe Smisky be all bravado with no nerve."

Suddenly, two men with hoods covering their heads, their handguns thrust outward, appeared inside the front door, the weapons scanning the dining area as if searching for a target. One by one, the clientele noticed the intruders. The sounds of a vibrant atmosphere became eerily silent. One of the hooded figures trained his revolver on our table and a voice cracked the motionless air. "Holmes, you monster! Prepare to meet your Maker!"

With that, four other men at a scattering of tables flashed weapons that were aimed at the two assailants. One of those men spoke authoritatively and loudly. "Drop the guns or we'll fire. I am Inspector Lestrade of Scotland Yard and you are both under arrest for attempted murder."

"Murder it will be, then!" the second hooded man bawled, squeezing off two rounds in the direction of the lawmen, missing them and sending the bullets over the scalps of the diners into the wall. The four officers cut him down with a volley of shots as the hooded man closest to Holmes wheeled and tried to escape. He was accosted by two more members of Lestrade's squad and engaged them in battle, killing one before the other policeman emptied his revolver into the belligerent's chest and abdomen.

The odour of sulfur penetrated the dining room, and the customers, especially the ladies, shrieked in horror before the pandemonium dissipated.

The officials removed the hoods from the heads of the deceased assassins and Holmes informed Lestrade that their names were Smisky and Kiefer.

"When I received your message this morning," Lestrade remarked, "I thought it was another of your wild goose chases. But I couldn't be certain, so I came, anticipating nothing of this sort."

"You should know better by now, Lestrade, that when I humble myself to ask for your assistance, I am certain," Holmes scolded. "This outcome was predictable. I told you as much."

The next morning, after reading the account of the gunplay in the *Times,* Holmes saw a separate article, a small item, about the death of an ex-convict, Gunther Williams, also known as Hobo Willie. The newspaper said the police reported he was gunned down by an unknown attacker in an alley behind the Southpointe Cafe in Pope's Court.

The writer speculated that the killing was an act of revenge perpetrated by an enemy who also had been an inmate at Dartmoor Penitentiary. "Leave it to the naive press, Watson, to jump to such a conclusion without having the data to support it," Holmes groused. "I shall make a contribution to the orphanage in Gunther's honour."

The Saviour of
Cripplegate Square
by Bert Coules

This play was commissioned by the BBC as the fifth episode in the first series of The Further Adventures of Sherlock Holmes, *sixteen pastiche mysteries based on some of the throwaway references to other cases which Conan Doyle scattered throughout the Canon. The shows followed the earlier dramatisations of all fifty-six short stories and four novels, the first time it had ever been done in any medium. Clive Merrison repeated his Holmes in the sequels, with Andrew Sachs taking over as Watson after the untimely death of Michael Williams.*

If you have the original broadcast, either on CD or as a download, and try following the script as you listen along, you'll notice a few minor differences. Things almost always get changed during the recording: cuts for time, clarifications of plot points, smoothing out of lines that have proved unexpectedly tricky to say, and so on.

Readers unaccustomed to radio scripts are sometimes surprised by the presence of detailed directions for movement and business, especially if they've imagined the studio sessions as a group of performers sitting round a table and acting to a single microphone. In fact the process is a very physical one: there are sets with practical doors, windows, staircases, and furniture which the cast can roam around, and most directors choreograph a scene in much the same way as they would for a stage, film or TV production. Action, even something as simple as crossing a room to open a door, is valuable for preventing a static feel, and even a gesture or the position of the head changes the voice and makes for aural variety as well as dramatic realism.

INT and EXT in the scene headings stand for Interior and Exterior, distinctions achieved not only by the addition of appropriate background effects but also by recording in different acoustics: purpose-built radio drama studios are divided into areas with contrasting wall, floor and ceiling treatments which radically affect the sound.

A note on dates: In general, I was careful not to be too specific about the dating of any of the Further Adventures. *Not only was I well aware that we had a loyal audience of extremely knowledgeable Holmesians eager to pounce happily (and good-naturedly) on any inadvertent inconsistencies with the canon – Conan Doyle is himself*

256

often vague or completely silent on the subject of dates – so I was following in the best possible footsteps. But having said that, this particular story's mood of reminiscence and revelation seems to sit nicely with the time of Holmes's reappearance from his wanderings and Watson's return to the old Baker Street rooms, twin events which in this instance Sir Arthur pins down exactly; so 1894 let it be.

The case at the heart of the story though took place long before. It happened shortly after Holmes's arrival in London following his years at university, when, as it says in the script, he would have been in his early twenties. And I'm happy to leave things at that.

Finally, a playscript isn't as easy to read as a story: the experience can feel disjointed as the eye and the brain moves from scene heading to character name to dialogue and directions. Any initial awkwardness usually disappears as the pages succeed each other and, with luck, as the world of the drama begins to form in the reader's imagination. I hope this happens for you, and you find yourself transported back to a stormy Victorian night with the rain beating against the windows, the wind howling in the chimney, the fire crackling in the grate and Sherlock Holmes in the mood to tell a dark tale of his earliest days as a detective.

THE CAST
in order of speaking

SMITH – Nathaniel Collington Smith, librarian at the British Museum. Mildly eccentric, soft-spoken, widely experienced and very wise in an unconventional sort of way: a mentor to the young Sherlock Holmes. Sixties or older.

WATSON – Doctor John Watson.

HOLMES – Sherlock Holmes.

JENNY – Jenny Snell, a working class cleaner and general household servant. Early teens.

GUTTRIDGE – A working class East Ender. Forties.

257

LANDLADY – Ruler of a rough working class pub in the East End of London.

WOMAN – A young working class mother. East End Londoner.

MRS. GUTTRIDGE – An East Ender from the upper ranges of the working class. Forties or older.

DOCTOR – Working in one of the most desperate and poor areas of the East End.

MAN – An East End local.

Plus a noisy bunch of **REGULARS** in the Landlady's pub

TEASER. INT. THE READING ROOM, THE BRITISH MUSEUM.

Huge, echoey. Very quiet atmosphere, occasional distant footsteps, the odd cough and similar. After a few moments, close and quiet:

SMITH: Look around you, my young friend. A library is a perfect reflection of the ideal world. Every single volume in my care has its allotted place in the great scheme of things. Move one, even by an infinitesimal degree, and you diminish its value.

What use is information if one cannot instantly obtain it, or see precisely how it fits into the universe as a whole? Nothing exists in isolation. It is the relationships *between* facts which give them their meaning. These connections may be subtle, they may be hidden, they may be . . . unexpected. But if you are to master the world of knowledge, it is these links which you must seek out and understand. However well concealed, the truth is always there to be . . . detected.

At least, that is my view – and I should like to think that you agree with me . . . Mr. Holmes.

Music: the opening sig.

Opening announcements.
The music fades into:

SCENE 1. INT. THE SITTING ROOM, 221b BAKER STREET.

It is the winter of 1894.

An almighty thunderclap right overhead. Rain lashes, wind howls.
Watson is off at a window, looking out.

WATSON: What a filthy night.

He pulls the heavy curtains shut. The sound of the wind and rain
becomes more muted.

(*Approaching*) God only knows what's going on under cover of that.

We become aware of the open fire crackling away.

HOLMES: Crime, you mean?

WATSON: (*Sitting*) Of course. (*He flexes his injured shoulder*) Damn
weather.

HOLMES: Not much, I'd wager. How's the old war wound?

WATSON: Making its presence felt. What do you mean, not much?

HOLMES: It's fog that's the criminal's friend. On a night like this, most
self-respecting villains are safely tucked up with a drink and a good
smoke.

WATSON: Both of which they probably stole from some honest, hard-
working citizen.

HOLMES: No doubt.

WATSON: Brandy?

HOLMES: Thank you.

259

The brandy is close at hand. Watson pours two glasses.
As he does so, Holmes idly picks up his violin and prepares to play,
quietly checking the tuning. He breaks off.

You don't mind?

WATSON: Of course not. Take my mind off my damn shoulder.

HOLMES: I'll do my best.

A moment as he composes himself.
Then he begins to play: a slow plaintive melody: The Shepherd's
Lament *from Wagner's* Tristan and Isolde. *After a few bars he breaks*
off.

WATSON: Don't stop.

HOLMES: Not too depressing for a cold winter's night?

WATSON: I wouldn't have called it depressing. Plaintive, yes.

HOLMES: Plaintive. The very word.

He starts again. As he plays:

A dying man lies alone, helplessly waiting for the woman he loves.
For her sake, he's turned his back on everything: his friends, his
country, his hopes for the future. And now he waits for her . . . and she
does not appear.

WATSON: What's it from?

HOLMES: *Tristan and Isolde.* A hymn to love and death.

He stops playing.

WATSON: He had a pretty bleak view of love, your Wagner.

HOLMES: It's a bleak emotion.

WATSON: Oh, come on.

HOLMES: The Elizabethans had the right idea. To them, love was a disease. If you caught it, you were doomed.

WATSON: I'll stick to my definition, thank you. Here.

He passes Holmes his brandy.

HOLMES: Thank you. Love is a positive force for good? Love brings out the best in man?

WATSON: I think so.

HOLMES: You should have met Tobias and Emily Guttridge.

WATSON: Who the devil were they?

HOLMES: The Guttridges of Cripplegate Square. They caught the disease.

WATSON: You mean they were in love.

HOLMES: It goes somewhat further than that.

WATSON: One of your cases?

HOLMES: Yes, before you and I met.

WATSON: Is it a . . . good story?

HOLMES: (*A smile*) Come on, Watson. If you want to hear it, say so.

WATSON: (*A smile*) Of course I want to hear it.

HOLMES: A dark tale for a dark night. Very well, Doctor. Keep the brandy to hand, light up a cigar and let me shatter your illusions about love.

Music: the Tristan *tune, this time as heard in the actual opera – the haunting, atmospheric sound of a solo flute.*

The music takes us into Holmes's tale. It runs under:

SCENE 2. INT. THE READING ROOM, THE BRITISH MUSEUM.

Nathaniel Collington Smith is checking a pile of books. Holmes is in his early twenties.

SMITH: *The Annals of Crime. Police Review. Criminals and Their Characteristics. A Survey of Delinquent Behaviour.* Your books, Mr. Holmes.

HOLMES: Thank you, Mr. Smith.

Smith slides the books across a counter.
The music disappears as we cut back to:

SCENE 3. INT. THE SITTING ROOM AT 221b, BAKER STREET.

HOLMES: I don't believe I've ever mentioned Collington Smith.

WATSON: Never.

HOLMES: Nathaniel Collington Smith. He worked in the library at the British Museum. When I came down from university I spent a good deal of time there reading up on various subjects.

WATSON: Like the history of crime?

HOLMES: It's an essential study for a detective. If they'd put in a book collection down at Scotland Yard, their success rate would soar.

WATSON: Only if you persuaded them actually to read the books.

HOLMES: Smith could have persuaded them. He had that rare combination: he not only possessed knowledge, he was able to enthuse others with the thirst for it.

Cut to:

SCENE 4. INT. THE READING ROOM, THE BRITISH MUSEUM.

SMITH: If I might make a small comment . . . .

HOLMES: Of course.

SMITH: *Criminals and Their Characteristics.* It is perhaps a trifle . . . unsound.

HOLMES: You've read it?

SMITH: Oh dear me no. Librarians don't read books, Mr. Holmes. They simply know about them.

HOLMES: (*Chuckles. Then:*) Unsound?

SMITH: That is the general opinion. Sloppily argued from some highly dubious data.

HOLMES: Then please take it back.

SMITH: Why?

HOLMES: I've no wish to clutter my mind with useless information.

SMITH: My dear sir. Your mind may not have elastic walls but it does at least possess both an entrance and an exit. Read the book. Decide for yourself what to retain. One can learn from the unsound as well as the sound, you know. Surely they taught you that, up at the university?

HOLMES: Mr. Smith, anyone foolish enough to have voiced that sentiment would have been rapidly removed from the building and confined as a lunatic.

263

SMITH: Really? Fascinating. What a good job I never went there.

HOLMES: (*A vocal smile*)

Cut to:

SCENE 5. INT. THE SITTING ROOM, 221b BAKER STREET.

HOLMES: He was a remarkable man.

WATSON: He sounds it.

HOLMES: I learned a good deal in that reading room, and by no means all of it from the books.

Cut to:

SCENE 6. INT. A GALLERY, THE BRITISH MUSEUM.

No-one is around.
Holmes and Smith approach, deep in conversation.

SMITH: This is the finest place in the capital to study one's fellow man. In the course of a single morning here you can observe more characteristics than in a week outside. Only the other day – (*I noticed a man . . .*)

Holmes interrupts, stopping their progress.

HOLMES: What was that?

SMITH: I heard nothing.

HOLMES: I was sure . . . Yes. Listen.

They listen.
For the first time, we hear:

JENNY: (*Off, muffled*) (*Crying*)

SMITH: That's a woman crying.

HOLMES: I thought I was right. Probably one of the cleaning staff. I'm sorry, you were saying?

SMITH: Mr. Holmes, you disappoint me.

HOLMES: In what way?

SMITH: I believe it's emanating from that store-room. (*Moving off*) Come with me.

Cut to:

SCENE 7. INT. A SMALL STORE ROOM, THE BRITISH MUSEUM.

The door opens.

JENNY: (*Stifles her tears*)

SMITH: My dear child, what are you doing in here?

JENNY: Sorry sir. It won't happen again, sir. I'll get back to work.

SMITH: You'll do nothing of the sort.

JENNY: Sir?

Cut to:

SCENE 8. INT. SMITH'S OFFICE, THE BRITISH MUSEUM.

Small, homely. Perhaps an unobtrusive clock ticks, sedately. Smith is pouring a cup of tea.

SMITH: Sugar?

JENNY: Sir?

SMITH: Do you take sugar?

JENNY: No, sir, no thank you.

SMITH: Very well. Mr. Holmes, kindly pass over that plate of biscuits, would you?

Holmes is a little nonplussed by all of this. It makes him uncomfortable.

HOLMES: Yes, of course. Here.

He passes over the plate.

I should be going.

SMITH: No, I think perhaps you should stay.

Something in Smith's voice makes Holmes change his mind.

HOLMES: Very well.

SMITH: Excellent. Now – I am Nathaniel Collington Smith and this gentleman is Mr. Sherlock Holmes. And you are . . . ?

JENNY: Jenny, sir. Jenny Snell.

SMITH: Drink your tea, Miss Snell.

JENNY: I shouldn't be in here. If Miss McCarthy finds out . . . .

SMITH: You may safely leave Miss McCarthy to me. Drink your tea, then Mr. Holmes will pour you some more and you can tell us what's wrong.

JENNY: (*Relaxing*) Yes sir. Thank you, sir.

She drinks, gratefully.

Cut to:

SCENE 9. INT. THE SITTING ROOM, 221b BAKER STREET.

HOLMES: That was typical of the man. She wasn't a servant to him, just a soul in distress.

WATSON: What was the matter with the girl? Obviously, it was nothing trivial.

HOLMES: How do you know that?

WATSON: If it were, you would hardly be telling me about it, would you? When do we get to the Guttridges of Cripplegate Square?

HOLMES: Patience, Doctor. Let the tale unfold at its own pace.

Cut to:

SCENE 10. INT. SMITH'S OFFICE, THE BRITISH MUSEUM.

Jenny takes another gulp of her tea.
She puts down the cup.

SMITH: That's better. Now, Miss Snell. What is it that's so upset you?

JENNY: I . . . can't tell you.

HOLMES: Is it something to do with your other job?

JENNY: How did you know about that?

HOLMES: I've observed you once or twice arriving here in the evenings as I was leaving. You always come wearing some sort of uniform. Obviously, you have other employment during the day.

JENNY: I'm a nursemaid. Well, not really a nursemaid. Just a sort of cleaner really. Like here. (*Panicky again*) Look, I've got to go.

She stands.

267

SMITH: Miss Smith, please try to stay calm.

JENNY: If anyone finds out . . . .

SMITH: No-one will learn anything from me. And my young friend here is the very soul of discretion. Do you know what a detective is?

JENNY: I think so, sir.

SMITH: Well you're looking at one. Guardian of secrets, seeker out of truths.

JENNY: Oh.

SMITH: Now please – sit down, compose yourself and tell us what's wrong. You must not fear.

Cut to:

SCENE 11. INT. THE SITTING ROOM, 221b BAKER STREET.

HOLMES: He had an almost hypnotic way with her. I'd never seen anything like it before.

WATSON: What was her story?

HOLMES: At first it seemed nothing. Just an oversensitive reaction.

Cut to:

SCENE 12. INT. SMITH'S OFFICE, THE BRITISH MUSEUM

JENNY: During the day I work at Guttridge's Private Orphanage in Clerkenwell. Have you heard of it?

SMITH: No.

JENNY: Mrs. Guttridge she's the owner. She takes in babies.

HOLMES: Orphans, presumably.

JENNY: No, sir, not orphans though most of them might as well be.

HOLMES: Then what?

SMITH: Unwanted children, Mr. Holmes.

HOLMES: Unwanted? For what reason?

SMITH: There are many. Cost, space, social stigma, general encumbrance.

HOLMES: Good God.

SMITH: Something else they didn't teach you at university?

HOLMES: (*Absorbing the idea*) Yes . . . .

JENNY: Anyway, the women bring their babies to Mrs. Guttridge, and she takes them in.

HOLMES: So she's a philanthropist.

SMITH: I think you'll find that money changes hands.

HOLMES: Ah.

Cut to:

SCENE 13. INT. THE SITTING ROOM, 221b BAKER STREET.

WATSON: (*Distaste*) Baby-farming. You're talking about baby-farming.

HOLMES: The concept was totally new to me then. It was quite a shock.

269

WATSON: It's a shocking practice.

HOLMES: No, I mean it was a shock realising how little I actually knew of life. A valuable lesson.

WATSON: Yes, I'm sure it must have been. (*A moment*) So – this girl Jenny worked for a baby–farmer.

HOLMES: Yes.

Cut to:

SCENE 14. INT. SMITH'S OFFICE, THE BRITISH MUSEUM.

JENNY: The women pay so much a week. Or sometimes, they just make one . . . donation.

HOLMES: And what happens to the children?

JENNY: Mrs. Guttridge looks after them until they're older. Then she finds people to take them.

HOLMES: I see. And something has happened to upset this arrangement?

JENNY: Yes sir.

SMITH: Something connected with Mrs. Guttridge?

JENNY: No, sir, not her. It's her husband. He's a nasty piece of work, sir, though I shouldn't say so.

Cut to:

SCENE 15. INT. THE MEDICINE ROOM, THE GUTTRIDGE HOUSE.

GUTTRIDGE: (*Very sharp*) Get out of here, girl. You've no business in here.

JENNY: Please sir, Mrs. Guttridge sent me to fetch some iodine, sir.

GUTTRIDGE: Iodine?

JENNY: Yes sir.

GUTTRIDGE: Very well.

Glass bottles clink as he takes one from a shelf.

You fetched this yourself, do you understand? I was not here.

He hands it over.

JENNY: Very good sir. Thank you sir.

GUTTRIDGE: Tell her otherwise and I'll see you're dismissed. Now go.

Jenny rustles away.

Cut to:

SCENE 16. INT. SMITH'S OFFICE, THE BRITISH MUSEUM.

HOLMES: Where did this conversation take place?

JENNY: In one of the store rooms, sir. Where the medicines and things are kept.

HOLMES: Interesting.

SMITH: Go on with your story, Jenny. Surely you're not so upset just because someone told you off?

JENNY: If I was, I'd always be crying, sir. No, it's more than that.

HOLMES: Give us the facts.

JENNY: Well . . . I'm not sure I can. Not real facts, like.

271

HOLMES: Without the facts, how can we help you?

JENNY: Well . . . . (*She trails off*)

SMITH: There's more to life than cold facts, Mr. Holmes. Jenny, suppose you tell us this in your own way?

JENNY: Yes, sir. Well, there's something wrong in that house. Something very wrong. If it was just Mrs. Guttridge, everything would be so different . . . .

HOLMES: But it's her husband who causes you this alarm.

JENNY: He hates them, sir. The poor little babies. He hates them!

Cut to:

SCENE 17. INT. THE PARLOUR, THE GUTTRIDGE HOUSE.

From a nearby room, three babies cry, noisily, insistently.

GUTTRIDGE: (*Wearily*) For the love of God. Can't you shut them up?

JENNY: Some of them are sick, sir.

GUTTRIDGE: Again?

JENNY: Mistress says they'll be over it soon.

GUTTRIDGE: Why she has to devote her life to this, I cannot tell.

JENNY: She says they need her, sir. They need her.

Cut to:

SCENE 18. INT. THE SITTING ROOM, 221b BAKER STREET.

WATSON: She was a rare woman. Most of them are only interested in the money. The babies come a very poor second.

HOLMES: You speak from experience?

WATSON: Indirectly. These people are supposed to be registered. Local doctors carry out regular checks. The stories I've heard . . . .

HOLMES: Perhaps this one will be different.

WATSON: I hope it is.

Cut to:

SCENE 19. INT. SMITH'S OFFICE, THE BRITISH MUSEUM.

JENNY: Mr. Guttridge's always complaining about the children, about his wife, everything.

HOLMES: And yet he helps her run the orphanage?

JENNY: Yes, sir. In some ways . . . in some ways he's just a quiet little man. He does whatever his wife tells him to. He only moans about things when she isn't there. (*She realises how relaxed she's become*) I shouldn't be talking about him like this. Promise me you won't tell! Please!

SMITH: We've already promised. Have no fears.

JENNY: I'll try, sir.

SMITH: That's the way. Well, Jenny – a husband who complains about his wife. I'm afraid that's something that goes on in a good few households, West End as well as East. Something else has happened, hasn't it? Something more serious.

JENNY: Yes. Yes it has.

Cut to:

273

SCENE 20. INT. A BEDROOM, THE GUTTRIDGE HOUSE.

A large room with many cots.
The babies are quiet. Gentle snores, snuffles, sleeping–noises.
Jenny is checking one particular cot.

JENNY: (*Approaching*) There, that's good. That's nice. (*Very low*)
He'll have nothing to moan about now, will he, the old misery?
(*Closer*) Feeling better, now, are you? Are you?

The baby is not moving. A long moment.

Oh no. No. Please, no . . . .

She runs out.

Cut to:

SCENE 21. INT. SMITH'S OFFICE, THE BRITISH MUSEUM.

HOLMES: (*Matter–of–factly*) How many of them were dead?

JENNY: (*Very upset*) Three. The three who'd been sick. And sir – (*low*)
This was the day after I saw Mr. Guttridge messing about with the
medicines. The very next day.

SMITH: Ah.

JENNY: As God's in his heaven, sirs. I . . . I think he killed them.

Cut to:

SCENE 22. INT. THE SITTING ROOM, 221b BAKER STREET.

WATSON: It wouldn't be the first time, I'm afraid. Were the babies
insured?

HOLMES: As usual, you cut straight to the heart of the matter. Yes,
they were.

274

WATSON: Was there a doctor's report?

HOLMES: Mrs. Guttridge did everything by the letter of the law. The doctor was sent for straight away.

WATSON: And?

HOLMES: "No obvious cause of death".

WATSON: It may not have been the most rigorous examination. Those East End practices are desperately overworked.

HOLMES: And some of the doctors there are not above taking money to turn a blind eye.

WATSON: That is a disgusting suggestion.

HOLMES: Which you know full well to be true. Every barrel has its rotten apples, Watson. It will always be so.

WATSON: (*Reluctantly*) Yes, I'm afraid you're right. (*A moment*) I take it you investigated this Guttridge man, then? Was it your first murder case?

HOLMES: Actually, I was reluctant to get involved.

Cut to:

SCENE 23. INT. SMITH'S OFFICE, THE BRITISH MUSEUM.

HOLMES: You must go to the police.

JENNY: The police! I can't! Don't you know what happens to servants who criticise their masters, sir? I'd be out on my ear and no character. Then what would happen to me?

HOLMES: You have your job here.

JENNY: Four hours work at fivepence a night? Could you live on that?

SMITH: No, he couldn't. I understand your problem, my dear.

JENNY: (*Very fearful*) There's something else, sir. Something I haven't said.

SMITH: And what is that?

HOLMES: She's afraid that Guttridge knows of her suspicions.

JENNY: That's it, sir. He knows I saw him doing it – whatever it was. With the medicines.

HOLMES: When was this?

JENNY: Five days ago.

SMITH: Have you been in to work there since?

JENNY: Every day. I'd get the elbow otherwise.

HOLMES: You are a very brave young woman.

JENNY: Brave? Not me, sir. I've been terrified, I tell you straight.

HOLMES: Has Mr. Guttridge said anything to you? Or done anything suspicious?

JENNY: No. But I've kept away from him best I could.

SMITH: Very sensible of you. (*A moment*) My young friend here will look into the matter.

JENNY: (*Gratefully*) Oh, sir . . . .

HOLMES: Smith?

JENNY: I'm ever so grateful, sir. I had to tell someone – I'm glad it was you.

Cut to:

SCENE 24. EXT. OUTSIDE THE BRITISH MUSEUM. NIGHT.

Quiet traffic, pedestrians.

SMITH: (*Deep breath*) Another fine night.

HOLMES: Why did you say that to the girl?

SMITH: My dear Mr. Holmes, surely you found the story . . . interesting?

HOLMES: Of course. The girl is observant and intelligent, and her suspicions are probably correct.

SMITH: And she appears to have great faith in your ability to help her. Which I share.

HOLMES: Thank you. But the fact remains I don't see what on earth I can do.

SMITH: You can stir yourself out from behind your books and look into the real world for a change. What sort of detective turns his back on a possible murder case?

HOLMES: I can hardly march up to this woman's . . . establishment and tell her I'm investigating three suspicious deaths.

SMITH: Of course you can't. But there are other ways. Put that brain of yours to use.

Cut to:

SCENE 25. INT. AN EAST END PUB.

Full, raucous and a bit frightening. Conversations, arguments, laughter.
Glass breaks. An ironic cheer goes up.
Closer, some of the regulars react to an incongruous sight . . .

REGULARS: Look what the cat dragged home / Slumming it, are you dearie? / Gordon Bennett, it's champagne Charlie hisself . . . .

The object of their attention makes it unscathed to the bar.

LANDLADY: Good evening sir. What's your pleasure?

HOLMES: Whisky, please. And have one yourself.

LANDLADY: Thank you sir. (*Louder, pointedly*) Pleasure to encounter a real gent, for a change.

REGULARS: (*Good–natured jeers*)

Holmes fishes out coins as the landlady pours his drink.

LANDLADY: There. Best in the house.

HOLMES: Thank you.

LANDLADY: (*Lower*) Now sir, what tickles your fancy? Big, skinny, ripe for the plucking, what're you after?

HOLMES: What I'm after is information.

LANDLADY: (*Suddenly cagey*) What sort of information?

HOLMES: Do you know a man called Guttridge?

Cut to:

SCENE 26. INT. THE SITTING ROOM, 221b BAKER STREET.

HOLMES: It was a mistake, of course. She shut her mouth and didn't open it again.

WATSON: They're very suspicious of strangers in those parts. Especially ones from up west.

278

HOLMES: Yes, so I discovered. It was a stupid miscalculation.

Cut to:

SCENE 27. INT. THE READING ROOM, THE BRITISH MUSEUM.

SMITH: Don't berate yourself. The basic idea was perfectly sound.

HOLMES: If you want the local gossip go to the local pub. (*Ruefully*) Just don't go dressed for the opera.

SMITH: I trust you didn't give up the quest quite that easily.

HOLMES: Of course not. I waited until it was full dark and went round to the house itself.

Cut to:

SCENE 28. EXT. OUTSIDE THE GUTTRIDGE HOUSE. NIGHT.

Cripplegate Square is not in a salubrious neighbourhood. Distant raised voices, dogs, perhaps even a muffled scream from well in the distance.

HOLMES (*over*): The area wasn't . . . pleasant. Guttridge's Private Orphanage was a rambling old building set back from the street. It must have been quite a place in its day.

WATSON (*over*): Didn't you feel even more conspicuous there than in the pub?

HOLMES (*over*): Oddly enough, no I didn't. Evening wear is ideally suited to hiding in the undergrowth. Every burglar should invest in a set of tails.

In the scene, the front door opens. Two women emerge.

279

WOMAN: (*Sobbing*)

MRS. GUTTRIDGE: Easy now. Easy. She'll be safe and well–cared for. And you can come and visit her whenever you want, I've told you that.

WOMAN: I don't think I could bear it. I really don't.

MRS. GUTTRIDGE: I understand. But if you change your mind, there's always a welcome for you here.

WOMAN: You're so kind. Without you, I . . . I'd have had to . . . .

MRS. GUTTRIDGE: Now there's no sense dwelling on might–have–beens. Will you be all right going home?

WOMAN: It's not far. I'll be quite safe. Oh . . . .

With a final rush of emotion, she hugs Mrs. Guttridge.

MRS. GUTTRIDGE: There, there child. It's mended. Everything's all right now.

Cut to:

SCENE 29. INT. SMITH'S OFFICE, THE BRITISH MUSEUM.

HOLMES: It was immensely frustrating. I could see in the front door, but I couldn't learn anything of use. And there was no sign of Mr. Guttridge at all. If I'm going to see this thing through, I need to get inside.

SMITH: And how exactly do you propose to do that?

HOLMES: I don't know yet.

SMITH: If I might make a small suggestion?

HOLMES: Please do.

SMITH: This could be an ideal opportunity to put some of that expensive university experience to good use.

HOLMES: Applied chemistry?

SMITH: That wasn't what I had in mind, no. Try to think in something other than straight lines.

Cut to:

SCENE 30. INT. THE SITTING ROOM, 221b BAKER STREET.

WATSON: So that's where you got it from.

HOLMES: Watson, you're interrupting my flow. Got what from?

WATSON: That infuriating expression. How many times have you told me to stop thinking in straight lines?

HOLMES: It's very good advice.

WATSON: Well, did it work?

HOLMES: Actually, yes, it did.

Cut to:

SCENE 31. EXT. AN EAST END STREET. DAY.

Holmes is in disguise. He's a market supervisor – working class but not the lowest rung.

HOLMES: 'Scuse me, mate.

MAN: Yeah?

HOLMES: I'm looking for Guttridge's Orphanage. D'you know it?

Cut to:

SCENE 32. INT. THE SITTING ROOM, 221b BAKER STREET.

WATSON: Are you really saying – (*that was the first time . . . .*)

Holmes is annoyed at yet another interruption.

HOLMES: Watson.

WATSON: Sorry. But this is fascinating. You're saying that was the very first time you ever used a disguise?

HOLMES: Exactly so. Thinking sideways, you see? What did I do at university apart from study – I acted.

WATSON: You've never told me that.

HOLMES: You've never asked me. May I continue?

WATSON: No more interruptions, I promise. What did you find when you got to the orphanage?

HOLMES: What I expected to find. My primary suspect.

Cut to:

SCENE 33. EXT. THE FRONT PORCH, THE GUTTRIDGE HOUSE. DAY.

Holmes is still in character.

GUTTRIDGE: Yes?

HOLMES: I want to see Mrs. Guttridge.

GUTTRIDGE: What makes you think she's here?

HOLMES: Look, mate, don't mess me about. This is Guttridge's Private Orphanage, right? Where else is she going to be?

GUTTRIDGE: (*Very suspicious*) Who are you?

HOLMES: (*Less aggressively*) I'm someone who wants to see the . . . proprietor. Look, please.

MRS. GUTTRIDGE: (*Off, inside*) Who is it, Toby?

GUTTRIDGE: Someone for you.

MRS. GUTTRIDGE: (*Approaching*) Then why didn't you send Jenny to find me? (*She sees Holmes. A moment*) Good afternoon.

HOLMES: Mrs. Guttridge? I was told . . . Look . . . .

A moment.

MRS. GUTTRIDGE: It's a chilly day. We'll be more comfortable inside.

Cut to:

SCENE 34. INT. THE PARLOUR, THE GUTTRIDGE HOUSE.

Mrs. Guttridge and Holmes sit.

MRS. GUTTRIDGE: That's better. Now, I expect you'd like some tea.

She rings a small handbell.

HOLMES: (*Hastily*) No, that's all right. Don't bother on my account.

MRS. GUTTRIDGE: It's no bother.

She rings again.

Where is that girl?

HOLMES: Look, really . . . .

The door opens. It's Jenny.

JENNY: Yes, ma'am?

MRS. GUTTRIDGE: Tea please, Jenny. And some of the cherry cake.

JENNY: Ma'am.

Cut to:

SCENE 35. INT. THE SITTING ROOM, 221b BAKER STREET.

WATSON: Did she recognise you?

HOLMES: I was sure she would. But no, she didn't. Quite a boost to my confidence, I can tell you.

WATSON: It's not easy to imagine your confidence ever needing a boost.

HOLMES: It was a long time ago.

Cut to:

SCENE 36. INT. THE PARLOUR, THE GUTTRIDGE HOUSE.

Mrs. Guttridge is pouring the tea.

MRS. GUTTRIDGE: Now, Mr. . . . ?

HOLMES: Hawkins, ma'am. Albert Hawkins.

MRS. GUTTRIDGE: Now, Mr. Hawkins. You drink your tea and I'll tell you why you've come to me.

HOLMES: Ma'am?

MRS. GUTTRIDGE: There.

She passes him the tea.
Both in and out of character, Holmes is a touch nonplussed.

HOLMES: Thanks. What do you mean, ma'am? *You'll* tell *me?*

MRS. GUTTRIDGE: My dear Mr. Hawkins, people only come here for one reason. The details vary, but the basic facts are always the same. Now let me see . . . You're in work, yes?

HOLMES: Market supervisor.

MRS. GUTTRIDGE: Decent enough pay but not enough to feed one more mouth. Am I right?

HOLMES: We've got five already. Look, no offence and all, but if there was any other way I wouldn't be here.

MRS. GUTTRIDGE: You're not alone, Mr. Hawkins. Oh no, you're definitely not alone. At least you're not contemplating something more . . . drastic.

HOLMES: I'll have nothing to do with that! And no more will my Elsie. I've seen what those butchers do.

MRS. GUTTRIDGE: And so have I, I'm sorry to say. We shan't mention it again. Does your wife know you're here?

HOLMES: Oh yes.

MRS. GUTTRIDGE: Good. Well, we do have space at the moment. Would you like to see round the house?

HOLMES: I wouldn't mind. Put my mind at rest, like.

MRS. GUTTRIDGE: Of course. Drink up your tea and I'll give you a tour.

Cut to:

SCENE 37. INT. A BEDROOM, THE GUTTRIDGE HOUSE.

The babies are asleep. Odd noises.

MRS. GUTTRIDGE: (*Low*) You've made a good choice, Mr. Hawkins. I never take in more babies than I can cope with, unlike some, I'm sorry to say.

HOLMES: (*Low*) We have heard stories, my Else and me.

MRS. GUTTRIDGE: And some of them are undoubtedly true, I'm afraid.

HOLMES: What happens if they get sick?

MRS. GUTTRIDGE: I can care for most common illnesses myself. And of course we're registered with a local doctor.

HOLMES: Good. That's good . . . And they do look all right, like. Look at 'em sleeping so peaceful. Happy, and that . . . . (*He can't continue, overcome with emotion*)

MRS. GUTTRIDGE: Oh, my dear young man. I realize how hard this must be for you.

HOLMES: Hard? Hard's not the half of it.

MRS. GUTTRIDGE: Of course it's not. And nothing I can say to you will ease the pain. But look around you, Mr. Hawkins. These babies are clean and well–fed and content. If I can give your little one those blessings, well, isn't that better than the life he'll face outside these walls?

HOLMES: Yeah. Yeah, it is. Course it is. (*A moment*) So – I suppose all I need to know now . . . Well . . . . (*He trails off*)

MRS. GUTTRIDGE: I think there's still some cherry cake downstairs. We can discuss the practicalities over some more tea. Come along.

Cut to:

286

SCENE 38. INT. THE SITTING ROOM, 221b BAKER STREET.

HOLMES: "The practicalities" turned out to be three-pence a day or a single payment of five pounds.

WATSON: (*A whistle*)

HOLMES: Yes, it was certainly more than the going rate, I checked. But it was a superior establishment.

WATSON: How many working class women could afford five pounds?

HOLMES: Well, when you consider the alternatives . . . .

WATSON: I'm afraid the alternatives are the only way for most people in that position. Something's going to have to be done, you know. Sooner or later.

HOLMES: I agree. But we are straying somewhat from the story.

WATSON: Sorry. Did you manage to see that medicine store room?

HOLMES: It would have been too out of character, I'm afraid. But I did at least succeed in getting another look at the alleged child–killer. He was summoned to show me out.

Cut to:

SCENE 39. INT. THE HALLWAY, THE GUTTRIDGE HOUSE.

Holmes and Guttridge approach.

HOLMES: Your wife's a wonderful woman, Mr. Guttridge.

GUTTRIDGE: So I'm constantly being told.

HOLMES: You must be proud of her.

287

GUTTRIDGE: There are perhaps . . . nobler ways to make a living.

HOLMES: I can't think of any. She's a real Godsend, she is.

Guttridge opens the front door.

GUTTRIDGE: Do you say so.

HOLMES: (*Leaving*) I do, sir. God bless her – and you too.

GUTTRIDGE: Good day to you, Mr. Hawkins.

He shuts the door.

(*Breathes deeply*)

Cut to:

SCENE 40. INT. SMITH'S OFFICE, THE BRITISH MUSEUM.

HOLMES: There's a definite undercurrent of . . . I'm not sure – hate, possibly. Weariness, distaste . . . But I'm not prepared to brand him as a murderer on the strength of it.

SMITH: I'm pleased to hear it.

HOLMES: I have to know what's in that medicine store.

SMITH: And how do you propose to find out?

HOLMES: I've thought of two separate ways. Neither of them is ideal. One is positively illegal.

SMITH: And the other?

Cut to:

SCENE 41. INT. A GALLERY, THE BRITISH MUSEUM.

Open and echoing.

JENNY: No! I can't!

HOLMES: Jenny . . . .

JENNY: Suppose he catches me?

HOLMES: I'll make sure he's out of the way.

JENNY: But I wouldn't know what to look for.

HOLMES: I'll give you a list.

JENNY: A list? Oh, sir . . . What good's a list to me?

HOLMES: (*Realising*) You can't read.

JENNY: Nor write. No, sir, I can't.

Cut to:

SCENE 42. INT. THE SITTING ROOM, 221b BAKER STREET.

WATSON: Thank God for it. Holmes, what the devil were you thinking of?

HOLMES: Collington Smith used exactly those words.

WATSON: Good for him. To put that child into danger . . . .

HOLMES: I had a perfectly foolproof diversion worked out.

WATSON: Did you.

HOLMES: (*A sigh*) As I said, it was a long time ago. I wouldn't do it now.

WATSON: Unless there was no other way.

HOLMES: The point is academic. I had to fall back on my second plan of attack.

WATSON: The illegal one.

HOLMES: Quite.

WATSON: I know exactly what it was.

HOLMES: Of course you do.

Cut to:

SCENE 43. EXT. REAR GARDEN, THE GUTTRIDGE HOUSE. NIGHT.

Very quiet and still.
Close, a glass–cutter does its stuff.
It stops. Tap . . . Tap . . . Tap . . . and part of a pane of glass comes away.
Suddenly, not far off, a dog barks.

HOLMES: (*Catches his breath*)

He freezes. But then a cat screeches and the barking and squealing recede together as the animals run off.
It was a coincidence. A moment of calm.

(*Breathes again*)

He reaches through the hole in the window and opens the latch.

(*Sotto, smug*) Ha. Elementary.

Cut to:

SCENE 44. INT. SMITH'S OFFICE, THE BRITISH MUSEUM.

SMITH: My dear Mr. Holmes. I cannot condone such blatantly criminal activity. (*A moment*) Unless of course it yielded the desired result.

HOLMES: Arsenic. He's been concentrating pure arsenic and storing it in unmarked bottles in a locked cupboard.

SMITH: Then young Miss Snell was quite correct.

HOLMES: It looks like it.

SMITH: What will you do now?

HOLMES: There's one more piece of evidence I need. Then my case will be complete.

Cut to:

SCENE 45. INT. THE SITTING ROOM, 221b BAKER STREET.

WATSON: I presume you were talking about the doctor.

HOLMES: Yes, I was. I had to be sure that the infants had died from arsenical poisoning. ["arse–EN–icle"]

WATSON: What about your theory that the doctor was in league with the murderer?

HOLMES: I was never said he was, Watson. I said he might have been. I had to hope that seeing him face-to-face would enable me to decide.

Cut to:

SCENE 46. INT. A DOCTOR'S SURGERY, THE EAST END.

Small, cramped, and with a lot of patients-in-waiting noise filtering in from the next room.

DOCTOR: A detective? Do you mean from Scotland Yard?

HOLMES: A private detective.

DOCTOR: Are you sick? Injured?

HOLMES: No.

DOCTOR: Sir, I have a room full of patients out there and a hundred more waiting to take their place. I don't mean to be rude, but I have no time to play games.

HOLMES: This is no game. You are the official medical examiner for Guttridge's Orphanage, are you not?

DOCTOR: What about it?

HOLMES: I have been commissioned to investigate the recent deaths of three infants.

DOCTOR: Mr. . . .

HOLMES: Holmes. Sherlock Holmes.

DOCTOR: Mr. Holmes, when you leave my rooms look around you. Look at the filth and the squalour and the hunger. And ask yourself which is the stranger – that children die or that they manage to live. Have you seen inside Mrs. Guttridge's establishment? Have you met the lady herself?

HOLMES: Yes, I have.

DOCTOR: Then you'll know that the children there live like royalty compared to most. I've seen Mrs. Guttridge take in babies who were more bone than flesh. If some of them don't survive, then look outside that house for the cause, sir, not inside it. (*A moment*) Now if you don't mind, I have to do my best to help these people.

HOLMES: Will you answer just two questions?

DOCTOR: If you will agree to ask them and then leave.

HOLMES: I agree.

DOCTOR: Then ask me your questions.

HOLMES: Did you conduct a thorough examination of the dead babies?

DOCTOR: As thorough as my time and my resources permitted, yes I did.

HOLMES: And did you detect any signs at all of arsenical poisoning?

DOCTOR: (*Taken aback*) Arsenic? Good God no. Not a trace.

Cut to:

SCENE 47. INT. THE SITTING ROOM, 221b BAKER STREET.

WATSON: You believed him.

HOLMES: I was impressed with him. I've said to you before now that when a doctor goes wrong he makes a formidable criminal.

WATSON: Yes, you have. I can't say I was flattered.

HOLMES: Then perhaps this will redress the balance. In all my life I've not met many people who were thoroughly decent, uncomplicated, good men. And of the ones I have met – several of them were doctors.

Cut to:

SCENE 48. INT. SMITH'S OFFICE, THE BRITISH MUSEUM.

SMITH: You appear to have arrived at something of an impasse, my friend.

HOLMES: Why else is arsenic there, if not to kill those children?

SMITH: Rats?

HOLMES: You can buy poison for vermin over the counter at any chemist's shop. If I read the evidence aright, that arsenic was being produced in secret, then hidden away.

SMITH: Then what do you propose to do now?

HOLMES: I suppose it could be nothing more than a coincidence . . . I have to talk to the girl again.

Cut to:

SCENE 49. INT. A GALLERY, THE BRITISH MUSEUM.

After closing time.
Jenny is mopping the floor, absorbed in what she is doing.

HOLMES: (*Close*) Jenny.

JENNY: (*Starts*)

HOLMES: I'm sorry. I didn't mean to startle you.

JENNY: It's not you, sir, it's me. I'm just frightened at any little noise, now. (*A sudden thought*) You're not going to ask me to spy on him again?

HOLMES: No, no. And . . . I'm sorry about asking you before. It was wrong. Please forgive me.

JENNY: Forgive you? Forgive . . . . (*She starts to cry*)

HOLMES: My dear Miss Snell . . . . Please stop crying . . . .

JENNY: Sorry, sir. I'm really . . . . (*She trails off*)

HOLMES: What's wrong?

JENNY: Nothing's wrong. It's just . . . Well, people like me don't get apologised to, that's all.

294

HOLMES: Ah. Then you do forgive me.

JENNY: Course I do, sir. You was only trying to help me, after all.

HOLMES: Thank you.

JENNY: So – what do you want this time?

HOLMES: I want to ask you this. When you surprised Mr. Guttridge with the medicines – can you remember what he was doing. Exactly what he was doing?

JENNY: Well . . . . (*She trails off*)

HOLMES: It might help if you tell me what he was working with. Do you remember?

JENNY: I'm not sure . . . .

HOLMES: Recall the scene. Mrs. Guttridge asked you to get some iodine.

JENNY: That's right.

HOLMES: So you had to stop what you were doing. What was that?

JENNY: I was washing the sheets. I'd just put the clean ones on the beds, and I was washing the old ones.

HOLMES: Very good. So you had to stop washing the sheets and you went to the medicine store. Was the door open or shut?

JENNY: (*Slowly remembering*) Shut. It was shut.

HOLMES: Excellent. You pushed open the door – and you saw Mr. Guttridge. Was he facing you?

JENNY: No he had his back to the door. That's right – he was bending over the table. He turned round . . . And he had . . . . (*puzzled*) flypapers. He was holding flypapers.

295

Cut to:

SCENE 50. INT. THE SITTING ROOM, 221b BAKER STREET.

WATSON: Flypapers.

HOLMES: Made by impregnating a strip of paper with a weak solution of . . .

WATSON: . . . arsenic. Soak the paper in water, boil the solution dry, and what's left is pure concentrated poison. Pretty damning.

HOLMES: Conclusive.

Cut to:

SCENE 51. INT. A GALLERY, THE BRITISH MUSEUM.

HOLMES: Excellent, Jenny. You've done well.

JENNY: Have I, sir?

HOLMES: Very well indeed. I fancy that what you saw was the very poison being prepared.

JENNY: No! That's so horrible.

HOLMES: I need to you do something else for me, now.

JENNY: I'll do anything I can, sir.

HOLMES: Continue to keep your eyes and your ears open. There's more to be discovered. If you see or hear anything else that might be important – anything at all – let me know at once. Do you understand?

JENNY: Oh yes, sir. I understand.

Cut to:

SCENE 52. INT. A SMALL ROOM, THE GUTTRIDGE HOUSE.

Jenny is bottle–feeding a baby.
It produces rhythmical sucking noises.

JENNY: There you are . . . Oh, not too fast, now. Good . . . .

MRS. GUTTRIDGE: When you've finished here Jenny, collect up the bottles and leave them to soak.

JENNY: Yes ma'am.

MRS. GUTTRIDGE: (*Going*) I'll be in the scullery if you need me.

JENNY: Ma'am.

Mrs. Guttridge has gone.
The baby continues to drink.

Yes you like that, don't you? Course you do. That's the way . . . .

GUTTRIDGE: (*From nowhere*) You, girl.

JENNY: (*Starts, very frightened*) Sir?

GUTTRIDGE: Stop that and come with me. I want to talk to you.

Cut to:

SCENE 53. INT. THE MEDICINE ROOM, THE GUTTRIDGE HOUSE.

Guttridge and Jenny approach from the corridor.

GUTTRIDGE: Get in there.

JENNY: No. No!

GUTTRIDGE: Quiet, girl. Go in, I say.

He pushes her in, follows her . . .
and closes and locks the door.

JENNY: (*Fights for breath, very scared*)

GUTTRIDGE: Stop that and listen to me. I want to know exactly what you saw in here the other day. You understand? Exactly.

Cut to:

SCENE 54. INT. SMITH'S OFFICE, THE BRITISH MUSEUM.

SMITH: I'm afraid I have some disturbing news.

HOLMES: What news?

SMITH: I've been speaking to the cleaning supervisor. Jenny Snell hasn't come into work for the past four nights.

Cut to:

SCENE 55. INT. THE SITTING ROOM, 221b BAKER STREET.

WATSON: Oh, God.

HOLMES: No, it didn't look good.

WATSON: What did you do?

HOLMES: I trusted that my disguise really had taken them in, and went round to Guttridge's Orphanage as myself.

WATSON: Quite a risk.

HOLMES: It had to be done.

Cut to:

SCENE 56. EXT. FRONT DOOR, THE GUTTRIDGE HOUSE. DAY.

HOLMES: Good afternoon. My name is Sherlock Holmes. I'm here to enquire about Miss Jennifer Snell.

A moment.

GUTTRIDGE: Then you'd better come in.

Cut to:

SCENE 57. INT. SMITH'S OFFICE, THE BRITISH MUSEUM.

SMITH: What happened?

HOLMES: I was presented with this. Here.

He produces a folded piece of paper.

Cut to:

SCENE 58. INT. THE SITTING ROOM, 221b BAKER STREET.

WATSON: But surely . . . .

HOLMES: Exactly. A fatal error.

WATSON: But what did it mean? Had he killed her, too?

HOLMES: The girl had been silenced. I'm afraid I could see no other explanation.

WATSON: What did you do?

HOLMES: To be honest – I wasn't sure what to do.

Cut to:

299

SCENE 59. INT. SMITH'S OFFICE, THE BRITISH MUSEUM.

HOLMES: I want to ask your advice.

SMITH: My advice? My dear sir, I'm just a tired old librarian, too rapidly approaching an unwilling retirement. What can you possible wish to ask me?

HOLMES: If I should go to the police with what I know, or confront the murderer myself.

Cut to:

SCENE 60. INT. THE SITTING ROOM, 221b BAKER STREET.

WATSON: What was Smith's advice?

HOLMES: To do neither.

WATSON: Neither? Why on earth not?

HOLMES: For a very good reason, which I'd completely overlooked.

Cut to:

SCENE 61. INT. SMITH'S OFFICE, THE BRITISH MUSEUM.

SMITH: You're too eager to show off your cleverness. A calculating criminal has made a slip and Sherlock Holmes has detected it. Am I correct?

HOLMES: Well, yes, I suppose you are. But if I'm right and the girl has been done away with . . . .

SMITH: Then justice must be done. Of course. But it seems to me, Mr. Holmes, that you're proposing to confront your villain with only half a case. You may have solved the new crime – but what of the old one?

Cut to:

SCENE 62. INT. THE SITTING ROOM, 221b BAKER STREET.

WATSON: The dead babies.

HOLMES: He was quite right, of course. I had nothing to link the three dead infants with the secret store of arsenic. No evidence whatsoever of foul play.

WATSON: What did you do?

HOLMES: Something you've seen me do many times. I just sat and smoked and thought. And eventually, I saw the truth. And then I knew exactly what course I should take.

Cut to:

SCENE 63. INT. THE PARLOUR, THE GUTTRIDGE HOUSE.

MRS. GUTTRIDGE: Mr. Holmes, I fail to see how I can help you further. I've given you Jenny's home address, I suggest you contact her at her father's.

HOLMES: I doubt if I should find her there.

GUTTRIDGE: What do you mean by that?

HOLMES: But I am not here solely about Miss Snell. I am investigating the recent deaths of three babies in your care, Mrs. Guttridge.

MRS. GUTTRIDGE: Those children died of natural causes, God rest their souls. I have the doctor's certificates.

HOLMES: I'm well aware of that.

MRS. GUTTRIDGE: Then what is there to investigate?

301

HOLMES: A very great deal. For instance – I know that your medicine store contains a hidden supply of concentrated arsenic.

MRS. GUTTRIDGE: What?

HOLMES: And I know that the arsenic was used to kill those infants.

MRS. GUTTRIDGE: But there was no trace of poison – (*in them . . . .*)

GUTTRIDGE: (*To Holmes*) You know that?

HOLMES: Oh yes. And finally, I know that Jenny Snell was unfortunate enough to stumble on to what was happening. And was killed, to keep her silent.

MRS. GUTTRIDGE: Jenny's dead?

HOLMES: Unfortunately for her killer, she came to me first.

MRS. GUTTRIDGE: She can't be dead. It's a lie. Toby, tell him.

GUTTRIDGE: I already have. She had to leave unexpected.

HOLMES: Oh yes.

He produces his sheet of paper.

"My Mum died sudden I have to go home" . . . .

MRS. GUTTRIDGE: There you are.

Holmes examines the paper.

HOLMES: Actually, it's quite well done. Except for one rather significant detail.

GUTTRIDGE: What are you on about?

HOLMES: Next time you forge a farewell letter, Guttridge, I suggest you first make sure that your victim knows how to write.

A long moment.

MRS. GUTTRIDGE: Tobias, tell me this isn't true.

HOLMES: What did you do with the body, Guttridge? There's newly-turned earth in the back garden – shall we go and dig it up?

MRS. GUTTRIDGE: Oh dear God.

HOLMES: I have you, Guttridge. There's no sense in denying it.

A long moment.

GUTTRIDGE: I'm not going to deny it.

MRS. GUTTRIDGE: Oh dear God. Oh dear Lord. How could you do it? Why?

HOLMES: Well? Will you tell her, or shall I?

A long moment. Guttridge reaches a decision.

GUTTRIDGE: I had to shut her up. She knew I killed those babies.

MRS. GUTTRIDGE: Toby!

GUTTRIDGE: Don't say nothing, Emily.

HOLMES: You admit it? You killed Jennifer Snell?

GUTTRIDGE: I said so, yes.

HOLMES: And the three children?

GUTTRIDGE: Yes.

MRS. GUTTRIDGE: Oh, Toby . . . .

HOLMES: How?

GUTTRIDGE: What do you mean, how?

HOLMES: It was brilliantly done. Not a trace of poison in their systems. Tell me how you did it. (*A long moment*) Very well then, tell me why.

Guttridge says nothing.

Perhaps it was for the insurance money.

GUTTRIDGE: Yes! Yes, that's it. The insurance.

HOLMES: The insurance money goes to your wife. I checked. I ask you again: just how were the murders done? (*A long moment*) You don't know. Of course you don't know – because you were not the killer.

GUTTRIDGE: I tell you I was.

HOLMES: You found the evidence. You knew there had been foul play even though you didn't know the method – and since then, you've done everything in your power to protect the real murderer. To protect your wife.

No–one speaks. A long moment.

Only she handles the children. Only she supervises their food and their medicines. And only she stands to benefit from their deaths.

GUTTRIDGE: No!

MRS. GUTTRIDGE: (*Moving off*) I've had enough of this.

HOLMES: Please remain exactly where you are. Thank you. Since one of you can't explain and the other won't, permit me. It's been done on adults before now, but never on children – so I congratulate you on a totally original crime. You start with the smallest of amounts – almost infinitesimal, I suppose, on an infant. Then you build up the dose, a fraction of a grain by a fraction of a grain, day by day – until you have a child hopelessly addicted to arsenic. Keep administering the drug

304

and the child lives. Withhold it – and the result is death. And not a trace of anything harmful to be detected. Clever – and diabolical.

A long moment.

MRS. GUTTRIDGE: You've got no proof.

HOLMES: I have abundant proof. It's here, in this house.

GUTTRIDGE: You'll find no arsenic here.

HOLMES: Of course I won't. You've destroyed it all, just as you destroyed that innocent young girl, and for the same reason – a perverted desire to protect your wife.

MRS. GUTTRIDGE: Toby, my dear . . . .

GUTTRIDGE: Don't say anything, Emily. You're right. He's got no proof.

HOLMES: Tell him, Mrs. Guttridge.

GUTTRIDGE: What? Tell me what?

HOLMES: Tell him the rest. Tell him that three wasn't going to be enough.

GUTTRIDGE: What?

HOLMES: Tell him that every single one of the babies in this house is already a drug addict – waiting to be casually snuffed out, the next time you felt the whim or the need for power or some ready cash. Tell him!

A long moment.

MRS. GUTTRIDGE: You are so wrong.

HOLMES: I don't think so.

MRS. GUTTRIDGE: A whim? Power? Money? (*A long moment. She sighs*) That's not why I do it.

GUTTRIDGE: Emily . . . .

MRS. GUTTRIDGE: Do you know what my babies have to look forward to, Mr. Holmes? Do you know about the factories and the workhouses and the filth and the squalour? Have you seen the children begging and stealing? Have you seen them selling their bodies on the streets for a penny a time?

HOLMES: I've seen them.

MRS. GUTTRIDGE: Well, before it comes to that – for a time – for a tiny, fleeting time – I can give them warmth and comfort . . . and love. And then . . . . Then, I can make sure the world doesn't get them and soil them and wear them down and finally destroy them like animals. And don't you tell me that what I do is wrong. It's the world that's wrong, sir. Forget about me, I don't matter. Do something about the world out there – if you can.

A long moment.

GUTTRIDGE: What are you going do with us?

HOLMES: Take you to the police.

MRS. GUTTRIDGE: And then it'll be the courts. And then the hangman.

HOLMES: I imagine so.

MRS. GUTTRIDGE: Then tell me this, Mr. Holmes: what will happen to my babies now? You tell me that.

Holmes has no answer.
A long moment.

Then cut to:

306

SCENE 64. INT. SMITH'S OFFICE, THE BRITISH MUSEUM.

SMITH: (*Sighs*)

HOLMES: I didn't know what to say.

A moment.

SMITH: I have one question.

HOLMES: What is it?

SMITH: The evidence of the other children – were you sure? Or was it just a bluff on your part?

HOLMES: It wasn't a bluff. One of the side-effects of progressive arsenic addiction is unnatural lethargy and calm, especially in the young. I'd seen the signs when she showed me round the house on my first visit. I just didn't recognize them for what they were until later.

SMITH: So – all the children are due for the same fate. Dear God.

HOLMES: The doctor thinks they can be slowly weaned off the stuff. They might live. If you can call the world that's waiting for them a life.

SMITH: Come now, Mr. Holmes. Whatever our experiences may suggest, I like to think that the world is basically a good place. There's still tolerance and warmth and humanity out there. Don't you believe that?

A long moment.

Cut to:

SCENE 65. INT. THE SITTING ROOM, 221b BAKER STREET.

WATSON: I'd very much like to meet that man.

HOLMES: I'm afraid that's not possible. He died, early last year.

WATSON: Oh. I'm . . . sorry.

A moment. Holmes doesn't like acknowledging an emotional bond to anyone. But eventually:

HOLMES: Thank you.

A moment. Watson deliberately breaks it.

WATSON: Why didn't the doctor recognise the symptoms in the other children?

HOLMES: I dare say I was lot more familiar with the signs of poisoning than he was. Besides, he had no reason to look for them. He saw clean sheets and good care and was grateful for it.

A moment.

WATSON: So – that was your story about love.

HOLMES: It was. Guttridge loved his wife, murderer or no. He loved her so much that he was willing to take her guilt on himself – and to kill to protect her. And she loved the children – and so she murdered them. Do you still insist that love is a positive force for good?

WATSON: Yes, of course I do. You can't argue from the particular to the general like that. It's . . . it's thinking in straight lines.

HOLMES: *Touché*, Doctor. A palpable hit.

A moment. The fire crackles.

WATSON: What a sordid business. Poor Jenny Snell.

HOLMES: The wrong place at the wrong time – she must have walked in on Guttridge at the very moment he discovered the arsenic.

WATSON: How can a young girl's life hang on such a slender thread?

HOLMES: How, indeed?

Wearily, he gets up.

(*Moving off*) (*An exhausted sigh*)

Distant, echoing, not in the scene, a solo violin plays the Tristan *theme.*

Holmes has moved to the window. He pulls aside the curtain and looks out into the darkness. A long moment.

Was Smith right, do you think? Is the world basically a good place?

WATSON: I believe so. Don't you?

HOLMES: I wish I could, my friend. I wish I could. (*A long moment*) I think the rain's stopped. (*He peers out*) Yes, it has.

A moment. The fire crackles.
Perhaps a not-too-obtrusive hansom cab clops by outside.

The music becomes the closing sig.
Closing announcements.
The music ends.
The End.

A Study in
Abstruse Detail
by Wendy C. Fries

"Good heavens, Watson, out with it already!"

It is a mark of my state of mind that at first I didn't hear my friend Sherlock Holmes, instead interpreting those words as my own frustrated thoughts.

It wasn't until a lean shadow cast itself over my work, and I looked up to see his scowling face looking down, that I realised he'd spoken.

I glanced at the papers in my lap, most with but a few notes, then scowled back at my companion. The January evening was cold, the fire burnt low, and I – too aware of Holmes's opinion on my record of his exploits – was in no mood to be chivvied again for my devotion to these "fairytales."

"I'm out of sorts and mumbling to myself. It's nothing."

Holmes collapsed into the chair across from me, peered over his steepled fingers. "My dear fellow, you've tapped out and recharged your unlighted pipe twice in thirty minutes, hoisted an empty brandy glass three times, and, most tellingly, taken four deep breaths and held them for long seconds at a time."

Already discontent, I took nothing of my usual delight in Holmes's attentions, so I'm afraid my reply was snappish. "And what of it? The surgery was dull, I don't much care for my new tobacco, and all this snow has given me a chill."

Holmes patted his chair and then himself, eventually unearthing a packet of shag, which he tossed to me. "You're writing, Watson," he accused. "Or rather, those are your tells when you're *not*."

Despite what my friend might say, I do see *and* observe, so I've both seen Holmes pick up my accounts of his adventures, and observed his frown as he scans the prose. I tossed the shag back to him and was about to make a bad thing worse, arguing for the sheer distraction of it, when Holmes stood again.

He moved with the quick and economic stride he so frequently uses to cover a crime scene, but that energy was this time expended in refilling our glasses with brandy. He glanced at my papers as he handed me mine. "Those are your notes for the Smith-Mortimer succession. What will you call this escapade?"

I recognised his solicitous tone. It was the same one he uses to relax over-excited clients, and I was resentful in the face of it. "That's just it! It wasn't an escapade at all, you barely rose from your chair or finished that terrible brew Scotland Yard has the nerve to call coffee!"

As I ranted, Holmes wandered to our dining table, peering at an experiment that looked to me like an effort to grow dirt.

"True enough, it was a very simple matter, even more so than that business with the Harpsichord Widow – really, who wouldn't have noticed the woman had no stoop? I expected more from Inspector Gregson. I don't know why I'm forever surprised by the incompetence of London's detective class." Holmes poked at the loamy black culture with his finger, then jerked it away at the sound of a faint hiss. With a pencil he pushed the vicious flora into the bin. "Present company excepted."

I recognised *this* solicitous tone, as well. It was the same one my companion uses when he's bored and wants distraction. I was about to take him to task for this obvious manipulation when I realised the bin was on fire.

"Holmes, the bin is on fire."

Before my companion could answer, I rose and upended my half cup of cold tea over the small blaze; a puff of smoke followed. I watched the grey cloud drift and felt sure I was about to channel its darkness, taking Holmes to task for his carelessness, when instead we both broke into gales of laughter.

Minutes later we were in repose again, me with my papers, Holmes slumped like a discontented idler in his chair. When possessed by his nearly-frantic energy, Sherlock Holmes's limbs are a whirlwind and it is all I can do to stay at his heels. When the torpor is on him, I have more than once given in to the impulse to see if he is breathing. By his splay-legged slouch, I knew an east wind of such discontent was coming, so decided my trifling problems could provide us both suitable distraction.

"If you've nothing pressing, I'll tell you what I have so far."

I gestured to Holmes for his tobacco pouch, which he dutifully sailed my way. "I seem to have accidentally murdered my black mould, and it'll be a few hours yet before the Mayflies hatch, so my schedule is yours. Share with me your fairytale, dear Watson, and I'll do my best to supply it with a few cold, hard facts."

Holmes hoisted his glass and I read aloud my evening's endeavours.

"'Ah ha!' cried Holmes."

311

I relit my pipe and waited.

Holmes gestured for the tobacco, which I tossed back to him. He smiled sly as he refreshed his briar. "Well done, you've pared back from your usual florid embellishments."

Rejecting the bait, I continued. "The problem as I see it, is that the case itself was solved so quickly that there's really nothing to it, yet I've been often asked about your involvement in this one, due to the famous lady involved."

Holmes waved his spent match, tossed it into the fire. "The morbid curiosity of gossips who feel ever justified in hounding the exceptional."

I won't go into whether Holmes's bitterness came from knowing this truth, for indeed the ordinary often think they have "a right to know" about the lives of the extraordinary – and Miss Mortimer was certainly that – or if his rancour was more personal.

"If you'd rather I not share these curious cases and how they highlight your talents, I promise you I'll cease this instant." I rose with my papers and stepped to the fire.

I have mentioned that Sherlock Holmes is sensitive to flattery, and he himself admits how much he enjoys the attention when a case affords the occasional dramatic moment, so I wasn't surprised when he waved his hand in the air.

"Oh, sit back down and stop encouraging my vanity. I understand why you share some of our adventures, adventures which might show the ease with which even the complex can be understood, but why this particular case? If I recall, we were at that same time sorting out the much more interesting problem of the Hammersmith Wonder."

While Holmes aimed blue smoke ceiling-ward I again took my chair. "Yes, but Mr. Vigor was neither rich, famous, nor a legendary beauty. Miss Mortimer was all three and was followed by many behind-the-hand whispers in her day. Your readers – "

"*Your* readers," Holmes corrected airily.

"My readers of *your* adventures have more than once taken me to task for mentioning but not detailing some of your more abstruse cases. And the many I don't mention at all are themselves mentioned by the press. For *their* absence I'm also lectured."

"An ungrateful public is a terrible thing," said Holmes, grinning.

"Laugh, but you can't deny it, if left to your own devices these two words – " I waved the small sheaf, " – would be the only colour in your report of Miss Mortimer's case. Yet what you call my florid embellishments are often nothing more than your method made clear."

Holmes swirled a long finger through a lazy cloud of smoke. I noted that his inflammatory mould had left a chemical burn and rose to fetch my bag.

"Then forget the Smith-Mortimer problem. That was the matter of noticing one or two abstruse details, as you say. How about 'The Affair of the Shooting Star' or 'The Conk-Singleton Forgery'?" he asked when I returned to treat his blistered finger.

"You know perfectly well that publishing anything of the first would lose a Lord his parliamentary seat, and an account of the second would take even less time to tell than Miss Mortimer's story. You solved that when Mr. Singleton said his watch had stopped at thirteen hundred and not at one pm. You're being no help."

Holmes conceded every fact with an insouciant shrug. "There's that matter of the Venomous Lizard. A fascinating array of chemicals in lizard venom," he said, inspecting his neatly-dressed wound.

"Really now! A murderously toxic creature that turned out instead to be perfectly harmless, unmasked in seconds when you tickled it with a feather."

Holmes chuckled, as if he himself had been poked with a bit of plumage. "I knew a herpetologist in Soho and once did a rather unsystematic study of her menagerie, which consisted of fifty-seven distinct species, including both the highly-toxic Gila monster and the beaded lizard. Each creature has a forked tongue, so it was but a matter to tickle the accused in this particular case and get it to stick out its blue, bulbous one at us."

Holmes sighed dramatically, as if unfairly put upon. "Oh, you're right as always, Watson. Sit down again and we'll craft things so that the Smith-Mortimer Succession offers a moment of distraction to your readership. Now refresh my mind on the case, would you? This January blizzard's wiped away its particulars completely."

Whether Holmes was truthful in his forgetfulness, "my" readers no doubt remember the extensive press given this case at the time, involving as it did a distinguished family and the right of succession to their family fortune.

The last of the Smith-Mortimer line, Miss Mariam Penelope Caroline Mortimer, was once a familiar name to every reader of *The London Leader* and the *Illustrated Courier,* both of which followed the young lady's world-travelling exploits, frequently spangling their pages with her elegant, cool-eyed image. That is, until Miss Mortimer disappeared from the City's social whirl under mysterious circumstance.

The lady's departure from the public eye of course aroused speculation and suspicion, from a love affair gone wrong, to behaviours too shameful to gossip about in polite company.

And then the poor woman was found dead in her large and lonely home, sitting in her favourite wingback chair, dressed for dinner and clutching new pearls. At first, foul play was suspected and once again Miss Mortimer was in every paper. It was soon discovered that criminal trespass had not cut the young lady's life short at thirty-two, but a sadly weak heart, legacy of the Smith side of her clan.

Soon after, it was discovered that this last scion of a proud family had no family after her and, despite an extensive search for cousins, nephews or nieces, none were found. Aunts and uncles, parents of parents, all had long since passed. Hope of a successor was thought lost, and within a month a new beauty captured public attention.

Then, not quite two years after, Dr. Lealand Bentham, the Smith-Mortimer's old family physician, sat nursing a gin at Simpson's long bar and let slip a very interesting fact to a very interested man.

The fact given away was this: Young Miss Mariam had been deaf upon her passing. Her hearing loss had begun soon after her thirtieth birthday, the garrulous physician told the obliging man buying his expensive drinks, and it was this early-onset deafness – a legacy of the Mortimer side of her line – that had lead the young lady to withdraw from society.

That was when the interested man, he called himself Stephen Smith Larkyns, devised a plan: He would pose as a lost member of the Smith-Mortimer clan. He knew he bore a striking resemblance to Miss Mariam herself, a fact that acquaintances had more than once remarked upon. As a matter of fact, over years of reading newspaper accounts of the family, and once exchanging a word with its matriarch, Larkyns had become more than half-convinced he must be related, and so was justified in succeeding Miss Mortimer to the family's fortune.

"Nothing gives a lie the varnish of truth quite like self-delusion, eh Watson? I remember the case now. Larkyns did indeed bear a striking resemblance to young Miss Mortimer, yet of course that wouldn't have been proof enough. He couldn't very well manifest the bad heart of the Smiths, but at all of twenty-six he did seem to suffer the early deafness of the Mortimers."

"The executors of the estate suspected he was lying, as did Gregson," I said. "They wanted only for a bit of proof, which you provided in seconds."

Holmes's small smile belied his words. "You give me too much credit, as usual. It was Inspector Lestrade who solved this particular case."

"I'm sure he'd be surprised to hear you say so."

"It's true. You may have noticed the good inspector is quite tone deaf, and yet often amuses himself by humming, whistling, and turning perfectly serene environments into music halls."

"He's even more bombastic when he thinks he has one up on Gregson!"

"Just so. Which explains why the inspector was lurking that day, whistling away. He was sure Gregson was about to blunder and wanted to be near when he did. Of course it was Mr. Larkyns, alias Stephan Plum, Hampton Bishop piano teacher, who did the blundering."

Holmes tapped out his pipe, placed it on the table beside him, then brushed stray ash from his dressing gown. After his housekeeping, he looked briefly thoughtful, then slumped in his chair, eyes closed, fingers laced over his heart, looking for all the world like a man settling down for a doze.

I checked my watch. It was only a bit past eight. As I've said, the winter night was cold and neither Holmes's mood nor mine were at their highest. Yet, we'd lived long enough together to learn how to cope with one another's fuss and foibles, so I knew that, with little more to do than wait for his Mayflies, Holmes craved distraction as much as I craved a good tale to tell.

I waved my papers until the rattling opened my friend's eyes. "I was there, I've written down the climax of that blunder perfectly. '*Ah ha!*' You unmasked the man easily, but I'm still not sure how."

Holmes pretended for a moment longer that he preferred a catnap to clarification, then he straightened slightly in his chair.

"It was the E-flat, Watson! You remember that Mr. Larkyns insisted that, though deaf, he could read lips well. You saw after our initial written introductions that we spoke face-to-face? As it will, this put us in fairly close proximity. While he busily insisted on his veracity, Inspector Lestrade lurked in the background, repeatedly hitting an F-sharp in the popular ditty he was whistling, instead of the E-flat for which he should have been aiming. Each time he did this and only when he did this, Mr. Plum's right ear shifted a fraction. It was after observing this that I realised how to prove our man could indeed hear. I quickly arranged what I needed, and then knew I need only depend on human reflex."

"Well, Mr. Plum seemed to lack at least one of those. I've never seen a man with no startle reflex."

I proved I had one when Holmes stood abruptly, shouting, "*Agaricus gardneri!*" No sooner had he risen than Holmes fell to his knees.

"Watson, move your knees!"

I bounded from my chair and Holmes immediately stuck his head under its skirting. He shouted, "My tea!" then reached out a long arm.

I handed him his half-empty cup, heard a triumphant crow, and then he emerged, smiling. "I was afraid my mushrooms had succumbed, but it seems luminous *Agaricus gardneris* is far more resistant to neglect than Mrs. Hudson."

Now, it's not uncommon for Sherlock Holmes to inform a room of his final deduction before he's granted us knowledge of his first, but often I can belatedly follow his logic. This was not one of those times. "Mrs. Hudson?"

Holmes dusted his knees, handed me his empty tea cup, then sprawled languid into his armchair again. "Haven't you noticed? When the clock went eight, our dear landlady started muttering. By a quarter past she began banging pots. By half eight her pique was so great she over-roasted the potatoes, which has only increased the muttering and the pots. Watson, we've again neglected to inform Mrs. Hudson when we want dinner."

The kitchen noises were indeed much louder than usual, and I hastened to go apologise to our landlady, when Holmes waved a hand.

"Sit, sit, she'll be up shortly and we can beg forgiveness then. We could no more prevent the dear lady from feeding us than we could hope to outwit every criminal in London."

"Lord knows you keep trying to achieve both," I said. While my friend laughed, I hesitantly approached my chair.

"It's all right. I moistened the mushrooms with my tea. It'll be interesting to see if a bit of milk fat fattens up the spores. Soon I'll be able to add an even dozen *Agaricus gardneri* to the Kew herbarium's sparse collection."

I resisted the urge to peek under my chair and took my seat, jotting *Agaricus gardneri* in the margin of my notes, never sure when just such abstruse detail might be useful later. "So, you were about to tell me how human reflex gave that imposter Plum away."

"I take it you thought it unusual that the man didn't startle when Constable Margola snuck up behind him, dropping that weighty book on the floor?"

"I know how powerfully the human body will protect itself. The instinct to snatch your hand from a candle flame or jump at an unexpected noise is all but impossible to resist."

Holmes tapped out his pipe, began cleaning the stem with a bit of wire. "'Unexpected' being the key! Constable Margola is an eighteen stone man. To be sure he moves with a rare grace, but you cannot be that large without affecting the things around you, even the air. Why do you think I became a consulting detective, Watson?"

Trusting this sudden deviation was driving a point home, I said, "Because you're very good at it."

"Precisely! My skill is for noticing small things, and for recognising when those things add up to something larger. The same goes for a man like Mr. Plum, who probably learnt early on that he had an exceedingly fine-tuned ear, that he could hear things others did not. Such as a student's misstep on the keys of a piano, the stealthy tread of a heavy man, or the slight gust of air as a large book falls to the floor. In short, Plum was prepared for the sound, which is why he did not startle."

"And this betrayed him?"

Holmes was now sitting fully upright. "A deaf man would have felt the vibration of that weighty tome striking the floor just behind him and turned – that same protective reflex of which you spoke. That Plum did not was all I needed. After I crowed '*Ah ha!*' the man realised his error. His immediate and simple human reflex was guilt – which was the same as an admission."

I sighed. "Of course! He could have passed off his error if he'd simply maintained his charade. It's always so simple when you explain, and I'm surprised that that still surprises me."

"Another human reflex, I expect," said Holmes, who then took up his position of a half-hour previous, peering at me over the tips of his fingers. "Now you have your account drawn up, all it needs are the romantic embellishments."

A harsh wind rattled the windowpanes and again the snow was falling thickly. I rifled through the notes in my lap. "On its own, the Smith-Mortimer Succession may be a bit short, perhaps we can flesh it out with another one of your small cases. What of that incident last week with the Grosvenor Square furniture van?"

Holmes slumped in his chair again. "Oh, Watson, I'm no help with these! That was so obvious, even the greengrocer suspected. I've no idea why the duchess came to me, though I was happy to pocket the fee. Barium of Baryta does not come cheap."

"Well, what of the Account of the Red Room? The problem of the Marques of Breadalbane? The Case of the Misplaced Gavel? How about – "

When Holmes scowled and slumped further in his chair I knew he was moments from a serious brood that might have him reaching for a particular diversion for which I have no fondness. "You once mentioned the case of Vamberry, the wine merchant. I recently asked Inspector Lestrade about it."

Holmes straightened in his chair the smallest bit, eyes narrowed. "Pray tell, what did the inspector say?"

"He said you solved the case because Vamberry was vain."

Holmes sat straight up in his chair. "As ever the inspector does not see what's in front of him waving the equivalent of semaphore flags! It was the smell of tar!"

As if that were that Holmes slumped again, and it was at this time Mrs. Hudson came in with a tray and pointedly did not look at either of us. She put a pot of tea on the crowded dining table, laying around it a Scandinavian repast of small plates. Beef, roast potatoes, bread, horseradish, pickled onions, sliced gherkins. She did this in silence, and in silence Holmes and I rose and came to the table. While I took my seat and made apologies for our neglect regarding supper, Holmes opened one of the innumerable drawers in his card cabinet and extracted a long packet, loosely wrapped in a pretty pale tissue paper.

"You are far more patient than we deserve Mrs. Hudson," he said, holding the packet toward her, "We've been saving these for just such a moment. Please consider them one of many future apologies for our being such trying tenants."

Mrs. Hudson looked at Holmes and then at myself. I mirrored Holmes's expression. There was nothing else I could do. I had no clue what was in the package.

Mrs. Hudson looked at the thin packet with a wary eye, then unwrapped it. "Oh, Mr. Holmes, Dr. Watson!" she said, face quickly spangled in smiles. Pushing newspapers, magazines, and dinner plates out of the way, Mrs. Hudson spread the contents of the packet on the table. Those contents were these: Feathers. Dozens of gleaming feathers from chaffinches, siskins, kingfishers, herons, and peacocks.

Suddenly I remember what I had seen but not quite observed on upward of twenty journeys to and from crime scenes: Holmes snatching something up from ground or a shrub, then pocketing it. Feathers. For months he had been collecting feathers.

"We hope these will suit your millinery efforts dear lady, and have assurances from the veterinarian at Holland Park that when the white peacock drops his finery he will save that bounty for you."

Mrs. Hudson looked from Holmes to myself again, then walked to the window. Shortly she buffed away a non-existent smudge on the glass, sniffing softly. After a few moments she nodded at us, collected her avian finery, said, "I already know just what to do with the chaffinch," and left.

As we settled down to our dinner Holmes said, "I sometimes think that good human relations are like detective work. If you observe but the smallest thing about someone and then perform a kindness related to it, most people are touched out of all proportion to your efforts."

As usual, Holmes seemed to underestimate the magnitude of his gifts. Instead of saying this, I thanked him for including me in his considerations to our dear landlady.

"Ah, but that's a small apology offered to you as well, Watson, for not only am I a trying tenant, I'm aware I'm not the most common of flatmates," my friend said, waving as if by example to the unseen mushrooms beneath my chair.

I did not tell Holmes it was just such small excitements that added the grace of colour to an often-dreary world.

"Pass the horseradish if you would Watson, and let's hear more of Lestrade's version of this story."

I did as asked, claimed the gherkins, and continued retelling the tale of Vamberry the wine merchant, just as I would tell it to you, dear readers.

"Vamberry was the Spanish Infanta's wine merchant, Mr. Holmes, reported to be her most loyal servant, above reproach, or so they thought until he scarpered with her small pleasure craft and only enough gold coin as he hoped would go unmissed!"

Sherlock Holmes stopped dead in the doorway of Scotland Yard.

"Sorry sir," said Inspector Lestrade, hastening forward, "I didn't mean to jump right in. We're a bit eager to have a solution to this mess. You know how things stand with Foria."

Sherlock Holmes followed Lestrade through Scotland Yard's busy corridors. "Strained as always. The Forian royal family seem to find the rest of humanity a disappointment, just so many idlers and dilettantes."

Lestrade gestured to a chair across from his desk, signaled a passing constable for coffee. Only once the steaming cups arrived did the men take a seat.

"I don't know much about that, but I do know this mess might make a mess of diplomatic relations. We've promised to not only find out why Vamberry fled, but why to England."

Holmes eyebrows rose and he replaced his cup upon its saucer. "Most interesting. The Infanta, like the Borgias from whom she descends, is famous for both her superb capacity to rule and her lack of sentiment to those who betray her. With a little effort, perhaps we can give the lady the answers she craves."

"Well you'd be the man for that, Mr. Holmes." Lestrade leaned across his desk, dropped his voice. "You may have noticed some of my men have a roughness about them. You employ softer ways, put people at their ease, and I'm afraid you will need that, as Mr. Vamberry is exceedingly tight-lipped. To be perfectly honest, I think we'd get more from a stone. Or at least another go at his boat."

Holmes steepled his fingers. "Tell me about it."

Lestrade shrugged, "The boat? Not much to tell. It's one of those new-fangled vessels that can be sailed by one man, though roomy enough for two. A pretty thing, all full of gilt and carved follies. Apparently the Infanta once let Vamberry take his boy and hers out on it."

"Interesting," said Holmes, leaning forward in his chair.

Lestrade placed his hands on his knees, ready to respond to a sudden burst of energy. Certainly Mr. Holmes would ask to see the boat now, or the suspect, perhaps someone's left shoe. It was never entirely clear where Sherlock Holmes would start an investigation, and so Lestrade had learned to expect anything.

What he got was nothing.

Instead of bounding to his feet, Sherlock Holmes leaned back, crossed his legs, and reached for the coffee that Lestrade had himself made – truly it was the only way to get a good cup.

While Lestrade is often startled by Mr. Holmes's tendencies to dash about a crime scene, falling upon his belly and looking beneath carriage wheels, this precise opposite of his usual behaviour was frankly disappointing. However, Lestrade is not an inspector at Scotland Yard for nothing. He's keen of eye and so he knew Sherlock Holmes was –

Holmes paused in pursuing a gherkin with his fork. "Did he call himself keen-eyed, Watson? Did he really?"

Even in her pique Mrs. Hudson makes a fine roast potato. I finished mine with relish, sipped some port. "Oh, he did indeed, as his retelling of the case advanced, both you and he gained ever-greater powers of cunning and deduction."

Holmes laughed and then looked at me side-eyed. Suddenly it was I who did the deducing. "Yes, Holmes, be glad Inspector Lestrade is not your biographer, for by the end of any story he told, I suspect you'd be able to fly, and he the wind beneath your wings!"

Eventually we'd finished with our supper and our laughter. Port in hand, we again settled by the fire. Holmes doffed a hat he wasn't wearing, "I find myself grateful for a restraint I never realised you show, dear biographer. Do please continue."

"Well, Mr. Holmes, don't you want to see the boat?" Lestrade asked. "As I said, we've gone over the craft carefully and found nothing."

"Soon. Tell me, what do you think of the Infanta's wine merchant?"

The inspector leaned over his desk again, keen to share his finely-observed opinions. "He will not look at any one of us, much less talk. I think there's something sinister about Mr. Vamberry."

"Why?"

"He's arrogant! Not once has he addressed me by title or name, he simply says 'you.' He's what I suspect you'd call imperious. He twice told me to fetch him tea. He's treated my men as if they are here to buff his shoes. And when I told him we'd called you and who you are, he said you'd be no better than a dancing bear at finding what he never took."

Holmes laughed, "That might prove quite true, one never knows."

"Don't be hard on yourself, Mr. Holmes. He doesn't know how well regarded you are here. Anyway, you might form your own opinion, as they're bringing the man himself through now. Mr. Holmes, this is Constable Hynes and Mr. Vamberry."

Sherlock Holmes stood to find standing before him two small, dark men. Only one looked off in the middle distance as if he were alone in the room.

It was to this one Holmes addressed himself. "Mr. Vamberry, I am Sherlock Holmes. I'm delighted to meet a member of the distinguished Infanta's household. I hope you'll answer a question or two for me."

321

Vamberry looked in the very opposite direction from Holmes. To no one in particular, he said in perfect English, "I still await my pomegranate tea."

Lestrade looked in exasperation at Holmes, at Hynes, at the same spot in the distance at which Vamberry stared. "I have told you Mr. Vamberry, we can offer you as much plain tea as you like. I really don't know where a man would find pomegranate tea in London."

Holmes interrupted me with a laugh. "Oh, it's a shame you weren't there then, Watson. You could have laid bare London's tea underbelly, you who has found in our city's byways shops to not only satisfy your taste for Afghan and Egyptian teas, but also located that awful sea salt brew you like from Ullapool."

Here Holmes shivered in memory at accidentally taking a sip of this north Scotland specialty when I had left my steaming cup near his microscope.

As if to wash away the memory, Holmes delicately sipped at his port, smacking his lips with relish. Momentarily he nodded at me in apology. "I'm sorry, do go on."

After his pronouncement regarding tea, Vamberry fell silent, ignoring any and all questions no matter from whom they came.

Holmes observed all of this in keen silence, and then said, "The Infanta is quite angry, sir."

For but a moment, Vamberry frowned then cleared his expression, blinking slowly as if bored.

"Perhaps if we could share with her why such a trusted servant has done this unthinkable thing, she would find within her mercy."

Another fiercer frown, this one chased away by a haughty lift of the chin.

"If you and the noble lady fall out, I'm sure her son and your fine boy will grieve."

At this all expression washed from Vamberry's face. And it was this response that helped Sherlock Holmes solve the mystery.

With a sigh I rose to refill my port glass. At the extended silence, my friend cracked open one fire-dozy eye.

"I'm afraid the inspector stopped the story there," I said, returning to my chair. "He quite belatedly said it was not his story to tell. Diplomatic secrets."

322

Holmes straightened in his chair, lifted his own glass. "Mr. Lestrade has unexpected wells of reserve, though tardy. He told you more than enough to un-secret this diplomatic secret. Ah, well."

At that, Mrs. Hudson quietly entered, and began serenely collecting our dinner plates. As we thanked her for the fine meal – I suspect we laid it on a trifle thick – my gaze went repeatedly to Holmes. When our landlady withdrew I leaned close, "Well, what happened? Why did Vamberry's lack of reaction to your remark about his son solve the case?"

"That last is the good inspector quoting something I said later and it's overstating the matter. I did not solve the case then. However, as with Plum, it was Mr. Vamberry's opposite response to the expected one – even greater arrogance – that told me we were close to his nest, so to speak.

"You must understand Watson, to Vamberry I was certainly no better than any other detective in that station – worse, in fact, as I'd been suddenly called from home that day after a fussy experiment left me with yellow-stained fingers, a singed collar, and a small plaster on my cheek. I looked disreputable. My discussing his royal employer in familiar terms rankled a man that class proud. The *lack* of his response when I was even more familiar in talking about his son – that told me this issue might be *about* his son. Following a brief viewing of his boat, it was *then* the case was solved."

Suddenly my friend bolted restless from his chair, then grousingly began pacing the sitting room, pushing aside rumpled dressing gowns, sheet music, and newspapers, careless of where they landed.

"I've told Mrs. Hudson I have a method and that her tidying – ah, here it is!" Tossing aside a bird's wing and a magazine on its belly, Holmes snatched up a blue waistcoat. Mumbling something about the secret pocket he'd only half-installed inside the snug silk, he settled again across from me with needle, thread, and thimble.

"So sorry, Watson, where was I? Ah yes, it was then that our small party of four decamped to the sailing vessel *Ayng*.

"Once onboard, there were two things of note. The first was the deplorable mess left by the police search. The narrow mattresses had been turned up, the dish cupboards ransacked, a child's small bucket been overturned, and its wet sand pawed through. Despite the disarray, I was assured no stolen coins had been found.

"The other thing of note was the familiar scent of tar. The very commonality of this odour is what likely prevented the good Inspector from perceiving it, or that the scent of it was especially strong. Yet, as Lestrade had mentioned, the boat was new. It was also a royal vessel, so no doubt kept in prime condition. So why had it been so freshly tarred the scent was strong?

"I'm afraid I then did that thing which seems to so alarm the tidy mentalities of Scotland Yard. I began climbing over the interior furniture of the little boat, and was quickly rewarded with what I sought: a fine black seam of tar at the bow. I dug into it with my thumbnail and within a few seconds had unearthed edge-on a gold coin, a bit more effort revealed a second.

"The inspector was jubilant, Vamberry unmoved, and here is where one of the more abstruse bits of deduction comes to the fore Watson. You must always remember that, though you've found what you're looking for, keep looking.

"While Lestrade went about the messy business of prying gold coins out of stiffening tar, I went about my business: I continued searching the boat. After a while I located in the hull near the stern another tar seam, this one better hidden and even thinner than the first. Two seams perpendicular to it also gave in to my nail. I knocked against the hull; the sound was hollow – and followed by a small-voiced whimper.

"Then, quoting Poe at his most grimly poetic, it was like 'a hideous dropping off of the veil.' All was clear, and I knew why this proud and trusted man had risked so much when he seemed to want for so little."

Holmes paused here to put on his freshly-tailored waistcoat. He spun in a slow circle, arms akimbo. Only after I assured him that I couldn't spy the location of the newly-installed secret pocket did my friend settle in his chair again and this time complete his story.

"I returned to the wine merchant. 'Mr. Vamberry, please allow us to help you.' Still the man said nothing, and so I said, 'Then I'm afraid we shall have to burn your boat.'

"At the bow of the boat, Lestrade stopped buffing gold on his trouser leg. 'Beg pardon, Mr. Holmes?'

"'The criminal is in hand Lestrade, and we have found the missing treasure. The *Ayng* is taking up valuable space in a dock already short of it. If I recall today's headlines, the 2nd Earl of Westfriars has requested berth in this same snug harbour and been denied. I say burn Mr. Vamberry's boat.'

324

"It was then Vamberry's iron spine crumbled. 'For the love of God, no!' he cried."

"Why, Holmes?" I cried, starting forward in my chair. "Why?"

"I didn't make the nest analogy lightly, Watson. Like a mother bird who flaps on the ground as if wounded, leading a predator away from her chicks, once Vamberry knew he was caught – and for diplomatic reasons Scotland Yard announced their intention of boarding his craft a full half hour before doing so – Vamberry flapped us away from his nest. He hid the coins at the bow, in sight of the observant, while at the stern he more carefully covered the seams of the hidden door cut into the *Ayng's* hull, and behind which lay his ill son."

"No!"

"Yes. Vamberry's child was desperately sick, and the wine merchant with not enough resources to help the poor boy. Vamberry's brother, a physician, lives in London, and so in desperation the Infanta's pleasure craft and a pittance of her gold were stolen, the boy secreted on board, and Vamberry sought safe haven for both of them here. When he knew he would be boarded, he hid his young son in what any diplomatic vessel holds: A hiding spot.

"Vamberry's failing in all of this was pride, Watson, which made him both blind and rash. Though it is true that the Infanta and her kin do not much truck with weakness, any good ruler understands mercy. Not only had this never occurred to Vamberry, but he, who hews so strictly to lines of class, did not believe the Infanta could hold him or his family in tender regard, so he simply never thought to ask for her help. Fortunately all ended well. Father, child, and boat were returned to Spain, and after a time the boy was made well. As a matter of fact, both Vamberry's son and the Infanta's son made the papers recently, together starting University at Oxford."

With a faint smile, Holmes nestled further in his chair. "And so you see, simple cases hinging on a few abstruse details. I hope they suit your needs, Watson?"

I agreed that they gave me more than enough to while away the rest of the cold winter evening.

And so it was, while Holmes dozed contentedly in his chair, I crafted the heart of each missive you've read here. It was a bit past midnight, and as I was banking the fire, that my friend woke with a start and shouted.

"The Mayflies will be hatching!"

325

Sherlock Holmes rose and ran to his water-filled jars lined upon the window sill and began to tut-tut at an experiment that would take him busily through the night.

For my part, I took down an encyclopaedia and began reading up on Mayflies.

The Adventure of
St. Nicholas the Elephant
by Christopher Redmond

It was a mild day near the end of March, in the year 1895, when Mr. Thomas Sexton appeared at the Baker Street rooms which I shared with my friend Mr. Sherlock Holmes. Holmes and I were lingering over one of the fine breakfasts provided by our landlady, whose imposing figure as she appeared in the doorway of our sitting-room to announce our visitor was promptly followed by the much smaller figure of Mr. Sexton himself. There was something a little comic about his old-fashioned and threadbare black suit, the jacket and waistcoat stretched to contain his rotund belly, with a smear of some greasy substance near the cuff of his right sleeve, while the firm jaw and solemn countenance above his double chin gave warning that, although he might be small of stature, he expected to be treated with some deference. And yet he was clearly in the grip of an intense agitation, as his writhing hands made evident.

"Come in, come in," said Holmes at once. "Pray have a seat, and perhaps your nerves will be no worse for a cup of Mrs. Hudson's not unsatisfactory coffee. What can be amiss in the affairs of the church to bring you out so early on a Saturday morning, Mr. – ?"

"Sexton, sir, Thomas Sexton. But how do you know I come from the church? I've heard of your wonderful guesses, Mr. Holmes, as we all have, but I have not said a word yet about the church – St. Nicholas the Elephant it is, sir, out in Lambeth, past Elephant and Castle. How could you guess that I was a churchman?"

"I did not guess," said Holmes. "When the available data justify no more than a guess, I remain silent and I observe. In this case, Mr. Sexton, I have observed a spot of what must be candle-wax on the sleeve of your coat. Your attire is otherwise immaculate, so that the stain has come there very recently, and you would hardly have been lighting and extinguishing candles for any household purpose on so bright a morning. Further, I recognize the distinctive if somewhat dull typography of the *Church Times* on the sheaf of paper protruding from your pocket. I conclude that you have been in church this morning, and that your name reflects your calling: that you are, in fact, a sexton."

327

"It's true enough," our caller replied, gratefully sipping the coffee that Mrs. Hudson had brought for him, "although the word *sexton* is one I don't care to have used, if it's all the same to you, Mr. Holmes. *Church-officer* is the right name nowadays, and church-officer at St. Nicholas is what I have the honour to be. Still, it's true that my grandfather and his fathers before him called themselves sexton. I dare say that may be why my family bears the name it does. Church-officer I have been at St. Nicholas for nineteen years this Whitsun, and never have I seen anything like what has happened this week. Witchcraft, I call it, witchcraft!"

"Tut, man, you call it nothing of the sort," said Holmes. "If you believed that it was witchcraft, you would hardly be here in Baker Street. You would be seeking help within the church itself, from the bishop's chaplain, or whatever the proper dignitary is called. You know very well that whatever has happened is the result of human agency, and so you rightly turn your steps to Baker Street. Or rather, not your steps, but the wheels of the Metropolitan Railway, if your journey is from far-off Lambeth. And so I ask you again: what is amiss, and what have you to tell that might be of interest to me?"

"Well, it may not be witchcraft in the end, but Mrs. Brickward calls it witchcraft," the little man replied, "and what else might anyone call it, with blood on the very steps of the church, and a page of the Bible burned there on the stone beside it?"

"Beside what, Mr. Sexton?" I interjected. "Beside the bloodstain?"

"Beside the body, sir!" he shot back. "Beside the body, there on the pavement. A page taken from the church's own Bible, that sits on the lectern for Mr. Brickward to read each Sunday. Now if there is no witchcraft in it, why would somebody have burned a Bible page, and a chapter of the Holy Gospel at that?"

Sherlock Holmes, who had shown some impatience when our visitor began to describe his problem, was now leaning forward in his chair, his long bony fingers rubbing together rapidly. "Why indeed, Mr. Sexton," he said. "Why indeed. I could suggest six, no, seven possible reasons at once, but without data I can hardly be expected to choose one. But you interest me much more when you speak of a body. What body?"

"That's just it," was the reply. "A body, a young woman, lying there dead, at the side door of St. Nicholas, in Moss Road. We didn't know who she was, not any of us, and nor did the police."

"Ah, the police?" said Holmes. "Of course, they would take an interest in the matter. For all the deficiencies that the police sometimes demonstrate, they can at least be relied upon to take note of a woman's body found at the door of a suburban church. Found when, Mr. Sexton?"

"On Sunday last, at twelve o'clock. We were coming out of Matins and we found it. Mrs. Brickward found it first, as she went round into Moss Street on the way to the rectory, and Mr. and Mrs. Wallace said she was crying and weeping beside it when they saw her. Mrs. Wallace was the first to see the Bible page there, burned so that all you could read were a few words at the bottom of the page. 'Cometh in his glory' it said, and that's all that was left that wasn't blackened, 'cometh in his glory'."

"I see," said Holmes, "and this Mrs. Wallace no doubt summoned the police? But no, she will have been fully occupied with comforting Mrs. Brickward – I take it that is the rector's wife? – and doubtless it fell to Mr. Wallace to go in search of a constable."

"Exactly."

"And when the constable came?"

"Well, Mr. Holmes, he told all the people to go home, all the people who had gathered round I mean, and he sent a messenger for an inspector to come. I waited to see if I could be of any assistance, but there were enough police to do everything, and after they took the body away in a waggon I locked up the church as I always do, and I went home to my dinner."

"Where, no doubt, Mrs. Sexton was all agog to hear every detail of the affair?" I put in.

"I am sorry to say that there is no Mrs. Sexton," said the little man quietly. "She died last year of a fever."

"A careful observer could have seen as much from a glance at our visitor," said Holmes. "I will not insult you, Watson, by mentioning the clues that you might have seen, had you only looked for them. Tell me, Mr. Sexton, as you waited in case your assistance might be required, what did you in turn observe?"

"Observe, Mr. Holmes?"

"Yes, man, observe! Mark, learn, and inwardly digest, to put it in words you must often have read in your Bible. What did you see? There was blood – was there a wound? How was the girl dressed? What did she look like?"

"As to that, I can't rightly say," was the response. "She seemed a fair enough girl, and dressed well enough. She did have a wound, for certain, for her shoulder and side were all wet with thick blood, such as I never saw but once, when a lumber-waggon overturned in Moss Road and there was a man crushed to death."

329

"Just so," said my friend. "If this woman's death on Sunday last made such an impression upon you, why have you waited until Saturday and then come in such haste to see me?"

"It was the Bible, Mr. Holmes. When we saw the burned page beside the body, we all knew it was from a Bible, of course, but it was only today, when I went into the church to make the candles ready for tomorrow and do my other Saturday tasks, that I glanced at the Bible on the lectern and saw the page had been torn from there. Of course I went straight to the rectory to tell Mr. Brickward, and Mrs. Brickward screamed out that it was witchcraft. When I came away and thought it over a little, I determined to come and see you at once."

"Hmph," said Holmes. "Well, Mr. Sexton, your story is an interesting one, and I do not object to looking into it briefly, for I am rather at loose ends since we put old Carstairs and his not-so-prepossessing son behind bars. Tell me, and then I will detain you no longer: what was the name of the police inspector who took charge of the case?"

"Hopkins, sir," said Sexton, and Holmes gave a brief nod of satisfaction, for I knew that he esteemed Stanley Hopkins more highly than any of the other official detectives. Thus I was not surprised when, as soon as our pompous little visitor had taken his leave, he rang for the pageboy and scribbled a telegram to be sent to Scotland Yard.

"Hopkins will not object to dropping round," he said, "and it may be that he can offer us transportation to south Lambeth this afternoon, as well as the benefit of whatever information the police have failed to overlook. We can at least be confident, I think, that they will have a better theory than witchcraft to explain matters – although, sad to say, little explanation may be needed, for a body at the side door of a church on a Sunday morning is the natural consequence of a quarrel or attack outside some nearby public house on the Saturday evening."

"But the Bible page?" I asked.

"I admit that is a little out of the ordinary," said Holmes. "What do you make of it, Doctor?"

I was flattered that my friend, who had spoken slightingly of my deductive skills just a few minutes earlier, was now eager to hear any suggestion I might be able to make. "I suppose," I said judiciously, "that we may disregard the words left visible at the bottom of the page, since whoever took the page and set it alight cannot have been able to guarantee how much would remain unburnt. 'Cometh in his glory' is hardly a very illuminating message in any case. But might the whole

330

page be some sort of message? It should not be difficult to find out what else should have appeared there."

"Indeed," said Holmes. "Then your theory would be that someone wished to point out a connection between the dead woman, or perhaps the reason for her death, and some incident or moral in Holy Writ? I have known something of the sort once or twice before. The difficulty in this case is the burning. If you seek to leave a written message, Watson, do you generally set fire to it and watch it shrivel to ash before it can be read? No, I think the explanation must be a little different – although I do agree that a message was sent, and indeed received."

He would say no more, and I was left to turn the matter over in my mind, and to occupy myself as best I could, while Holmes leafed through the day's newspapers and cut out two or three items with his black, long-bladed scissors, for later pasting into his steadily growing commonplace-books. I glanced at the cuttings later, but could make nothing of them: one was a report on glue manufacturing in some Midlands town, while another discussed the anticipated marriage of a Member of Parliament to the daughter of a Professor of Poetry.

Shortly after luncheon, however, Stanley Hopkins was announced, and both Holmes and I greeted him as the old friend he had become through a succession of odd and once or twice dangerous adventures together. "So it's the Lambeth case, is it?" said the inspector with a smile, as he sat easily in the chair where we had seen him so often before. "Well, you won't find much in your line this time, Mr. Holmes. A dead girl in south Lambeth is nothing so unusual, you know. I say a 'girl' by habit, for so many of those we find dead on the streets are very young, as you know, but this one can't have been less than thirty."

"The girls you find dead on the streets are not so often on the doorsteps of churches, or marked by torn pages from a Bible," Holmes observed. "And I note that you speak of this particular girl as 'the Lambeth case', although there is, as you say, never any lack of cases in Lambeth."

"You have me there," Hopkins grinned. "As a matter of fact, the matter has been on my mind all this week, although I have not been able to spare so much as a constable to look into it since Sunday afternoon. There was something just a trifle odd about the matter."

"The lack of a weapon, for example?"

"I see you know a little about it already," said the inspector. "That was certainly a striking feature, although it may mean nothing, for a knife is a valuable thing to some of the roughs who can be found on the

331

streets thereabouts. I have a little time to spare this afternoon; would you care to ride down to Lambeth with me and see the place for yourself? I can't offer to show you the body itself, for we had it buried on Wednesday in the usual way."

Holmes and I accepted the offer with alacrity, and as we rode through London and across Westminster Bridge, Hopkins gave us, in response to my friend's request, a brief sketch of the personalities at the church of St. Nicholas the Elephant, apart from the church-officer, our caller of a few hours earlier. Ambrose Wallace, the churchwarden, Hopkins dismissed as an elderly busybody, and his wife as a nonentity. "The rector and his wife are another thing altogether," he said, "and I gather that there has been a good deal of talk about them, although it may be no more than the usual gossip in any church, or any pub for that matter, when a young man comes to take the place of an old one. Mr. Brickward is no more than five or six-and-twenty, fresh from the theological college up in Durham, and of course a London parish is a difficult place for a man from the north. Then his wife is a northerner too, and she is said to be a sulky young woman, with a dark eye and a hot temper, who has been slow to seek friends and slower to find them. If Mrs. Wallace had not been nearby to take a motherly interest, she would be entirely without female company."

"An admirable thumbnail sketch," said Holmes. "And she is the one who discovered the body, our client told us. I should be very glad to meet Mrs. Brickward."

However, when the carriage stopped in Moss Road and we rang the bell at the rectory, it was the Rev. Mr. Brickward himself who answered the door. I wondered at the lack of a maidservant, but Hopkins murmured to me that the girl who had been employed at the rectory had left the previous week with Mrs. Brickward's screams of fury ringing in her ears. "A matter of burnt toast, I was told," he added.

"I may have a question or two for you, and also for your wife if she is at home," Holmes told the rector, "but first, it would be a great kindness if you would allow us to see the interior of the church. I dare say these modern bricks conceal stonework and woodwork of some real antiquity and artistic merit, do they not?"

Mr. Brickward, who at first had appeared far from gracious, brightened at once, and in a moment had snatched up a key and was escorting us to the north door of the church, chattering all the way about mediaeval tracery, Elizabethan carvings, and Georgian re-pointing. Inside the building it was so dark, even on a bright spring afternoon, that my eye could distinguish little, and when Mr. Brickward pointed into the gloom and spoke ecstatically about the foliated rood-screen, I nodded mutely. Holmes made even less pretence of taking an interest in the architecture, but made a beeline for the brass-and-oak lectern, where he pulled out his thick magnifying lens, struck a match, lit a stub of candle, and bent to peer closely at the great Bible which lay there. As he moved the flame from side to side, then up and down the open page of the book, I heard a gasp from the back of the church, and realized that the church-officer, our client, had joined us. I chuckled at his anxiety, knowing the care with which Holmes avoided so much as touching, let alone scorching, anything that might yield a clue to his extraordinarily keen eye.

"Thank you, I think that will do," he called, joining us again near the doorway. "Now if Mrs. Brickward can spare us a moment, her clarification of one or two points might be most illuminating."

Mr. Brickward led us back along the path we had taken from the rectory, stepping carefully to avoid the stone flag on which I could still detect a pale brown stain that doubtless represented the dead woman's blood. "Jennie!" he called as we entered the rectory. "Jennie, these gentlemen would like a word with you."

We took seats a little awkwardly in the parlour, all of us save Holmes, who propped his lean frame against a bulging bookcase beside the mantel and surveyed the heavily furnished little room with a keen eye. In a moment the rector's wife appeared before us: a slight, dark woman, as Hopkins had said, neatly though inexpensively dressed in a pale blue costume. Dark shadows beneath her eyes reminded me of the strain this mysterious bloodshed, with the curious and even sinister desecration that had accompanied it, must be imposing on a young couple not yet much tried in the fires of life. It crossed my mind that the young rector, through his ecclesiastical training and no doubt an innately religious cast of mind, must have resources for facing the proximity of death that were not available to his more delicate wife. Seated together on a horsehair sofa, her little hand resting gently on her husband's arm, they seemed a picture of courage in time of sorrow.

Hopkins introduced us, Thomas Sexton adding with a note of pride in his voice that as church-officer he had taken the responsibility of asking Mr. Holmes to look into the affair. Holmes murmured a soothing word or two to Mrs. Brickward, then asked her to tell how she had found the body on Sunday morning.

"I had slipped out of church during the last hymn," she explained. "I

333

know it seems dreadful of me, and I always do stay long enough to listen to John preach, but I do feel so alone in the middle of the congregation sometimes, and suddenly I thought, 'I can't bear to listen to *Alleluia! Alleluia!* one more time. I'll just leave quietly and have a few things started for luncheon before Mr. and Mrs. Wallace arrive, since I don't have Mary Ann to help me any longer.' So I did that, and when I came round the side of the church to the rectory path, I saw the woman lying there on the stone step, with the blood splashed out around her like – oh, like a red cape!"

Her low voice rose in pitch and her dark eyes seemed wider than ever; I saw her husband's protective arm reach around her. "Mr. Holmes," he said, "I hope you will forgive me if I say that my wife is overwrought; she is really not able to discuss this dreadful affair."

"I have only one other question of importance to ask," said Holmes. "Mrs. Brickward, when did you first recognize Ellie?"

The rector's young wife stared at Holmes in horror, rose to her feet, gave a little shriek and crumpled to the floor.

"It was obvious from the first that someone closely connected to St. Nicholas had killed the young woman," Holmes explained as he, Hopkins and I rattled homeward in the inspector's cab. "If you will forgive me for saying so, friend Hopkins, street brawls that end in sordid bloodshed are most unlikely to take place on a Sunday morning, when the public houses are closed and their denizens asleep in their lodgings or under Lambeth Bridge. As soon as I saw the place, I recognized that if there had been a body in Moss Road before the service began, someone among the good people of St. Nicholas would certainly have seen it, perhaps the diligent Mr. Sexton himself. It followed that the murder was committed during the time of the service itself.

"The most important indication, however, was the page from the church's Bible. We may dismiss witchcraft – a suggestion which, I strongly suspect, Mrs. Brickward put forward as a desperate attempt at misdirection. Likewise it was apparent from the beginning that there must be an excellent reason for someone to have ripped a page from the great Bible in the church itself, when so many other copies of scripture are easily at hand.

"You spoke, Watson, of a message being conveyed by the page. Indeed it was, but through no work of the printer or any divine hand. Asking myself why that particular page was torn from the volume, I looked in the volume itself to see what remained, and in the margins of the next page after the torn stub, my candle revealed deep and irregular impressions. It was not difficult to tell that words had been scrawled on the missing page, and I was able to read them: 'John, I have returned. Meet me in Moss Road after the service ends. Ellie.'

"Evidently it was a message for Mr. Brickward, which he was to find when he looked at the Bible during the service on Sunday. The writer, this Ellie, cannot have anticipated that he would find it beforehand, presumably when he came in to see that all was in readiness for Sunday morning, or that he would tear it out, for fear that others might see it – still less that he would confide in his wife. On the contrary, she must have assumed that he would keep his wife in darkness, and even abandon her for the sake of the one who had 'returned'.

"Of course we do not yet know exactly what had been the relations between Mr. Brickward and this woman, but it is clear that despite her husband's remarkable willingness to show her the letter, Mrs. Brickward perceived Ellie as a serious threat and was prepared to take drastic action to keep her from ever meeting her husband.

"Taking the page from the Bible is not, of course, the same thing as murder, but the one led to the other. Again, the opportunity to be in Moss Road during the service is the vital indication. Mr. Brickward himself was, if I may say so, under close observation by the entire congregation throughout the service. Much the same must be true of Mr. Sexton, the church-officer.

"Mrs. Brickward says that she left the service early, and that in itself might have given her the opportunity to find Ellie. It must have taken some little time, however, to have words with her, stab her dead, and conceal the knife somewhere. I dare say, your constables will find it in the cellar or kitchen-garden about the rectory if they take the trouble to search. More than that, however, she also needed a moment to burn the Bible page beside Ellie's body."

"I cannot see why she took the trouble to do that," Hopkins remarked.

"I should think," said Holmes, "that she intended her husband to recognize the remains of paper and to realize what had happened. Her heart told her that he would feel himself as much to blame as she, and the secret of Ellie's death would bind them close together. Burning the page, of course, would also ensure that no stranger could read the pencilled message.

"Doing all these things must have taken more than the few seconds by which Mrs. Brickward preceded other churchgoers into Moss Road, and for a moment or two I wondered whether the young woman had, in fact, been killed earlier than I thought. But then Mrs. Brickward herself gave us the explanation. You will recall her remark that the service had included the words '*Alleluia! Alleluia!*' again and again.

"It is many years since I was compelled to attend Sunday School classes as a boy, but I do recall being told with determination, as a matter of great importance in the mind of the maiden lady who instructed me, that in the austere season of Lent, those words are never used in the liturgy. Here we are in March, a fortnight before Easter, and so it is Lent. Mrs. Brickward cannot have heard the congregation repeating *Alleluia!* this Sunday morning – because the prayer book told them not to say it, and because she was not in church at all. I knew that she was not telling the truth, and the matter was settled. Unnoticed by the other churchgoers, for she had no friends to look for her, she was not in the church, but in Moss Road, where she waited for Ellie, killed her, and burned her last message to John Brickward."

"It seems very straightforward as you set it out," said Hopkins. "If only I had had a few minutes to consider the case, I should have come to the same conclusion on Monday last, and you need not have been troubled."

"Ah," laughed Holmes, "and so my hours have made good your minutes. It was a trivial matter, certainly, and yet not without interest, particularly for the novelty of the message written on a leaf of the Bible. Watson, I recall hearing that some device of the sort was used in one of the romance novels of your friend James Barrie. I must look into it one of these days, although I understand that his works are written in a Scots dialect which is perhaps more congenial to you than it is to me."

The Lady on the Bridge
by Mike Hogan

Sherlock Holmes pushed back his chair, stood, and laid his napkin on the table. "Settle up, would you, old chap? I have a small errand to run." He weaved among the tables of the restaurant and disappeared through the main entrance doors.

I pulled out my pocket book and sighed. Our finances, as often at the end of the month, were at a low ebb, but at Holmes's insistence we had travelled from Baker Street to Sydenham on a blustery afternoon to take an early dinner at a fine French restaurant in the Byzantine court at the Crystal Palace. The decor was as highly stylised as the menu prices were highly inflated.

And Holmes's attention had not been on the food. Even as we were ushered into the room, his eyes had flickered around as if looking for someone, and between courses he had glanced at his pocket watch as if gauging whether he had time to make a rendezvous.

I requested the bill and peered at a note in tiny print explaining that the charge had been calculated according to a Continental system by which a seven-per-cent gratuity had been added. It occurred to me as I received my change from the sharp-eyed waiter that a gratuity should be precisely what the word suggested, a token of appreciation from a satisfied customer, not a levy. However, under the supercilious gaze of the waiter and with the *maître d'hôtel*, hovering with an elderly couple anxious to possess our table, I made a swift mental calculation and left an appropriate amount in the saucer as a 'tip'. The waiter peered at the thru'pence coin and its ha'penny companion with disdain, the maître d'hôtel sadly shook his head, and the gentleman waiting for our table shared a condescending half-smile with his lady companion. Undaunted, I stood and marched to the entrance of the restaurant, where I found Holmes leaning against an iron pillar deep in his *Evening News*.

He folded the newspaper and tucked it under his arm. "Nothing yet, but there is still the final edition."

I frowned. "What are you expecting?"

"Did you take the receipt?" he asked.

337

I handed it to him. "The price included a seven-per-cent charge for service. It was clear from the attitude of the restaurant staff that a further amount was expected as a tip."

Holmes considered. "Fourpence three-farthings would have been an adequate addition to the charge to make it consistent with your usual practice. Come."

I followed him out of the restaurant, counting surreptitiously on my fingers, and into one of the huge galleries in the iron-framed glass building. A crystal fountain glistened in the sunlight streaming through the tremendous glass walls and curved ceiling high above us, and I stood in awe as I gazed at the long vista before me. Tall trees brushed the ceiling of the central nave, and massive monuments from antiquity and gigantic engines from the present day occupied the aisles and transepts.

I looked for Holmes and found him reading his paper in the shade of a palm tree in what was clearly a Roman or Greek themed exhibition. A dozen ladies sat before a row of plaster statues of naked, ivy-leaved young males, while a spade-bearded gentleman discoursed on features of ancient sculpture. One young lady seated at the end of the row of students flicked her eyes along the line of sculptures and then past them to me. I blinked at her, and she smiled. It would have been boorish in the extreme not to return such a charming smile, however inappropriately offered, and I – "

"Watson?"

"The Palace is a virtual university," I said as Holmes led me away. "A very useful institution, especially for young ladies of artistic inclinations."

Desiring to smoke after our meal, Holmes and I strolled the extensive gardens on what had become a balmy, early spring evening and found a bench where we sat, lit our pipes, and watched the Palace come alive with glittering electric lights.

The sky darkened and Holmes looked at his watch, tapped out his pipe and stood. He led me to a gate to one of the special garden exhibits, where he displayed our restaurant receipt to an attendant and we were waved in, *gratis*.

A newspaper boy ran up to Holmes holding out a copy of the *Evening News* late edition. Holmes grabbed it from him and flicked through the pages in the light of a gas lamp, humming softly to himself. He folded the newspaper in half and held his hand out to me. "Pencil?"

I reluctantly gave Holmes my propelling pencil and peered at the boy. On one invasion of our rooms by Holmes's band of ragamuffins, his

Baker Street Irregulars, I had lost not only my propelling pencil, but a signed score of *The Lost Chord* by Sir Arthur Sullivan. I was understandably wary of nefarious activity by any boy under Holmes's direction.

Holmes ringed a paragraph in the paper and handed it to me, then he leaned down and fixed the newspaper boy with his steady gaze. "You know what to do?" he asked.

The boy grinned up at Holmes, turned and sped away.

"In the Personals," I said, holding out my hand for my pencil. "To Ajax. *'Seven is impossible – Tower Bridge at nine; agent must wear red carnation and carry a newspaper. One Fearfully Wronged'*."

I shook my head. "What silly names; she (we must assume a she) is loquacious, even when paying by the word."

I was talking to thin air; Holmes was on the move. "Come," he called back. "It's ten minutes to seven."

I scurried after him. "We'll not get across London to the Tower in time, Holmes, it must be several miles. It is a physical impossibility, unless you have engaged a private balloon!"

Holmes skirted an ornamental fountain and came to a stop at a magnificent floral display. He plucked a red carnation bloom and slipped its stalk through my button hole.

"I say, old chap," I remonstrated.

He handed me his *Evening News* and propelled me into a large grassy enclosure, the principal feature of which was an artificial lake crossed by a bridge illuminated with coloured electric globes.

I recalled that some years previously, the promoters of the hideous Tower Bridge across the Thames had built a wood and plaster, quarter-scale model of the structure in the gardens of the Crystal Palace, no doubt hoping that the public would get used to a Gothic monstrosity almost as uncouth as the ridiculous iron tower that defiled the centre of Paris. The model had proved a popular attraction, especially when illuminated on spring and summer evenings. Young couples perambulated the lake and crossed the bridge, no doubt focussed on each other and oblivious to their less than scenic surroundings.

I followed Holmes to the arch that marked the start of the bridge walkway. Close to, the model was sadly dilapidated. Bare wood showed through the paintwork, and the suspension wires hanging from the twin towers were visibly bent and frayed, and it was with trepidation that I followed Holmes onto the creaking deck and we joined the crowd crossing and re-crossing the structure. A police constable stood by one of the towers, but he seemed content to chat with a flower seller rather than enforce any rule of the road. Holmes and I took the leftmost tack as having fewer people walking against our direction.

"Keep an eye out," he enjoined me in a murmur.

"What for?"

My question was immediately answered. Coming towards me against the flow and at a stately pace was an oddly-dressed figure, a lady, who, despite the mildness of the evening, was wrapped in a voluminous grey cape. On her head she wore a grey, flowery hat and her face was hidden, veiled in net. She stopped before me and slipped a hand into her reticule.

I blinked at her, started at a huge bang, and looked up as a firework bloomed high above me in the shape of a bright red carnation.

Holmes stepped between the lady and me and took her arm. "Madame," he said softly. "I urge you not to take such a foolhardy step."

More fireworks thundered over us as Holmes drew the lady to the side of the bridge. He made no move to bid me join them, and I stood uncertainly and in a state of utmost confusion as the crowd swirled past me staring up, mouths agape. An instinct of delicacy drew me away from my friend and the lady, and I took a position on the opposite side of the bridge against the balustrade and out of the flow of pedestrians. I could only glimpse Holmes and his companion through gaps in the passing throng and in the bursts of light from the fireworks as if in a jerky, slow-motion Kinematograph. Holmes bent towards the veiled lady and spoke most earnestly, emphasising his words with sharp gestures.

A thickening of the crowd hid them from me for a few seconds, and Holmes was beside me and the lady gone.

"Holmes," I exclaimed. "You arranged a rendezvous for me with that lady!"

The newspaper boy reappeared, handed Holmes a rolled up newspaper, and disappeared into the crowd.

"In a manner of speaking." Holmes unrolled the newspaper and disclosed a pocket pistol. "She intended to assassinate you." He smiled. "Come, let's take the train home and smoke a pipe or two in the safety of our comfortable den in Baker Street." He took me by the arm and steered me towards the station.

"Miss Berthoud said that she was sorry to have bothered you, but she cannot see very well without her spectacles, especially through her veil and in the glare of the electric lamps and pyrotechnics, and your

340

luxurious moustache is very like that of her oppressor. I advised her to go home and lay the matter before us in the morning."

I dropped both newspaper and boutonniere into a bin. "Bothered, Holmes?" I said, somewhat sharply. "Yes, I dare say a bullet through the breastbone might have been bothersome."

Holmes kept his counsel during our ride home, over late supper, and for the rest of the evening, and I went to bed with no more idea of why I had been targeted by the veiled lady than I had on the bridge.

I came down to breakfast the next morning and found Holmes in his dressing gown, reclining on the sofa, puffing on his morning pipe, and sipping coffee. A newspaper-wrapped parcel lay on the floor beside him.

"I feel that I am owed an explanation, Holmes," I said as I poured my coffee.

"I am sure you do, old man," he answered amicably. He leaned towards me and held out his cup for a refill.

"I think it only right that I should know what the devil is going on," I said stiffly. "Oh, good morning, Mrs. Hudson."

"Language, Doctor," our landlady said as she placed fresh dishes of scrambled eggs, bacon, and kidneys before me on the table. "Naming calls. Billy will bring your toast, hot-and-hot."

"I expect Murchison did what I should have done in his circumstances," Holmes said as the door closed behind her. "He bribed the boot boy (or boot girl as Miss Berthoud resides in an exclusive ladies' hotel in Bayswater) to slip a note under her bedroom door. The note referred her to the *Evening News* Personals and gave the gentleman's *nom de plume*, Ajax."

The bell rang in the hall downstairs.

"Who is this Murchison," I asked. "And how did you become involved in the matter?"

Billy appeared at the door as I was about to tuck into my bacon and eggs.

"Where's the toast?" I asked.

"Which, I didn't bring it, Doctor, on account of the lady in the waiting room come to see Mr. Holmes."

"But, what about breakfast?" I exclaimed.

Holmes jumped up. "Clear the table, Billy, then show her up."

"I am a wronged woman," Miss Berthoud said in a charmingly French-lilted English. "I was harried from my home, driven from my

341

position as a nanny with a titled family, and hounded and threatened by a fiend who will stop at nothing to ruin me."

Our visitor was a fresh-faced young lady of twenty or so, again in grey, but she had exchanged her cape and veil for a well-fitting, tailored ensemble in the latest fashion, and on her head was a tiny grey and pale yellow hat that clung to her tightly coiled hair like a budgerigar to its perch. She refused refreshment and took Holmes's place on the sofa while he and I sat in our usual chairs before the empty grate.

She folded her hands in her lap. "There are moments, gentlemen, when one has to choose between living one's own life, fully, entirely, completely – or dragging out some false, shallow, degrading existence that the world in its hypocrisy demands. I grasped that moment yesterday when I saw you on the bridge, Doctor. I was determined to destroy he who stands between my dear Alfie and me."

Holmes sniffed. "But, you must consider, Miss Berthoud, that you would undoubtedly have been apprehended. Your costume, although admirably conceived for hiding your identity, was too voluminous for speedy escape, and a constable was at hand. You must have been caught and inevitably hanged for murder."

Miss Berthoud seemed about to contradict Holmes, but he overrode her. "I see you frown. Although your English is excellent, I deduce from your accent (and your name) that you are French by birth, and you may not be aware that on this side of the Channel the courts do not have the option of excusing a murder as a *crime passionel*. Our Judiciary is not known for its Romantic conceptions; no, no, it would have meant the rope."

"I say, Holmes – " I interjected.

"If I might accept your offer of refreshment, Doctor?" Miss Berthoud asked softly.

"Of course, tea or coffee?" I asked.

"A reviving brandy and soda for our guest, Watson," Holmes said firmly. "And a whisky for me while you're at the Tantalus."

I poured the drinks, handed them and helped myself to a whisky.

"Tell me more of the target of your assassination attempt," Holmes requested. "This Reverend Murchison."

"Your oppressor is a clergyman?" I asked. "Not of the established church, I trust."

"Of the Church of Scotland," Miss Berthoud answered. "He retired to Boulogne, as do many of his countrymen, particularly professional gentlemen."

She took a dainty sip of brandy. "Although my family was of aristocratic status, we lost everything in the turmoil at the end of the last century. My great-grandfather opposed the tyrant Napoleon, and our family was proscribed. After the death of my father, my mother was obliged to sell what remained of our property and set up a lodging house in Boulogne. A very genteel establishment, you understand, catering to elderly ladies and retired gentlemen, several of them from Britain, as the town has a reputation as a welcoming place for such people: we have an English bookshop, several tea rooms, and a subscription library with the latest newspapers and periodicals from London. I left school in order to assist my mother in the business."

"Your English is most remarkable, Miss Berthoud," I said.

She bowed. "In France I received a typical education for a girl of my class and background, but I had the good fortune to make the acquaintance of an English lady who boarded with us. She took me under her wing and tutored me in your language."

Her voice took on a more severe quality as she continued. "My life changed forever when an elderly man in clerical hat and clothes appeared at our door enquiring whether we had rooms. He rented the second floor front bedroom, with the use of the necessary facilities on that floor and freedom of the downstairs sitting room where my mother and I spent our quiet evenings, sewing or reading improving literature."

She sighed a most affecting sigh. "From the moment Reverend Murchison entered our household, I had not a moment's peace. At first, he dined with the other lodgers, but soon he was invited to share our supper *en famille*, and he ate with my mother and me every night, without fail. During meals, he did not take his eyes from me."

Miss Berthoud leaned across and grasped my hand. "I was a caged bird, Doctor!"

I squeezed her hand in a reassuring gesture as she continued. "I must explain that in Boulogne, the English men who reside or holiday there are considered prime matches for young girls of the town; the gentlemen are usually elderly and are thought to be wealthy (at least in comparison the local *ouvriers*). My mother forced the man upon me. I had nowhere to go, and no funds of my own, but I knew that I could not endure being Reverend Murchison's wife."

"*Ouvriers*," said Holmes, "labourers."

I frowned at him.

"I represented to my mother that the reverend gentleman was of a certain age and an ungenerous disposition, and that I was but nineteen,"

343

Miss Berthoud continued with a long sigh. "But she would hear nothing against him. She even sought occasions when she might leave us alone together, and I was obliged to endure his vile advances."

I stood and stroked my moustache. "He did not, ah – "

Miss Berthoud pursed her lips. "Reverend Murchison did not force himself upon me, no. But in every other way he bound me to him with chains of iron. He visited our sitting room morning and afternoon, visibly annoyed if other persons, such as our neighbours, Monsieur Sublier and his wife, or other lodgers were present."

"You made your escape," Holmes suggested.

"With the help of that kind English lady, since Passed Over, who knew of my travails and offered her wise counsel. I replied to an advertisement in an English newspaper, offering the position of nanny to a young lady of good character who could teach French. As you were kind enough to remark, my English was good (it has improved in the two years I have worked here). My benefactor provided a letter of introduction to Lord and Lady Muntley (for that is the name of my erstwhile employers) that served in lieu of an employment reference, and I happily accepted the position on adequate terms and conditions. I fled Boulogne for my safe haven in the town of Frome, in Wiltshire."

Miss Berthoud blinked sadly at me, and I offered her another glass of medicinal brandy, which she reluctantly accepted.

"I will not say that my life was idyllic," she continued, "although Frome is a pleasant location, and my employers were kind, but – " She sighed. "I hope that you will not judge me too harshly, gentlemen, when I admit that I am not one of those women who dote on children; in fact, I found no charming traits whatsoever in the baby boy in my care, or in the twin girls, his older sisters."

"Reverend Murchison sought you?" Holmes asked.

"He somehow found me out and settled at an inn in the town. He followed me whenever I left the house, even to church on Sunday. He plagued me with bouquets of meadow flowers and boxes of inferior chocolates."

"The hound," I said.

"Frome is a small town, gentlemen, a village really, and Reverend's Millward's activities were noticed." Miss Berthoud frowned down at the clenched hands in her lap. "He wrote to me, often daily."

"The fiend!" I cried.

"I think we might accept Reverend Murchison's villainy as a given, Watson," Holmes said, turning to me, "requiring no further expostulation."

I sniffed and sipped my whisky in a decided manner.

"One day," Miss Berthoud continued, "earlier in the summer, the youngest child of the family was out of sorts, and our physician in Frome recommended the waters of Bath. We took lodgings there."

Miss Berthoud seemed lost in thought for a long moment.

"And?" Holmes asked sharply.

She looked up. "I met Lieutenant Lord Alfred Bartholomew by chance in a small park where he played at quoits with some of his brother officers from *HMS Atropos*, his armoured cruiser. She is in the second rate of that class, but Alfie and I are convinced that she is the most effectively armed of her sisters, as she has no less than five six-inch quick firers, all Armstrong guns. He is Third Officer."

Miss Berthoud smiled at me, and Holmes tut-tutted for her to continue.

"Alfie proposed, but I hesitated. I did not care to exchange one kind of domestic slavery for another; to become an officer's wife living at the admiral's manor house while my husband was in China or the Cape, with my contentment dependent on the goodwill of my mother-in-law. No, no, that would never do. But my beloved convinced me that the Navy is quite different from the Army, in that wives may follow their husbands to foreign stations and set up a home, if they have sufficient means."

She took a sip of brandy and smiled again. "Admiral Lord Charles Bartholomew is very well situated, and Alfie has high expectations."

"Reverend Murchison discovered your attachment to Lieutenant Bartholomew?" Holmes asked.

"He did. My tormentor followed me as I wheeled Baby to the park in his perambulator. I refused to enter into communication with him, but he sent me messages through the Personal Columns in which he avers in veiled terms that he will do everything in his power to sever relations between Alfie and me. If I will not be his, he is determined that I shall have no future with another, that I shall die an old maid."

"The brute!" I exclaimed, and Holmes gave me a reproving look.

"He is determined to ruin my happiness," Miss Berthoud said, sobbing into her hands. "The wedding is on Saturday at ten in the morning at the church in Rowland's Castle, a village in Hampshire close to Admiral Bartholomew's estates. Reverend Murchison requires me to

345

submit to him within forty-eight hours or he will write to the admiral and acquaint him with his prior claim to my hand."

"Very well," said Holmes, rubbing his palms together in what I thought a rather callous gesture. "I must now ask if there is anything known to Murchison that might cause unease if it were relayed to the admiral."

"Nothing! He will make something up. He is the Devil incarnate. Alfie's father would instantly forbid the match if he detected any taint of impropriety. Lady Bartholomew is of a frail disposition of mind. I fear for her sanity if any shadow of scandal adhered to the family name."

"I must press you, Miss Berthoud," Holmes said coldly. "If I am to help you in this matter, I must know everything."

Miss Berthoud looked down and wrung her hands. "You must understand that I was very young, Reverend Murchison was very persistent, my mother entreated me, and I could conceive of no alternative to accepting his proposal."

"You did so?" Holmes asked.

"In a manner of speaking."

"There is written proof of your acceptance of Reverend Murchison's offer?"

"There were certain allusions in one short note I wrote to Reverend Murchison," she answered. "Nothing untoward, you understand, but they might be taken as a statement of assent."

"To marriage with him?"

Miss Berthoud nodded unhappily.

Holmes stood. "We have but two days before the deadline and four before the nuptials. We must act. Watson?"

I stood.

"Perhaps you might see Miss Berthoud to her conveyance."

I offered Miss Berthoud my arm and accompanied her downstairs and to the omnibus stop.

I returned to our sitting room, and found Holmes leaning against the mantel smoking a cigar from my packet and undoing the string on the parcel I'd seen earlier.

"An interesting lady," I suggested, "who mixes the delicacy of her sex with an admirable streak of determination; think on the pistol."

"She is One Cruelly Used," Holmes exclaimed, throwing his arms up in a melodramatic gesture.

"Are you quite well, Holmes?"

346

"We could visit the fellow as friends of Miss Berthoud and warn him that his behaviour is intolerable," I suggested later in the day as we rumbled towards the West End in a four-wheeler. Holmes was dressed in the uniform of a district messenger. On my knees was a picnic hamper.

"Reverend Murchison is already in a paroxysm of jealousy over the naval lieutenant," Holmes answered. "I fear that his Scots intransigence would meet your own well-documented pugnacity and lead to fisticuffs. He boards at the Langham Hotel in Portland Square, a genteel establishment whose staff might look askance if violence (however justified) were offered to one of their guests. No, we must adopt a more circumspect approach."

"How did you come across the correspondence in the *Evening News*, Holmes?" I asked.

"You know that the Personal Column is the first I turn to in every paper. The thread of messages between Ajax and One Cruelly Wronged intrigued me. She refused to countenance a face-to-face meeting with Ajax to discuss the matter between them. He suggested instead a rendezvous on the bridge with a go-between. Miss Berthoud accepted, and I intervened and sent a message to Ajax putting the meeting back and signing it – "

"One Cruelly Wronged."

"Exactly." Holmes sniffed. "I believe Miss Berthoud saw through Reverend Murchison's ploy of confidential agents and knew that the reverend himself would accost her on the bridge. She was prepared to end the matter there and then."

"Would she have shot her adversary?"

"French women are unencumbered by notions of propriety."

I frowned.

"There was no danger, my dear fellow; everything was under my control," Holmes said. "On my orders, the newspaper boy at the Palace contacted a local band of pickpockets and gave them a commission to dip the lady's reticule as she stepped onto the bridge." He smiled. "Two hours later, the same band accosted a gentleman carrying a folded *Evening News* and wearing a carnation buttonhole," Holmes continued. "The newspaper boy delivered a parcel early this morning in exchange for twelve-and-six from our contingency fund, plus omnibus fare and refreshments."

Holmes displayed a silver pocket watch, a spectacle case, an empty wallet, a bill for accommodation at the Langham Hotel at the clergy rate, and an unopened, unstamped letter addressed to Admiral Bartholomew, care of the Railway Hotel, Rowland's Castle, Hampshire.

"So, we not only have the reverend's address, we have the letter he intended to give to Miss Berthoud to show that he was in earnest." Holmes slit the envelope open with a pocket knife.

"I say, old man, you can't just – "

"The envelope is not franked; it is unprotected by law."

I muttered something about the inviolability of private property while Holmes held the letter to the light from the cab window. He offered it to me, but I waved it away.

He shrugged. "It is as vile as we might expect. Miss Berthoud, however circumspect she has been with the truth, is under threat from this man."

"Will Reverend Murchison not take precautions after his things were stolen?"

"No, no," Holmes answered. "He was prey to a band of ragamuffins who will throw the letter away, take the cash, and sell the empty wallet, spectacles and watch."

The cab turned off Regent Street and halted in Portland Place "We must return Reverend Murchison's possessions," I said. "And pray that no more contingencies occur this month."

We stepped down from the cab, and I sat on a bench under a tall plane tree just across from the grand entrance to the Langham Hotel.

"I expected you to infiltrate the hotel in the guise of an aged clergyman," I said as I peered into the hamper, but Holmes was already out of earshot and halfway to the cab stand on the corner. I poured myself a cup of wine and sipped it as I watched Holmes chatting with the drivers in his guise as district messenger. He nodded farewell to them and climbed the steps to the hotel entrance.

"The task before us may be divided into several stages," Holmes said when he returned to the bench some minutes later. "The first is already accomplished: we have the address and room number of our mark and, after a moderate distribution of silver to the cab stand and the hotel door and boot boys, we will soon note his routines. The second stage is the letter he threatens to send to the groom's father and how we may prevent it reaching its recipient."

Holmes accepted a chicken leg and a cup of wine. "Word from the cab drivers is that the reverend gentleman is of a choleric disposition, prefers to travel by omnibus, and frequents Madame La Rout's establishment in Jermyn Street."

I heaved myself up. "And the hound has the effrontery to pursue Miss Berthoud, despite her clear revulsion. I should take a horsewhip to him, reverend or no. He is a disgrace to the Kirk and, and – "

Holmes handed me an apple. "Calm, old man. Let us plan our dispositions."

I subsided onto the bench.

"The letter, then," Holmes said. "According to the door boy, Reverend Murchison is a prolific letter writer. He drops a bundle of envelopes into that letter box before dinner each evening." Holmes indicated an iron post box on the pavement a few yards from the hotel entrance. "He uses no other."

"He does not employ the hotel mail service?" I asked.

Holmes smiled. "Reverend Murchison is clearly a man of frugal habits. If he posts the letters himself, he saves a tip."

"Merely dipping the letter from his pocket will not answer," I said, "as Reverend Murchison will simply write another letter and take better care when he posts it. What other measures may we adopt?"

Holmes considered. "Lead line and plumb, with tar or glue on the plumb bob, dropped into the letter box slit just after he posts the envelope to fish it out. Or fit a bag inside the slit. Or we can just set fire to the letters. Do you want the last boiled egg?"

I listened to Holmes's suggestions with mounting unease. "Set fire to Her Majesty's mails! I say, Holmes."

He shrugged. "Very well. According to the cab drivers, the postman has no less than seven mouths to feed on his wage, and he moonlights as a knocker upper."

"I refuse to countenance bribery of an official of the Crown," I said stiffly. "You speak of criminal activity with the insouciance of a Hoxted costermonger."

"Perhaps you could offer a more benign solution to our problem, Doctor?" Holmes said, taking the last boiled egg. "Miss Bertaud's deadline expires at midnight tonight."

We returned to Portland Place at eleven-thirty, and I sat in a four-wheeler cab parked across the road from the hotel. Holmes, now in the guise of a London postman, was opposite me.

He smiled. "Three-and-six to a specialist firm in Lambeth for rent of the uniform and post box key."

"The expenses in this case are mounting," I said, noting the rental cost on my shirt cuff.

At two minutes to midnight, the hotel door opened and a stooped, elderly man with a thick walrus moustache emerged and paused at the top of the steps, peering around myopically and sniffing the air. He wore clerical weeds and a flat vicar's hat and carried an umbrella. Seemingly satisfied with the balmy weather, he strode down the steps to the pavement, marched to the letter box, and without a moment's hesitation slipped an envelope inside. He turned and sauntered back to the hotel entrance, humming a tune and with his umbrella clicking rhythmically on the steps.

"*Pinafore*," I murmured, frowning. "Murchison looks nothing like me."

Holmes put his finger to his lips as we watched Reverend Murchison re-enter the hotel lobby. Holmes instantly leapt from the cab, raced to the post box and unlocked it with his key.

I glanced down at my watch. We had met the regular postman, Mr. Willis, at his local public house earlier in the evening before he started his round. He had blankly failed to comprehend the hints and innuendos that Holmes employed, and Holmes did not dare make a plain offer in case the man informed the authorities. We had fallen back on an alternative plan which required Holmes to retrieve the letter before Willis collected the mail at midnight.

I stiffened as Holmes, kneeling beside the post box, struck a match, but he stood, relocked the box, hurried across to the cab and leapt inside just as a tricycle turned into the square. It stopped beside the post box and Willis emptied the post into his sack.

Holmes tapped on the cab roof with his stick and we set off for home.

"I thought for a moment you were going to set fire to the letters," I said with a soft chuckle.

"I would not dream of interfering with Her Majesty's mails," Holmes answered.

I frowned.

"Reverend Murchison will expect his letter to arrive at the admiral's villa in Hampshire tomorrow," Holmes continued. "The reply, probably by telegraph or express letter, should reach him no later than Friday afternoon, the day before the wedding. If Murchison does not receive that reply, he will gird his financial loins and spring for a telegram."

"He will not use the Langham Hotel telephone service?"

"Too expensive." Holmes smiled. "And I checked the directory. Admiral Bartholomew does not possess a telephone."

We arrived back at Baker Street and settled in our sitting room.

"Take down Bradshaw would you, old man?" Holmes requested. "I want a Portsmouth train stopping at Rowland's Castle not later than nine-thirty on Saturday morning. That gives Murchison time to have his breakfast (included in his room charge and not to be missed by our frugal friend), take a 'bus to Waterloo and get to Rowland's Castle before the wedding starts at ten."

Holmes sat at his writing table, took a sheet of notepaper from an envelope, dipped his pen and wrote in silence for a few moments.

He looked up and handed me the note. "I have made an appointment for Reverend Murchison to meet Admiral Bartholomew on the morning of the wedding – that will appeal to the reverend's sense of drama. He will relish his power to destroy the happiness of Miss Berthoud and her naval swain."

"This is The Railway Hotel, Rowland's Castle notepaper, Holmes."

"A touch of authenticity courtesy of Wiggins' Uncle Silas, confidential printer, and purveyor of slush paper to the Quality at tuppence a sheet."

I made a note.

We were on our bench opposite the Langham at six-thirty on Saturday morning.

"Reverend Murchison has checked out," said Holmes. "And, here he is, curtly spurning the offer of a porter to carry his carpet bag and stalking head down towards the omnibus stop."

"He is not as sprightly as he was two nights ago," I remarked as we stood and picked up our bags. "He seems to be in a gruff mood."

"I want Reverend Murchison in a lather," Holmes said, rubbing his hands together. "I did not destroy his letter to Admiral Bartholomew, I merely crossed out the address and marked the envelope 'return to sender'. Oddly, when the letter was returned to the Langham in yesterday's morning post, the admiral's reply came in the same delivery. Reverend Murchison has had a confused night. Come, we will go on ahead to Waterloo by cab."

"What if he takes a Portsmouth train from Victoria Station?" I asked as we crossed the square to the stand.

"He will not. That service does not stop at Rowland's Castle. He would have to buy a separate ticket from Portsmouth and incur more expense. No, no, we shall wait for him at Waterloo."

Holmes purchased our tickets at the kiosk in Waterloo Station and instantly disappeared into the crowd. I looked about me and started as Reverend Murchison strode purposefully from the arched exit from the omnibus stands, bought a second-class ticket at the kiosk, and headed towards the Departures Board.

Holmes reappeared beside me dressed as a railway porter.

"Holmes!" I cried. "He is here. What now?"

He passed me a ticket. "Stick precisely to my plan, of course."

I stalked my prey as he squinted up at the Departures Board and at the station clock hanging from the roof above us.

"What platform for the eight-oh-four to Portsmouth?" I called across Reverend Murchison to Holmes lounging against a porter's trolley.

"Moved to platform seven, sir," Holmes answered.

"Stopping at Rowland's Castle?" Reverend Murchison asked in a gruff tone tinged with Scots.

"Number seven, sir. You'll have to hurry."

Reverend Murchison reached towards his empty watch pocket and frowned. "I will do no such thing. I have thirty minutes or more."

Holmes pulled out a brass pocket watch and checked it with the clock above us. "Five or less, sir. It's just gone eight."

"My watch says eight and a bit," I said truthfully. "We'll have to run!" I hefted my Gladstone bag and raced towards Platform Seven with Reverend Murchison grumbling at my heels.

A group of schoolboys milled about the entrance to the platform with a harassed looking master attempting to bring them to order. I pushed through them and waved my ticket at the attendant guarding the platform entrance. A line of a dozen or so carriages stood behind him with the engine in front hissing and puffing out billows of steam. The attendant glanced at my ticket and indicated with a jerk of his head that I and my clerical companion might proceed.

"Have I time to get a paper?" I asked.

"You have not, sir. She's away any moment."

"Come now, boys," the teacher cried in a shrill voice. "You heard the man, you must come along. The train is leaving."

The gate attendant chuckled. "He'll never get that lot on; he's herding cats."

Reverend Murchison and I pushed through the mass of boys, who seemed to take delight in obstructing us. I lost my stick in the

352

commotion, which was probably just as well as I would have been sorely tempted to use it on the brats. I saw that Reverend Murchison's hat was askew and his umbrella had become unfurled.

At a harsh cry from the teacher, the boys came instantly to attention, and I was able to struggle through to clear ground on the platform beyond with Reverend Murchison close behind, rolling up his umbrella.

"We must make haste," I cried, pointing to the guard with his flags in his hand marching along the side of the train and closing the last few doors. Reverend Murchison and I raced behind a gentleman in a top hat and overcoat also running for the train. We three jumped through the first open door, which the guard slammed behind us. The reverend and I sat on either side of the compartment, he opposite the gentleman, who snapped open his *Times* and disappeared behind it.

Reverend Murchison nevertheless addressed him, and my heart sank.

"Excuse me, sir, this is the eight-oh-four to Portsmouth, I collect?"

A shrill whistle sounded and the train jerked into motion. The man put down his paper, stood and smiled at me. "Come, my dear fellow."

Holmes opened the door and we stepped out onto the platform. I closed the door behind us. The train picked up speed, and as it left the station and curved west, a walrus-moustached face squinted from the window of our compartment.

The harassed schoolmaster came up to Holmes with his charges.

"A shilling each boy," Holmes murmured in my ear, "and three bob for the cat herder."

I fumbled in my waistcoat for the necessary coins, paid the master and boys and glared down at one schoolboy who held out my stick.

"Reverend Murchison may have some difficulty with the guard before he arrives in Exeter," Holmes remarked.

"Exeter!" I exclaimed.

"He is on the seven-thirty-eight non-stop to Exeter without his watch and spectacles and with my *Times* and the wrong ticket." Holmes smiled. "He might go on to the coast in this fine weather."

"I trust you will post his things back to him, or hand them in at the Lost and Found."

"I will post them. I want him to know that Miss Berthoud (soon to be Mrs. Bartholomew) has friends."

I threw my Exeter ticket into a bin, took out my watch and corrected the time. "Where did you find such brats, Holmes? Are they the Crystal Palace gang?"

"No, no. I applied to the nearest Doctor Barnado's Home and borrowed a dozen of their inmates. Before they became Barnado's cherubs, the boys were street Arabs; I am happy to see they have not lost their skills."

I took out my pencil and made a note of our expenses on my shirt cuff, tut-tutting to myself.

Holmes took my arm. "Come, we have twenty minutes before the Portsmouth train." He indicated the railwayman's uniform he wore under his coat. "I must change, and then let us have a celebratory coffee."

I had a sudden thought. "But will Reverend Murchison not pull the communication cord, at the next station and stop the train?"

"And incur a hefty fine?"

Rowland's Castle was a picturesque village nestled around a green, with a Railway Hotel and a church, where I was roped in to give Miss Berthoud away during a short and very simple service. After the requisite photographs at the lynch gate, the groom, Lieutenant Bartholomew, having unaccountably disappeared, I took it upon myself to take the bride's arm and lead the wedding party across the green, where wickets were being set up for a cricket match, to the hotel.

We joined Holmes in a pleasant room adjoining the bar, and the newly minted Mrs. Bartholomew took glasses of Champagne from a waiter and handed one each to Holmes and to me. I proposed a toast to the happy pair, which Mrs. Bartholomew acknowledged with a gracious bow. "I cannot thank you gentlemen enough," she said, tears glistening in her eyes. "I should have been lost without you."

"What are your plans?" I asked.

She smiled as she dabbed her eyes with her handkerchief and regained her composure. "Alfie and I leave immediately on the mail packet for our honeymoon in Grenoble, then to Gibraltar and our new life."

"Grenoble?" Holmes asked in a musing tone. "Not Paris? I thought you might like to revisit your old haunts. The Moulin Rouge is very entertaining, or so I am told."

Mrs. Bartholomew regarded Holmes through narrowed eyes.

"Of course, you will want to put Daisy behind you," Holmes continued. He lifted his glass again. "To a fresh start for you with Lieutenant Lord Alfred Bartholomew and a very happy life together."

Holmes bowed and left us, passing through the front door and onto the village green.

I blinked at Mrs. Bartholomew.

"I will indeed start anew with Alfie," she said stiffly. She considered for a moment, smiled and continued in an accent more reminiscent of Balham than Boulogne. "And I suppose I owe you the truth, Doctor, now that things are all hunky dory, as they say. I met my beloved in Paris, not Bath." She giggled. "Not at the Moulin Rouge neither. No, no, my little establishment was not at that level, 'though we had a show."

Mrs. Bartholomew smiled up at me. "*Poses plastiques et tableaux vivants.* Alfie visited the house with some other officers. They took a girl each upstairs and left, but Alfie stayed watching the show, and he called me to his table."

She frowned and looked around the room. "Where is he?" She turned to me. "Do you have a cigarette, Doctor?"

I opened my case with a cold gesture and Mrs. Bartholomew took a cigarette and lit it with a match from a passing waiter. "Alfie was polite and handsome, and he wanted to take me out for supper."

She blew out a long stream of smoke. "He saw me home to my lodgings after, with no 'how's your father' expected. On the third evening, he proposed, not only marriage, but a cycling trip through the Camargue. I accepted."

"You went on holiday alone and unchaperoned with a man you had known a bare three days?" I asked.

Mrs. Bartholomew laid a hand on my arm. "What a darling you are, Doctor. Alfie was a perfect English gentleman. You remind me of him."

I smoothed my moustache.

"After a very jolly holiday, he brought me here to London and set me up at a ladies hotel. I provided myself with a suitable wardrobe, and I met Admiral Bartholomew and his dear, but delicate wife at their London home."

She squeezed my arm. "What I told you of Reverend Murchison's unwelcome attentions was true, Doctor. The wretch bombarded me with *billets-doux* in Paris, wouldn't take *non* for an answer, and followed me to England. What better way to get him off my back than to persuade the great private detective, Sherlock Holmes, to deal with him? Your stories in the *Strand Magazine* gave me the idea of hooking Mr. Holmes by insisting that Murchison only contact me through the Personals."

She chuckled. "*One Cruelly Used*! Ha!" She frowned again. "Where is Alfie? He should be with me, the attentive husband and all." She leaned towards me. "He's been a might skittish today. I suppose he was

355

afraid of a scandal if Murchison turned up. Men are such cowards. They outrage every law of the world and are afraid of the world's tongue."

I sniffed and looked away.

"Oh, Doctor, do not judge me. You don't know what it is to fall into the pit, to be despised, mocked, abandoned, *sniffed* at!"

Mrs. Bartholomew took a silk handkerchief from the sleeve of her bridal dress and blew her nose. "One pays for one's sin, and then one pays again, and all one's life one pays. But let that pass."

"If Mr. Holmes had not turned up," I asked. "Would you have used your pistol?"

Mrs. Bartholomew looked around with a *moue* of annoyance. Guests, mostly female, were in small clusters around the room, looking rather nonplussed. "Where the devil has the boy got to?"

I found Holmes on the village green in a deckchair under an umbrella, drinking a pint of ale and watching the cricket match. "Should we not meet the groom and family?" I asked.

Holmes waved me to a chair beside him and ordered a pint of ale from a boy in sailor suit and a bright scarf.

I settled back in my chair. The afternoon was warm, mellowed by a cooling breeze that brought the smell of new mown grass and the scents of spring flowers across the green. There was a thwack of leather on willow, and the ball arched across the cloudless sky and was deftly caught by an elderly gentleman in cover.

"I should have expected a more Naval wedding; an arch of cutlasses and so on," I said as we applauded.

Holmes chuckled. "What a minx it is, Watson."

The boy arrived with my beer, and I paid him, took a sip of deliciously refreshing ale, and frowned. "Miss Berthoud, I mean Mrs. Bartholomew? Have we met her before? Who is this Daisy?"

"You mentioned once that you saw Oscar Wilde's *Lady Windemere's Fan* a few years ago."

I shrugged. "In '92, if I recall, while you were gadding about Asia. A lot of high flown, airy nonsense, I thought. Very clever, of course, but not my cup of tea."

"Our Daisy Watts was not on the boards that night, but she was in the wings as understudy for the part of Rosalie, the maid. I saw Daisy play the role of Lady Windermere at a private performance in the residence of the Apostolic Nuncio in Montpellier in '94."

"Watts?"

"An East End costermonger family of ancient lineage."

"Not French?"

Holmes laughed. "The taste in the bordellos in Paris, and, I dare say, Boulogne and Montpellier, is for English roses, or Daisies in this case. She crossed the Channel to try her chances, picking up a smattering of the language and the sultry accent she deployed against us. I recognized her purple prose as shadows of passages from the Wilde play, snipped and fitted for her new role as One Cruelly Wronged."

I blinked at my friend, and a new and unpleasant thought struck me. "But what of the wedding, Holmes? Have we not set the young officer up for a terrible fall when he discovers Daisy's true identity?"

He smiled. "You wanted to meet the groom, old chap? There he is."

A lithe young man in cricket whites with a full, imperial beard raced towards his opponent at the far wicket, swung his arm in a blur of motion and let the ball loose. It bounced just before the feet of the batsman, but he was able to deflect it, with a satisfying thwack, across the green towards the church.

"Well played, sir!" I cried. "Both of you, actually."

I turned to Holmes and frowned. "But I just gave Daisy Watts away under the name of Miss Berthoud! Can that marriage be valid? And isn't her impersonation highly illegal and my involvement culpable?"

"Do not fret, my dear fellow; few things in life are what they seem. You were involved in a form of words, a charade for the admiral and his wife. The legal wedding took place *sub rosa* at dawn this morning in the Library of the Railway Hotel. It was presided over by the chaplain from young Bartholomew's ship and attended by his brother officers."

"How did you – oh, the boot boy."

Holmes smiled. "The only servant up at the time. He was bribed to silence and commandeered to serve the Navy rum in which the officers toasted the happy pair. I re-bribed him to paint the scene in his own words; the ceremony was, by his account, very affecting."

Holmes reached into his pocket and waved a cheque at me. "On Hoare's in the Strand and for a hundred guineas. Lieutenant Bartholomew buttonholed me in the bar of the hotel before the church wedding and congratulated me on keeping Murchison away (he mentioned that he had a horsewhip handy if the reverend had turned up). Ha! Daisy's husband is not quite as easily gulled as she thinks."

Holmes pocketed the cheque. "And we dine at the Amati's tonight."

Another crack came from the cricket field and the bails of the nearer batsman's wicket flew apart. Lieutenant Bartholomew waved a languid hand in acknowledgement of the congratulations of his teammates and the crowd's applause. He bowed to the elderly gentleman fielding in cover.

"Admiral Bartholomew," Holmes said. He lifted his glass. "Any man who can forsake his bride on her wedding day to play a taut game of cricket deserves a salute from us. I very much doubt that Daisy knows what she's taken on, but let us wish them both the greatest happiness."

I raised my glass. "The Navy, Holmes!"

"And Daisy," he answered.

The Adventure of the
Poison Tea Epidemic
by Carl L. Heifetz

We were residing at the time in furnished lodgings close to a library where Sherlock Holmes was pursuing some laborious researches in Early English charters – researches which led to results so striking that they may be the subject of one of my future narratives.
    – The Adventure of the Three Students, April 1895

After the adventure that took place at the onset of the Great War in August 1914, during a quiet time over Scotch and soda, my friend Sherlock Holmes finally gave me the permission to publish the event that brought us to one of England's great universities in a search for clues to another mystery – The Adventure of the Tea Epidemic. The name of the university and its locale must still be concealed due to the fact that some of the principals in the story, published as "The Adventure of the Three Students," are still alive, though elderly. I pray that my readers will forgive my occasional use of spellings and references more appropriate to an American, but my language has been contaminated by my three-year sojourn in Baltimore, Maryland obtaining a fellowship in neurological diseases at Johns Hopkins University School of Medicine.

If I recall, the story that I will name "The Adventure of the Poison Tea Epidemic" began in the early spring of 1895. March had been particularly cold and dry that year, and we were welcoming the anticipated sunshine and warmth of April, only to experience a week of torrential rains. Being alone after the sad occasion of the death of my dear Mary, I had retaken residence in my old home on Baker Street with Mr. Sherlock Holmes. Since most doctors were unavailable after surgery hours, I was often called upon during those times to render emergency medical service. In addition, I was serving two shifts in the neuroscience facility at St. Barts to keep my hand in and to provide additional income for entertainment.

I had been sitting in my favorite chair by the window, although the heavy downpour impeded the light to some extent. I had just finished *Lancet*, the *British Medical Journal*, and several treatises on experimental neurosurgery, when I noticed that Holmes had installed his large capacity curved briar into his mouth. This signaled the need to organize his papers, which were strewn into every corner of our sitting room, into his notebooks and files. Unimpeded, after a few hours work, he would have our quarters as neat as a pin. Since this was much to my liking, I thought it best to sneak off of the premises. Otherwise, seeing my presence, he might feel impelled to narrate one of his old adventures instead of completing the organizational task. I glanced at the huge grandfather clock that had been a gift from the King of Scandinavia, and noted that it was past three p.m.

I quietly tip-toed to the door and was approaching the stairs, when glancing back, I saw Holmes remove his pipe after taking a large inhalation. He said, "Have a nice evening." He smiled briefly, as was his custom, and returned to his chores.

As I entered the street, I noticed that the rain had temporarily ceased and the sky was finally clearing. I encountered a messenger and gave him a note to deliver to my old friend Thurston, stating, "Thurston, old man, are you up to a nice dinner at our club, a few drinks, and several rounds of billiards? If so meet me at our club. I will be there in less than thirty minutes."

After that, I beckoned a hansom cab over, and went on a short, splashy ride to my club. I climbed the flight of stairs, entered the reading room, and ordered a Scotch and soda to while away the time and read the *Guardian*.

After only a brief interlude, I spotted Thurston wiping his feet at the entrance to the chamber, his hat still dripping from the renewed downpour. After the servant had removed his rain gear, I noticed that my friend was still thin and well built. He looked as if he could still command his platoon as he had done in Afghanistan. His smile revealed bright teeth under his red moustache that was spotted with specks of gray. I ordered a Scotch and soda for him, and he sat next to me.

Picking up the drink from the intervening table, after we shook hands and seated ourselves, he took a sip and said, "Just the thing after a hard day of filing taxes for the lords and ladies of the kingdom. I'm happy to see you for a long savored relaxation." He continued in his deep baritone voice, just slightly showing the deleterious effects of age on its timbre, "I hope that you are ready for a serious match. I haven't played in two weeks, and I'm anxious to deprive you of some of your money."

After downing our cocktails, we were notified that our table was ready for our dinner of rare prime rib with tasty potatoes and vegetables, and a bottle of Bordeaux. Afterwards, satiated, we went up the one flight of old oaken stairs to the beautiful mahogany paneled billiard room. We were enjoying a leisurely game of three cushion billiards and our second aged cognac when a melee burst out at the entrance to the portal.

Our play was interrupted by one of the servants. He made me aware of the fact that the commissionaire, whom I had known for many years, had invaded the facility. Unlike the usually staid demeanor of the former non-commissioned officer in her Majesty's marines, the commissionaire came bursting into the billiard room. Gone was he usual military bearing and stiff upper lip. Instead, he was trembling all over. His usually stern face was red with grief and his eyes flush with tears.

He exclaimed in a loud voice, "My youngest child, Edith, is dying from pneumonia. She is burning with fever and can scarcely breathe. She is shaking all over her little body. My doctor expects her to die by morning."

Obviously, it was my ethical duty to comply with this urgent call to service. I scooped up my bag, said a hasty farewell and apology to my opponent, and rushed down the stairs, following my old commissionaire, whom I had known for many years, and who had always provided faithful service. I dashed out the door to find a four wheeler peopled by the commissionaire, an old woman, and a tiny infant wrapped in woolen blankets. Without a second's delay, I yelled to the cabbie, "Off to St. Barts as fast as you can go. If you make it in twenty minutes you will earn an extra sovereign."

My stethoscope informed me that the female infant was in the last stages of pneumonia. She was barely breathing and her lungs were congested. Also, I didn't need the assistance of a thermometer to determine that she was highly febrile. I knew there was only one chance for her: the new experimental serum being developed at the Serology Institute in the research area of St. Barts. The rabbit antiserum containing antibodies to all three strains of *diplococccus* was her only hope. When we had entered the new facility, I summoned the colleagues with whom I had researched for several years prior to switching to neurology. They quickly arrived, all five of them, from the areas in which they were working. My medical colleagues and I spent all night ministering to the baby with multiple intravenous injections of serum, an ice bath, and aspirin. Finally, at two in the morning, she reached the expected climax. By God's willing answer to my prayers and the power of the new medication, the fever broke, and she was again spirited and well. Joyfully, I left her and her father in the loving care of the hospital staff. I

361

trudged out into the deep night, after promising to return at noon to see how she was faring. Finally, finding a cab, I made my way back to Baker Street, not recalling how I made it up the stairs and into my bed.

I didn't arise until a quarter past eleven a.m., if you can believe the old grandfather clock that was provided by the King of Scandinavia. I was in desperate need for a cup of hot coffee, and was grateful that the smell of fresh beverage filled the air. However, my ability to obtain this beverage was retarded by my colleague's actions. Now, I may have certain character flaws, but when it comes to plucking out a thick facial hair at the breakfast table, I draw the line. Not only was Sherlock Holmes performing that less-than-elegant act that should have been restricted to the bathroom, but he was using the highly polished coffee pot as his mirror.

"Holmes, if you don't mind, I would like to have the coffee pot. Maybe you could find a mirror in your bedroom for your preening," I said with some asperity.

Holmes turned to me with a smile, handed me the coffee pot, and said, "I see that you made a late night of it. What did you and Thurston do after leaving the club? Did you seek female companionship? I tried to leave a message for you, but my courier could only say that you rushed out."

"Holmes, what did you want me for? You weren't busy when I left for supper and billiards. I'm busy now. I must eat a quick breakfast and hurry off to St. Barts. I have a pneumonia patient," I replied. "When I return, you can tell me why you went to the trouble to summon me."

Holmes replied, "All will be revealed. Here is a sandwich that Mrs. Hudson made for me. Take your coffee with you and eat in the cab."

Grateful to Holmes for the thoughtfulness he occasionally showed when appropriate, I was even more grateful that my miniature patient had now recovered. However, I was shocked the commissionaire had left the facility and the child was being ministered to by the previously seen elderly woman.

"Where is Bracket?" I asked loudly, "and who are you?"

Smiling gently as she stroked the child, the gray haired woman said, "Don't fret doctor, I am Edith's aunt, Teresa. Mr. Bracket is my brother. He rushed off after seeing another doctor. I don't know why or where."

I rushed out to the nurse's station, yelling, "What happened to the commissionaire? What has caused him to leave his daughter, who is just now recovering from pneumonia?"

362

A beautiful, young, blonde-haired nurse, whom I had often visited for conversation, walked over to me and said, "It's Mr. Bracket's wife and other two children, a boy of two and a girl of five. They seem to be suffering from a severe poisoning. You may find them in the women's ward. Follow me."

I walked behind her, admiring both her figure and her control of the situation. She said, pointing to the left, "Go this way. The doctors are in with them now. Perhaps you would like to take charge of the case, since the men ministering to them are only young interns."

She turned and smiled at me, and then quickly left for her station as I reluctantly watched her go. "Well, another time would be more propitious," I thought.

As I entered the room, I quickly sized up the situation. Bracket was sitting in a chair, his head in his hands. His wife and two children were shaking all over, in an obviously nervous state. The young interns rose to greet me, and then recognizing a senior colleague backed away as if awaiting my orders.

"These people are obviously suffering from a poisoning. Their moans indicate a state of hallucination. It appears to be some type of food poisoning, since there are no wounds on the bodies or bleeding, as I can tell from your notes. You must clear their bodies as quickly as possible. Pump their stomachs, apply enemas, flush with copious amounts of water, and then administer activated charcoal and very strong tea."

"No tea! It's poison!" yelled Mrs. Bracket, as she sat upright in the bed. Then she quickly fell back to her supine position.

I ordered, "Cancel the tea until further notice. Continue with the other instructions."

Observing the patients more closely, I began to recognize their symptoms as I slowly recalled the lectures I had received many years ago. They had undergone seizures, hallucinations, tremors, and now they expressed that they were nauseous. There was no diarrhea that one would expect from typical food poisoning. I hypothesized that they were suffering from a mild case of ergotism. I turned to my youngest colleague, an Indian, and said, "Mr. Singh, please run to the chemists and bring me amyl nitrite solution. Have the woman inhale 0.3 ml. and give the children 0.1 ml."

Turning to the other two men, I said, "Mr. Riley and Mr. Addison, please watch them carefully and keep me abreast of their progress."

As my young colleagues were ministering to my new patients, I went over to the commissionaire. Kneeling next to him, I asked "What is happening? Why are your wife and children ill and you are not? Did you drink any tea? Did it have a strange taste?"

He responded with a tremulous voice, "We were just sitting down to tea when I had to rush Edith off to the hospital. Thus, I had no tea. When I was at Edith's bedside, talking to my sister, a doctor took me away to see my family in this state. They were yelling and convulsing. No one knew what to do."

"Fortunately, I have neurological training and I recognized signs of chemical poisoning. Has anyone eaten freshly baked rye bread or anything unusual?"

He replied, "No sir. We had eaten nothing until tea was served. I left with Edith and told them to continue the tea service while I rushed to find you. Fortunately, I know where you often go when you are not in Baker Street, and I knew that it was not one of your work nights."

I said, "So it would appear that the tea was contaminated with rye bearing the ergot fungus. That is most unusual and surprising. Please stay here and watch your family. I will ask the nurse to bring you Edith on my way out. Now I must summon Mr. Sherlock Holmes. This sounds like a rare mystery that is beyond my power to discern," I said as I turned to leave.

Running out to the busy street, I spotted my friend, the cabbie Jonathon. Handing him five shillings, I shouted, "Bring Mr. Sherlock Holmes. Tell him that Bracket's family has been poisoned, and such a criminal act requires his immediate attention. Other people may be at risk."

While I awaited Holmes visit, I noticed that the victims were recovering from their attack. Finally, Mrs. Bracket turned to me and said, "Dr. Watson, thank you very much for saving our lives. We must get that tea out of the house before anyone else gets sick."

"Where did you buy the tea? We must retrieve any that they sold or still have in hand, in case there are more poisoned lots. Also, did it taste unusual?"

"Well, Doctor, I didn't purchase the tea. It was a gift from one of my husband's employers, John Alexander. She said that he hadn't bought the tea, but that it was a gift from his employer's neighbor, Sir James Green, who had given it to Mr. Alexander."

"So the tea wasn't originally intended for you. It was originally intended for Mr. Alexander," I stated.

364

"That is correct, Dr. Watson. But the tea tasted a little like rye bread. I really didn't like it, but you can't look a gift horse in the mouth."

Just then, Holmes rushed in and took over the scene. He turned to the commissionaire and said, "I have a very important job for you. Get as many men as you can and go to the shop that sells this brand of tea, locate all of the recent customers, and bring all you can find to my lodgings on Baker Street. Here are several shillings to get the necessary cooperation. Tell the proprietor that Sherlock Holmes thinks that they are selling poisoned tea."

Relieved that he now had an important assignment, and that his entire family was recovering and in the hands of medical professionals, Bracket resumed his normal erect stature and bearing, and marched out of the room quickly with precise steps.

Holmes and I made the short carriage ride to Bracket's abode to see if we could find any other evidence that would point to a source of poison or, as I thought, ergot contaminated rye. We arrived at the small lodging, contained on the third floor of a brown brick building in the working class neighborhood housing the workers who served the local hospital and medical offices. Holmes quickly penetrated the building entrance and the door to the apartment without requiring a key, using methods that he had acquired from his more nefarious colleagues. The only thing out of place were the turned over chairs at the kitchen table, some liquid tea drying on the wooden floor, and tea cups containing the dregs of the teas that had not yet been ingested. Otherwise, there was no evidence of foul play. We scoured the two bedrooms, the bath, sitting room, and kitchen without finding anything suspicious. It was obvious that, as good parents, anything hazardous to children was safely under lock and key. We took the used teacups back with us for further examination. Holmes poured the residue of the tea into small glass containers, and secured the opened carton of tea in a canvas bag that he had brought for that purpose.

As we were exiting, Holmes turned to face me and asked, as a teacher does to a student, "You have examined the contents of this abode. Using your powers of observation and deduction, do you think the Bracket was the kind of man that would purposely poison his wife and children?"

I replied, "Not at all, Holmes. His bed was made with military precision. One could bounce a shilling off of it. His children's beds were covered with care and were warmly dressed. Although one wall in his sitting room was decorated with mementos of his military service, the

365

larger bore many images of his family that far exceeded his personal effects. Also, based on my training as a neuroscientist, I would declare that his grief for his toddler's pneumonia, and his reaction to his other family members' illness, was genuine and palpable. Have I missed anything? Do you agree?"

"Watson," he declared with a smile. "You are coming along nicely. You make an excellent detective's associate. I agree with your analysis and trust the commissionaire completely."

As soon as we had arrived at our lodgings, Holmes quickly got to work. First he smelled the package of tea and invited me to do the same.

"It smells like rye bread," I said. "I never have experienced that odor in tea before."

Then he cleared his chemical apparatus from the deal topped table and installed a high powered microscope on its surface. Using a forceps, he carefully teased a portion of the solid dregs onto a glass slide. Then he applied a thin cover slip. He slowly lowered the objective to the top of the cover slip, and then raised it until he had what he wanted to see in focus. He smiled and said, "I think that your diagnosis was correct. Take a look."

I carefully repeated his actions until the material was brought into sharp focus. It didn't take me long to recall the lessons that I had learned many years ago. There were tea leaves and what could only be stands of rye stipules.

"Holmes, what I find most revealing are fruiting bodies of the ergot fungus *Claviceps purpurea*. I never thought that I would ever need this knowledge." I said, "My physical diagnosis was correct. I'm pleased that I was able to predict the appropriate therapy."

Holmes replied, "Yes, Watson, you are to be congratulated for medical acumen. Tomorrow I will need to visit the purveyors of this tea for a conversation. I'm certain that they have closed their facility for the night, but I will visit them early in the morning. Meanwhile, you must tell your assistants not to alert the police. If they want to publish this account in a house medical proceedings and report it in Grand Rounds, where it will disappear from public sight but serve to further their careers, that would be fine."

I responded, "Why not bring in the police? They can help us gather evidence."

Holmes retorted, "If my supposition is correct, Bracket will benefit financially from my solution to the crime. If the perpetrators are jailed, which may be unlikely unless we can find more direct evidence tying

366

them to the actual crime, no one will benefit from the misfortunes suffered by his wife and children."

Having accomplished all that we could, Holmes and I had our own high tea, being careful to inspect the label, sniff the contents, and to settle down for a rest. I was pleased by our conversation and in a relaxed frame of mind during the entire evening. As we sat, I asked Holmes why we didn't go to the tea merchant ourselves to get the information. He replied, "Everyone likes Commissionaire Bracket. They all use his services and trust him. Had we shown up, we might have encountered suspicion and resistance. Also, I think that I would like to light a pipe and cogitate upon the issues. Why would someone give John Alexander poisoned tea? Or if we are to believe his wife, why would someone give it to Sir James, or if we want to take it a step further, was the commissionaire's family the ultimate target? Then, is there a large supply of poisoned tea in the market? I'm certain that Bracket and his cohorts will round up all of the supplies. Then, we will need to scour the papers that I asked Billy to pick up for us as we enjoyed our tea and crumpets. And finally, why did the tea have a rye taste? I have a monograph on two-hundred-twenty-six blends of tea, including the appearance of cooked and raw leaves, and a description of each flavor. I have never encountered a tea that is flavored with rye, and I can't see why anyone would want it. Tomorrow, we will have accumulated enough data to guarantee a meaningful conversation."

Holmes's last act for the evening was to send our buttons out to acquire copies of all of the newspapers before he allowed the lad to leave for the evening.

I awoke at my usual late hour to find Holmes deeply studying the newspapers that were piled up next to his ham, eggs, and coffee mug. He had a glint in his deep gray eyes and a devilish smile in his face that predicted a bad ending to the perpetrators of this mischief. I quickly ingested my breakfast and left for my morning shift at St. Barts. Also, I needed to see to my four patients and handle any financial issues. Sherlock Holmes guaranteed that he would add this expense to whoever would end up paying for his investigative services.

As I left, Holmes said, "Are you up to a trip? I need to do a search of ancient British charters and you might enjoy the environs. We leave this afternoon from Baker Street Station."

I replied, "I will be packed quickly, a skill I learned in the army medical service." Then I rushed down to the street to get the cab that our buttons had reserved for me.

367

I arrived on time at St. Barts and met with my staff. I congratulated my students for a job well done and warned them about avoiding publicity. I brought a sample of the tea dregs for them to evaluate as background for their report, but told them that the source of the materials was still under investigation and could not be revealed. Then, with my interns in tow, I examined my patients, saw that they were now recovered from their travails, and released them from their involuntary hospital confinement. I informed Bracket and his wife that the poisoning incident must be kept secret so that Mr. Holmes is able to adjudicate the issue and obtain remuneration for them.

After two hours of patient rounds, I bid farewell to my staff, wished them a good day, and returned to my Baker Street lodgings for a well-deserved lunch and nap. However, the nap was not to be. As I arrived, my nose was overwhelmed by the strong odor of tea that masked the pungent smell of his vile pipe tobacco. Holmes's chemical table bore five opened cartons of Paladinium Tea, the same brand that was the source of the ergot poisoning the previous day. The entire surface of his work table was covered with microscope slides and cover slips.

Holmes said, "Ah Watson, you are just in time for our next pieces of evidence. All five cartons of tea that were recently delivered are free of rye particles and fungal spores. Only the box delivered to Sir James Green, who had later given it to Mr. Alexander, was so contaminated. It was not a random event. So, the source of the poisoned tea goes at least as far back as Sir James Green. Although it's possible that the servants despoiled the samples, I suggest that that is not the case. I sent the buttons to question Mrs. Bracket, and she said that the box did not look as if it had been opened, or if it had been, it was very well done.

Then he showed me the papers. In the interior pages of the *Guardian*, in the section devoted to agriculture, there was a brief account of cattle poisoning in a rye field near his famous university.

He cried out, "Quick, eat your lunch! A cab awaits our voyage of discovery."

And off we went on a journey that I found out would take us to the city where resides one of England's great universities, and former scholastic residence of Sherlock Holmes before he left to complete his degree at London University and St. Barts.

As we dashed onto the train and entered the last available first class smoking carriage, I asked Holmes, "Where are we going? What is the purpose of this journey?"

He replied, "We are traveling to the area where I first encountered my university training. Therein is a library replete with official land charters, and a nearby field in which some poor cattle died from eating rye contaminated with the fungus of ergotism. These documents, and ownership of the land, may provide further information on the motive for the ergot poisoning that we discovered by accident, and the possible source of the deleterious material."

I immediately understood his objective, but I couldn't understand how this data would apply to a criminal event in far-off London. As usual, I was forced to stay on the sidelines, exploring the buildings and town of a university that was foreign to me, while my friend spent hours on the diligent search through dry records that may date back to the formation of the English nation itself. My perambulations and isolation, except for mealtimes, was only interrupted by the brief adventure concerning the copying of the Greek scholarship exam. After only two more days, Sherlock Holmes grabbed me off of the street. In his right hand he held a plethora of documents that were rolled in a bright blue ribbon.

"Come Watson, we must pack our belongings. I now have the solution to the mystery of the devious ergotism event!" he cried. "We must return to London before the trail turns cold!"

We ran for the train just as the whistle was blowing and the conductor yelled, "All aboard."

We hurried into a first class smoker and settled down for the long journey to Baker Street. Holmes busied himself with several newspapers that he had acquired from Professor Soames, and then began studying the documents that had been carried under his long, thin arms.

Knowing that my companion would not permit any conversation as he studied the papers in his hands, I sought out the dining car, had two glasses of dry white wine, and fell into a stupor. The gentle monotonous chug of the locomotive and the delightful view out of the window, after I had returned to my carriage, must have lulled me to sleep. I felt a gentle tap on my shoulder as the conductor cried out, "All off!"

I noticed that Holmes had now unfolded all of the documents and tied them into a neat pile. The newspapers were shoved under his seat. The edges revealed that several pages had been sampled with a pair of scissors. A smile on Holmes's face indicated that someone was not going to be happy in a day or two. The look of concentration thwarted my attempts to converse with him, and I quietly followed him to a hansom cab and our final ride to our quarters.

After we strode up the seventeen steps to our suite, Holmes immediately went to his desk and began writing telegrams. I noted that he was also withdrawing his special expensive formal stationery and writing notes with his neat hand. He then called out, "Billy, drop these telegrams at the post office and pay for a reply to each. Then take a cab and hand deliver these to the addresses on the linen envelopes."

With that, Holmes looked at me and said, "Watson, as you see, I have been very busy. Please forgive me for ignoring you, but time was of the essence. Please get together your best set of city clothes. We will be entertaining tomorrow at high tea at five p.m. at the Paladinium Tea Room, in their special tasting room. I expect that we will make the acquaintance of two leaders of our society who, unbeknownst to our friends, have some dark dealings in their past."

"Should I call Gregson or Lestrade?" I asked.

"No, Watson, I think that justice will be served better without the intervention of the constabulary. Just be prepared to leave tomorrow at four-forty p.m."

Then, opening his violin case, he continued; "Now, it is time for sweetness and light. Please fix each of us Scotch and soda while I supply some music before we order our supper from Mrs. Hudson."

The following day, I arose a trifle late, even for me, full of a desire to question Holmes about our coming adventure, but alas, he had already stepped out. I was required to fill the day as best I could, walking to Marble Arch and listening to the orators, and then returning for a solitary lunch of fish and chips, and a bitter ale.

Holmes arrived at four p.m. already attired in his conservative business dress. He glanced at my selection of dark frock coat, silk tie, and grey striped pants. He nodded in affirmation of my attire. We each picked up our most ornate walking sticks, walked down to the street, and retrieved a four-wheeler that our servant had secured for us.

Holmes winked at me and said, "We will make a stop along the way."

Then, we stopped at the residence of Bracket, who was now very elegantly attired in his military dress uniform. Our threesome pulled up at the chic entry to the most expensive tea room in the West End. A liveried footman emerged, opened our carriage door, and guided us past the little old ladies who populated the front room of the shop. We then were escorted up the stairs to the palatial rooms reserved for the special guests. The fashionable décor indicated that we appropriately dressed for the surroundings. The tables were set with glistening silver spoons and stylish imported tea cups and saucers, with matching pitchers and lemon service. The walls were adorned with masterworks of art, among which were several oil paintings by Holmes's great uncle, M. Vernet.

The heralded proprietor of the Paladinium Tea Room, Mr. Brooks, was garbed in afternoon formal attire. He greeted each of us individually as an honored guest. His thin moustache accented a very narrow nose on a slight well-shaven face that matched his slim build and tiny feet. He carried himself with the grace expected of a doyen of such a fine establishment.

When he approached Sherlock Holmes and shook his hand, he said, "Mr. Holmes, I have always wanted to meet you. I have been following your exploits closely."

Turning in my direction, he extended his hand and gave me a firm shake. "Doctor Watson, I'm extremely pleased to meet the famous author and biographer of Mr. Holmes."

He also greeted the Commissionaire with the respect usually afforded an aristocrat, shaking his hand and thanking him for his courage and service to our Queen. He then motioned to a tray of small glasses and invited us to join him in a sherry as we awaited our other visitors.

The two additional men arrived about five minutes later, separately, and each was accompanied by his man servant. After the valets removed the top hats and light overcoats of our visitors, they took away the walking sticks and went down the stairs to the servants' area. Sir James Green and Mr. John Alexander were men of a type who could be considered aristocrats and men of affairs. In many ways, they resembled Holmes's former school mate, Musgrave. Their attire was in the latest fashion from the best tailors. Their shoes were glistening in the light of the tea room. They were both very pale of skin, and had fair hair. They held their noses up as if to avoid any foul odors, and their faces bore the obvious signs of disdain. As they approached the earlier residents of the room, they bowed formally as a sign of recognition. However, they did not offer their hands. They especially looked askance at the uniformed military figure of Commissionaire Bracket, who gave each a military salute.

The man identified as Sir James Green said, "Mr. Brooks, I thought that this was to be a private showing. What are the other men doing here?"

Brooks responded as courteously as well as he could under the circumstances saying, "I thought that you would enjoy the company of other noted gentlemen at this event."

371

Mr. Alexander said, "Let's get this over with. As long as we are here, I can stand the company of Sir James Green for this short time. Next time, please make certain that you meet us separately. The other men are welcome to join us."

With that, Mr. Brooks clapped his hands and a waiter appeared, pushing in a large carboy sloshing hot water. The men were invited to take seats of their choice, and were each provided with a dollop of tea in a strainer. He then poured hot water through each.

Immediately, Sir James burst out, "Are you trying to kill us? This tea is poisoned!"

Shocked by this outburst, the other men pushed their chairs back. Sherlock Holmes asked, "How do you know this tea is poisoned? Is it the smell of rye?"

Sir James shouted, "Are you accusing me of something?"

"No," retorted Sherlock Holmes, "You are accusing yourself." And with that, Holmes finished preparing his cup of tea and began to drink. "Is it the smell of rye? I thought that this was a very pleasant taste."

At Holmes's signal, Bracket and I also drank our tea. Seeing that there was no danger, Mr. Alexander also consumed his tea. Chagrined by this, Sir James followed suit, but with some degree of trepidation.

"What is this about?" asked Sir James angrily. "You tricked me!"

"You tricked yourself," replied Holmes. "Now please seat yourself. I have a story to tell you."

Sir James stood up and attempted to leave. "I have no interest in your tales, you busybody. I'm leaving."

"We three will hold you in here until we have concluded the business of the evening. Mr. Brooks, I think that the Scotch and soda that I brought would be better suited to what follows. Thank you very much for your courtesy. Please sit and listen, since what follows many also be of interest to you."

Mr. Alexander said, "Yes, stay. I want to know what this is about."

After each man had been supplied with their alcoholic beverage, Sherlock Holmes began his recitation. "I received a desperate call from Dr. Watson that Sergeant Major Bracket's wife and children were stricken with ergot poisoning. Now, Dr. Watson is an expert in nervous system disorders. He was able to save the lives of the three individuals, all of whom had ingested tea smelling of rye. Neither Mr. Bracket nor his daughter was affected because they went to the hospital before they could drink any tea, due to an attack of pneumonia suffered by the youngest child. When Dr. Watson and I inspected Mr. Bracket's domicile, we noted a strong smell of rye. Subsequently, we examined the tea dregs in my laboratory and saw, in the microscope, fragments of rye wheat and *Claviceps purpurea* therein."

"What has that to do with me," yelled Sir James. "I don't even know this man or his family."

As he started again to leave, Holmes, Bracket, and even Alexander threw him back in his chair saying, "Somehow, I think that tea was meant for me. My cook told me that it was sent over and I refused it, telling her to destroy it."

"You have been after me all of the years as well. But you can't prove that I'm the source of the poisoned tea."

Sherlock Holmes resumed his professorial manner and continued. "According to Mrs. Bracket, she received the tea from Mrs. Alexander, who thought that she was doing a kindness. But the tea, which wreaked havoc with the Bracket family, was clearly intended for Mr. Alexander."

"Then where did the ergot in the tea come from?" asked Sir James belligerently.

"Thank you for the next entry to my story. It seems as if land belonging to you is infested with rye wheat contaminated with ergot."

With that, Sherlock Holmes passed around material clipped from the *Guardian*, and more detailed accounts of cattle poisoning from the local press in Holmes's university town. Holmes said, "I also visited the area with Dr. Watson, and looked at all of the land holdings in the area. You, Sir James, had access to the ergot-contaminated rye."

"If you think that is the case, why don't you turn this over to the police?"

"Because, I do not plan to besmirch your name or that of Mr. Alexander in the press. The society pages would have a field day. Also, it would harm the excellent and hard-earned reputation of the Paladinium Tea Room and its proprietor Mr. Brooks. I have another story that you may find interesting as well." went on Sherlock Holmes.

He continued, "I researched ancient English charters, almost to the beginning of our nation from the Norman conquest. There was a brave and ferocious knight who served William the Conqueror. As a reward for his service, the man was first made a baron of the realm, and later was awarded the position of Earl. This gentleman had a succession of heirs, each bearing the noble title and serving the kings of England. Unexpectedly, one of the men had twin sons. He died before the land could be officially awarded to the appropriate heir. After that time, descendants of both have quarreled over the ownership of the estates.

373

Gentlemen, those men were your ancestors. Your quarrel dates back to that time. You gentlemen are of the same blood, first cousins several generations removed from the great Earl, who is your ancestor. I now have the copies of all of the documents and land grants. I suggest that you join together in a court action and split the properties equitably, and to cease these useless attempts to murder each other."

"That is good news, Mr. Holmes. I had no idea that we were kin. I only knew that we each were told that the entire tract of land was ours to fight over," said Mr. Alexander. "It does not behoove us to fight each other when, in tandem, we can join our forces and reap the harvest that we deserve. James, I forgive your attempt to harm me if you can see it in your heart to do the same for my past actions."

Sir James stood up, held out his hand and said, "Cousin, it is time that we were partners. We are both very clever at affairs and could reap a great harvest. By now, the value of the land itself is far less valuable that our holdings in properties, money, and investments. "

To everyone's surprise, the two cousins shook hands in friendship and said, in unison, "To making our fortunes." Then, they embraced each other and started to leave arm in arm.

Sherlock Holmes ordered, "Just a minute, gentlemen. I'm satisfied that you have made a friendly alliance, but there is still the matter of Mr. Bracket and his family, who were the innocent victims of your rivalry. Mr. Bracket, thank you for your attendance. Now I wish to speak to the cousins in private, with only Doctor Watson as a witness. Mr. Brooks, would you please see the Commissionaire to a cab and pay his fare? I will reimburse you soon."

As they left, Mr. Brooks said, "It is the least I could do for saving my reputation."

After they left, Sherlock Holmes took some very formal looking documents from his pocket. He handed a copy to each gentleman, saying, "Here are contracts that I have had formatted by my attorney, binding you to an agreement to provide financial remuneration to Mr. Bracket's family. Please read them carefully. You may have a solicitor read over them, but I am firm on the requirements. You will collectively provide money to support a suitable home for Mr. Bracket and his family, and scholarships to excellent schools and a university education for his children."

Both gentlemen carefully read the short document, nodded their agreements, and quickly signed both copies.

Sherlock Holmes said, "Thank you gentlemen for your cooperation. I'm happy that everyone will benefit by this day's events. I will have my solicitor finalize these contracts for my signature, along with Dr. Watson, as witnesses."

Both men smiled broadly. "Thank you, Mr. Holmes. You are truly a miracle worker," said Sir James.

"Yes," added Mr. Alexander. "The words of Dr. Watson's narratives ring true. If ever I am troubled with a serious problem, I will contact you. Expect a check for one-thousand pounds for your expenses."

"I will add the same amount to that." Said Mr. Alexander, as he two aristocrats strolled off arm in arm.

Sherlock Holmes turned to me and said, "Now for some great food, wine, and repartee. We have both been invited by brother Mycroft to join him at his club for dinner."

I turned to Holmes and asked, "How does he know about this?"

Holmes replied, "Brother Mycroft seems to always know what is going on, sometimes before it takes place."

Then off we went seeking transportation to the guest dining room at the Diogenes Club.

The Man on
Westminster Bridge
by Dick Gillman

I – Meeting Anthony Stewart

It was an occurrence during a cab ride, as we returned to Baker Street one pleasant evening in the latter half of May 1895, that was to begin the case that I have here recorded as that of "The Man on Westminster Bridge."

Holmes had become increasingly frustrated over the past weeks as nothing of great note had occurred to stimulate the great machine within his head that needed a constant challenge. For the last few days, he had prowled our rooms in Baker Street like a caged beast, avidly devouring *The Times* each day, hoping to find a case worthy of his talents. Each day I had found the newspaper torn and tossed aside in disgust.

In an attempt to distract Holmes, I had suggested an outing to one of the Royal Parks. Holmes, after a great deal of persuasion, had grudgingly agreed. In truth, he himself could recognise that he was close to the edge of that abyss that would surely take him if his mind remained unchallenged and turned in upon itself.

We had spent a pleasant enough time strolling for perhaps an hour in the sunshine and, although the physical exercise had helped Holmes, the machine inside his head continued to race towards destruction. Having done all that I could, we hailed a cab and set off back towards Baker Street.

Throughout the journey, Holmes had remained silent and looked straight ahead, seeming oblivious to his surroundings. It was as we crossed Westminster Bridge that he suddenly cried out, "Stop!" and began hammering on the roof of the cab. The cabbie in response pulled back hard on the reins and the cab slewed to a stop. Holmes leaped from the cab and ran full tilt towards the stone balustrade of the bridge. For one dreadful moment, I thought that he had decided to end it all and leap headlong into the Thames.

As quickly as I could, I followed crying out, "Holmes! Holmes! For pity's sake, wait for me!" but it was to no avail. Holmes by now had mounted the balustrade and was seen to be reaching down towards something below him.

As I grew near, I heard him say, "You seem to be having some difficulty climbing back from there, friend. Allow me to help you." After a few moments, and as I watched, I saw a hand reach up and grasp the one offered by Holmes. Gradually, its owner came into view and Holmes assisted the figure back over the balustrade.

The figure before us was that of a middle-aged man and clearly in some distress. He was dressed as one would for The City, although some of his clothes had become unbuttoned and flapped like limp, black wings in the evening breeze. Looking at his face, I noted it was streaked with tears, and his eyes were wild with emotion. He nodded to Holmes, saying, "I do not know whether to thank you, sir, or curse you."

It was at that moment he collapsed before us. We were barely able to grasp his limp figure to prevent his head smashing onto the stone flagstones of the pavement. Propping the lifeless man against the balustrade, I reached for my hip flask and poured out a sizeable measure of medicinal brandy into the silver cup of the flask. Holmes took the cup from my grasp and poured a little into the mouth of the limp figure before us. Almost instantly the man coughed and became animated as the fiery spirit trickled down his throat.

Holmes grasped the fellow beneath one armpit and I followed suit. Together, we staggered with him towards the cab and somehow managed to seat him inside. I rode with him whilst Holmes joined the cabbie at the rear.

By the time we had reached Baker Street, our fellow traveller was much improved and was able to climb the stairs to our rooms almost under his own steam. Once inside, I immediately rang for Mrs. Hudson and asked her to provide a pot of tea.

Our guest sat on our settee, and for the first time he seemed able to make some sense of his hosts and the surroundings in which he found himself.

Blinking slightly, he said, "I am most grateful for the help you have given me this evening, gentlemen. It is far more than I deserve, for I am a wretched man. I do not deserve your kindness. Had you implored me not to jump, then I fear that that would have been the trigger for me to end it all. I don't even know your names, or indeed where I am. Allow me to introduce myself. My name is Anthony Stewart."

I looked towards Holmes and I could see that he was nodding in agreement. Holmes began thus, "I am Sherlock Holmes, and this is my friend, Doctor John Watson. You are a guest in our rooms in Baker Street."

A slight knock at the door announced the arrival of Mrs. Hudson with the tea, and after pouring out three cups, we settled back and sipped in silence. After perhaps five minutes had passed, Holmes leant forwards slightly, asking, "What has brought you to this position, Mr. Stewart?"

Our guest regarded Holmes with a face full of woe. "Mr. Holmes, I am a weak man. I have a good position in The City, but I have a weakness that clouds all my judgement and is the ruin of me. I am a gambler and, Lord help me, it has ruined me . . . or one accursed man has. I have lost everything: my wife, my children, my home . . . everything. I know it is my fault, but he has taken everything in a way that is against all the odds. He is a cheat . . . I know it, but it is nothing I could prove . . . and it is not just *my* life that is forfeit. He has ruined others' too."

I could see a spark of interest in Holmes's eyes as he listened to our guest's story. "Who is this man that you accuse?" asked Holmes.

Stewart's face hardened. "His name is Cooke, Major Tobias Cooke. He is a retired army officer, and I rue the day I ever set eyes upon the man. He appears to have the luck of the Devil himself."

Holmes sat back in his armchair, his fingers steepled against his lips. "And where does this gambling take place?" asked Holmes.

Our guest looked up wearily, saying, "At a gentleman's club. Bairstow's, in Westminster."

Holmes's eyes now burned. He obviously knew the name and was eager to involve himself in this matter. "And where will you sleep tonight, Mr. Stewart?"

Stewart shook his head, saying, "I am unsure . . . I left the small amount of money that I have, together with a letter to my wife and children, in my rented rooms in Putney. I believed that this was to be my final day on Earth."

Standing, Stewart continued, "I have taken too much of your and the good Doctor's time. I must make my way back to Putney somehow."

Holmes reached into his pocket and from it he took half a crown. This he pressed into the hand of our guest, saying, "This will be sufficient for your cab fare, Mr. Stewart. Your story intrigues me. Have no fear, we will meet again, and I will enquire further into this Major Cooke."

Our guest was clearly moved by Holmes's gesture, and he took Holmes's hand, saying, "Have a care, Mr. Holmes, for the Major is a violent man towards those who do not pay their debts or have crossed him."

Holmes nodded and guided Mr. Stewart to the door. With a nod to Holmes, he was gone.

I sat a little bemused by the evening's happenings. "This Major Cooke seems to be something of a scoundrel, Holmes. What do you propose?" I asked.

Holmes had returned to his armchair and had taken up his pipe. Drawing steadily upon it, he replied, "I think I need to have some breakfast with my brother." Having said this, Holmes took a page from his notebook before dashing off a telegram and ringing for Mrs. Hudson.

This reply was of no help and did little to enlighten me . . . but I would have to wait until the morning and breakfast with Mycroft.

II – Major Tobias Cooke

I arose quite early and was looking forward to the visit of Mycroft to our rooms for a little breakfast. Often the intellectual interplay between the two brothers was sufficient to provide at least some small stimulation for Holmes. However, a brief look towards Holmes suggested that the previous evening's events had seemed to have only provided a temporary relief from his depression.

Mycroft arrived promptly at eight o'clock and I welcomed him on the landing outside our rooms. In a few brief words, I recounted my concern for his brother's health. I could see from Mycroft's face, as I took his hat and coat, that he had, with a single glance into our sitting room, immediately assessed the situation.

With a nod in my direction, Mycroft proceeded to seat himself on our settee and fill his pipe. Holmes was firmly ensconced in his leather armchair, his old dressing gown draped over his shoulders. He looked up briefly as Mycroft sat but uttered not a word of welcome. I rang the bell for Mrs. Hudson to bring up the breakfast tray and sat in my own chair and waited.

Mycroft moved forwards a little on the settee, saying, "I am most grateful for your invitation, Sherlock, for I, too, have something I wish to discuss with you."

Holmes did not look up. He simply blew out a cloud of blue smoke from his pipe and followed this with an unintelligible grunt. Mycroft looked across at me and I nodded to him in encouragement.

Mycroft continued. "This fellow at Bairstow's, I need to have your opinion of him."

Holmes again said nothing, but I was pleased to see some slight spark of interest appear upon his features.

"Bairstow's?" I questioned, as the name now seemed unfamiliar to me.

Holmes had shrugged off his dressing gown and looked towards me. "Come along, Watson. It is the Gentleman's Club by the river in Westminster that Stewart spoke of. What is it, Mycroft? Has he also taken a liking to the club's silverware?" asked Holmes, somewhat testily.

Mycroft gave a wry smile, saying, "Would that it were so simple. There are a handful of members at the club who like to place wagers against each other on the results of horse races. There is one member in particular, the one whom you mentioned in your telegram, who has had spectacular luck of late and has, in a matter of weeks, won some tens of thousands of guineas."

Holmes cried out, "Luck? Pah! As you well know, there is no such thing, Mycroft! The man is plainly a cheat and a scoundrel!"

Mycroft was now sitting back on our settee and nodding. "Yes, those are entirely my thoughts, Sherlock, but as of yet, I have been unable to determine how he does it."

Our conversation was halted by a knock at the door of our rooms, followed by Mrs. Hudson entering with a handsomely spread breakfast tray. Three places had already been laid at our dining table, and we were soon tucking into rashers of home-cured bacon, fresh farm eggs, and freshly baked bread. I have to say that I was greatly relieved to see that Holmes was enjoying the meal to the full. His appetite had recently dwindled to almost nothing. After the meal, we sat almost in silence and enjoyed a cup of Darjeeling. I could see that Holmes's interest had been piqued and he was now fully alert.

"Tell me more of this 'lucky' fellow, Mycroft, for I am intrigued," demanded Holmes.

With the briefest of raised eyebrows in my direction, Mycroft proceeded thus: "Well, Major Tobias Cooke is a retired cavalry officer. From what I have seen of his military record and my discreet enquiries at the War Office, he appears to have retired under somewhat of a cloud. Apparently, there seems to have been some unpleasantness regarding 'irregularities' in the officers' mess accounts."

Holmes nodded briefly before asking, "How and where does this gambling take place?"

Mycroft drew upon his pipe before answering, "There are, perhaps, five members of the club who gather in one of the side rooms off the main lounge, usually once or twice a week. Here they will select a race and, after consulting the runners and riders, they will wager against each other. It appears that they may place a bet at any time before the result of the race is known, even up until the very last second before the envelope is opened."

I was troubled. "Envelope? What envelope is this, Mycroft?" I asked.

Mycroft turned to me slightly, saying, "There is no telegraph at the club. A messenger boy is sent to a telegraph office nearby, and an arrangement has been made with the telegraph company whereby they will receive the result of the race and seal it in an envelope which is then brought to the club by the messenger boy."

Thinking for a moment, I asked, "I presume, then, that no-one will know the result of the race until the envelope is opened?"

Mycroft nodded, saying, "Quite so."

Holmes looked thoughtful. "This envelope, is it possible that it is opened and the contents conveyed to Major Cooke before the winner is announced?"

Mycroft slowly shook his head. "No, those were my first thoughts but I have seen it for myself. The chairman of the club was so concerned by the losses of some club members that he took me to one side and asked me to observe the proceedings. I was shown the envelope privately before it was opened publicly and all was intact."

Holmes had drawn his knees up to his chest and was now deep in thought. "What of the members? Are they free to leave the premises at all?"

Mycroft again shook his head. "They have agreed amongst themselves that none of them may leave the club once the race has started and until the result is known. This fellow, Major Cooke, has wagered thousands of guineas on horses with poor form only to have them win." Mycroft paused for a moment before continuing, "It is a bad business, Sherlock. Some of the members cannot afford these losses and may well be ruined if they continue."

Holmes blew out a thin stream of smoke, saying, "Yes, that poor wretch Stewart, for one! I have little pity for gamblers, Mycroft, but I detest cheats. I would like you to arrange to invite Watson and me to the club, as your guests, the next time these fellows meet."

381

Mycroft smiled. "It is already arranged. You are expected at half past three today. Their next wager is to be on the result of the four o'clock race at Lincoln."

Holmes could not help but rub his hands and smile, crying, "Splendid!"

Mycroft rose, gathered his hat and coat and, with a nod to me, he was gone. I have to say that I was indeed relieved to see that my friend was once more animated and looking forwards to the challenge ahead. It was apparent from his posture, his knees drawn up tightly to his chest and his eyes half closed, that even now he was considering a multitude of possibilities.

III – A Visit to Bairstow's

That afternoon, we dressed formally and made our way down the stairs to Baker Street. Holmes quickly hailed a hansom and gave the cabby an address in Westminster. Once on our way, I was curious about how these wagers were made, and asked Holmes to enlighten me.

Holmes sat forwards slightly in the cab, saying, "In my experience of these things, a group of fellows will wager on the winner of a race and perhaps also take bets on the minor placings. It is commonplace not to consider the bookmakers odds, but merely place or accept a bet on the horse's position at the finish."

I nodded . . . but in truth, I was still a little unsure.

Holmes saw my confusion, sighed, and then continued. "Suppose, then, that I think horse number three will win and I announce a wager of five hundred guineas. You may accept the wager and if it wins, you must pay me five hundred guineas. If it loses, then I must pay you five hundred guineas. Of course, these fellows will know the previous form of the horse and so they will place or accept bets accordingly."

Again I nodded, confident that I now, at least, knew the rudiments of placing a wager.

In but a few minutes, our cab slowed to a stop at the kerb outside the rather grand façade of a fine Victorian building, having one side facing the river. A discreet brass plaque to one side of the arched and fluted stone doorway said simply "Bairstow's," and beneath that, "Members Only." On our approach, a liveried doorman touched the brim of his top hat with his gloved hand and opened the heavy, half-glazed, oak front door.

Once inside, I was immediately aware of the fine crystal chandelier that lit the elegant atrium. Sparkling brightly, it sent out shards of coloured light that highlighted the moulded plaster ceiling and the half panelled walls. We were clearly strangers and were straightaway approached by one of the staff who took the card proffered by Holmes. Almost immediately, we were whisked away to a smoking room where the familiar figure of Mycroft Holmes could be seen, seated in a deep-buttoned leather Chesterfield chair, drawing contentedly on a fine Havana cigar.

Upon our arrival, Mycroft rose from his Chesterfield and beckoned us to sit in the two empty chairs beside him. "Ah, Sherlock, may I offer you a little refreshment? I am told that they serve a very passable glass of sherry."

Holmes held up his hand, saying, "Thank you, no, but I would like one of your fine Havana's, Mycroft. A little sherry for you, Watson?" he questioned.

I nodded, replying, "Err . . . yes, a 'fino' would be most pleasant." I smiled and nodded at Mycroft.

With barely a raised finger, Mycroft summoned one of the ever alert waiters, ordering a glass of 'fino' sherry for me and a Havana for Holmes. Within moments, the waiter returned with a small silver tray which bore my sherry in a lead crystal glass, and beside it a fine Havana cigar. I carefully took the glass of straw-coloured sherry and sniffed at it before taking a sip. It was indeed very pleasant, like a mouthful of Spanish sunshine.

Holmes had taken the cigar from the tray and had used the cigar cutter proffered by the waiter to slice the very tip from the rounded end of his cigar. He now took a Vesta from his silver case, struck it, and then carefully toasted the end of the cigar before drawing contentedly upon it.

It was as we sat there that Mycroft reached over and touched the sleeve of Holmes's jacket. Inclining his cigar slightly, he used it to discreetly point towards a gentleman who was standing some ten feet away at the entrance to the room and now framed by the doorway, saying quietly, "That is Major Cooke, Sherlock."

I looked towards the doorway and there stood an impressive figure, every inch a military man, well-dressed and finely groomed. He stood some six feet in height, with hair that was iron grey. His slightly ruddy face was lined and bore fine almost mutton chop, whiskers. Looking around him, he gestured to three seated gentlemen who rose and left the room. With a sweep of his gaze, he left, seeming to have ensured that no-one else remained whose presence he required. As we watched, another member joined the group and the five now disappeared from our view into a side room.

Holmes turned slightly, saying, "An interesting fellow. The polo injury must be quite painful in the damper months."

Mycroft nodded. "Yes, those thirty-guinea, hand-lasted shoes, undoubtedly from Harrison and Ball of Old Bond Street, must give his ankle some vestige of support, I would imagine."

Holmes nodded, saying, "Yes, but it is what he carries in his right-hand jacket pocket that intrigues me, Mycroft."

Mycroft nodded sagely in agreement. I sat amazed looking simply from one brother to the other. I, as had they, had only seen the man for, perhaps, barely twenty seconds. I had a brief impression of his face and clothes, whilst they had observed so very much more. As we sat, it became clear to me that Mycroft had chosen his position in the smoking room very wisely. From our chairs, we had a clear view of the atrium, and also the door to the side room where the five club members had gathered to place a wager and await the result of the race.

The rather grand, gilded wall clock in the atrium struck four o'clock. I had finished my sherry whilst Sherlock and Mycroft were still drawing contentedly upon their Havanas. It was a few minutes after four when I noticed that Major Cooke had hurried out of the side room, had turned left, and was now climbing the fine mahogany staircase. Holmes laid aside his cigar in the ashtray beside him and immediately gave chase . . . at a respectable distance. Perhaps two minutes later, the Major was to be seen hurrying down the stairs and heading towards the side room, followed by a now frowning Holmes.

Holmes approached us, clearly deep in thought. He sat for a moment in silence before turning towards the atrium, clearly impatient for something further to happen. I observed Holmes straighten and his jaw become firm, as a messenger boy crossed the atrium and walked towards the side room, clutching an envelope. Within moments, there could be heard a muted cry and, a minute or so later, the members from the side room emerged from their conclave.

As I watched, the faces of the five men were a testament to their fortunes. One was holding his head and, seemingly, almost in tears; another's face clearly showed anger and was almost scarlet, his fists clenched tightly by his sides. A third looked resigned to his loss, whilst the Major and another fellow were clapping each other on the back and had beaming faces.

Holmes turned slightly and stood with his back to the Major. Leaning forwards towards his brother, he said quietly, "I want to meet this fellow, Mycroft."

Mycroft nodded and waved a hand in the direction of the Major and shouted "Cooke! Come and meet my brother." The Major looked towards Mycroft, raised his hand in greeting, and he and his companion approached. Holmes still had his back to the Major and just as he drew level, Holmes turned abruptly and bumped awkwardly into him.

Holmes cried out, "Oh, I'm so sorry. I was tending to my cigar." Holmes smiled broadly and proffered his hand, saying "Sherlock Holmes, and this is my friend, Doctor John Watson."

The Major looked us both up and down with a somewhat wary eye and shook our hands. Holmes continued, "My brother Mycroft, he is the sensible one, says that you like a flutter on the horses. My friend Watson also has a penchant for such things, don't you, Watson?"

In truth, I was flabbergasted by this sudden change in persona by Holmes. He had become this brash, casual fellow that I certainly did not recognise as my friend. I somehow managed to mutter, "Err . . . yes, I have been known to wager a few sovereigns."

"Nonsense, Watson! I have known you to drop a thousand or two at one go," cried Holmes.

I could only nod and smile, but, as Holmes said this, I could see that the Major had suddenly become interested in my wagering habits. Smiling broadly, the Major said, "Well, Doctor, as it happens, we are having a small wager on the outcome of the half past three race at York tomorrow. Would you like to join us?"

I looked towards Holmes and was about to open my mouth when he cried, "Of course he would. However, we are, of necessity, required to be elsewhere tomorrow, but Watson would be pleased to oblige the day after!"

The Major smiled, saying, "Splendid! We are having another wager *that* day on the result of the half past three race at York."

"Excellent! Come along, Mycroft, I will treat you to some tea." Grasping his brother's arm, Holmes hurried from the room with me smiling and nodding a "good bye," and then hurrying in his wake.

As we left Bairstow's, Mycroft reached out and held Holmes's arm, asking, "What is it, Sherlock? Why this charade? Do you know how he does it?"

Holmes was once more his old self. Nodding, he replied, "I believe so . . . but I need a day to confirm my suspicion. I would be grateful if you were to meet Watson here in two days' time when he places his wager." Holmes paused for a moment before asking, "I take it, Mycroft, that you do not mean to ruin the man, but simply to recoup the other members' losses and warn him off?"

Mycroft nodded. "Quite so. The members do not want a scandal."

Holmes nodded and, after a good bye to his brother, Holmes quickly hailed a cab to take us back to Baker Street.

IV – Surveying the Course

Once more back in our rooms and settled in our respective chairs, I began to reflect on the events at Bairstow's. "Tell me, Holmes, what did you make of our new friend, Major Cooke? I am intrigued to know more of his polo injury."

Holmes blew out a cloud of blue smoke and laughed heartily. "After seeing him approach, it was clear that he was right-handed and lame in his left leg. From his slightly restricted movement in his right arm, he also suffers from arthritis. Now, a cavalry officer may carry a sword into battle, but as there have been none of late, it is much more likely that the damage to his shoulder is from the repeated use of a polo mallet."

I nodded, although in truth, I was still unconvinced. Holmes, of course, observed my troubled expression and added, "However, the Major's cufflinks which bore the distinctive crest of the Marylebone Polo Club did, to some extent, support my deduction."

On hearing this, I burst out laughing and then asked, "And the item in his jacket pocket?"

Holmes now grew more serious. "Now that is an interesting object, Watson. I managed to grasp it briefly when I engineered to collide with the Major. I have an idea as to what it is, but I need to return to Bairstow's early in the morning to confirm my suspicions."

Upon this, Holmes would say no more. We retired, and early the next morning, after a hearty breakfast of a pair of Scottish kippers, coffee, toast and some rather fine Seville marmalade, we made our way downstairs and out onto Baker Street. Holmes hailed a cab, and I was perplexed when he directed the cabbie to take us to Westminster Bridge. During our ride, Holmes looked straight ahead and purposefully avoided my eye. It was clear that he wished not to be questioned as to what was afoot.

Arriving at the bridge, Holmes directed the cabbie to drive towards the centre span, almost at the point where we had saved Anthony

Stewart. Here, he called out, requesting the driver to stop. Getting down from the cab, Holmes moved to the stone balustrade of the bridge and then withdrew from his jacket pocket a pair of field glasses. Raising them to his eyes, he used them to sweep, and then carefully examine, the buildings that abutted the bank of the Thames. As I watched, he paused in his observations. Looking towards one particular building, a thin smile appeared upon his lips. Replacing the field glasses, he leapt back into the cab, calling out to direct the driver to take us once more to Bairstow's.

Our cab ride was but brief, and before long we were once again within the atrium of Bairstow's. As we stood for a moment, we were approached by a tall, grey haired, slim gentleman, dressed very formally. His waistcoat was a delicate shade of dove grey, and it was adorned with a heavy gold Belcher chain and fob. His face was oval and sported a fine moustache. His eyes were bright, almost piercing – no, enquiring – and he spoke in a precise way.

Nodding briefly to us, he extended his hand and began thus, "Good morning, Mr. Holmes, Doctor Watson. I am Sir Terence Walters, the Chairman of the club. Your brother and I have already had conversations regarding your assistance in this matter, and I am at your complete disposal."

Holmes and I shook Sir Terence's hand and allowed him to guide us towards a more private area of the atrium. Holmes, I could see, was at complete ease with Sir Terence, and it took me but moments to recall that Sir Terence had, until but a few years past, been a senior figure at the bar.

Gesturing us to be seated, Sir Terence sat forward on his chair, seemingly eager for Holmes to begin.

Holmes paused for a moment and then asked, "What do you know of this Major Cooke, Sir Terence?"

Sir Terence pursed his lips slightly. "Well, I know something of his military career, as all our members are scrutinised before being allowed to join the club. However, the business regarding his retirement from the regiment was obscured from us and only came to light, thanks to your brother. He is from an honourable family that has a country seat in Lancashire. His father bred racehorses, I believe, so I would imagine the Major's penchant for a wager stems from there."

Holmes nodded and from his expression, he seemed quite satisfied with this new information. "Yesterday afternoon when we were here, Sir Terence, Major Cooke took his leave from his companions and ascended the staircase to the first floor, disappearing into a room with an unmarked door. I was reluctant to follow, you understand, and I would be grateful if you might show me the room."

Sir Terence nodded and his face bore a slight smile as he led the way. Crossing the atrium, we passed through the lounge, where I could see the fine mahogany staircase with its scarlet Wilton carpet runner and brass stair rods ascending to the next floor. At the top of the stairs, Holmes pointed across the landing to a plain mahogany door. As I watched, Sir Terence's smile broadened, saying, "This way, gentlemen."

Passing through the doorway, we found ourselves in a panelled anti-room. Along one wall were arranged a row of dull, brass coat hooks. On the opposite wall was a large, mahogany-framed, bevel-edged mirror. Below the mirror were three wash basins which were furnished with a glass soap dish, together with a collection of colognes and lavender water. The third wall comprised a waist-high Travertine marble-topped counter. Behind the counter stood a liveried attendant with a small pile of freshly laundered towels. The final wall was simply panelled and contained a further door, behind which I was sure that I knew what I might find.

Sir Terence smiled broadly, saying, "You see, gentlemen, we all, at some time, must answer the call of nature. The outer door bears no name for our 'facilities,' as all the members know of its purpose and where it leads."

Holmes's face showed no humour. "I wonder, Sir Terence, if I might venture a little further and then, if you will allow, I would like to question your attendant?"

Sir Terence nodded and held out his hand with his palm to one side as a sign of his agreement. Holmes nodded politely and disappeared from our view through the second door. Within a minute he returned and walked over to where the attendant stood waiting. The attendant offered Holmes a towel but he declined, saying, "Thank you, but there is no need. I would, however, like to ask if you were on duty here yesterday afternoon."

The attendant looked towards Sir Terence for permission. Sir Terence nodded, saying, "These gentlemen are my guests, Wilson. You may speak freely and honestly to them as though you were answering to me."

The attendant looked relieved and answered Holmes. "Yes sir, I was here from one o'clock until late evening. I am employed here for six days per week."

Holmes smiled. "You, of course, know all the members here?"

Wilson nodded, saying proudly, "Oh yes, sir, I have been here these many years. I know them all."

Holmes smiled again, asking, "I was here at the club at a little after four o'clock yesterday, and I happened to pass a gentleman on the stairs whom I thought I recognised: Major Cooke?"

The attendant's smile became positively radiant. "Why, yes sir. You are correct. It was Major Cooke. I think of him as one of my regulars. You can almost set your watch by him, sir. He uses the facilities a few minutes past the hour or the half hour of an afternoon."

Holmes looked towards me with a knowing smile. Thanking the attendant, we left and returned downstairs with a rather bemused Sir Terence.

Once more in the atrium, I looked towards Sir Terence and noticed him rubbing his chin. He looked at Holmes, saying, "As a barrister, I am unsure as to what your questions might have revealed, Mr. Holmes."

Holmes replied, "Not a great deal in themselves, Sir Terence, but they are another piece of the puzzle which has dropped neatly into place. Tell me, if you would, which telegraph office provides the results for the races?"

Sir Terence thought for a moment before replying, "I believe it is the office on the corner of Bridge Street, a few paces from Westminster Bridge."

Holmes now had a grim smile on his face. "Thank you, Sir Terence. Doctor Watson and Mycroft will be joining the gentlemen who gamble tomorrow. I would be grateful if you might make yourself available at a little after half past three . . . just in case there is any unpleasantness."

Sir Terence looked a little bemused but he readily agreed. Taking our leave, Holmes rushed out into the street, hailed a hansom, and tossed the cabbie a florin to race us back to Baker Street.

V – A Job for Wiggins

The journey was swift and uneventful, and barely had we reached our rooms when Holmes dashed to the window, opened it and shouted "Wiggins!" at the top of his voice. Barely two minutes passed before there was knock at our door and a lanky street urchin, accompanied by a clearly disapproving Mrs. Hudson, entered our rooms.

Mrs. Hudson looked Wiggins up and down before saying, "This person said you had shouted for him, Mr. Holmes. Shall I send him away?" I watched as she began to roll up her sleeves.

Holmes smiled and then cried out, "No, no, Mrs. Hudson. Wiggins is quite correct, I did summon him. Thank you."

Wiggins curled his lip and Mrs. Hudson gave him a look which, had it been in Biblical times might, I believe, have turned him to stone.

Wiggins smiled at Holmes, saying, "Alright, Mister 'Olmes, what d'yer need?"

Holmes sat in his armchair and began to fill his pipe whilst saying, "A little detective work, Wiggins. I want you to go and keep a watch on the telegraph office on the corner of Bridge Street, just across the road from Big Ben. Be there by half past three."

Wiggins nodded and with rising excitement asked, "What you expectin'? A robbery? A murder?"

Holmes's face had a wry smile upon it. "Not quite. Something a little more comical, perhaps. I want you to watch for anyone acting strangely, follow them to wherever they go next, and then send me word."

Wiggins nodded. "Usual rates, Mr. 'Olmes?"

Holmes again smiled and tossed Wiggins a shilling. With a touch of his cap, Wiggins was off, clattering down our stairs two at a time. I am certain that this display of bravado was only done to spite Mrs. Hudson!

After a delightful light luncheon of cold meats, pork pie, and pickles, we sat replete. I was eager for there to be developments in the case and, after half an hour, I began to pace irritably. Holmes, however, was the picture of serenity, sitting back in his armchair reading *The Times* and puffing contentedly upon his pipe.

Looking up from his paper and seeing my agitation, he gently rebuked me, saying, "Calm yourself, Watson. We will hear nothing until, I believe, four o'clock."

I consulted my pocket watch, and as this was some two hours hence, I forced myself to sit and read. I must have dozed off somewhat, as the next thing I knew was our door bell ringing wildly and the clock in our sitting room now showed five minutes past four. The copy of *The Lancet* that I had been reading had fallen from my lap, and the thunder on the stairs announced the imminent arrival of young Wiggins.

Within seconds, Wiggins had burst through our door, his face wreathed in smiles. "You won't believe what I've seen, Mister 'Olmes!"

Holmes held up his hand to silence Wiggins and he turned to me, asking, "Be a good fellow, Watson, and go out and buy me a copy of the evening paper."

390

I looked at Holmes in shock. I was as keen as he to know what Wiggins had observed. Holmes inclined his head slightly and raised an eyebrow. Sighing, I took this to be a signal that he wanted to hear from Wiggins in private. "Very well, Holmes, I will be but a few minutes."

Having purchased the newspaper, I returned from my errand to find that Wiggins had completed his report and left. Holmes was now playing furiously upon his beloved Stradivarius. "What is that, Holmes?" I shouted above the tumult of sound that engulfed me.

Holmes smiled and paused briefly, saying, "What? You do not recognise it? Beethoven's "Battle Symphony", Opus 91. It celebrates Wellington's victory. I thought it quite apt for Major Cooke!" Holmes continued for perhaps two further minutes before sitting down, exhausted from his frantic bowing.

I must confess that I was relieved when he stopped. "Do I take it, then, that Wiggins provided some valuable intelligence?" I asked.

Holmes smiled and slapped the arm of his armchair, saying, "We have him, Watson! We have him! It is now down to you, old fellow, for tomorrow you must play your part as the innocent and inept gambler if we are to succeed."

I was now extremely concerned. It seemed that the whole case rested upon my shoulders. I frowned, saying, "You will have to coach me in this, Holmes, for I have no experience in these matters."

Holmes leant forwards and patted me on my forearm. "There is nothing to learn, Watson, all you must do is be confident. Watch as the Major leaves the room, as he surely will, and on his return, listen to him. I expect him to make an outrageous wager. You must then engineer, in some way, to raise the wager against him to twenty thousand guineas."

On hearing this, my mouth fell open. "Good Lord, Holmes! That is a fortune. He will never accept such a wager!"

Holmes wagged his finger in my direction, saying, "On the contrary, Watson. He will leap at the chance. Mycroft and Sir Terence will be present to see that all is proper, have no fear."

Although I was still unsure, I was comforted by the thought of their presence, given the Major's reputation for violence.

The following morning, Holmes and I breakfasted, and I watched as he sent off a telegram to Lestrade. He then excused himself, saying only that he would meet me at Bairstow's at four o'clock. I watched, bemused, as he placed a pair of white, opera gloves into his jacket pocket before leaving. I have to say that I was nervous for the entire morning. I could not settle and could barely manage a bite at luncheon before dressing for Bairstow's.

The cab ride was uneventful, and on entering the club, I was greeted warmly by Mycroft. Smiling, he held out his hand in greeting, saying, "Ah, Watson. A sherry, perhaps?"

I shook my head, replying, "Thank you, no, Mycroft. I would prefer a large brandy."

A wry smile crossed Mycroft's face as he said "Ah, I see you are getting into role."

I looked at him in a querying way. I imagined, from this comment, that he must already have had some communication with his brother, something to which I was not privy.

VI – Placing a Wager

At twenty minutes past three, Sir Terence joined us, shortly followed by Major Cooke. On spying me, the Major cried, "Ah, Doctor Watson! I am so pleased to see that you have been able to join us. Come this way." I was a little concerned when he took my arm and led me towards the small private room used by the group.

Once inside, the door was closed. The other four members that I had seen earlier were already assembled . . . plus another figure that at first I did not recognise. Looking more closely, I saw that towards the back of the group stood Anthony Stewart. I was about to greet him when a hand touched my sleeve. Looking towards its owner, I saw that Mycroft was very slightly shaking his head.

The room itself was expensively furnished with velvet covered chairs and rich, red velvet drapes. In the centre of the room there stood a large, oval mahogany table with eight dining chairs. To one side stood a drinks table, upon which there stood a silver tray and an array of bottles of spirits from which the group helped themselves. I felt the need for some Dutch courage and poured myself a large brandy. It was as I replaced the brandy decanter that I saw a sly grin form on the Major's face.

The members of the group all sat around the table and I joined them, unsure as to what was to happen next. I introduced myself to the gentlemen either side of me and nodded to the others.

Beside each person was a small pad of paper and a pencil. I took it that this was rather like a marker, showing the amount that you had wagered and to whom. Mycroft and Sir Terence stood some little

392

distance apart, against the rear wall so that they could clearly observe the proceedings.

The clock in the room struck the half hour and the Major stood and addressed the group. "Gentlemen, today we are wagering on the half past three race at York. The race has begun. Who will place a wager?"

There then began some small wagers among the members: wagers of, perhaps, fifty or a hundred guineas. Slips of paper were passed between them as the wagers were made. I made a small wager of twenty guineas on horse number four with a gentleman sitting to my right.

It was then that the Major suddenly gripped his stomach, made an excuse and walked swiftly from the room. I looked about me and I was about to rise to see if I could be of some assistance when the gentleman to my right put his hand on my forearm, saying, "Do not concern yourself, Doctor. I have been told that the Major has some slight intestinal problem, apparently from his service overseas. The excitement of the moment aggravates it, but he will return shortly."

As predicted, the Major returned within four or five minutes. Apologising, he sat and then again addressed the group, saying, "I feel that good fortune is smiling upon me today, gentlemen, and although the horse has little form, I wager one thousand guineas on number seven. Are there any takers?"

I looked around at the incredulous faces of the group. A single voice spoke out . . . one that I immediately recognised as that of Anthony Stewart. "I fear it stands little chance today, Major. I am willing to wager five thousand guineas that it is not the winner."

The Major's smile was now like that of a wolf. "I thought you might have had enough, Stewart, betting against me. If you are so confident, will you not wager ten thousand?"

There was a gasp from the other members around the table as they waited for Stewart's reply. After a few seconds Stewart nodded, saying, "Very well, here is my marker." Stewart quickly wrote the amount of ten thousand guineas and signed it, passing it to the Major."

I felt it was now time to follow Holmes's instructions. I raised my brandy glass in salute to Stewart, took a hefty swallow from it and holding the glass aloft, cried, "This is an opportunity I cannot let slip. I will double that amount. I wager twenty thousand guineas that number seven is not the winner. I feel the young gentleman has luck on his side today."

The gentleman to my right held my arm, saying, "Be silent sir, it is the brandy talking!"

The Major's eyes burned as he rubbed his hands together as if he were washing them. "Let him be! He has made the wager and we have all heard it. It will stand." Turning to Mycroft, the Major demanded, "Is he good for the money, should he lose?"

Mycroft nodded. "I will stand guarantor for the amount, Major . . . if need be."

It was at that moment that the slightest shadow of doubt passed over the Major's face. He shook his head as though to clear it and then looked once more supremely confident. I, however, was trembling like a leaf. If, somehow, Holmes's plan had failed, then Mycroft would stand to lose twenty thousand guineas and I would be ruined.

For the next few minutes, the atmosphere in the room was stifling. I finished my brandy and found that I was still shaking. Several of the other members were easing their collars and mopping their brows waiting, as we all were, for the knock on the door that announced the arrival of the messenger boy with the envelope of results.

Suddenly, there was the knock and the Major moved to open the door, but his progress was blocked by Sir Terence, saying, "I think, Major, given the high stakes, an independent person should open the envelope."

Major Cooke's face was puce, but he kept control and managed to stammer, "Yes, yes . . . of course, Sir Terence."

The Major stood back and Sir Terence opened the door. Framed in the doorway was a uniformed messenger boy holding out an envelope. This Sir Terence took and, sliding his finger beneath the sealed flap, he opened it. There was a collective intake of breath as he withdrew the single sheet of paper from within it. Clearing his throat, he announced, "York, three thirty, First . . . number five, second . . . number eight, third . . . number twelve."

Major Cooke lunged forwards, tearing the telegram from Sir Terence's grasp and reading it again to himself. "This is not possible! It is a trick!" Turning towards me, he screamed, "You are a ch – "

Sir Terence placed his hand firmly on Major Cooke's chest before he could say more. "Have a care what you say, Cooke! The libel laws in England are punitive, and I would happily represent any one of these gentlemen, for no fee, should you venture to tarnish his reputation. Be sure to leave a cheque for the full thirty thousand guineas in my office before you leave. Your membership of Bairstow's has been revoked."

Major Cooke glared malevolently at me and then at Sir Terence before storming from the room. The other members were still sitting open mouthed, unable to comprehend what had occurred. In truth, I would not have been able to enlighten them.

A few moments later, a familiar voice called out to me from the open doorway, "Ah, Watson! I understand that you are now a very wealthy man!"

Holmes laughed heartily and clapped me on the back. From across the room a figure approached with his hand outstretched. It was Anthony Stewart. Shaking Holmes's hand, a very grateful Stewart said, "Thank you, Mr. Holmes. I am forever in your debt and I swear never to gamble again."

Holmes's face was without emotion as he replied, "I will take you at your word, Mr. Stewart."

Holmes nodded towards Mycroft and Sir Terence, and I reached for my cheque book to pay the twenty guineas I had wagered. The gentleman who had been sitting to my right picked up the slip I had signed and, with a wink, he tore it up.

VII – A Pair of White Gloves

Taking Anthony Stewart by the arm, Holmes led the way out of Bairstow's, hailed a cab, and together we returned to Baker Street. I must admit I wanted to know everything, but Holmes would say nothing until we all were sitting with a steaming cup of tea.

Sitting back, I ran through my mind all that had happened. "Tell me, Holmes, how was this achieved?"

Holmes sipped his tea and began thus, "I became suspicious of the Major when I detected, in his jacket pocket, what appeared to be a small telescope. Now, why would one carry such a thing to a gentleman's club? Whilst Bairstow's is located on the banks of the Thames, it does not face it . . . except for one side . . . and why would a seemingly healthy man suddenly, and so predictably, have to make use of the club's facilities?"

I thought back to our first visit to the club, and how Holmes had questioned the washroom attendant. "Whilst in the washroom, you left Sir Terence and me whilst you investigated further. What did you discover, Holmes?"

Holmes smiled, "Tell me, Watson. Where in a gentleman's club might you be sure not to be disturbed and have perfect privacy . . . especially if you feigned to have an intestinal problem?"

It took me but a moment to realise. "Of course! In the lavatory!"

Holmes nodded, saying, "Quite so, Watson. I discovered that the rear wall of the toilet cubicles face the Thames, and have small, frosted, sash windows. I opened one briefly and had a most excellent view of the Thames and the bridges crossing it. Do you recall our cab ride to Westminster Bridge, Watson?"

I nodded and waited for Holmes to continue. "As I stood at the centre of the bridge with my field glasses, I was able to see clearly the frosted glass of the lavatory windows of Bairstow's. Therefore, a person in Bairstow's would have a similarly clear view of the centre of Westminster Bridge."

I scratched my head, as I was still unsure how this discovery could benefit the Major. "Tell me, Holmes, how does this observation relate to the intelligence from young Wiggins?"

Holmes began to fill his pipe, asking, "Do you also recall the conversation with Sir Terence when we sought information on the background of the Major? Sir Terence thought the Major had developed his liking for a wager through his family connection to horse racing. Bookmakers who take wagers at a race course have to ensure that they can communicate with each other to ensure that they are all offering similar odds. They often have to do this over a distance of a hundred yards or more. How then is this achieved, Watson?"

I thought back to a race meeting I had attended at Epsom and suddenly remembered. "Hand signals! They communicate by some strange system where they wave their hands and pat the top of their heads . . . and . . . and they wear white gloves! Ha! The opera gloves! But why, Holmes?"

Holmes drew contentedly upon his pipe and blew out a thin stream of blue smoke. Pointing his pipe stem in my direction, he asked, "Why does a Robin have a red breast? To be seen, Watson! To be seen! The white gloves show up clearly against a dark background and the hand signals can be read over a long distance. Young Wiggins observed a man leave the telegraph office on Bridge Street, just as a messenger boy was leaving. The fellow ran to the centre of Westminster Bridge, where he was seen to wave his arms wildly in the air whilst wearing white gloves. Wiggins thought the poor man to be demented!"

I had almost forgotten about our guest until he suddenly shouted out, "So that was how it was done! Somebody received the results of the race from the telegraph office and then conveyed them, using hand signals, to the Major, who was using his telescope to observe from the lavatory window at Bairstow's!"

396

Holmes nodded, saying, "Precisely! That 'somebody' was a servant in the Major's employ. Wiggins followed him back to a house in Wimbledon which had the name 'Major T. Cooke' emblazoned above the bell-pull at the front door."

I was still puzzled. "But . . . but . . . that does not explain how you were able to deceive the Major today."

Holmes wagged his finger, saying, "Not so, Watson. Wiggins had described this fellow to me, and I determined that we were of similar height and stature. My telegram to Lestrade ensured that when this fellow appeared at the telegraph office and collected the results, a somewhat burly constable detained him. When I questioned him, he quickly told all. I had studied the bookmaker's code and from a distance of over a hundred yards, I would be indistinguishable from the Major's man. At any event, the Major would be concentrating hard upon my hand movements, not my identity. It was a simple matter to ensure that the number of the winning horse was changed in my message to him."

Anthony Stewart clapped his hands in delight. "Wonderful! Whilst Mr. Holmes was away from you this morning, Doctor, he tracked me down at my lodgings in Putney. He kindly offered me the chance of rebuilding my life by regaining all the losses I had made to the Major. He informed me of the part I was to play but, like you, I had not the slightest idea as to how the deception was to be accomplished."

Holmes leant forwards slightly towards me, saying, "I am indeed sorry that I was unable to tell you all, Watson. It was imperative that the Major's suspicions were not aroused by anything that you might inadvertently let slip. It was vital that you made the wager as though you believed it to be genuine and, it appears, you played the part perfectly!"

I shook my head. "Holmes, you will never comprehend how real that wager was to me. The prospect of being indebted to your brother for the rest of my life hung over me like the sword of Damocles."

On hearing this, Holmes slapped the arm of his chair and roared with laughter. After finishing our tea, we said goodbye to Anthony Stewart and earnestly hoped that he would honour his solemn promise to never gamble again.

Of the Major, we heard no more except for a mention in a note from Mycroft confirming that the cheque the Major had lodged on leaving Bairstow's had been honoured. Sir Terence had used the funds to make good the losses of the other members and, as a result of the Major's 'excesses', gambling was now prohibited at Bairstow's.

It was one morning, perhaps a week or so later, as I began to record this case in my notebook, that I remarked to Holmes that saving a man's life and bringing him back to his family was something of which to be proud. I noticed that Holmes almost blushed as I said this.

He shook his head, saying, "No, Watson. I take no pride in this. I saw it as my moral duty, for I, too, have been to the edge of the abyss on occasions . . . and, in any case, we have been amply rewarded for our endeavours. See what came in this morning's post!"

Holmes tossed an envelope to me and on opening its contents I read, *"Dear Mr. Holmes, I am most grateful for your recent assistance. In recognition of this, it is my privilege, as Chairman of Bairstow's, to offer both you and Doctor Watson a lifetime's membership of the club for the great service you have rendered."* The letter was signed, *Terence Walters.*

"I trust that you will accept, Holmes?" I asked.

Holmes's eyes twinkled. He appeared to consider my question for a brief moment before replying, "Yes, I believe so . . . if only to spite Mycroft!"

About the Contributors

The following authors appear in this volume
The MX Book of New Sherlock Holmes Stories
Part II – 1890-1895

Matthew Booth is the author of S*herlock Holmes and the Giant's Hand*, a collection of Sherlock Holmes short stories published by Breese Books. He is a scriptwriter for the American radio network *Imagination Theatre*, syndicated by Jim French Productions, contributing particularly to their series, *The Further Adventures of Sherlock Holmes*. Matthew has contributed two original stories to *The Game Is Afoot*, a collection of Sherlock Holmes short stories published in 2008 by Wordsworth Editions. His contributions are "The Tragedy of Saxon's Gate" and "The Dragon of Lea Lane". He has provided an original story entitled "A Darkness Discovered", featuring his own creation, Manchester-based private detective John Dakin, for the short story collection *Crime Scenes*, also published by Wordsworth Editions in 2008. Matthew is currently working on a supernatural novel called *The Ravenfirth Horror*.

J.R. Campbell is a Calgary-based writer who always enjoys setting problems before the Great Detective. Along with his steadfast friend Charles Prepolec, he has co-edited the Sherlock Holmes anthologies *Curious Incidents, Curious Incidents 2, Gaslight Grimoire: Fantastic Tales of Sherlock Holmes, Gaslight Grotesque: Nightmare Takes of Sherlock Holmes*, and *Gaslight Arcanum: Uncanny Tales of Sherlock Holmes*. He has also contributed stories to Imagination Theater's Radio Drama *The Further Adventures of Sherlock Holmes*, and the anthologies *A Study in Lavender: Queering Sherlock Holmes* and *Challenger Unbound*. At the time of writing, his next project, again with Charles Prepolec, is the anthology *Professor Challenger: New Worlds, Lost Places*.

Peter Calamai, BSI, a resident of Ottawa, was a reporter, editor and foreign correspondent with major Canadian newspapers since 1966. For half those years he has worked five minutes' walk from the Rideau Canal and the Commissariat Building. When editor of the Ottawa Citizen's editorial pages, Calamai had the good fortune to spend an afternoon interviewing canal historian Robert Legget. He has been an active Sherlockian since the mid-1990's, concentrating on Holmes and the Victorian press. Honours include designation as a Master Bootmaker by Canada's leading Sherlockian society and investiture in the *Baker Street Irregulars* as "The Leeds Mercury", a name taken from *The Hound of the Baskervilles*.

Bert Coules wandered through a succession of jobs from fringe opera company manager to BBC radio drama producer-director before becoming a full-time writer at the beginning of 1989. Bert works in a wide range of genres, including science fiction, horror, comedy, romance and action-adventure but he is especially associated with crime and detective stories: he was the head writer on the BBC's unique project to dramatise the entire Sherlock Holmes canon, and went on to script four further series of original Holmes and Watson mysteries. As well as radio, he also writes for TV and the stage.

Catherine Cooke BSI is a Librarian with Westminster Libraries who divides her time between maintaining and developing the Libraries' computer systems and the Sherlock Holmes Collection. She is a Fellow of the *Chartered Institute of Library and Information Professionals*, Joint Honorary Secretary of the *Sherlock Holmes Society of London*, a member of the *Baker Street Irregulars*, and of the *Adventuresses of Sherlock Holmes*. She won the Baker Street Irregulars' *Morley-Montgomery Award* for 2005 and the Sherlock Holmes Society of London's *Tony Howlett Award* in 2014.

Bill Crider is a former college English teacher, and is the author of more than fifty published novels and an equal number of short stories. He's won two *Anthony* awards and a *Derringer* Award, and he's been nominated for the *Shamus* and the *Edgar* awards. His latest novel in the Sheriff Dan Rhodes series is *Between the Living and the Dead*. Check out his homepage at *www.billcrider.com*, or take a look at his peculiar blog at *http://billcrider.blogspot.com*.

Carole Nelson Douglas is the author of sixty New-York-published novels, and the first woman to write a Sherlock Holmes spin-off series using the first woman protagonist, Irene Adler. *Good Night, Mr. Holmes* debuted as a *New York Times* Notable Book of the Year. Holmes and Watson have been Douglas' "go-to guys" since childhood, appearing in a high school skit and her weekly newspaper column. Seeing only one pseudonymous woman in print with Holmes derivations, she based her Irene Adler on how Conan Doyle presented her: a talented, compassionate, independent, and audacious woman, in eight acclaimed novels. ("Readers will doff their deerstalkers." – *Publishers Weekly*) Those readers pine in vain for a film version of the truly substantial and fascinating Irene Adler that Holmes and Sir Arthur Conan Doyle admired as "The Woman." Now indie publishing, Douglas plans to make more of her Irene Adler stories available in print and eBook. *www.carolenelsondouglas.com*

Sir Arthur Conan Doyle (1859-1930) *Holmes Chronicler Emeritus.* If not for him, this anthology would not exist. Author, physician, patriot, sportsman, spiritualist, husband and father, and advocate for the oppressed. He is remembered and honored for the purposes of this collection by being the man who introduced Sherlock Holmes to the world. Through fifty-six Holmes short stories, four novels, and additional Apocryphal entries, Doyle revolutionized mystery stories and also greatly influenced and improved police forensic methods and techniques for the betterment of all. *Steel True Blade Straight*

Steve Emecz's main field is technology, in which he has been working for about twenty years. Following multiple senior roles at Xerox, where he grew their European eCommerce from $6m to $200m, Steve joined platform provider Venda, and moved across to Powa Technologies in 2010. Steve is a regular trade show speaker on the subject of mobile commerce, and his time at Powa has taken him to more than forty countries – so he's no stranger to planes and airports. He wrote two novels (one bestseller) in the 1990's and a screenplay in 2001. Shortly after he set up MX Publishing, specialising in NLP books. In 2008, MX published its first Sherlock Holmes book, and MX has gone on to become the largest specialist Holmes publisher in the world, with around one hundred authors and over two hundred books. Profits from MX go towards his second passion – a children's rescue project in Nairobi, Kenya, where he and his wife,

Sharon, spend every Christmas at the rescue centre in Kasarani. In 2014, they wrote a short book about the project, *The Happy Life Story*.

Lyndsay Faye, BSI, grew up in the Pacific Northwest, graduating from Notre Dame de Namur University. She worked as a professional actress throughout the Bay Area for several years before moving to New York. Her first novel was the critically acclaimed pastiche *Dust and Shadow: An Account of the Ripper Killings by Dr. John H Watson*. Faye's love of her adopted city led her to research the origins of the New York City Police Department, as related in the *Edgar*-nominated Timothy Wilde trilogy. She is a frequent writer for the *Strand Magazine* and the Eisner-nominated comic *Watson and Holmes*. Lyndsay and her husband, Gabriel Lehner, live in Queens with their cats, Grendel and Prufrock. She is a very proud member of the *Baker Street Babes, Actor's Equity Association, Mystery Writers of America, The Adventuresses of Sherlock Holmes*, and *The Baker Street Irregulars*. Her works have currently been translated into fourteen languages.

Wendy C. Fries is the author of *Sherlock Holmes and John Watson: The Day They Met* and also writes under the name Atlin Merrick. Wendy is fascinated with London theatre, scriptwriting, and lattes. Website: *wendycfries.com*.

Mark A. Gagen BSI is co-founder of Wessex Press, sponsor of the popular *From Gillette to Brett* conferences, and publisher of *The Sherlock Holmes Reference Library* and many other fine Sherlockian titles. A life-long Holmes enthusiast, he is a member of *The Baker Street Irregulars* and *The Illustrious Clients of Indianapolis*. A graphic artist by profession, his work is often seen on the covers of *The Baker Street Journal* and various BSI books.

Bob Gibson, graphic designer, is the Director at Staunch Design, located in Oxford, England. In addition to designing the covers for MX Book publications, Staunch also provides identity design and brand development for small and medium sized companies through print and web for a wide range of clients, including independent schools, retail, financial services and the health sector. *www.staunch.com*

Dick Gillman is a Yorkshire-man in his mid-sixties. He retired from teaching Science in 2005 and moved to Brittany, France in 2008 with his wife Alex, Truffle the Black Labrador, and two cats. He still has strong family links with the UK, where he visits his two grown up children and his grandchildren. Dick is a prolific writer, and during his retirement he has written fourteen Sherlock Holmes short stories and a Sci-Fi novella. His latest short story, "Sherlock Holmes and The Man on Westminster Bridge" was completed in July 2015, and is published for the first time in this anthology.

John Atkinson Grimshaw (1836-1893) was born in Leeds, England. His amazing paintings, usually featuring twilight or night scenes illuminated by gas-lamps or moonlight, are easily recognizable, and are often used on the covers of books about the Great Detective to set the mood, as shadowy figures move in the distance through misty mysterious settings and over rain-slicked streets.

Jack Grochot is a retired investigative newspaper journalist and a former federal law enforcement agent specializing in mail fraud cases. He lives on a small farm in southwestern Pennsylvania, USA, where he writes and cares for five boarded horses. His fiction work includes stories in *Sherlock Holmes Mystery Magazine, The Sherlock Holmes Megapack* (an e-book), as well as the book *Come, Watson! Quickly!*, a collection of five Sherlock Holmes pastiches. The author, an active member of *Mystery Writers of America*, can be contacted by e-mail at *grochot@comcast.net*.

Carl L. Heifetz Over thirty years of inquiry as a research microbiologist have prepared Carl Heifetz to explore new horizons in science. As an author, he has published numerous articles and short stories for fan magazines and other publications. In 2013 he published a book entitled *Voyage of the Blue Carbuncle* that is based on the works of Sir Arthur Conan Doyle and Gene Roddenberry. *Voyage of the Blue Carbuncle* is a fun and exciting spoof, sure to please science fiction fans as well as those who love the stories of Sherlock Holmes and *Star Trek*. Carl and his wife have two grown children and live in Trinity, Florida.

Jeremy Holstein first discovered Sherlock Holmes at age five when he became convinced that the Hound of the Baskervilles lived in his bedroom closet. A life long enthusiast of radio dramas, Jeremy is currently the lead dramatist and director for the Post Meridian Radio Players adaptations of Sherlock Holmes, where he has adapted *The Hound of the Baskervilles, The Sign of Four*, and "Jack the Harlot Killer" (retitled "The Whitechapel Murders") from William S. Baring-Gould's *Sherlock Holmes of Baker Street* for the company. He is currently in production with an adaptation of "Charles Augustus Milverton". Jeremy has also written Sherlock Holmes scripts for Jim French's *Imagination Theatre*. He lives with his wife and daughter in the Boston, MA area.

Mike Hogan writes mostly historical novels and short stories, many set in Victorian London and featuring Sherlock Holmes and Doctor Watson. He read the Conan Doyle stories at school with great enjoyment, but hadn't thought much about Sherlock Holmes until, having missed the Granada/Jeremy Brett TV series when it was originally shown in the eighties, he came across a box set of videos in a street market and was hooked on Holmes again. He started writing Sherlock Holmes pastiches about four years ago, having great fun re-imagining situations for the Conan Doyle characters to act in. The relationship between Holmes and Watson fascinates him as one of the great literary friendships. (He's also a huge admirer of Patrick O'Brian's Aubrey-Maturin novels). Like Captain Aubrey and Doctor Maturin, Holmes and Watson are an odd couple, differing in almost every facet of their characters, but sharing a common sense of decency and a common humanity. Living with Sherlock Holmes can't have been easy, and Mike enjoys adding a stronger vein of "pawky humour" into the Conan Doyle mix, even letting Watson have the second-to-last word on occasions. Mike is British, and he lives in Italy. His books include *Sherlock Holmes and the Scottish Question*; *The Gory Season – Sherlock Holmes, Jack the Ripper and the Thames Torso Murders* and the Sherlock Holmes & Young Winston 1887 Trilogy (*The Deadwood Stage*; *The Jubilee Plot*; and *The Giant Moles*), He has also written the following short story collections: *Sherlock Holmes: Murder at the Savoy and Other Stories, Sherlock Holmes: The Skull of Kohada Koheiji and Other Stories*, and *Sherlock Holmes: Murder on the Brighton Line and Other Stories*. *www.mikehoganbooks.com*

Roger Johnson BSI is a retired librarian, now working as a volunteer assistant at Essex Police Museum. In his spare time he is commissioning editor of *The Sherlock Holmes*

Journal, an occasional lecturer, and a frequent contributor to the Writings About the Writings. His sole work of Holmesian pastiche was published in 1997 in Mike Ashley's anthology *The Mammoth Book of New Sherlock Holmes Adventures*, and he has the greatest respect for the many authors who have contributed new tales to the present mighty trilogy. Like his wife, Jean Upton, he is a member of both *The Baker Street Irregulars* and *The Adventuresses of Sherlock Holmes*.

Ann Margaret Lewis attended Michigan State University, where she received her Bachelor's Degree in English Literature. She began her writing career writing tie-in children's books and short stories for DC Comics. She then published two editions of the book *Star Wars: The New Essential Guide to Alien Species* for Random House. She is the author of the award-winning *Murder in the Vatican: The Church Mysteries of Sherlock Holmes* (Wessex Press), and her most recent book is a Holmes novel entitled *The Watson Chronicles: A Sherlock Holmes Novel in Stories* (Wessex Press).

David Marcum first discovered Sherlock Holmes in 1975, at the age of ten, when he received an abridged version of *The Adventures* during a trade. Since that time, David has collected literally thousands of traditional Holmes pastiches in the form of novels, short stories, radio and television episodes, movies and scripts, comics, fan-fiction, and unpublished manuscripts. He is the author of *The Papers of Sherlock Holmes Vol.'s I* and *II* (2011, 2013), *Sherlock Holmes and A Quantity of Debt* (2013) and *Sherlock Holmes – Tangled Skeins* (2015). Additionally, he is the editor of the three-volume set *Sherlock Holmes in Montague Street* (2014, recasting Arthur Morrison's Martin Hewitt stories as early Holmes adventures,) and most recently this current collection, *The MX Book of New Sherlock Holmes Stories* (2015). He has contributed essays to the *Baker Street Journal* and *The Gazette*, the journal of the Nero Wolfe *Wolfe Pack*. He began his adult work life as a Federal Investigator for an obscure U.S. Government agency, before the organization was eliminated. He returned to school for a second degree, and is now a licensed Civil Engineer, living in Tennessee with his wife and son. He is a member of *The Sherlock Holmes Society of London*, *The John H. Watson Society* ("Marker"), *The Praed Street Irregulars* ("The Obrisset Snuff Box"), *The Solar Pons Society of London*, and *The Diogenes Club West (East Tennessee Annex)*, a curious and unofficial Scion of one. Since the age of nineteen, he has worn a deerstalker as his regular-and-only hat from autumn to spring. In 2013, he and his deerstalker were finally able make a trip-of-a-lifetime Holmes Pilgrimage to England, where you may have spotted him. If you ever run into him and his deerstalker out and about, feel free to say hello!

William Patrick Maynard was born and raised in Cleveland, Ohio. His passion for writing began in childhood and was fueled by early love of detective and thriller fiction. He was licensed by the Sax Rohmer Literary Estate to continue the Fu Manchu thrillers for Black Coat Press. *The Terror of Fu Manchu* was published in 2009 and was followed by *The Destiny of Fu Manchu* in 2012 and *The Triumph of Fu Manchu* in 2015. His previous Sherlock Holmes stories appeared in *Gaslight Grotesque* (2009/EDGE Publishing) and *Further Encounters of Sherlock Holmes* (2014/Titan Books). He currently resides in Northeast Ohio with his wife and family.

Sidney Paget (1860-1908), a few of whose illustrations are used within this anthology, was born in London, and like his two older brothers, became a famed illustrator and painter. He completed over three-hundred-and-fifty drawings for the Sherlock Holmes stories first published in *The Strand* magazine, defining Holmes's image forever after in the public mind.

Chris Redmond, BSI, is editor of the website *Sherlockian.Net*, and the author of *A Sherlock Holmes Handbook, In Bed with Sherlock Holmes,* and other books, as well as many Sherlockian articles. He is a member of the *Baker Street Irregulars, The Bootmakers of Toronto, The Adventuresses of Sherlock Holmes,* and other societies. He lives in Waterloo, Ontario, Canada.

Robert V. Stapleton was born and brought up in Leeds, Yorkshire, England, and studied at Durham University. After working in various parts of the country as an Anglican parish priest, he is now retired and lives with his wife in North Yorkshire. As a member of his local writing group, he now has time to develop his other life as a writer of adventure stories. He has recently had a number of short stories published, and he is hoping to have a couple of completed novels published at some time in the future.

Sam Wiebe's debut novel *Last of the Independents* was published by Dundurn Press. An alternative private detective novel set in the Pacific Northwest, *Last of the Independents*, won the 2012 Arthur Ellis Award for Best Unpublished First Novel. Sam's short fiction has been published in *Thuglit, Spinetingler, Subterrain,* and *Criminal Element,* among others. Follow him at @sam_wiebe and at *samwiebe.com*.

Marcia Wilson is a freelance researcher and illustrator who likes to work in a style compatible for the color blind and visually impaired. She is Canon-centric and her first MX offering, *You Buy Bones,* uses the point-of-view of Scotland Yard to show the unique talents of Dr. Watson. She can be contacted at *gravelgirty.deviantart.com*

Vincent W. Wright has been a Sherlockian and member of *The Illustrious Clients of Indianapolis* since 1997. He is the creator of a blog, *Historical Sherlock,* which is dedicated to the chronology of The Canon, and has written a column on that subject for his home scion's newsletter since 2005. He lives in Indiana, and works for the federal government. This is his first pastiche.

The following authors appear in
The MX Book of New Sherlock Holmes Stories
Part I – 1881-1889 *and* Part III – 1896-1929

Mark Alberstat, BSI, has been a Sherlockian based in Nova Scotia since his early teens, when he began reading the stories from his father's two-volume Doubleday edition. When he discovered the wider world of Sherlock Holmes, he was fortunate enough to become a regular correspondent with American John Bennett Shaw, who encouraged Mark to start a local club, which he did while still in high school. That club, *The Spence Munros,* continues to meet and is the Sherlockian achievement of which Mark is most proud. In addition, Mark, and his wife, JoAnn, edit *Canadian Holmes,* the quarterly journal published by *The Bootmakers of Toronto.* At the January 2014 Baker Street Irregulars dinner, Mark was given the investiture name of *Halifax.*

Peter K. Andersson is a Swedish historian specialising in urban culture in the late nineteenth century. He has previously published a collection of Sherlock Holmes stories, *The Cotswolds Werewolf and Other Stories of Sherlock Holmes*.

Hugh Ashton was born in the UK, and moved to Japan in 1988, where he has remained since then, living with his wife Yoshiko in the historic city of Kamakura, a little to the south of Yokohama. In the past, he has worked in the technology and financial services industries, which have provided him with material for some of his books set in the 21st century. He currently works as a writer: novelist, copywriter (his work for large Japanese corporations appears in international business journals), and journalist, as well as producing industry reports on various aspects of the financial services industry. Recently, however, his lifelong interest in Sherlock Holmes has developed into an acclaimed series of adventures featuring the world's most famous detective, written in the style of the originals, and published by Inknbeans Press. In addition to these, he has also published historical and alternate historical novels, short stories, and thrillers. Together with artist Andy Boerger, he has produced the *Sherlock Ferret* series of stories for children, featuring the world's cutest detective.

Deanna Baran lives in a remote part of Texas where cowboys may still be seen in their natural habitat. A librarian and former museum curator, she writes in between cups of tea, playing *Go*, and trading postcards with people around the world. This is her first venture into the foggy streets of gaslit London.

Kevin David Barratt became a fan of Sherlock Holmes whilst at school. He is an active member of the *The Scandalous Bohemians*, a group who meet regularly in Leeds and for whom Kevin has contributed an essay on *Sherlock Holmes and Drugs* (which can be read at *www.scandalousbohemians.com*). Kevin is also a member of *The Sherlock Holmes Society of London*. He is married with two grown-up children and lives in Yorkshire.

Claire Bartlett is a writer and journalist who has worked extensively in comics and magazines. With her regular writing partner, Iain McLaughlin, she has worked on several radio and audio series, including *Doctor Who* and *UNIT* for Big Finish Productions and Imagination Theater's horror anthology series, and *Kerides the Thinker*, which she co-created and co-writes with McLaughlin. They have also written novels for Big Finish Productions, Telos Publishing, and Thebes Publishing. She is currently working on a non-fiction book for publication in 2015. Claire lives in Dundee, Scotland.

Derrick Belanger is an author and educator most noted for his books and lectures on Sherlock Holmes and Sir Arthur Conan Doyle, as well as his writing for the blog *I Hear of Sherlock Everywhere*. Both volumes of his two-volume anthology, *A Study in Terror: Sir Arthur Conan Doyle's Revolutionary Stories of Fear and the Supernatural* were #1 best sellers on the Amazon.com UK Sherlock Holmes book list, and his *MacDougall Twins with Sherlock Holmes* chapter book, *Attack of the Violet Vampire!* was also a #1 best selling new release in the UK. His novella, *Sherlock Holmes and the Adventure of the Peculiar Provenance*, is forthcoming from Endeavour Press. Mr. Belanger's academic work has been published in *The Colorado Reading Journal* and *Gifted Child Today*. Find him at *www.belangerbooks.com*.

Bob Byrne was a columnist for *Sherlock Magazine* and has contributed to *Sherlock Holmes Mystery Magazine* and the Sherlock Holmes short story collection *Curious Incidents*. He publishes two free online newsletters: *Baker Street Essays* and *The Solar Pons Gazette*, both of which can be found at *www.SolarPons.com*, the only website dedicated to August Derleth's successor to the great detective. Bob's column, *The Public Life of Sherlock Holmes*, appears every Monday morning at *www.BlackGate.com* and explores Holmes, hard boiled, and other mystery matters, and whatever other topics come to mind by the deadline. His mystery-themed blog is *Almost Holmes*.

Leslie F.E. Coombs is a true polymath whose interests include the writings and work of Conan Doyle, and he is a Holmes devotee. He has a keen interest in the social and technical history of Victorian Britain, and has extensive knowledge of military weaponry and ergonomics, and of naval, military, aviation and transport technologies. In addition to his writing of books and articles for magazines, he has written extensively on aviation and steam locomotion, and he is an editor and publisher's reader. Leslie Coombs's fictional writing has already produced two collections of Holmes short stories, and "The Royal Arsenal Affair" is one of a number of short stories which will appear in his third collection, to be published shortly.

David Stuart Davies BSI is a long time Sherlockian. He is a member of *Sherlock Holmes Society of London* and an invested *Baker Street Irregular*. He is a writer and editor and author of six Sherlock Holmes novels – the latest being *Sherlock Holmes: The Devil's Promise* (Titan), and two books on the films of the Great Detective. He has also penned two plays about Holmes and *Bending the Willow*, a volume about Jeremy Brett playing Sherlock. David is a member of the national committee of the *Crime Writer's Association* and edits their monthly magazine, *Red Herrings*. He has edited various collections of mystery & supernatural fiction and is the author of two crime series: one set in the Second World War featuring the detective Johnny One Eye, and another based in Yorkshire in the 1980's with DI Paul Snow. The latest novel in this series is *Innocent Blood* (Mystery Press).

C. Edward "Chuck" Davis was born and raised in New Jersey, and has lived in Colorado since 1993. He worked for over forty years as a draftsman and technical illustrator for AT&T, Sikorsky Aircraft, Exxon Engineering and Research, and Lockheed-Martin/Federal Aviation Administration. Additionally, he provided research, editing, illustrations, and technical advisory services for a number of publications, and is currently working on several projects, including *The Lunarnauts: The Rescue of Professor Cavor* (A sequel to the 1901 H. G. Wells novel *The First Men in the Moon*), *The Years of Infamy: The Japanese Invasion of Hawaii*, and *The Lion of the Sea (Il Leone di Mare)*, a historical fictional novel based upon the experiences of his late father-in-law who served in the Italian Navy during World War II.

Stuart Douglas runs Obverse Books *www.obversebooks.co.uk*, a small genre publisher. He has written short stories for many imprints, and his debut novel, *Sherlock Holmes: The Albino's Treasure* has just been released by Titan Books.

Séamas Duffy lives and works in Glasgow. His areas of interest are crime fiction, historical fiction, social history, and London writing. He has contributed articles to the

London Fictions website and to the *Baker Street Journal*, and wrote the Foreword for *The Aggravations of Minnie Ashe* by Cyril Kersh, published by Valancourt Books in January 2014. His first collection, *Sherlock Holmes In Paris* was published Black Coat Press in February 2013, and in May 2015 *Sherlock Holmes and The Four Corners of Hell* was published by Robert Hale of London. A third novel *The Tenants of Cinnamon Street* will be published in autumn 2015. This is historical crime fiction set in 1811, centred on Aaron Graham – a real Bow Street Magistrate – who investigated the Ratcliff Highway Murders. Séamas Duffy is also a musician and composer with an interest in Irish Language and History, and has produced *Tairngreacht Na nDraoideann* ("A Druid's Prophecy") in Irish and *Ó Ghartan Go Ghlaschú: Odaisé Colm Cille* ("From Gartan to Glasgow: Odyssey of Colm Cille") in Irish and Scottish Gaelic – both suites of Celtic music and song celebrating aspects of early Celtic culture, the latter emphasising the shared cultural heritage of Scottish and Irish Gaels.

C.H. Dye first discovered Sherlock Holmes when she was eleven, in a collection that ended at Reichenbach Falls. It was another six months before she discovered *The Hound of the Baskervilles*, and two weeks after that before a librarian handed her *The Return*. She has loved the stories ever since. She has written fanfiction, but this is her first published pastiche.

Matthew J. Elliott is the author of *Lost in Time and Space: An Unofficial Guide to the Uncharted Journeys of Doctor Who*, *Sherlock Holmes on the Air* (2012), *Sherlock Holmes in Pursuit* (2013), *The Immortals: An Unauthorized Guide to* Sherlock *and* Elementary (2013), and *The Throne Eternal* (2014). His articles, fiction and reviews have appeared in the magazines *Scarlet Street, Total DVD, SHERLOCK*, and *Sherlock Holmes Mystery Magazine*, and the collections *The Game's Afoot, Curious Incidents 2, Gaslight Grimoire*, and *The Mammoth Book of Best British Crime 8*. He has scripted over 260 radio plays, including episodes of *The Further Adventures of Sherlock Holmes, The Classic Adventures of Sherlock Holmes, Doctor Who, The Twilight Zone, The New Adventures of Mickey Spillane's Mike Hammer, Fangoria's Dreadtime Stories*, and award-winning adaptations of *The Hound of the Baskervilles* and *The War of the Worlds*. Matthew is a writer and performer on *RiffTrax.com*, the online comedy experience from the creators of cult sci-fi TV series *Mystery Science Theater 3000* (*MST3K* to the initiated). He's also written a few comic books.

James R. "Jim" French became a morning DJ on KIRO (AM) in Seattle in 1959. He later founded *Imagination Theatre*, a syndicated program that is now broadcast on over 120 stations in the U.S. and Canada, and also heard on the XM Satellite Radio system all over North America. Actors in French's dramas have included John Patrick Lowrie, Larry Albert, Patty Duke, Russell Johnson, Tom Smothers, Keenan Wynn, Roddy MacDowall, Ruta Lee, John Astin, Cynthia Lauren Tewes, and Richard Sanders. Mr. French states, "To me, the characters of Sherlock Holmes and Doctor Watson always seemed to be figures Doyle created as a challenge to lesser writers. He gave us two interesting characters – different from each other in their histories, talents and experience but complimentary as a team – who have been applied to a variety of situations and plots far beyond the times and places in the Canon. In the hands of different writers, Holmes and Watson have lent their identities to different times, ages, and even genders. But I wanted to break no new ground. I feel Sir Arthur provided us with enough references to locations, landmarks, and the social conditions of his time, to give a pretty large canvas on which to paint our own images and actions to animate Holmes and Watson."

Jayantika Ganguly is the General Secretary and Editor of the *Sherlock Holmes Society of India*, a member of the *Sherlock Holmes Society of London*, and the *Czech Sherlock Holmes Society*. She is the author of *The Holmes Sutra* (MX 2014). She is a corporate lawyer working with one of the Big Six law firms.

Paul D. Gilbert was born in 1954 and has lived in and around Lindon all of his life. He has been married to Jackie for thirty-eight years, and she is a Holmes expert who keeps him on the straight and narrow! He has two sons, one of whom now lives in Spain. His interests include literature, ancient history, all religions, most sports, and movies. He is currently employed full-time as a funeral director. His books so far include *The Lost Files of Sherlock Holmes* (2007), *The Chronicles of Sherlock Holmes* (2008), *Sherlock Holmes and the Giant Rat of Sumatra* (2010), *The Annals of Sherlock Holmes* (2012), and *Sherlock Holmes and the Unholy Trinity* (2015). He has just started work on *Sherlock Holmes: The Four Handed Game.*

Phil Growick has been a Sherlock Holmes fan since he watched a black and white Basil Rathbone and Nigel Bruce on his grandparents' TV when he was five. His first Holmes novel was *The Secret Journal of Dr. Watson.* It has a surprise ending that no one, as yet, expected, and left everyone demanding to know what happened to all the major characters; primarily, of course, Holmes. Ergo, he wrote the sequel, *The Revenge of Sherlock Holmes,* which answered all the questions the readers of the first book were asking. His greatest joys are his wife, his sons, his daughters-in-law, and his grandsons.

Dr. John Hall has written widely on Holmes. His books includes *Sidelights on Holmes*, a commentary on the Canon, *The Abominable Wife*, on the unrecorded cases, *Unexplored Possibilities*, a study of Dr. John H. Watson, and a monograph on Professor Moriarty, "The Dynamics of a Falling Star". (Most of these are now out of print.) His novels include *Sherlock Holmes and the Adler Papers, The Travels of Sherlock Holmes, Sherlock Holmes and the Boulevard Assassin, Sherlock Holmes and the Disgraced Inspector, Sherlock Holmes and the Telephone Mystery, Sherlock Holmes and the Hammerford Will, Sherlock Holmes and the Abbey School Mystery,* and *Sherlock Holmes at the Raffles Hotel.* John is a member of the *International Pipe-smoker's Hall of Fame,* and lives in Yorkshire, England.

John Heywood (not the author's real name) was born in Gloucestershire in 1951, and educated at Katharine Lady Berkeley's Grammar School and Jesus College, Cambridge. After graduating, he supported himself in many different ways, including teaching, decorating, house-sitting, laboring, and mowing graveyards, while at the same time making paintings, prints and drawings. He continues to make art, and his work is now in collections in Europe and America, and is regularly exhibited. He currently lives in Brixton, South London, and works as a painter and as a teacher of art and English in adult education. In 2014, his first book, *The Investigations of Sherlock Holmes,* was published by MX Publishing. It was enthusiastically received by the critics, and has recently been issued in India.

In the year 1998 **Craig Janacek** took his degree of Doctor of Medicine at Vanderbilt University, and proceeded to Stanford to go through the training prescribed for pediatricians in practice. Having completed his studies there, he was duly attached to the University of California, San Francisco as Associate Professor. The author of over seventy medical monographs upon a variety of obscure lesions, his travel-worn and battered tin dispatch-box is crammed with papers, nearly all of which are records of his fictional works. To date, these have been published solely in electronic format, including two non-Holmes novels (*The Oxford Deception* and *The Anger of Achilles Peterson*), the trio of holiday adventures collected as *The Midwinter Mysteries of Sherlock Holmes*, and a Watsonian novel entitled *The Isle of Devils*. His next project is the short trilogy *The Assassination of Sherlock Holmes*. Craig Janacek is a *nom de plume*.

Leslie S. Klinger BSI is the editor of *The New Annotated Sherlock Holmes* and many other books on Holmes, Watson, and the Victorian age.

Kim Krisco, author of three books on leadership, now follows in the footsteps of the master storyteller Sir Arthur Conan Doyle by adding five totally new Sherlock Holmes adventures to the canon with the recently released *Sherlock Holmes – The Golden Years*. He captures the voice and style of Doyle, as Holmes and Watson find themselves unraveling mysteries in America, Africa and around turn-of-the-century London that, as Holmes puts it, "appears to have taken on an unsavory European influence." Meticulously researched, all of Krisco's stories read as mini historical novels. Indeed, he traveled to the UK and Scotland in May of 2013 to do research for his most recent book. The five novellas all take place after Holmes and Watson were supposed to have retired. *Sherlock Holmes – The Golden Years* breathes new life into the beloved "odd couple," revealing deeper insights into their protean friendship that has become richer with age . . . and a bit puckish. Krisco's diverse career fashioned a circuitous route to his becoming a full-time writer. He has taught college, written and directed TV and films, and served in corporate communications. He has two writing desks: one in a travel trailer on a river in the Rocky Mountains of Colorado, and the other in a *pequeña casa* on an estuary in La Penta, Mexico.

Luke Benjamen Kuhns is a crime writer who lives in London. He has authored several Sherlock Holmes collections including *The Untold Adventures of Sherlock Holmes* (published in India & Italy), *Sherlock Holmes Studies in Legacy*, and the graphic novel *Sherlock Holmes and the Horror of Frankenstein*. He has written and spoken on the various forms of pastiche writing, which can be found in the *Fan Phenomena Series: Sherlock Holmes*.

Michael Kurland has written over thirty novels and a melange of short stories, articles, and other stuff, and has been nominated for two Edgars and the American Book Award. His books have appeared in Chinese, Czech, French, Italian, German, Japanese, Polish, Portuguese, Spanish, Swedish, and some alphabet full of little pothooks and curlicues. He lives in a Secular Humanist Hermitage in a secluded bay north of San Francisco, California, where he kills and skins his own vegetables. He may be communicated with through his website, *michaelkurland.com*.

Andrew Lane is a British writer with thirty-odd books to his credit, a mixture of fiction & non-fiction, Adult & Young Adult, and books under his own name and ghost-written

411

works. Most recently he has written eight books in a series (sold in translation to more than twenty countries at the last count) imagining what Sherlock Holmes would have been like when he was fourteen years old. The third of these books, *Black Ice*, is referenced in passing in his story for this anthology. *A Study in Scarlet* was the first book that Andrew Lane bought with his own pocket money. He was nine years old at the time, and the purchase warped his life from that moment on.

James Lovegrove is the author of more than fifty books, including *The Hope, Days, Untied Kingdom, Provender Gleed*, the *New York Times* bestselling *Pantheon* series, the *Redlaw* novels, and the *Dev Harmer Missions*. He has produced three Sherlock Holmes novels, with a Holmes/Cthulhu mashup trilogy in the works. He has also sold well over forty short stories and published two collections, *Imagined Slights* and *Diversifications*. He has produced a dozen short books for readers with reading difficulties, and a four-volume fantasy saga for teenagers, *The Clouded World*, under the pseudonym Jay Amory. James has been shortlisted for numerous awards, including the Arthur C. Clarke Award, the John W. Campbell Memorial Award, the Bram Stoker Award, the British Fantasy Society Award, and the Manchester Book Award. His short story "Carry The Moon In My Pocket" won the 2011 Seiun Award in Japan for Best Translated Short Story. His work has been translated into over a dozen languages, and his journalism has appeared in periodicals as diverse as *Literary Review, Interzone* and *BBC MindGames*. He reviews fiction regularly for the *Financial Times*. He lives with his wife, two sons, cat, and tiny dog in Eastbourne, not far from the site of the "small farm upon the South Downs" to which Sherlock Holmes retired.

Bonnie MacBird has loved Sherlock Holmes since breathlessly devouring the Canon at ten. She has degrees in music and film from Stanford, is the original writer of the movie *TRON*, won three Emmys for documentary film, studied Shakespearean acting at Oxford, and divides her time between her home in Los Angeles and a hotel room in Baker Street. She runs *The Sherlock Breakfast Club* and a playreading series in Los Angeles, where she also teaches writing at UCLA Extension. Her first novel, *Art in the Blood* (HarperCollins 2015) features a kidnapping, murder, and an art theft, and challenges Holmes's artistic nature and his friendship with Watson to the limits.

Iain McLaughlin has been writing for a living since 1985. He has worked on numerous comics in the UK, and was editor of the *Beano* for a time. He has written novels, short stories, radio plays, and some TV episodes, often working with regular writing partner Claire Bartlett. He wrote several stories in the "Doctor Who" universe, beginning with 2001's *The Eye of the Scorpion*, which introduced the character of Erimem. He has also written audios for *Blake's 7*, and radio plays of legendary sleuth Sherlock Holmes. Additionally, he has written numerous horror radio plays, and created and wrote every episode of Imagination Theater's *Kerides The Thinker* radio series. His *noir* novel, *Movie Star*, was released by Thebes Publishing in 2015. He was born and still lives in Dundee on the east coast of Scotland.

Lyn McConchie began writing professionally in 1990. Since then, she has seen thirty-two of her books published, and almost three hundred of her short stories appear. Her work has been published to date in nine countries and four languages, which she says isn't bad for an elderly, crippled, female farmer. Lyn lives on her farm in the North island of New Zealand where she breeds coloured sheep, and has free-range geese and hens. She shares her 19th century farmhouse with her Ocicat, Thunder, 7,469 books by other authors, and says that she plans to write forever or die trying.

Daniel McGachey Outside of his day job – which, over the past quarter century has seen him write extensively for comics, newspapers, magazines, digital media, and animation – Scottish writer Daniel McGachey's stories first appeared in several volumes of *The BHF Book of Horror Stories* and *Black Book of Horror* anthology series, and *Filthy Creations* magazine. In 2009, Dark Regions Press published his first ghost story collection, *They That Dwell in Dark Places*, dedicated in part to M.R. James, whose works inspired the creation of the collected stories. Since 2005, he has reviewed television and radio adaptations of James's stories for *The Ghosts and Scholars M.R. James Newsletter*, while his sequels to several of James's original tales appeared as the Haunted Library publication *Ex Libris: Lufford* in 2012. Moving from M.R. James to his other lifelong literary hero, his 2010 Dark Regions Press collection pitted Sir Arthur Conan Doyle's rational detective against the irrational forces of the supernatural in *Sherlock Holmes: The Impossible Cases*. His radio plays have been broadcast since 2005 as part of the mystery and suspense series *Imagination Theater*, including entries in its long-running strand of new Holmesian mysteries, *The Further Adventures of Sherlock Holmes*. He is working on a new "impossible case" for Sherlock Holmes and Dr. Watson in the novel, *The Devil's Crown*.

Adrian Middleton is a Staffordshire born independent publisher. The son of a real-world detective, he is a former civil servant and policy adviser who now writes and edits science fiction, fantasy, and a popular series of steampunked Sherlock Holmes stories.

Larry Millett worked for thirty years as a newspaper reporter in St. Paul, where he lives, while building a parallel career as a mystery novelist and architectural historian. He has written seven mysteries featuring Sherlock Holmes, all but one of them set in Minnesota. His first novel, *Sherlock Holmes and the Red Demon*, appeared in 1996. His second novel, *Sherlock Holmes and the Ice Palace Murders*, was adapted in 2015 into a play that performed to full houses at a theater in St. Paul. He is now working on a new mystery featuring Holmes that will be published in 2016 by the University of Minnesota Press.

Steve Mountain is a "born and bred" native of Portsmouth in the UK. Married with two grown-up children, he works for a local Council as a civil engineer, trying to retro-fit cycle riding facilities into roads not originally built for the purpose. This is usually, but not always, successful. Seeing his name in print is nothing new, although to date this has been mostly in articles in the local newspaper complaining about the effect of said cycle facilities on other road users. Having helped his daughter solve a problem with one of her Holmes pastiches, he caught the fiction writing bug himself. He has self-published one of his early stories with *Lulu*.

Mark Mower is a crime writer and historian and a member of the Crime Writers' Association. His books include *Bloody British History: Norwich* (The History Press, 2014) and *Suffolk Murders* (The History Press, 2011). His first book, *Suffolk Tales of Mystery & Murder* (Countryside Books, 2006), contained a potent blend of tales from the seamier side of country life – described by the East Anglian Daily Times *Suffolk* magazine as ". . . a good serving of grisliness, a strong flavour of the unusual, a seasoning of ghoulishness and just a hint of the unexpected . . . ." Alongside his writing, Mark lectures on crime history and runs a murder mystery business.

Summer Perkins is a film student who lives in Portland, Oregon, and has been a fan of the various incarnations of Sherlock Holmes for many years. Though no stranger to writing in the world of Holmes, this is Summer's first published piece. In addition to writing, Summer can be found reading, watching films, and studying various eras in history.

GC Rosenquist was born in Chicago, Illinois, and has been writing since he was ten years old. His interests are very eclectic. His eleven previously published books include literary fiction, horror, poetry, a comedic memoir, and lots of science fiction. His latest published work for MX Books is *Sherlock Holmes: The Pearl of Death and Other Stories* (2015). He works professionally as a graphic artist. He has studied writing and poetry at the College of Lake County in Grayslake, Illinois, and currently resides in Lindenhurst, Illinois. For more information on GC Rosenquist, you can go to his website at *www.gcrosenquist.com.*

Martin Rosenstock studied English, American, and German literature. In 2008, he received a Ph.D. from the University of California, Santa Barbara for looking into what happens when things go badly – as they do from time to time – for detectives in German-language literature. After job hopping around the colder latitudes of the U.S. for three years, he decided to return to warmer climes. In 2011, he took a job at Gulf University for Science and Technology in Kuwait, where he currently teaches. When not brooding over plot twists, he spends too much time and money traveling the Indian Ocean littoral. There is a novel somewhere there, he feels sure.

Geri Schear is a novelist and short story writer. Her work has been published in literary journals in the U.S. and Ireland. Her first novel, *A Biased Judgement: The Diaries of Sherlock Holmes 1897* was released to critical acclaim in 2014. The sequel, *Sherlock Holmes and the Other Woman,* will be released by MX Publishing in November 2015. She lives in Kells, Ireland.

Denis O. Smith's first published story of Sherlock Holmes and Doctor Watson, "The Adventure of The Purple Hand", appeared in 1982. Since then, numerous other such accounts have been published in magazines and anthologies both in the U.K. and the U.S. In the 1990's, four volumes of his stories were published under the general title of *The Chronicles of Sherlock Holmes,* and, more recently, a dozen of his stories, most not previously published in book form, appeared as *The Lost Chronicles of Sherlock Holmes* (2014), and he wrote a new story for the anthology, *Sherlock Holmes Abroad* (2015). Born in Yorkshire, in the north of England, Denis Smith has lived and worked in various parts of the country, including London, and has now been resident in Norfolk for many years. His interests range widely, but apart from his dedication to the career of Sherlock Holmes, he has a passion for historical mysteries of all kinds, the railways of Britain and the history of London.

Carolyn and Joel Senter ("Those Sherlock Holmes People in Cincinnati") were the founders of *Classic Specialties*, which they operated for more than a quarter century, as "North America's leading purveyor of items appertaining to Mr. Sherlock Holmes and

His Times." After retiring *Classic Specialties* in 2014, the Senters have maintained their contact with The Sherlockian Community via membership in several scions and Sherlockian societies, continued participation in numerous Sherlockian gatherings and, primarily, through their monthly (almost) internet newsletter, *The Sherlockian E-Times.* Their previous contributions to the world of Sherlockian printed literature have included the compiling and editing of *The Formidable Scrap-Book of Baker Street*, the publication of three full-length Sherlockian books, and the authoring of articles for various Sherlockian periodicals.

Shane Simmons is a multi-award-winning screenwriter and graphic novelist whose work has appeared in international film festivals, museums and lectures about design and structure. His best-known piece of fiction, *The Long and Unlearned Life of Roland Gethers*, has been discussed in multiple books and academic journals about sequential art, and his short stories have been printed in critically praised anthologies of history, crime and horror. He lives in Montreal with his wife and too many cats. Follow him at eyestrainproductions.com and @Shane_Eyestrain

Tim Symonds was born in London. He grew up in Somerset, Dorset, and Guernsey. After several years in East and Central Africa, he settled in California and graduated Phi Beta Kappa in Political Science from UCLA. He is a Fellow of the *Royal Geographical Society*. He writes his novels in the woods and hidden valleys surrounding his home in the High Weald of East Sussex. Dr. Watson knew the untamed region well. In "The Adventure of Black Peter", Watson wrote, "the Weald was once part of that great forest which for so long held the Saxon invaders at bay." Tim's novels are published by MX Publishing. His latest is titled *Sherlock Holmes and The Sword of Osman*. Previous novels include *Sherlock Holmes and The Mystery of Einstein's Daughter*, *Sherlock Holmes and The Dead Boer At Scotney Castle*, and *Sherlock Holmes and The Case of The Bulgarian Codex*.

Amy Thomas is a member of the *Baker Street Babes* Podcast, and the author of *The Detective and The Woman* mystery novels featuring Sherlock Holmes and Irene Adler. She blogs at *girlmeetssherlock.wordpress.com*, and she writes and edits professionally from her home in Fort Myers, Florida.

Will Thomas is the author of seven books in the Barker and Llewelyn Victorian mystery series, including *Some Danger Involved, Fatal Enquiry*, and *Anatomy of Evil.* He was nominated for a *Barry* and a *Shamus*, and is a two time winner of the Oklahoma Book Award. He lives in Broken Arrow, Oklahoma, where he studies Victorian martial arts and models British railways.

Daniel D. Victor, a Ph.D. in American literature, is a retired high school English teacher who taught in the Los Angeles Unified School District for forty-six years. His doctoral dissertation on little-known American author, David Graham Phillips, led to the creation of Victor's first Sherlock Holmes pastiche, *The Seventh Bullet*, in which Holmes investigates Phillips' actual murder. Victor's second novel, *A Study in Synchronicity,* is a two-stranded murder mystery, which features a Sherlock Holmes-like private eye. He is currently completing a trilogy called *Sherlock Holmes and the American Literati.* Each novel introduces Holmes to a different American author who actually passed through London at the turn of the century. In *The Final Page of Baker Street*, Holmes meets

Raymond Chandler; in *The Baron of Brede Place,* Stephen Crane; in *Seventeen Minutes to Baker Street*, Mark Twain. Victor, who is also writing a novel about his early years as a teacher, lives with his wife in Los Angeles, California. They have two adult sons.

Stephen Wade has a special interest in crime history, having published widely on regional crime. His book, *The Girl who Lived on Air* (Seren) was a Welsh Book of the Month for Waterstones last year. He was formerly a lecturer in English, and also worked as a writer in prisons for six years. His latest book is a short story collection, *Uncle Albert* (Priory Press). The current fiction project is a collection of crime stories featuring Lestrade.

MX Publishing

MX Publishing is the world's largest specialist Sherlock Holmes publisher, with several hundred titles and over a hundred authors creating the latest in Sherlock Holmes fiction and non-fiction.

From traditional short stories and novels to travel guides and quiz books, MX Publishing caters to all Holmes fans.

The collection includes leading titles such as *Benedict Cumberbatch In Transition* and *The Norwood Author* which won the 2011 *Tony Howlett Award* (Sherlock Holmes Book of the Year).

MX Publishing also has one of the largest communities of Holmes fans on *Facebook*, with regular contributions from dozens of authors.

www.mxpublishing.co.uk (UK) and *www.mxpublishing.com* (USA).

Lightning Source UK Ltd.
Milton Keynes UK
UKHW011430290520
364087UK00001B/13